Note for Readers

I wrote this book to help empower readers who are dealing with the aftermath of sexual assault and/or relationship violence.

Within these pages, you will meet a 16-year-old rape survivor. The story also involves domestic violence, bullying, and suicide.

Some of these issues may be uncomfortable to read about, especially if you've experienced them in real life.

It's okay to take breaks from reading, talk to someone if this book upsets you, or even stop reading altogether.

If you are in the United States, you can also call these hotlines if you need to talk to someone.

NATIONAL SEXUAL ASSAULT HOTLINE
1-800-656-4673
NATIONAL TEEN DATING ABUSE HOTLINE
1-866-331-9474
1-866-331-8453 (TTY)
NATIONAL SUICIDE PREVENTION HOTLINE
1-800-273-8255
TREVOR PROJECT CRISIS LINE (LGBT/YOUTH)
1-866-488-7386

REINVENTING HANNAH

Jack A. Ori

Heroic Muse Books

1732 1st Avenue #20990 New York, NY 10128

Paperback Edition April 11, 2020

ISBN: 978-1-7345211-1-5

REINVENTING HANNAH

Jack A. Ori

HEROIC MUSE BOOKS   NEW YORK

Red Ribbon Week

1 – A Fateful Decision

"SO, WHICH IS it going to be, Hannah?" Molly asked. "Trunk or Treat or the crazy party in Eastwood?"

Hannah twisted a bead on her Friends for Life bracelet, looking around the section of the library where after-school tutoring took place. The tutoring center was dead except for her and her two friends. Molly had creamy white skin, green eyes, and red hair that was always tied back into a loose ponytail, while Sierra had eyes the same shade of light brown as her skin, framed perfectly by silver-rimmed glasses, and her hair was done up in millions of tight braids that were bunched together.

No matter how hard Hannah looked, there were no other faces in the whole library except for theirs, and Mr. Collins', of course. He sat at a desk at the front, grading papers. Since no one else was there, Hannah's choices were to keep talking with her friends or stare at the childish Halloween decorations on the wall:

Brightly colored ghosts and tombstones that they should have outgrown in third grade.

A skeleton in the corner that was sort of scary looking.

And a chain made of construction paper she and Molly had hung from the ceiling along with a wall sign reminding people to avoid alcohol and drugs this Halloween.

The sign didn't look like it fit with everything else, and Hannah was sure no one was looking at it.

"I don't know," she said, staring down at her hands. Her fingers were too long and her nails were uneven. She didn't like looking at them. "Maybe neither."

"I do know," Sierra interjected from the other side of the table. "You're going to come with me and have an awesome time instead of wasting the night away giving out candy to a bunch of snot-nosed kids and pretending to smile at their lame costumes."

"Sierra!" Molly said.

"I'm just saying." Sierra pulled on Hannah's sleeve. "Come on, Mouse, don't you want to live a little for once? Jake said I could invite anyone I want. And I bet there'll be a ton of hot guys there. This is your chance to meet someone amazing."

"I doubt that," Hannah said weakly, leaving out that she wasn't too happy to hear that Jake was involved. Jake was Sierra's boyfriend, sort of. More than once Hannah and Molly had to stay up all night listening to Sierra cry her heart out after one of their fights, but within a few days Sierra always took him back and gushed about how sweet he was and how stupid she was to ever let him go.

"You won't know until you try." Sierra turned to Molly. "Give her one good reason why she should go to your stupid babysitting party instead."

"Um, because she just put up this thing," Molly said, gesturing toward the sign, "and all week long she's been putting red ribbons on people's lockers to encourage them to stay sober."

Hannah looked away. Molly was right. It didn't look good for the Vice-President of Students Against Destructive Decisions to go to a party where everyone would be drinking, especially not during Red Ribbon Week. "I'm not going to drink," she said. "So, it'll be fine."

"Yeah," Sierra said. "Hannah doesn't give in to peer pressure. You're just jealous because she's not afraid to live a little, unlike some people."

"I'm not afraid to live," Molly said. "I just actually have common sense. Don't do this, Mouse. Come. . ."

"Do what?" a voice said, and Hannah knew before she looked up that it was Brad's voice. It was a little higher than most boys' voices, but still deep enough to be masculine, and he had a stronger New York accent than she did.

"Oh," Hannah said, ignoring how much faster her heart had started beating when she looked up at Brad's oval face. He was tall, which was fine with her because she was too, and had sandy brown hair that looked blond when the light hit it right.

Hannah fidgeted with her hands, twisting them together and drawing way too much attention to them. They felt too big to her suddenly, and she was sure Brad thought so too. "I'm going to a party tonight, but Molly doesn't like it."

"Wow." Brad's eyes widened and Hannah couldn't tell if he was impressed or worried. "I didn't think you were the partying type."

"Oh, I'm not. Usually, I mean. I'm more the kind of girl who discourages it." Good going, Hannah. Make yourself sound like some stuck-up goody-two-shoes, why don't you? "But Sierra's going, and I want to make sure she's okay."

"Really?" Brad tried to raise one eyebrow but only succeeded in scrunching up his entire face, making Hannah's heart do flip flops again. "Hey, you got the math homework? I lost where I wrote it down."

Oh. That was all Brad wanted. Of course he didn't want to talk to Hannah just to talk to her. Her heart sank while she felt stupid for hoping. "Of course," she said, keeping her feelings firmly in check. "I put it in my phone right away. You should do that too, so you don't lose it again." Her fingertips brushed Brad's as she handed him the phone. Had she done that on purpose? Not that it mattered, because she was sure he didn't like it. . . or did he?

"Thanks." Brad grabbed a pen off the table without asking and wrote the assignment on his hand. The black ink stood out against his white skin, and Hannah wondered if he had any tattoos. He seemed like the kind of boy who might.

"Brad!" Hannah said as he gave her back her phone. "Use paper!"

"I'll lose it again. Can't lose my hand, right?"

"That's a shame," Sierra said, prompting Hannah to glare at her. "Now if you're done wasting Hannah's time, do you mind moving out of the way?"

"Sierra," Hannah said, but her voice wasn't as forceful as she wanted it to be. It never was. That was why her friends called her Mouse, a nickname she secretly hated but pretended not to.

"Not 'til I do this." Brad took a step forward, looking Hannah in the eye, and for one terrible, wonderful second, she thought he was going to try to kiss her. "You sure you want to go to this party tonight?" he asked, and her heart sank again. "Cause my friend Mark's doing this thing, and you'd be welcome. If you want, I mean."

Whoa. He was asking her out. Hannah hadn't expected THAT. "A thing?" she asked, trying to play it cool, but she couldn't help smiling a little anyway.

"Nothing big," Brad said, looking away from her. "We're just gonna chill and watch a couple cheesy horror movies and laugh at how dumb they are. Costume optional."

"She's not interested," Sierra said. "Trust me, Mouse, you're not. Chill's code for 'get stoned out of your mind,' and he's going to be pushing you to do it too. You don't want that."

Hannah didn't like the way Sierra was talking, and anyway, there was going to be worse than weed at Jake's party, from what Molly said. "I hope Sierra's wrong about the weed," she said to Brad, feeling she had to do her duty as Vice-President of SADD and encourage him to stay sober. "It's not good for you." Brad's eyes narrowed and she realized too late how judgmental that sounded. "Anyway, it sounds great and I'd like to come, but I already made plans with Sierra, so. . . "

"Right." Brad played with the pen, flicking the button to open and close it over and over. "Sure you don't want me to write my digits on your hand in case you change your mind?"

"She's positive," Sierra said before Hannah could answer. "And give us our pen back."

Brad's eyes flashed. "Whatever," he said, throwing the pen down. "Have fun watching this one's back," he told Hannah. "Hope she gets someday that you're a way better friend to her than she deserves."

"Brad. . ." Hannah began, but Brad turned and walked away, his feet hitting the floor hard enough that she was sure they could hear it down in the cafeteria. She slumped down in her seat. "Sierra! You just ruined the only chance I'm ever going to have with him!"

"I just saved you, you mean," Sierra said. "You can do way better than him, trust me." She pulled her purse over her shoulder. "Let's get out of here. He and his lame excuses for talking to you are the only ones who have been here all afternoon and the sooner we go, the sooner you can meet Mr. Right instead."

Hannah felt like shoving the table hard enough to knock it over, but of course, she didn't do that. "Fine, whatever. Let's go have fun."

"YAY!" Sierra said, loudly enough that Mr. Collins looked up from the papers he was marking. "Come on, bestie," she added, lowering her voice slightly. "Tonight's the night we really start to live."

What have I got myself into? Hannah picked up her backpack and followed Sierra out of the tutoring center.

2 – Mouse Girl

BOUT TWO HOURS later, the girls finally made it to the party. Hannah was wearing a blue dress that was way too see-through and way too low-cut for her liking, but it was the only thing in Sierra's closet that was anything close to what Hannah thought Estella Havershim from Great Expectations would wear, so she'd borrowed it anyway. Sierra had also lent her a tiara and a pair of glasses with no lenses in them and put a French braid in her hair for her.

Sierra was dressed as Cleopatra, or so she said. She had tucked her hair into a short wig and was wearing a dress that was much too revealing for Hannah's liking: all white with a top that looked like a bra, nothing covering her belly, and a skirt so short that Sierra would have been sent home if she'd worn it to school.

"Here we are," Sierra said, parking halfway down the block. "It's the last house on the right. Number 1917."

Hannah laughed, nervously. "Last chance to turn around so we don't both get grounded for a month."

Sierra rolled her eyes. "Don't chicken out on me now."

"I'm not," Hannah said, shouting to be heard over the loud music coming from the end of the block. "This music's tearing the block apart. I can feel it as we walk."

Sierra said nothing, and Hannah was sure she was pretending not to have heard her. She felt like the neighbors were all watching her from their darkened windows as she hurried down the block, trying to ignore the goosebumps growing on her legs and anxious to get out of this cold weather. The house they wanted was at the end of the block; it was the only one that had any lights on at all.

They walked up a driveway to an open door.

"Here goes," Sierra said, and Hannah got the sense she was as nervous as Hannah was. She smiled at Hannah and said, "You look gorgeous. There's nothing to worry about." Then she turned the doorknob and gestured to Hannah to go first. It reminded Hannah of that time they'd gone to a haunted house and neither one of them had wanted to be the first one to walk in, but Hannah had decided to be brave and push her way through.

She took a deep breath and let it out slowly as she walked through the door of the party house.

There were people everywhere, and most of them had plastic cups or cans of beer in their hands. A couple of guys, obviously stoned, were sitting on a couch playing video games. Some people were dancing. Everyone else's costumes, if you could call them that, were even more revealing than Sierra's.

"Where's Jake?" Hannah asked, yelling over the too-loud music.

Sierra shrugged. "He's here somewhere. It's his house."

Some guy with a realistic-looking grizzly bear costume came out of nowhere, jumping in front of Hannah and growling. She flinched. The guy laughed and took off the bear head. He was a white guy with curly, dark hair that had got all messed up by the bear costume. He hadn't shaved, or at least, was wearing one of those awful beards that looked like stubble.

"You made it!" he said, and Hannah could smell the beer on his breath. Sierra scrunched up her nose as he leaned in to kiss her. But she kissed him back, so Hannah guessed she wasn't too disgusted. "Who's your friend?"

"This is Hannah," Sierra said. "Don't ask who she's dressed as. She's one of a kind."

"Cool. Cool." Jake looked Hannah up and down. "I didn't know she was gonna be so hot. Hot Hannah." He giggled.

Hannah stiffened. Sierra, oblivious, said, "Where's the beer? We need to loosen up some."

"Beer's in the cooler. There's other stuff in the kitchen too if you're more of a wine girl or whatever, Hannah."

"I'll just have water, thanks," Hannah said.

"Whatever floats your boat. Kitchen's that way." Jake bounced off after gesturing vaguely over his shoulder.

Sierra grabbed Hannah's hand. "I'm so glad you finally met Jake. Come on, let's go get drinks so you can start mingling."

Since when was Sierra into drinking? Hannah didn't ask, just let her lead her to the kitchen. Sierra opened a cooler that was under the table and grabbed two cans of beer.

"Seriously?" Hannah said as Sierra tried to hand her one of the cans. "I told you I wasn't drinking, and you shouldn't either."

"Don't be so uptight. It's a party, isn't it?" Sierra pressed the can into Hannah's hand. "Look, I know at school you're like, the queen of sobriety or whatever, but we're not at school now. We're at a party full of cool people who really ought to get to know how awesome you are, and you're not going to meet anyone standing there scowling and refusing to even try to fit in."

Maybe I don't want to fit in. Hannah slammed the can down on the table and turned her back on Sierra so she could open the fridge. It was full of six-packs and wine coolers. No water anywhere except the sink, and Hannah doubted Jake had a filter.

"You should try one of those," Sierra said, gesturing toward the wine coolers. "They're like lemonade. You'll like them."

"Yeah, whatever." Hannah took a peach-flavored wine cooler out of the fridge and went back into the living room.

She didn't know where to go or what to do. She looked around for a spot where there weren't too many people and decided on the couch where the guys were playing video games. One of the guys kind of reminded her of Brad. He didn't look like him, at least not up close. He was rounder and shorter, but he had the same hairstyle and face shape.

Hannah watched the not-Brad-but-close-enough guy play a racing game. She wished there was a potted plant or something she could pour the wine cooler down. The more she stood there, the more she felt like taking a sip to see what it was like, and she didn't want to break the contract she'd signed as a SADD officer promising to be a positive, sober role model. She leaned against a wall saying nothing and wondering if Not-Brad even knew she was there.

He looked up. "I thought someone was watching me, but I didn't think I had such a beautiful stalker."

"I. . . I wasn't stalking you," Hannah stammered. "Honest. I just wanted to see what you were playing."

Not-Brad laughed. "Relax. I was complimenting you. Here, let me get your drink for you." He took it and opened it before Hannah could tell him she didn't want him to.

"Thanks," Hannah said. "But I don't actually want it. I was just holding it so no one would offer me a drink."

Not-Brad giggled. "That's different. But hey, it's cool. If you don't want it, I'll take it." He took a sip. "You sure you don't want any? It's just a wine cooler. It won't get you all that fucked up."

Hannah did. She wanted it more than anything. "I can't," she said. "I'm sort of the designated driver." It wasn't a total lie. Since Sierra was drinking, she wasn't going to be able to drive them back. This guy didn't need to know that that meant ordering a Lyft because Hannah only had a learner's permit.

"Look at you being all responsible," Not-Brad said, smiling the same relaxed smile Brad did when he was fooling around in class. God, he was cute! "You got a name, responsible girl?"

"Hannah, but my friends call me Mouse."

"Mouse." Not-Brad took a sip of the wine cooler. "Like in that kids' story about the lion." He took another sip. "What'd you say your other name was?"

"Hannah. What's yours?"

"Uh uh uh." Not-Brad pointed the wine cooler toward Hannah. "If you want to know, you have to take a sip of this."

Hannah took a step back. "Then I guess you'll stay anonymous."

Not-Brad nearly doubled over laughing. "You're hilarious. Hilarious Hannah Mouse." He threw his head back and downed the rest of the wine cooler. Hannah was sure that was not what you were supposed to do with it, but she didn't care. Better it was in him than in her. "Come sit next to me," he said, "and let's see if you can beat me at racing." Hannah did and he said, his voice slurred a little, "You know what I like about you? You're the kind of girl who knows exactly what you want. That's awesome. Too many girls just go along with whatever anyone tells them to do, and it's like, don't be so weak, you know?"

"You're hanging around the wrong kind of girls, then." Hannah picked up the video game controller. "I want to know your name. If I win, which I will because you're too drunk to play properly, you have to tell me."

"Okay. But if I win, you have to kiss me."

Hannah wasn't sure she wanted her first kiss ever to be with some guy who had beer on his breath, but it probably didn't matter because it wasn't going to happen.

She focused intently on the controller, playing hard so that she would win and get the guy's name out of him, and almost forgot she was at the kind of party she wasn't supposed to be caught dead at. This wasn't so bad. What had Molly been so worried about?

They played three rounds. Hannah learned the guy's name was Jamie and that he went to Cedarwood Community College. That made him too old for her, but she didn't care. It wasn't like she was ever going to see him again after tonight anyway.

After the third round, Jamie said, "This is no fair. Are you sure you don't want to get just a little fucked up, so I have a chance?"

Hannah shook her head. "I'm having too much fun sober. Why ruin a good thing?"

Jamie laughed. "So funny," he said. "Does that mean I have a chance to kiss you even though I lost?"

"I'll think about it." Hannah's heart pounded. She knew if she sat here any longer, she'd give in, and that scared her even though there was nothing to be scared of. Jamie was nice even if he had had way too much to drink, so what was the big deal? "Tell you what," she said. "Let me just get something to drink and then we'll try again."

"I'm corrupting you already." Jamie smiled. "Go ahead, Mouse Girl."

Hannah went into the kitchen and looked around, not sure how long she could stay in here before Jamie realized she was hiding from him and came looking for her. She grabbed a wine cooler from the fridge without knowing why she was doing it. There were some red cups on the counter next to the sink that she hadn't noticed before and a pitcher of something that looked like iced tea. "Is this actually tea?" she asked Jake, who had come into the kitchen. "Like, not alcoholic?"

"Oh yeah," Jake said. "It's for mixing, but if you want just tea, go for it. I won't tell anyone." He winked.

Hannah hurried to put ice in her cup and put the tea in it. Her best friend's boyfriend shouldn't have winked at her, and she didn't like the vibe she got from him.

She went back out into the living room. "There you are," Jamie said. He glanced at the guy next to him, a skinny-as-a-pencil dude whose skin was super pale and who was wearing alien antennas on top of his head. "Told you she hadn't gone for good."

"Go ahead and play," Pencil Boy said. "I play winners. And when I play, the winner has to kiss the loser." His eyes sparkled. "I'm Ty, by the way."

Hannah put her cup down on the table and picked up her controller. "Well, Ty, maybe I'll let Jamie win."

Ty scowled. "Shut up and play, bitch."

Hannah leaned forward, determined to block out her awareness of this asshole who was ruining her fun. Ty got up but she was barely aware of him walking behind her. She could feel people watching as she made her race car go faster and faster. She made it go so fast that she lost control and couldn't get into the other lane fast enough when a car was in her way.

"You lose," Jamie said happily. "Now you have to kiss me."

Hannah's heart pounded. "Let me just. . . " She picked up her cup. "Dry mouth."

She drained the cup before she turned toward Jamie. She could smell the beer on his breath, and it turned her off as much as it had before. So, when he leaned in, she turned and kissed his cheek.

"Hey!" Jamie said.

"I said a kiss. I didn't say where." Hannah fidgeted, feeling bad. "I just don't like the taste of beer on your breath. Maybe some time when you're more sober, I'll give you a real kiss."

"It's cool," Jamie said, laughing slightly, but Hannah could tell he was upset. "Like I said, you're a girl who knows what she wants. But I want another beer, so that's what I'm going to have." He walked away.

"Jamie, wait! I didn't mean. . ." But Jamie was already gone.

"Don't look so sad," Ty said. "How about. . ."

Hannah walked away before he could finish, wishing she knew where Sierra was so she could get her to take her home. She felt like the biggest loser in the world. Going to this party was stupid. She didn't belong here. She didn't fit in. And she'd ruined things with the only cool guy she'd met.

Suddenly, she was dizzy, and her hands and feet wouldn't move the way she wanted them to. "What the fuck?" she mumbled. She wanted to find Sierra and tell her something was wrong, she was sick or something, but she couldn't remember how to get from the living room to the kitchen to see if she was there. She began pushing through the crowd anyway as fast as she could, stumbling and trying not to fall.

"Whoa," someone said. "Talk about wasted."

"I'm not," Hannah mumbled. Her voice sounded slurred like she'd had a stroke or something.

She needed Sierra. NOW.

She pulled her phone out and stared at it. There were buttons to press to put letters on the screen and make them into words, but she'd forgotten how to make it work. She stumbled around the living room instead, going in circles because she couldn't find the way out.

"It's okay," a guy said, putting his hand on her shoulder. It was the pencil guy from before.

Hannah wished it was the other one, the one she liked a lot, but she couldn't remember what you were supposed to do if you didn't want someone to touch you, so she let him. "It's just your first time drunk, that's all. Come sit with me. I'll help you relax."

"Okay." Hannah leaned on Pencil Guy and let him lead her to the couch. He sat down first, smiling slightly. "Put your head on my lap. Lying down'll help."

That seemed like a good idea to Hannah, so she did.

He stroked her hair, laughing to himself as he leaned over and kissed the top of her head. Then he put his hand over her breasts and squeezed them through the fabric while he kissed her for real. Hannah lay there frozen, her panic growing because she couldn't move, while the guy pulled her arms up over her head and began unbuttoning her dress . . .

3 – The Morning After

PURPLE BUTTERFLIES ON the curtains. Glow-in-the-dark stars stuck to the ceiling here and there. A heavy blue comforter wrapped around her.

This was Sierra's room, not Hannah's.

Hannah sat up, blinking hard and trying to remember how she'd got here. But no matter how hard she tried, she couldn't remember leaving the party last night. She remembered playing video games with Jamie, pulling away when he tried to kiss her, getting some iced tea from the kitchen. . . and then waking up here, her mouth dry and her body aching like the last time she had the flu.

"Sierra?" she whispered, but Sierra was fast asleep and didn't respond. Hannah got up, slowly. She was sore in weird places, like between her legs, as she tiptoed toward the bathroom.

Had she packed a toothbrush? she wondered as she took a Dixie cup from the dispenser on the side of the sink. Her mouth was so dry that she didn't care she was drinking tap water, from the bathroom no less, as she filled the cup and gulped gratefully. But then she caught sight of herself in the mirror.

It wasn't that her hair was limp and uncombed or that she looked extra tired. It was early in the morning and she doubted she'd got much sleep last night. But there were bruises on her neck, three of them, and the nightgown she didn't remember changing into was cut low enough that she could see another one on the top of one of her breasts. She put her hand under the nightgown, feeling gingerly.

There were tiny indentations all over her breasts. She pulled the collar of her nightgown down as far as it would go without ripping the fabric so she could see better. The indentations looked like teeth marks, like someone had bitten her over and over.

What the hell???

Hannah glared at herself in the mirror, trying to remember what she'd done to herself and getting mad because she couldn't. The bathroom door, which she'd left open a crack, creaked open more and she hurried to pull her nightgown on properly.

Dylan, Sierra's older brother, started to come in. Hannah could see him in the mirror: a tall black guy the same age as the boys she'd met last night. Dylan's ears stuck out a little too much from his skull, or maybe she noticed it more because he'd shaved his head recently.

"Oh!" he said, jumping back a little. "Sorry, Hannah. I didn't know you were in here." He frowned. "You okay?"

"Yeah. Just really confused. I don't remember coming back last night."

"I'm not surprised. You and Sierra were both totally wasted, you worse than her. You tore your dress a little, by the way, but nothing major. It just needs a couple stitches."

Hannah nodded, trying to process all that. She rubbed her head and said, "Wait. You're not making sense. I. . . I couldn't have been drunk."

Dylan shrugged. "It's okay. It happens. I told Sierra I'd cover for you guys this time, but no more parties like this, okay?"

"I won't, believe me. I feel awful. And I have all sorts of bruises and stuff that I don't remember getting." Hannah's heart pounded as she saw Dylan's eyes narrow. He pressed his head forward, slightly, and looked her in the eye. Hannah had a feeling he was putting on his EMT face. She made herself go on, "I don't remember drinking at all. The only thing I remember having is a cup of iced tea."

"Iced tea? You're sure it didn't have alcohol in it?"

"Positive."

"Okay." Dylan ran his hands through what little hair he had on top of his head. "Okay. Come out of the bathroom, and let's talk more about this."

"About what?" Hannah was confused.

Dylan let his breath out slowly. "This isn't easy to say and it's not gonna be easy to hear." He put his hand on Hannah's shoulder. "Anyone ever talk to you about date rape drugs?"

"Date rape. . . ? What?" Hannah's eyes widened. It kind of made sense. "You're saying someone. . . no."

"It fits." Dylan's voice was gentle. "Look at the evidence, Hannah. You were totally out of it without touching alcohol, you have bruises everywhere, your dress was torn. So . . . "

Hannah turned away from him. "I'm not talking about this anymore!" She blinked back tears. "It didn't happen. You're wrong."

"Let's see what the doctors say." Dylan's voice was calm, too calm, pissing Hannah off. "That'll tell the story."

"No. I'm not going to the hospital. They'll call my parents and I'll get grounded for going to the stupid party that I wish I'd never gone to."

"They can't call your parents without your permission." Dylan's voice was still soft. "Hannah, listen to me. I'm not trying to boss you around, but if I'm right, there's stuff you need to take care of. You could get an infection or get pregnant, and the only way to make sure that doesn't happen is if you go to the hospital. So if you won't let me take you, I have to tell your parents what I think happened to you so that they can take care of you."

"That's blackmail!" Hannah glared at Dylan, but he didn't back down, just looked her in the eye like she hadn't said anything. "Okay, fine, I'll go to the hospital. Can I at least get dressed first?"

"Of course."

Hannah ran down the hall. She was madder at Dylan than she'd ever been at anyone in her entire life, and she didn't like feeling that way. She'd always thought Dylan was cool. He treated her like she was as much his sister as Sierra was and he never made her feel embarrassed, not even the time he overheard her telling Sierra she had a crush on him. He let her down gently and then six months later, she was the first person he ever told he was gay.

And now he knew she and Sierra had gone to the wrong kind of party and that instead of watching Sierra's back like she was supposed to, Hannah got all messed up. And worse, he wasn't totally on her side like he was supposed to be.

Hannah came back into Sierra's room and threw herself onto her comforter, then made herself get up and look for some clothes to wear. Obviously, she wasn't wearing her torn dress, wherever it had ended up. She found the pair of jeans and sweater she'd worn to school under the desk; Sierra had kicked them there after they had changed because she was in such a rush to get to the party.

"What's going on?" Sierra mumbled sleepily, rolling over onto her back.

"Nothing. Go back to sleep." Hannah squeezed the sweater, liking the feeling of the fabric under her fingers. "D-dylan thinks. . ." she began but didn't go on. She couldn't tell Sierra that Dylan thought she'd been date raped. Sierra would understand better than Molly would, but she still would be shocked. Plus, she might not believe it.

"Dylan thinks what?" Sierra sat up. She groaned and rubbed her head. "I way overdid it but tell me anyway."

Hannah swallowed hard, thinking, trying to figure out what she could say that wasn't the whole truth. "He doesn't think I was drunk. He thinks someone put pills in my iced tea. Crazy, right?"

Sierra's mouth dropped open. "I don't know. You were so adamant about not drinking, and then you were so messed up. You were saying things that didn't make sense, and you did whatever Dylan told you, no questions asked. It was like you were a robot. Your answer to everything was 'Okay.'"

"I was? I don't remember any of that." Hannah turned her back on Sierra so she could put her shirt on. "Don't look," she said, feeling Sierra staring at her. "I don't like it."

"My glasses aren't even on. I can barely see you."

"Just look the other way, will you?" Hannah hurried to get dressed. Putting her jeans on kind of hurt but she ignored it. "There. Now Dylan can take me to the hospital so they can tell me he's wrong."

"Wait up," Sierra said. "I'm coming too."

"You don't have to. . . "

"Yes, I do. I'm your best friend, and it's my fault you were at the stupid party in the first place. Besides, afterward, I can make him take us out for pancakes so that the note I leave for Mom and Dad won't be a total lie."

Pancakes were the furthest thing from Hannah's mind. Getting dressed exhausted her and her stomach hurt a little. "Whatever," she said. "Get dressed before he loses his patience. I don't want him calling my parents."

"He'd better not," Sierra said. "And I don't have to get dressed. I was too drunk to get changed last night and slept in my clothes." She went over to the vanity and pulled a brush through her hair. "There. I'm presentable. Comb your hair so we can go."

Hannah didn't feel like combing her hair, but she took her comb out of her purse and did it anyway so that Sierra would have nothing to say.

4 – The So-Called SAFE Room

"**Y**OU DON'T HAVE to wait with me," Hannah told Sierra while they were in the waiting room. She'd just given Dylan her forms to hand into the intake person so that she wouldn't have to deal with her, and now it was a matter of getting called back to see the doctor. "You guys got me to the hospital. You don't have to waste your whole Saturday morning on this."

"I'm your best friend," Sierra said. "Of course I'm waiting for you." She fidgeted with her hair. "L-look what happened to you cause of . . . "

"We don't know anything happened. Besides, I told you, I wanted to go to the stupid party."

"The only thing you wanted was to watch my back and we both know it. You could have been having the time of your life with Brad, and instead, your first time was with some drunk loser you didn't want touching you."

Hannah stiffened. Just then, Dylan came back and she said to him, "What did you tell her?"

"He didn't," Sierra said. "I figured it out. That's all. The bruises on your neck make it obvious. Remind me to show you how to cover those with makeup, by the way. The last thing you need is your parents asking questions."

"I don't know. It seems like lying." Hannah touched one of the bruises, gingerly. If her parents saw them, she'd probably be grounded for the rest of the school year for making the kinds of stupid choices Mom had warned her over and over she'd better not make. "But maybe just this once."

Sierra shrugged. "What your parents don't know won't hurt them." She glanced at Dylan, who was frowning. "What? It's not like you're not covering with ours for me."

"I know." Dylan sighed. "It's just, you sure your parents wouldn't understand if they knew that some guy - "

"We don't know how far he went yet!" Hannah snapped even though she was getting surer by the second that whatever asshole had done this to her hadn't stopped at her neck and chest. "And no, they wouldn't. If they knew I went to a party like that they'd be more disappointed in me than they've ever been in my life."

"Or," Dylan said, "they might be mad that someone did this to you and give you a ton of support."

"Don't be an asshole," Sierra said. "When you tell Mom and Dad you're gay, you can talk about other people telling their parents stuff. 'Til then, leave Hannah alone."

Hannah wanted to yell at the top of her lungs that she was capable of talking for herself, but instead, she said, quietly, "Dylan's just trying to help."

"Yeah, well, he's doing the opposite," Sierra said.

"He did us a favor. He got us home safe from the stupid party. So, leave him alone."

The door to the exam rooms opened and a nurse called, "Hannah Kollman."

Sierra started to stand up when Hannah did, but Hannah said, "They called me, not you."

"I can tell them how you were last night. You don't remember, how can you . . ."

"If they want to know, they'll call you in. I'll be fine."

Sierra looked away from Hannah. She fiddled with one of her braids. "Okay, Mouse. If that's how you want it."

Hannah felt bad about hurting Sierra's feelings, but she swallowed hard and made herself follow the nurse anyway. This was something she had to do by herself, and Sierra needed to understand that.

Her anger melted into anxiety as the nurse took her down a hallway. She hoped she wouldn't be dumped in a room full of people. The ERs in Florida were like that, or at least Mom said so after that time she'd come out of the hospital. She said there were two dozen patients in one room separated only by curtains and you could hear what the doctors were saying to everyone else. But that was a long time ago and in another state. Maybe New York ERs weren't like that, if Mom had even been telling the truth and not exaggerating to make an impression.

The nurse took Hannah to a small room. The door had the words "SAFE Room" marked on it in tiny white letters with a black background, so small it was like reading a whisper. The nurse let her in, and she looked around, surprised that the so-called safe room didn't look any different than the examining room at her regular doctor's.

"Have a seat if you'd like," the nurse said. Hannah's eyes darted back and forth between a small chair and the edge of the exam table. She decided on the exam table since she was sure she'd have to be examined eventually and sat there, taking in the nurse with her eyes. The woman was white with dark hair like Hannah's, but she had a pixie cut instead of dark curls bouncing off her shoulders. It looked good on her even though she was Mom's age or older. Her eyes were blue, but they went with her hair well. Hannah wondered if that was her natural color but didn't want to be rude by asking, so instead, she traced the letters on the woman's lab coat with her eyes, over and over: E Keller, ANP.

"Let me introduce myself," E. Keller, ANP said, apparently oblivious to the fact that Hannah had already read her name off her coat. "My name is Elizabeth Keller. I'm a nurse practitioner that specializes in helping people who have been attacked in the way that you were attacked."

Hannah nodded. Her mouth was dry, and she didn't feel like talking anyway.

"I'd say it was nice to meet you, but I know you're here because of something terrible that happened that shouldn't have," E. Keller, ANP went on while Hannah argued with herself about whether she was supposed to call her by her first name or call her ANP Keller. "I'm going to begin by getting your medical history. Let's start with your full name and date of birth." Hannah gave those to her and answered her questions about childhood illnesses. There wasn't much there since Hannah had never been hospitalized or had anything worse than chickenpox.

Then ANP Keller asked about her family history.

Hannah hugged herself tightly, pressing her arms against her already-too-tender-breasts. "My mom was hospitalized once when I was little, but I don't want to talk about it."

"That's fine. And your dad?"

Hannah's eyes darted all over the place. "I don't know who he is." She looked down at her beat-up sneakers. They were dirty and her laces were frayed.

"I see," ANP Keller said, and Hannah wasn't sure whether she was judging her or not. "Have you ever experienced violence at home or in any relationship you've ever been in?"

Hannah's head jerked up. "Never."

She wasn't sure that ANP Keller believed her, but she guessed she did because she just moved on to asking Hannah if she was sexually active.

Hannah blinked back tears. "I was. . . I mean, I AM. . . a virgin. I-I want. . . wanted. . . not 'til college."

ANP Keller made a note. "Later on, we'll talk more extensively about your next steps, but I want you to know that there are counselors that can help you work through your feelings about what happened to you. In fact, we have social workers on staff here who can talk to you before you leave today."

Hannah had a sudden flash of memory. Ambulance lights flashing in the window. Grandma holding six-year-old Hannah on her lap as Mama was loaded into an ambulance. Grandma telling her she couldn't go to Mama now.

She blinked hard to get rid of the unwanted memory. "I don't need to talk to anyone."

ANP Keller frowned, but she said that was up to Hannah and asked her a few more questions, like the date of her last period and when the last time she'd seen a doctor was. Then she said, "Time to talk about the elephant in the room. I need to ask you about what happened to you. That'll help me understand what medical treatment you need as well as provide a statement that we can share with the police if you choose to report the assault."

Hannah hugged herself tighter. She'd never even thought about the cops being involved. If she told them, they'd probably want to talk to her parents. "I-I don't know about the police."

"That's okay. We'll hold onto whatever you give us, and if you decide later you want to make a complaint, you can give your consent for us to share it with them." Hannah nodded again, and ANP Keller asked, gently, "Can you tell me what happened to you?"

"No. I. . . I don't remember. . . " Hannah stared at the ground. "I went to a party last night I had no business being at and. . . "

"That doesn't make this attack your fault," ANP Keller's voice was too soft like she was afraid Hannah was going to shatter into a million pieces right in front of her if she talked like a normal person. Hannah glared at the floor, wanting to say that she wasn't fragile but not sure ANP Keller would believe her because she was such a mess and not like herself at all. ANP Keller said, "Tell me the last thing you remember."

Hannah rocked back and forth. "Video games with. . . um, I think his name was Jamie. I should have kissed him." A tear rolled down her face. "I could smell beer on his breath."

"Is he the boy who attacked you?"

"No! Maybe? He left. I think." Hannah rocked back and forth some more. "Maybe I picked up the wrong cup?"

"Cup of what?"

"Tea. I mean, mine was." Hannah hugged herself. "It was on the table and I downed it. Then. . . ." Hannah squeezed her eyes shut, trying hard to remember. "Then I was dizzy. I think. Dylan thought I was drunk."

"Who's Dylan?"

"Sierra's brother. I woke up all sore, and I had to convince him I hadn't been drinking and then he took me to the hospital."

ANP Keller nodded as she wrote that down. "I need to ask you, were you drinking alcohol at all?"

"I just said I didn't!" Hannah wasn't sure she had, but whatever. "And anyway, I signed a pledge to be a sober role model, and I take it seriously."

"It's not an accusation. I promise. I just needed to know so I can evaluate your symptoms properly. I suspect from what you're telling me that your attack was drug-facilitated, and if you'd been drinking the drugs would have affected you more seriously more quickly."

"Drug-facilitated," Hannah repeated. The words felt cold and hard to her. "Right. Well, I wasn't drinking. Period."

"I believe you." ANP Keller wrote yet another note on her pad. "I can run blood and urine tests on you to try to catch exactly what's in your system. But first, I want to take a look at your injuries. I'll give you a sheet to cover yourself while you get undressed, and I'll only look at what I need to look at. Is it okay with you if we do that?" Hannah's ears were ringing as she nodded. "By the way," ANP Keller went on, "are these the clothes you were wearing last night?"

"No. My, uh, my dress was torn so. . . ."

"That's okay. You can always bring it to the police station should you decide to file a report. Just don't wash it before you do. What about your underwear and socks?"

Hannah's face felt so hot she thought she might be running a fever. "I didn't change those."

"Is it okay if we hold onto them? We can give you new ones."

"Okay. . . " Hannah felt dizzy. She lay back and let ANP Keller put a white sheet over her so she could get undressed. Her heart pounded and she wasn't sure that it hadn't skipped a beat as she peeled her clothes off.

ANP Keller kept asking her if she could do stuff: look at her injuries, take photos, use a UV light to look for fluids the rapist might have left behind. Hannah only said 'Yes' because she was too exhausted to say 'No' but she felt more and more uncomfortable with every step.

Finally, ANP Keller promised this was the last thing. She let Hannah put on a hospital gown but told her to lie down again so that she could examine her vagina. ANP Keller said something about bruising and swelling down there and asked if she could take more photographs and also if she could put something called a speculum inside Hannah to see if she could extract DNA.

Hell no! But Hannah wanted to do whatever the doctor thought she should, so she squeezed her eyes shut and held her breath.

But when ANP Keller put her instrument inside Hannah's vagina, it hurt so bad she couldn't stand it. "Stop. . . it hurts."

"Okay," ANP Keller said and withdrew the speculum. "It's okay. We don't have to. Let's have you sit up and we'll talk."

Hannah nodded, ashamed of the tears in her eyes.

ANP Keller adjusted the exam table so Hannah was sitting again. "There's no question that your attack included sexual intercourse you couldn't consent to. Your hymen is torn. There's bruising and swelling around your genitals, and there's a little bit of blood in your underwear that you probably didn't even notice."

"S-so I'm really not a virgin anymore." Hannah's voice was flat.

"I'm sorry. I can't stress enough that it isn't your fault. Someone drugged you—we'll find out exactly what sedatives were used—and took away your ability to say 'No'. Now, since your attack did include intercourse and we don't know if he wore a condom or not, there's a risk of pregnancy."

"Pregnancy?" Hannah put her hand under her gown, feeling her stomach. "No. I can't be. . . "

"I'm not saying it's definite, just that it's possible. As I'm sure you know, unprotected heterosexual intercourse can lead to pregnancy, and the fact that you couldn't and didn't consent to it doesn't change that. Now, there is a pill called Plan B we can give you that can help prevent it. Since it's only been about twelve hours, the likelihood is very high that if you take this pill, it will stop an egg from fertilizing at all or implanting in your uterus if it has been fertilized. Is that something you want to do?"

Hannah nodded. Her mind was going fast--so fast she thought she was going crazy. If she got pregnant she'd be just like Mom, having a baby with some guy whose name she didn't even know. Only Mom had been older, she'd met him in a bar or a hotel or something, and if it hadn't been for that stupid one-night stand with a guy who didn't even stay 'til morning, there'd have been no Hannah at all. And Hannah had been careful. She'd been so, so careful because she didn't want to do the same stupid things Mom had. Until she'd decided to go to the party, she'd never done a single thing that could get her in trouble.

How could this be happening to her?

ANP Keller was still talking, saying something about needing to give Hannah a shot for Hepatitis B. Hannah wasn't really listening, but she nodded anyway. She felt weird as she signed the consent forms like she was floating on the ceiling watching herself read over and sign them.

ANP Keller patted her shoulder and said, "I'll be right back. We'll do the pee test, and then I'll give you the pill and the vaccine."

When ANP Keller was gone, Hannah leaned back as far as she could on the exam table, wishing she knew how to adjust it so she could lie flat. Her cheeks felt tight like she was going to throw up, but she told herself sternly that she was going to do no such thing.

She couldn't keep track of her thoughts. There were too many of them all at once. Sierra would want to know everything, and Dylan would want to know why she hadn't told ANP Keller to call the cops since he already thought she should tell her parents.

Why didn't you? A voice in her head said.

I can't, she answered herself. *I'll get grounded and probably Mrs. Marino will kick me off the SADD leadership team because even going to a party like that is the opposite of what officers should do.*

That was only half of it too. She didn't trust the cops to believe her. They might think she was just embarrassed about getting high and having sex that she regretted now and was making the whole thing up, and wasn't it illegal for her to even go to this kind of party? Couldn't they write her a ticket or maybe even arrest her? Besides, nobody knew for sure she hadn't wanted to have sex, did they? So, what if she called it rape and it turned out it wasn't?

But you were drugged, the voice in her head said. *You heard ANP Keller, you couldn't consent.*

Hannah breathed in sharply, afraid again she was going to puke. She felt like there was a war going on inside her head between the quiet girl that her friends called Mouse and another girl who was so mad she wanted to trash the exam room. Mouse was crying that she was scared of telling the cops and that she wanted to forget the party ever happened. At the same time, Hannah was screaming that what happened to her was wrong and she wanted to do something about it.

Hannah breathed in and out, trying to keep the puke at bay, trying to decide. She put her hand over her stomach. *What if I'm pregnant? I can't stay quiet then, can I?*

That was the answer. It was the only one that made sense.

If she wasn't pregnant, no one besides Sierra and Dylan would have to know she'd even been attacked this way, and she could just go on as if nothing had happened.

No police report, she told herself firmly, ignoring the other voice in her head that said she was a coward. *Not unless I'm pregnant because then I don't have a choice.*

The pukey feeling went away and not a second too soon either because ANP Keller was opening the door.

She said, "I need to do the pee test first so that the medication doesn't contaminate the results."

"Okay," Hannah said. She felt numb like she was just going through the motions, but at the same time, she felt good about having made a decision. Now all she had to do was hope the pill she was going to take in a minute worked so that nothing messed up her plan.

5 – Nobody Needs to Know

BY THE TIME Hannah was done at the hospital, she was in an awful mood. She had to wait forever to get discharged and before that, ANP Keller told her she was going to have to see her regular doctor in three weeks to get an STD test, and if she didn't get her period, she would have to have a pregnancy test then too. She didn't know which was worse: having to deal with all this crap because of what some asshole had done to her or having to wait because it was too early to find out how messed up she was because of him. ANP Keller had brought up the counselor again too. She backed off when Hannah said 'No' and gave her a list of therapists in case she changed her mind, but the fact that she thought Hannah was so screwed up that she needed to talk to a therapist made her feel worse.

ANP Keller gave her a paper to bring to the front desk to check out. The check-out person said that under New York law, some state office paid for this kind of exam, which Hannah was glad for because she hadn't even thought about how much it would cost. The only thing they charged her for was the pill to prevent pregnancy. Her ears were ringing as she signed the little screen to authorize her debit card to be charged for it, and she asked three times whether they were sure her parents wouldn't get a bill in the mail because she was scared of them finding out.

"All done?" Sierra asked when Hannah finally came back to the waiting room. "My legs are stiff from sitting, not that's the most important thing. How are you?"

Humiliated. Angry. Exhausted. "Can we just go?"

Sierra and Dylan exchanged glances. Dylan said, "Yeah, okay. Let's put this whole thing behind you. Sierra wants to go out for pancakes. You up for it?"

Hannah's stomach felt tight with anxiety. "I don't really feel like eating," she said weakly, praying she didn't throw up right here in the waiting room. "You guys go ahead. I'll just wait at the house."

"You have to eat," Sierra said. "Come on, Hannah, let's do what we would have done if this guy hadn't ruined your morning. Don't let him win."

"I said I don't want to!" Hannah snapped. Sierra's eyes narrowed and Hannah looked away. "Sorry. I didn't mean to get mean, I just. . . I'm not feeling good and. . . "

"We understand," Dylan said. "Of course you're emotional after something like this."

"Right," Hannah said, feeling even more anxious as they headed toward the door. She realized suddenly her coat was unzipped and she was about to go out into a chilly morning. Zipping it tight, she said, "About that. . . can I count on you both not to tell anyone?" Her eyes met Sierra's, then flitted away. "Especially not Molly. She tried to talk us out of going to the party, and I don't want to hear whatever she has to say now."

"Yeah, of course," Sierra said. "The last thing you need is Miss Goody-Two-Shoes going on about how nothing would have happened if we'd gone to her stupid, boring Trunk-or-Treat."

Sierra shoved the metal bar to open the door. The cold got under Hannah's coat as soon as she did and she pulled on her gloves, glad that the bitter wind gave her an excuse not to talk anymore. She walked slowly to the car, taking in all the bare trees and the leaves on the ground. Everything was exactly the way it was before she'd gone to the party. It was only her that was different, and she couldn't really put how she felt into words so she couldn't explain it, not that she felt like talking anyway.

When they got in the car, Hannah asked Dylan to take her to get her things so she could go home. Sierra begged her to let her cover her bruises with makeup. They had to stop at CVS first, so she could get the right concealer for Hannah's skin tone. Sierra ended up buying three different ones because Hannah didn't feel up to going in, and she wasn't a hundred percent sure what the right color was. Hannah knew she should offer to pay Sierra back for the makeup, but she didn't have the energy to ask how much it cost.

It turned out one of the bottles Sierra bought was perfect. After she had covered up all the bruises on Hannah's neck and slipped the concealer into

Hannah's purse so that she could redo it herself every morning until they healed, Dylan offered to drive Hannah home. Sierra wanted to do it instead, and Hannah let her.

Sierra's mom was in the kitchen, washing dishes, when the girls were ready to go out to the car. Sierra looked just like her except her mom's face was round like Dylan's and her hair was short, almost a pixie cut, and all tight curls.

"Leaving so soon?" she asked.

"Yeah," Hannah's heart pounded, and she hoped Mrs. Dunlap couldn't tell something was wrong with her. "Thanks for having me, but I need to go home and study for AP Chemistry." It wasn't a total lie. She did have to study so that she wouldn't be embarrassed if she got called on randomly to answer a question on Monday.

"Aren't you studious? I sure wish some of that would rub off on Sierra."

"Sierra's smarter than me. She doesn't have to study so much."

"Smart or not," Mrs. Dunlap said, "you've got to work twice as hard as other people, Sierra. Otherwise, you're not going to get anywhere. I know it's not fair, but I told you, people will . . . "

Sierra rolled her eyes. "I have to get Hannah home. Can this lecture wait 'til I'm back?" She pushed the back door open without waiting for an answer. "Come on."

***

Hannah's apartment looked the same as always when she dragged herself inside. There was still the same beat-up leather couch Mom had bought at Goodwill pushed up against the ledge separating the kitchen from the living room and the same big screen TV they couldn't really afford taking up the whole wall over the fireplace. And in the kitchen, the painting Hannah had made in third grade still hung from the refrigerator as if time had stopped and Mom had forgotten that the sweet little eight-year-old girl had grown up into a young woman, sixteen years old and bouncing back and forth between dreaming Brad Ashton would come to his senses and kiss her and dreaming of the new life she'd start in two years when she went away to college. Nothing had changed. Nothing was out of place, and yet everything felt different.

"There you are," Mom said, coming out into the living room as Hannah dropped her purse on the ledge. "How was the sleepover?"

"Okay." Hannah didn't like how easily the lie slipped off her tongue, but it wasn't like she had a choice.

Mom frowned and Hannah thought, not for the first time, how different she and Mom looked. Mom's pale white skin burned rather than tanned in the summer, and she had straight blond hair, no hint of a curl anywhere, and sea blue eyes. Hannah must have got her easy-to-tan skin, dark curls, and gray eyes from her father, whoever he was.

"You're way too quiet after having spent a night with your best friend," Mom said. "What's wrong?"

"Nothing. I'm just tired, I was up late and. . ." Hannah stopped herself just before she let the real story out. She rubbed her temples and said, "I woke up with a headache too. I think I'm going to take a nap."

"Go ahead," Mom said, even though her eyes were narrow and she had a tight-lipped expression on her face. "I'll be here all day if you feel like talking. I know it's against teenage law to hang out with your mom, but I can see something's bothering you."

Hannah's stomach sank. Mom knew. Somehow without her saying a word, she knew. "I'm fine," she said weakly. "I just wish I hadn't gone last night. I'm gonna be so behind in school."

Mom shrugged. "You can't just study all the time. You need time for fun too."

"Fun. Right." Hannah's eyes flitted away from Mom's. She made herself yawn. "I really am tired. I'd better. . . "

"Are you sure you don't need to talk? Sleeping won't fix it, you know. It'll still be there when you get up."

Give it up, Mom! God! "Good night," Hannah said firmly, being careful not to raise her voice so that Mom wouldn't think something was even more wrong than she did. She hurried into her bedroom and closed the door, then collapsed into her bed.

She tossed and turned, too angry to sleep. Her thoughts were all jumbled up and she couldn't stop thinking about the party and Mom and Sierra all at once. The front door creaked open and then shut, and she knew Eric was home. However, she didn't know how much time had passed. She sat up and reached for her phone, then realized she'd left it in her purse, which was still on the ledge in the living room.

"I'm sure you're overreacting," her stepfather was saying as she came out into the hall. "Maybe she really is just tired."

"She's my flesh and blood! I can tell when something's wrong with her!" Mom snapped, and Hannah froze. "When I was her age, I was wild and out of control, and what if she goes down the same path? Then what?"

"I doubt that's the case. I doubt she's even hungover. That's probably your fear talking. Anyway, look, we'll get her to talk. Tomorrow's Sunday, so let's . . . "

Hannah came into the room just then, and suddenly, her parents stopped talking. She could feel them staring at her as she got her purse from the ledge. She looked away, wanting to laugh even though nothing was funny. Well, Eric was, kind of. He was shorter than Mom, so seeing him reach up to put his hand in her hair was amusing. He and Mom were quite a pair. He was more peach while she was almost porcelain white, and he only came up to her shoulder. His wavy hair was brown with streaks of gray in it.

"Forgot this," Hannah mumbled. "Don't let me interrupt."

"You're not," Eric said. His eyes met Hannah's and she had this weird feeling like he was trying to x-ray her. "You feeling any better?"

Hannah shrugged. "My head still hurts," she said, rubbing her temples, "but I'm sure I'll be fine."

"That's too bad. I thought since we're all home, maybe we could do something as a family. How about we spend the afternoon playing a board game and then go out to dinner?"

"You love *Clue*," Mom added, "so I'll suffer through it if you'll come play with us."

Hannah's legs felt wobbly, and she realized suddenly she hadn't eaten anything since the party. "I don't think I'm up for it," she said weakly, going to the fridge to try to find something that wouldn't be hard on her stomach. "Besides, I have to try to study, headache or no headache."

She stared into the refrigerator, but nothing looked good to her. There was bread on the top shelf, and she remembered suddenly how when she was little and had the flu, Grandma would give her toast and jam and let her eat it in front of the TV. They had all lived together then, she and Mom and Grandma, but New York was too cold for Grandma, and she'd stayed in Florida when Mom and Hannah moved. Now she only came up once or twice a year and never in November.

She missed her grandmother taking care of her so much that tears welled up in her eyes.

Hannah grabbed the loaf of bread, annoyed with herself. It wasn't like they'd moved here yesterday. She'd been a New Yorker since fifth grade. What was wrong with her?

She threw the bread onto the counter and looked for jam. There were about five thousand jams on the door of the fridge, and half of them only had one spoonful in them. That made Hannah madder. Why couldn't Mom finish one jam before opening another like normal people did? Thanks to her, there were too many on the shelf and trying to decide which one to take felt overwhelming.

"It's 20 degrees out," Eric said. "Do you really need to cool off in the fridge?"

Hannah grabbed a jam at random and slammed the fridge shut. It was raspberry, her least favorite flavor, but whatever. At least she'd get something in her stomach that hopefully, she could keep down. She took a big spoonful and spread it over the bread, not caring that she was making crumbs.

"I think you're missing something," Mom said as Hannah slammed the two pieces of bread together. "How are you going to have the energy to study without any protein? Put some peanut butter on that sandwich."

"If I wanted peanut butter, I would have taken it without you telling me to!" Hannah snapped. She threw the sandwich onto a plate and stomped out of the room, almost forgetting her purse again and having to stop and grab it.

As she went down the hall, she heard Mom say, quietly, "Still think nothing's wrong? I've never seen her so irritable in all my life."

Eric said something that Hannah couldn't quite hear but which she was sure was about agreeing that she was hungover.

Good. Let them think that. Let them punish her for it. She deserved to be punished for going to the party anyway.

And yet, Dylan said she needed them, that she couldn't deal with this alone.

She hesitated, her hand on the doorknob to her room.

She wished again that her grandmother was here. She could crawl into her lap like she was still a little girl and tell her what happened, and Grandma would comfort her even if she was mad at her for doing something stupid.

But Grandma wasn't going to be here until Passover, and that was months and months away. In the meantime, Hannah was stuck with Mom and Eric, and they would be so disappointed in her and so mad at her. Mom would cry and send Hannah to her room like she was still in second grade, and later Eric would come talk to her in a quiet voice about how she broke their trust and had to be grounded even though he hated to punish her.

She didn't care about the punishment. She'd lied to them and gone to a party she knew she had no business going to.

But the looks on their faces and the tears in Mom's eyes if she told. . .

She couldn't handle that.

She hurried inside her room and slammed the door closed before Mom or Eric could come after her to question her about what she'd been up to.

6 – Sunday Morning Breakfast Lecture

THE NEXT MORNING, Mom wanted Hannah to come to the diner with her and Eric for breakfast. She wouldn't take 'No' for an answer, and Hannah couldn't explain that she didn't want to run into anyone from school and that the diner was popular with sports teams, even on Sundays. So, she had to go.

"Fine," she said, "but you'll have to wait 'til I change my shirt."

"What's wrong with what you've got on?" Mom asked. "It looks cute on you."

"It's too fancy for the diner," Hannah said, not wanting to explain that the lace collar was cut way too low and she didn't want anyone seeing her cleavage. "Be out in a sec." She closed her door and stared at her closet. She had rows and rows of shirts in every color and style, and she couldn't figure out where to begin looking for something that might make her feel more comfortable. She ran her finger along the hangers, feeling stupid about how anxious she was getting over something that mattered so little.

Mom knocked and told her to hurry up. Hannah grabbed something and put it on without looking. She double-checked to make sure her bruises were still covered. They were, and better yet, her plaid button-down shirt made it looks like she didn't have any breasts at all.

***

Hannah kept her eyes down as she followed the hostess and her parents to their table a little while later. There were people at every table as they passed by, and she could feel them all staring at her.

They knew what had happened to her. She was sure of it. Either that or they were thinking about the outline of her breasts under her shirt and what they wanted to do to her.

She threw herself into her seat, wishing more than ever that she was at home where nobody could look at her. Mom glanced at her, frowning, but said nothing.

"Well," Eric said, rubbing his hands together. "What looks good to you, Hannah?"

"I know what she wants," Mom said. "Smoked salmon and eggs with wheat toast, just like always."

Hannah grabbed a menu. "Maybe I'll try something different this time."

"That'll be the day," Mom said.

Hannah stared at the menu, pretending to read it. This was the way it was every time they went to the diner. Eric always asked her what she wanted, and Mom always teased her about ordering the same thing. It had never annoyed her before, but today she could barely stand it.

She scanned the breakfast choices with her eyes. The eggs she always got would probably be easier on her stomach than the pancakes with the fruit compote on top that looked so good to her, but she wanted the pancakes so bad and all of a sudden, she wanted hot chocolate too even though she considered it a Christmas season drink and it wasn't even Thanksgiving yet.

A waitress showed up to take their orders. Hannah argued with herself about the pancakes or the eggs while her parents ordered. "And what about you, hon?" the waitress asked, and Hannah surprised herself by asking for the pancakes with a double helping of cinnamon apple compote and a hot chocolate.

"Well!" Mom said. "I never thought I'd see the day."

"I know all that sugar's terrible for you, but I wanted it," Hannah said weakly.

Mom shrugged. "You're too young to worry about it. Life's short, enjoy yourself."

Last time I tried that, it didn't go so well. Some kids at the next table were coloring, and Hannah had an impulse to ask the waitress for a kids' menu and a cup full of crayons so she could color too. She bit her lip, telling herself she was way too old for that.

Eric picked up his glass of water. "Let's toast to Hannah's restored health. I'm so glad you're feeling better this morning, sweetheart." Hannah's face got hot as he and Mom clinked glasses.

"Well?" Mom said. "Aren't you going to join in?"

"No, thanks," Hannah said. "I'm already dying of embarrassment."

Eric sighed as he put down his water. Mom said, "You want to. . . "

"Not really, but we might as well get it out of the way," Eric said. Hannah's heart pounded as he turned to her. "We had an ulterior motive in taking you to breakfast this morning. Yes, we want to have a nice time. But we're also worried about you, and we thought it would be easier to talk about over the kind of meal you always look forward to."

Hannah wriggled. "There's nothing to worry about. I'm fine."

"Are you?" Mom said. "It seemed to me you were more than a little hungover yesterday."

Hannah picked at a corner of her placemat. "What?" she said, offended even though she knew that's what they thought and had made a pact with herself to let them think it. "You think I was drinking? Come on, Mom, don't you know I'd never . . . "

"I know a hangover when I see one!" Mom snapped. "Now don't lie to us, Hannah, how much did you . . . "

A busboy came to deliver their drinks and Mom cut herself off. Hannah's hot chocolate didn't have whipped cream on it like it was supposed to, but she said nothing even though she wanted almost desperately to have it. Instead, she took a sip while the busboy poured coffee for her parents, not bothering to wait for it to cool. She burned her tongue, but she didn't care.

The busboy went away, and Hannah said, awkwardly, "What did you order, Mom?"

"I'm having the egg and potato special with bacon and sausage," Mom said, "but don't think I forgot what we were talking about before the waiter came. How much did you drink? Or, should I say, how much did Sierra talk you into drinking?"

Hannah hesitated. She could pretend she drank that wine cooler she gave Jamie, she guessed, and leave out where she got it from. But that was going too far. Letting her parents think she'd been drinking when she hadn't was one thing, but actively making up a story was another. Hannah wasn't ordinarily a liar and she'd broken her parents' trust enough without trying to keep track of some fake story.

She took a deep breath, trying to build up her courage. "All right," she said. "You're going to be super disappointed in me, but. . . "

"No matter how disappointed we are, we'll still love you," Eric said. "And we're already disappointed because you drank and then tried to cover it up. But once we know the whole story, we can figure out together the best way to help you bounce back from this. Now, what is it you're scared to tell us?"

Hannah looked over her shoulder to make sure no one she knew was at any of the nearby tables. "Sierra and I weren't watching scary movies Friday night. We went to a Halloween party."

"A party," Mom repeated, her lips a thin line. "What party?"

"The kind you wouldn't want me at." Hannah stared down at the table. "W-with older people w-who were drinking and . . ."

"A frat party?" Mom's voice rose. "You let Sierra take you to a FRAT party? You'd better start learning to stand up to her, young lady. You knew better, and you let what she wanted to do override your common sense. How much did you drink, Hannah? One beer? Two? Do you even know?"

"Do you have to be so loud?" Hannah snapped. "The whole restaurant can hear."

"Oh, are you embarrassed? Too bad, Hannah, if you hadn't done something so stupid, you'd have nothing to be embarrassed about."

Hannah slumped down in her seat. "I'm not embarrassed," she said, even though she was. "I just don't want us to get kicked out of here before we even get our food, that's all."

Eric put his hand over Mom's. "Don't exaggerate, Hannah. We're not nearly loud enough to cause trouble." He sipped his coffee. "Anyway, maybe Mom's right that you let Sierra talk you into this and maybe she's not. It doesn't matter. You still broke the rules, and you still lied to us about what you were planning to do that night. All of that is on you no matter what Sierra thought you should do."

The food came before Hannah could answer. She stared at her pile of pancakes as the waiter put it down in front of her. They were huge with chocolate chips in them and baked apples in syrup on the top. *I don't deserve something as nice as this,* Hannah thought as she picked up her fork.

Mom and Eric should have made me stay home while they went out, or better yet, made me order toast and butter, nothing more.

"Can we finish breakfast before you punish me?" she asked.

Eric sighed. "Your mom and I need to talk over what to do about this, and the food's here, so we might as well try to enjoy ourselves. But if there's anything else we need to know about this party, you'd better tell us now."

Hannah's hands were suddenly cold. She cupped them around her hot chocolate while she tried to think. "I didn't drink," she said. "That's not what happened."

Mom's eyes narrowed and Hannah knew she didn't believe her. "It wasn't!" she said. "I told you, I didn't drink. Sierra made me take a wine cooler but -"

"Wine coolers are still alcohol," Mom interrupted.

"And I gave it away!" Hannah snapped.

Eric and Mom looked at each other. Eric said, "Hannah. You had a lot of symptoms that looked an awful lot like a hangover yesterday. If you have some other explanation, you need to offer it. Otherwise, we're going to have to assume that you were drunk and that you're scared to admit it."

"You have it all wrong," Hannah said flatly, "and that's all I'm going to say." She picked up her fork. "Now can we drop this? Please?"

Eric looked her up and down like he was trying to figure something out. "There's something you're not telling us, but okay. We'll drop it for now."

"Eric," Mom said.

"If she doesn't want to talk, she doesn't want to talk. We can't make her. But what we can do is decide how we're going to handle what she did tell us. So, Hannah can stay home for the rest of the day while we figure that out and we'll take it from there. Now, let's eat before all of our food gets cold." Eric stabbed his scrambled eggs with his fork.

Hannah stared down at her pancakes. It was obvious there was no talking to her parents. They didn't even believe she hadn't been drinking, so there was no way they'd ever believe the rest of it. She blinked back tears, feeling betrayed by her parents even though she also felt like she was the one who betrayed them.

"How're your pancakes?" Mom asked as if nothing had happened.

"Fine," Hannah said, even though between the apples, the powdered sugar, and the chocolate chips, they were sickeningly sweet, and she had no appetite anyway. "Everything's fine." She hurried to cut some more of her pancakes and eat them so that Mom wouldn't guess that she was lying.

7 - Back to School

WHEN HANNAH'S PARENTS called her into the living room later that afternoon, the disappointment and worry on their faces were worse than knowing she was about to be grounded. Mom's eyes were all red and irritated and Hannah knew she'd been crying, and Eric had creases in his forehead as he told her, his voice quiet, how sneaking around was not like her, and that she had to be punished for breaking their trust.

She stared at the floor as he said he knew she wasn't telling the whole truth even now and that he and Mom were worried about her. Mom's voice shook as she begged Hannah to tell her what was going on with her, and it hurt Hannah so badly to know she'd made Mom cry that she almost gave in. But when she looked up at her parents' faces, she knew they'd be a hundred times more disappointed than they were already if they knew she'd been stupid enough to let her drink out of her sight so some guy could drug her and have sex with her. So, she just mumbled that she wished she hadn't gone to the party and that she felt like she betrayed everyone who looked up to her by being a poor role model.

Mom kissed the top of her head. "You're always so hard on yourself, baby. All you have to do is own up to making a mistake and move on from here."

"Mom's right," Eric agreed, while Hannah's eyes darted everywhere so she wouldn't have to look at her parents. "That's how I want you to think of your punishment. As an opportunity to do some thinking, so you can make a better choice next time." Hannah's eyes burned with tears for no reason as he added that she was grounded for the next two weekends and not allowed to ride to school with her friends, either.

Hannah guessed that was fair, but when Sierra texted her the next morning while she was brushing her hair and offered to meet her by the bus stop so they could ride together without Mom and Eric knowing, she agreed without a second thought.

What was wrong with her? First the party, now this. She was becoming an expert at sneaking around behind her parents' backs. She threw her hairbrush down and got her stuff, sick of looking at herself in the mirror.

***

Molly wasn't in the car when Sierra picked Hannah up. Hannah asked if she was coming, and Sierra said that Molly was riding with Jen, her girlfriend.

"I'm kind of glad," Hannah said, twisting a stray lock of hair around her finger. " I still haven't decided what to say if she asks me about the party."

"Can you do me a favor? When you figure it out, leave out how I'm the world's worst friend. I don't want her to hate me."

Hannah pulled a hair tie off her wrist and tied her hair back without bothering to adjust the mirror so she could see what she was doing. "That's easy because you're not. And don't start about how you pushed me to go to the party. I told you, I wanted to go! I wanted to meet people, I wanted to have fun. So, stop acting like you dragged me there at gunpoint or something because that's not what happened!"

"All right. Sorry. It's just. . . if you hadn't gone, if I hadn't talked you out of going to Brad's instead . . ."

Brad. Hannah sat up straighter, her heart beating hard. Brad had been so hurt she turned him down, and now she had to sit next to him in math and pray he didn't think any less of her than he had before the party.

"Maybe it wouldn't have been better," she said weakly. "Like you said, he only cares about smoking weed, so. . . " But she didn't believe a word she was saying. She turned up the music so she wouldn't have to hear whatever Sierra's answer was.

A few minutes later, they were at school. It looked the same as always with the faded letters over the front door spelling out that this was Dwight D. Eisenhower High School and the tiny knots of people milling around outside like they had no idea it was freezing out.

Of course it was the same as always. Just because Hannah was different didn't mean the world was. She fiddled with her seatbelt, pretending it was stuck, so she didn't have to get out yet.

"What are you doing?" Sierra asked.

"Nothing. I'm just dreading going out into the cold, that's all."

"We'll go inside. Let's just make sure Molly's not waiting for us under the tree." In nice weather, Hannah, Sierra, and Molly hung out under an oak tree on the edge of the campus. It was far enough away from everyone and everything else to feel like it was private, and somehow everyone knew it was theirs, or at least, didn't try to horn in on it while they were there.

"I'm sure Molly has too much sense to hang out under the tree when it's negative fifteen hundred degrees out," Hannah said, opening her seatbelt. "Let's go."

The wind was blowing right in Hannah's face. She pulled her hood tighter around her face as she pushed against it.

When was almost at the door, someone wolf-whistled at her and said loudly, "Looking good for an ugly girl, Hannah!"

Hannah stiffened. She turned to face her attacker. It was Nathan, of course, a pale, almost pasty white boy who was constantly bothering her. Hannah thought he looked liked the Pillsbury Doughboy, only too skinny to poke your finger into his stomach, but she was too nice to say so. He was wearing a wool cap that covered his yellow hair and his blue eyes made her feel even colder as they met hers.

"Ignore him," Sierra said under her breath, "and for God's sake, stop walking all hunched over like you deserve to get messed with."

Hannah's eyes narrowed. "Way to be on my side," she mumbled.

"Come on, Ms. Grouchy-Groucherton. Let's go get some food in your stomach." Sierra pulled open the steel door at the front of the school and gestured for Hannah to go ahead of her.

Hannah's stomach felt tight and sore and she doubted she could eat anything, but she didn't bother to say so as she followed Sierra into the building.

In the cafeteria, Sierra snagged them their usual table in the corner by the far door. That table had been Hannah's idea on the first day of freshman year. Being so close to the door meant they could get to their lockers faster than anyone else when the bell rang. But today, Hannah was in no hurry to go anywhere, and she was glad when Sierra offered to go buy food for both of them so they wouldn't lose the table. She sat and stared, watching everyone else.

There was a group of girls sitting in the opposite corner. One of them, an Asian girl with blonde streaks in her long black hair, had a backpack that was so huge she had to put it on the table to make room for her friends to sit. That was Katie, the President of SADD. Hannah didn't know her very well. She wondered how Katie got away with carrying that huge bag without people making fun of her.

She looked away before Katie caught her staring. Instead, she watched Brad's table from across the room. Brad doubled over laughing at something his friend, a guy Hannah didn't know whose claim to fame seemed to be long red hair, said. Hannah wondered if that was Mark and what they were laughing about. Not her, she hoped, even though there was no reason for them to be laughing at her. They didn't know she was watching, and she was sure Brad had got over her turning him down the second he got weed smoke in his lungs.

Sierra came back with two plates of eggs and two drinks. "Chocolate milk's for me," she said, handing Hannah a small container of skim milk. "I won't get you anything that's not good for you ever again. Don't worry."

Hannah wanted chocolate milk so bad it hurt, but she just mumbled her thanks and opened the container Sierra handed her.

***

When she got to homeroom, Molly was already in her seat. "There you are," she said. "It feels like forever since I've seen you even though it's only been the weekend. How was the party?"

"It was," Hannah said. "Now it's over, and it's a new week. How was Trunk or Treat?"

"It was what?" Molly asked. "Come on, Hannah, since I didn't go I want to live it through your eyes. Tell me everything."

"Wait," the boy on Hannah's other side interjected "You're THAT Hannah? I heard some girl named Hannah got totally wasted at a party

Friday night and jumped into bed with a rando, but I didn't think it could be you. Aren't you in charge of all the sobriety pledges and shit?"

"It wasn't me," Hannah said. "I went to a party, but I didn't drink."

"That's not what I heard," a girl said. "I heard you were the life of the party, a real slut, coming on to one guy after another."

Hannah looked toward Molly for help, but Molly was staring into space, her lips thin. Of course she was. She wasn't there, she didn't know what had happened. So how could she be of any use whatsoever?

"That's not true," Hannah whispered, panicking so hard that she could barely speak. "That's not what happened at all."

"But you did go to the party, right?" the guy on her left said.

"Yeah. But I didn't break my pledge." Hannah was sure she was protesting too much and that no one believed her, so she made herself shut up.

The bell rang, and a teacher Hannah had never seen before walked in. The new teacher was a tall black woman whose hair was piled up on top of her head. She wore three or four bracelets on one arm that jingled as she walked.

"Sorry I'm late," she said. "My name is Ms. Prentiss. I'm subbing for Mrs. Wolfe today. Now, I have the roster, so please raise your hand when I call your name. And please don't fool around and pretend to be one another."

People were snickering under their breath, laughing at the sub for no reason. Hannah wanted to tell them to cut it out, but she didn't have the energy even though she felt bad about not standing up for the woman.

Molly said under her breath, "That poor woman's going to have a hard time today."

She's not the only one. Hannah slid down in her seat, wishing the sub would somehow forget to call her name so that no one would know she was there.

8 – Gossip and Lies

HANNAH TOOK SO long arguing with herself at her locker about whether Brad believed the rumors and whether she gave a fuck if he did that almost all the seats in the front half of her Chemistry classroom were full by the time she got to class. The only seat left was next to Molly, who was the only other girl in the class, and Hannah had to walk past Nathan to get there. She felt like she was wading through quicksand as she forced herself into the room.

Molly lowered her voice as soon as Hannah sat down and asked her if it was true that she'd got drunk at the party.

"Molly!" Hannah's head hurt and her throat felt tight. "How can you think I'd ever . . ."

"I don't want to! But you won't tell me anything about the party and neither will Sierra, and it's obvious something happened. I don't care if you did drink or whatever else. I'm still your best friend. You can tell me."

Hannah pretended to be having a hard time unscrewing her pen cap while she thought about it. "I didn't drink," she said firmly, "and the rest of it isn't something I want to talk about."

The bell rang and Mr. Dawson came in. Thank God.

"Today's not a lab day, is it?" Hannah whispered to Molly as Mr. Dawson started the lesson.

Molly shook her head slightly but said nothing, and Hannah wasn't sure if it was because Mr. Dawson might call them out for talking or because she was mad at her.

Mr. Dawson wrote an equation on the board. "Which one of you wants to be the brave soul who tries to balance this chemical reaction for us and risk everyone discovering you know nothing?"

Hannah rubbed the back of her neck, trying to get rid of her headache. Mr. Dawson said things all the time about everyone being stupid. He made it sound like a joke, but it wasn't funny. Hannah's worst fear was him calling on her and her not knowing the answer.

"How about you, Hannah?" Mr. Dawson said. "Come up to the board and show us if you learned anything over the weekend, though I highly doubt it."

As Hannah got up, her heart pounding, Nathan said, "I bet the only chemical equation she knows is what happens when a penis meets a vagina." He and his friend Paul, who was sitting next to him, both doubled over with laughter.

Mr. Dawson's eyes landed on them for half a second, and Hannah thought he might actually have the decency to tell them to cut it out, but Mr. Dawson just said, "We're waiting, Hannah. Come on."

Hannah walked up to the board, holding her head up as high as possible to show Nathan he wasn't going to get to her. She looked at the problem.

$$N_2(g) + H_2 (g) \rightarrow NH_3 (g)$$

After she was grounded, Hannah had spent the rest of Sunday in her room studying chemical equations, but now it was like she'd never seen one before. She picked up the dry erase marker, but she couldn't think because in her head she was hearing the boy in homeroom asking her if she'd really got drunk and slept with a bunch of guys and Molly begging her to tell her what happened at the party and Nathan basically calling her a slut too.

She let her breath out slowly and told herself to forget that and focus. There were two nitrogen atoms on one side, so it was easy to balance that. All she had to do was put a two in front of the NH_3. She did, then stared at the problem. She just needed to balance it now, and she knew exactly what to do. But she was half thinking about how long it was going to take all the people who called her Saint Hannah to be mean to start calling her Slut Hannah instead, and by accident, she wrote the three in front of the N instead of the H and had to erase it.

"You're going to win a lot of science competitions with that speed," Mr. Dawson said. "Sit down, Hannah, you're clearly guessing."

Hannah ignored him, picking up the marker again. But Mr. Dawson said, "I said, sit down. Let someone who knows what they're doing do that." He took a step toward her, and Hannah dropped the marker before he could touch her.

"Leave me alone!" she said.

Everyone was laughing except Molly. Nobody was bothering to hide it. Hannah said, "For your information, the correct coefficients are one, three, and a two on the other side. I'm not stupid like you think I am." She hurried back to her seat and threw herself into it before anyone could say anything.

Mr. Dawson said, as if nothing had happened, "Nathan, you're on the hot seat next. Show us how it's done, will you, and try not to cry if it's hard." All the boys giggled as he turned to write another equation on the board.

Molly leaned over and whispered, "Hey. You okay?"

"No talking, girls," Mr. Dawson said, saving Hannah from having to explain herself to Molly for the second time in one class period. "Especially you, Hannah. Pay attention and you might actually learn something."

Hannah's eyes narrowed and she wrote the new problem on her paper, determined to solve it faster than Nathan. It seemed to her that he took twice as long at the board as she had, but Mr. Dawson didn't say anything, so she guessed she was wrong.

"Excellent," Mr. Dawson said when Nathan finally finished, even though Hannah had had the right answer for ten minutes already.

Nathan smirked as he passed Hannah's desk. "Looks like I'm gonna beat your grades this quarter, huh, Slut Hannah?"

Hannah ignored him. Instead, she glared at the back of Mr. Dawson's head as he erased the board.

When the bell rang, Hannah jumped up and left while Molly was still packing her notebook. She spent hcr free period in the library where she grabbed a random book off the fiction shelf and tried to get lost in it like she used to when she was little and needed to forget how sad she was that Mom was in the hospital.

It wasn't working today. She was too aware of other people in the library and the rumors people were spreading about her in the halls, and she kept losing her place and reading the same sentence over and over. When the bell rang, she left the book on the table, not caring that someone else would have to put it away and braced herself for the trip down the hallway to her next class.

Two more class periods went by and then it was time for Precalculus. Hannah wasn't in the mood for whatever stupid thing Brad was going to say, but she decided she'd rather be brave than live up to her nickname. She held her head up as high as she could as she walked into the classroom. She could feel everyone staring at her as she slipped into her seat between Brad and Jen, but she told herself she didn't care.

Jen flipped her rust-colored hair over her shoulder and stared at Hannah as she sat down. "You all right?" she whispered. "Everyone's saying you got drunk last weekend."

"Well, I didn't!" Hannah snapped. "And I'm fine. Mostly, anyway. I just don't want to talk about the stupid party, all right?"

"Whoa! I'm your friend, not your worst enemy, but whatever."

"Sorry." Hannah could feel Brad staring at her and she didn't like it. "It's just, I've been hearing stupid rumors all day, and I'd rather talk about something else. When did you and Molly become official?"

"After Trunk or Treat." Jen's eyes sparkled from behind her big, round glasses. "We went out for a late-night snack, and Molly gave me a promise ring." She held out her hand to show Hannah. The ring had three purple stones on it, which Hannah was sure were fake, but they looked pretty. The silver band stood out against Jen's peach skin.

"That's great," Hannah said, making herself smile.

The bell rang. "All right, everyone," Mrs. Marino said. "You all have worksheets on your desk. Please work on them individually for the next ten minutes, and then we'll break up into groups to go over them."

"Hannah," Brad whispered as she flipped her worksheet over.

Hannah turned her head despite herself. "What? There wouldn't be any rumors if I'd gone to your party, is that what you were gonna say?"

"Bzzzt," Brad said. "Thanks for playing, but you're dead wrong, even if you did miss the most awesome Halloween party ever." He leaned forward. Hannah shrank back, not wanting him in her space.

Brad lowered his voice and said, "I know the rumors are a bunch of BS that some jealous asshole started. I'll help you spread the word if you want."

Hannah hesitated. She wanted to tell Brad she could handle this on her own, but at the same time, she didn't. Plus, the world was backward. Brad, who never took anyone or anything seriously, totally rejected the rumors, while her best friends were falling all over themselves to help her through the hangover that hadn't actually happened.

"Sit up, please, Brad," Mrs. Marino said, sounding weary.

Hannah said, "We'll talk later," even though she didn't intend to continue this conversation at all.

Brad nodded as he sat up. Hannah bent over her worksheet, pretending she was totally absorbed in finding the coordinates of the center of a circle on a graph even though it was the least important question running through her mind.

S IERRA TEXTED HANNAH while she was at her locker after school that she couldn't give her a ride because she needed to meet up with Jake.

Hannah bit her lip, not sure she liked this. Jake hadn't done anything to her, but it was his party, and that meant he probably knew the guy who had. Maybe they were even good friends. And what did a twenty-one-year-old want with a high school junior anyway?

"Do you think we need to worry about Sierra dating Jake?" she asked Molly.

Molly shrugged. "It won't last. It's almost that time of the month where they break up again, and maybe this time we can finally get through to Sierra to keep it that way." A shadow crossed her face. "She's the one who should be grounded. It's not fair that you are, and she gets off scot-free."

"She didn't tell her parents. I did."

"And you got punished for telling the truth! That's messed up."

"Right." Hannah looked away. "I guess I'd better go before I miss the stupid bus." She let Molly hug her goodbye, and then she hurried away.

Brad was sitting on the ledge around the raised flowerbed by the pick-up circle. He called her name.

Hannah was going to ignore him, but for some reason, she didn't. She came over and stood a safe distance away, crossing her arms against her chest. "What's up?"

"Nothing." Brad grinned. "I just like getting you to turn around by calling your name."

Hannah rolled her eyes. "I'm gonna miss my bus, so if you need the homework, hurry up and ask for it."

"That's not what I wanted." Brad picked up a book that was taking up space next to him. "Come sit a sec."

Hannah didn't want to sit, but she came a little closer. Brad said, "We got interrupted earlier, and it was kind of important. I meant what I said. I don't believe for a second that you got drunk, and I want to help you fight it."

"There's nothing to fight. If I ignore them for long enough, they'll find something else to talk about."

"I wish." Brad looked away. "They don't forget. Trust me. Even when they find someone else to gossip about, they still don't." He played with the buckle to his backpack strap, flipping it open and closed over and over. "I don't know what you heard, but I don't actually bite. Sit down, will you?"

Hannah threw herself down next to Brad, annoyed. "Fine. I'm sitting. Now, what's so important?"

"You okay, Hannah? Really?" Brad's voice was soft. "I mean, I'm used to being on the receiving end of bullshit, but you're the ultimate good girl. People saying crap has to be getting to you."

Hannah stiffened. "Can everyone stop asking me that? I went to a party. It's not like I broke my neck skydiving."

"Way to go to extremes." Brad smiled suddenly, and Hannah couldn't help loving his smile. It was so bright, so full of life. It made her think things she had no business thinking, especially not after what some asshole had done to her. "So," he said, "how was the party you blew me off for anyway?"

Hannah's heart pounded. "It was. . . a mistake. I'd have had more fun with you." She fidgeted, desperate to know what Brad thought of her and not wanting to know at the same time.

"I bet you would." Brad slid a little closer and Hannah slid back, pressing her arms tight against her chest. Brad looked her up and down. "Something terrible must have happened there," he said. "When you're not jumping down someone's throat, you're jumping away like you just saw a ghost."

Hannah's ears were buzzing. "I didn't fit in there," she said carefully. "I was the only one who wasn't drinking, and the guys all wanted to do stuff with me I didn't want to do." She touched the makeup over the bruises on her neck, gingerly, hoping Brad couldn't see them.

"Sucks." Brad stared into space, saying nothing. Then out of nowhere, he said, "I got arrested last summer."

"What?" Hannah was shocked on top of being confused.

"Yep. That's the kernel of truth in all the dumbass rumors you hear about me. It was for weed. I was dumb enough to buy it off some guy I didn't know, and I got caught."

Hannah had a billion questions, but she just asked, "Why are you telling me this?"

"I dunno. I just felt like it." Brad's eyes sparkled. "But since I told you a deep, dark secret, maybe you can tell me one. What really happened at the party?"

Hannah shook her head. "You wouldn't understand."

"Why? Cause I'm a dude?"

"That and cause I can't. . . " Hannah sighed. "It's too hard to talk about."

Brad's eyes widened. Hannah had never thought that seeing the wheels turn was a real thing before, but she could tell he was figuring things out. She looked away from him again, not wanting him to be able to see right through her.

Brad said, "Wait a sec. Some guys wanted you to do stuff and now you're all freaked out. . . no way. . . " A shadow darkened his face. "Who do I need to beat up?"

"Nobody!" Hannah slid further away. "Why do guys think that's the answer to everything?"

"I don't," Brad said. "I'm just trying to sound all tough and cool. Seriously, though, if some dude did what I think he did to you. . . " He pounded his palm with his fist. "I hate it as much as I hate the thought of someone doing it to my sister."

His sister. So that's how Brad thought of her, as another sister. Hannah was so disappointed it made her chest hurt even though there was no reason to be sad. It wasn't like she had a chance with Brad anyway.

"You have a sister?" she asked.

"Not the point, but yeah. Her name's Emily. She's away at college." The light went out of Brad's eyes suddenly, and he looked down at the ground. Hannah wondered what that was about, but she didn't dare ask. "Listen," Brad said, tapping the book in his lap, "you think you could tutor me in English? I can't make myself get through the first page of this book, never mind the whole thing, and Mr. Collins already kept me after once to talk to me about wasting my potential."

Hannah glanced at the book to buy herself some time. The title was upside down, but she recognized the cover for *The Scarlet Letter*. "Sure," she said cautiously. This was a safer topic of conversation, but tutoring Brad might mean spending a lot of time with him alone, and she wasn't sure that was a good idea. "But you have to read it, I'm not going to just summarize it for you."

"I'll try," Brad said, "and if I can't, there's always Wikipedia." He grinned. "Thanks, Hannah, you don't know what a lifesaver you are."

Brad was sitting close to Hannah, and she had this feeling like he wanted to hug her. It scared her enough to make her scoot back.

Mr. Collins suddenly showed up. "If either of you needs a bus, better get to it now," he said.

"I was just about to, thanks," Hannah said, her eyes darting everywhere. "Meet me in the library second period tomorrow if you still want tutoring, Brad." She got up and walked away, then turned her head over her shoulder.

Mr. Collins had sat down next to Brad and was talking to him. Brad had his arms crossed and was kicking his feet against the bottom of the ledge. Hannah couldn't tell what they were saying because the wind was blowing in her face again, but whatever had happened, it was not good.

Her stomach hurt suddenly. She hoped she hadn't got Brad in trouble somehow on top of everything else.

10 – In the Library

THE NEXT MORNING, Hannah waited her entire free period in the library for Brad, but he never showed up. Molly said he was a flake or maybe he got high, but Hannah was sure she was wrong. Whatever happened had to do with what Mr. Collins had to say. She was sure of it.

Sure enough, Mr. Collins kept her after English so he could tell her that he'd sent her to the bus because he could tell Brad was making her uncomfortable.

"It won't happen again," he said. "I talked to Brad and made sure he understands that his behavior was inappropriate."

Hannah knew she should be grateful, but she was irritated. No one had asked Mr. Collins to get in her business, and now there was no way to explain the real reason she'd been so freaked out because there was no way in hell she was telling him what happened to her.

She gave Brad space for the next week, not sure how to bring this up to him and hoping that he would approach her first. But he didn't.

"Course not," Sierra said one morning while they were at their lockers. "He thinks he made you uncomfortable. How's he gonna know any different if you keep avoiding him?"

Hannah guessed she was right, but she still felt too shy to talk to Brad. She put a note on his desk during Precalc telling him to meet her in the library the next day if he still wanted tutoring.

The next morning, Molly came with her to the library.

"Mind if we talk about Key Club while we're waiting?" she asked. Key Club was another community service club that Hannah and Molly belonged to, though Hannah had skipped the last few meetings and told Molly it was because she was grounded.

"I guess," Hannah said.

"Cool." Molly flipped a page. "We talked last week about co-sponsoring the All Nighter. Has SADD started planning yet?"

Last year's All Nighter had been so much fun. Twister—the game Sierra had suggested even though she wasn't even in SADD—was a huge hit and so was the dance marathon. Hannah danced with Dylan and even him letting her down gently at the end of the night hadn't really ruined anything, not after he told her why. And best of all, Hannah could drink as much punch as she wanted without worrying that someone had spiked it because it was a totally drug-free event.

Or was it? Could someone sneak pills in and do the same thing to her all over again?

"Earth to Hannah," Molly said. "Have you started your planning or not?"

"Sorry. No, we haven't." Hannah could feel Molly's eyes on her as she picked at her Friends for Life bracelet. "What?"

"Nothing," Molly said. "It's just, if you're going to ask Brad, make sure he knows it's a drug-free event."

Hannah picked at her bracelet."Oh. I'm. . . I doubt I'm going. I mean, I'll help plan, but. . . "

"What? Why wouldn't you go?"

"That thing at Jake's sort of soured me on parties." Hannah looked up., "Anyway, there's Brad. Finally."

"So, you did decide to bother to show up," Molly said as Brad came up to the table. "Hannah was worried you'd bail on her again."

"Molly!" Hannah said, her teeth gritted.

"Just saying," Molly said. "Anyway, I'll leave you two to study or whatever." She walked off.

Hannah slumped down in her seat. "Molly's usually not like that, I swear. I don't know what's got into her."

Brad shrugged. "She's just looking out for you cause of me flaking out last time. I want you to know it wasn't cause I don't like you. I swear. It was. . . "

"Mr. Collins. I know. I set him straight."

"Cool." Brad dug around in his backpack. "Damn it, I thought I put the stupid book in here. Now he's gonna get on my ass about not having it with me on top of everything else." He slammed his backpack on the table.

"We are in a library," Hannah said. "I'm sure there's another copy floating around somewhere."

"You think?" Brad's half-smile was even cuter than his full one. It made him look like he was up to something. Hannah looked away to stop her heart from beating harder than it had any right to beat. "I'd ask you if you wanna walk through the shelves with me," Brad went on, "but someone's gotta save the table."

"Through the aisles," Hannah corrected. "Through the shelves would be like if we were ghosts." Stop that! Now he's going to think you think he's stupid!

"That would be awesome!" Brad said. "We'd get to go through walls and shit and on top of that we could haunt people." His eyes sparkled. "I'd start with Mrs. Marino. That bitch is always picking on me for no reason."

"I noticed." Mrs. Marino wasn't a bitch, and anyway, Hannah didn't like it when guys used that word. But she didn't feel like correcting Brad for a second time in as many minutes. "What's up with that?"

Brad shrugged. "To be fair, I give as good as I get. I wouldn't wanna have to deal with me day in and day out either."

"Why?" Hannah asked. "There's nothing wrong with you."

"Glad someone thinks so." Brad flipped the edges of his notebook with his thumb. "I'd better go look for that book, so I don't waste any more of your time. Who's it by again?"

"Nathaniel Hawthorne."

Brad looked her up and down. "There anything you don't know?" he asked. "You should try out for *Jeopardy!* or something."

Hannah's face grew hot and she couldn't look at Brad. "Thanks, but no thanks."

Brad headed for the shelves. He was zigzagging and not looking at the labels on the ends of the bookcases, which meant it might be a while. Hannah kind of hoped so. It was the first time she'd been alone all day.

She took out her Chemistry notebook so she could study while she was waiting, but she couldn't concentrate. For some reason, she kept having this fantasy about going to search for Brad and the two of them kissing. Before the party, she'd always imagined her first kiss would be in the library, surrounded by the books she loved almost as much as she loved her boyfriend. But Brad thought of her as a sister, so that was a lost cause. Besides, he wouldn't be her first kiss, not anymore.

She slid down until she was almost under the table. She didn't want Brad to see her. She didn't want anybody to see her.

Brad's footsteps thudded toward her. Hannah sat back up so he wouldn't ask too many questions.

"Did you find the book?" she asked, making herself smile.

"Yeah." Brad sat down. He spun the book around and around, staring at it. "Reading this last night put me to sleep. Why can't teachers ever give us anything good to read?"

"This is good," Hannah said. "You just have to get through the first few pages." She opened it and read a few lines aloud. "He's just setting the scene before he starts. It's sort of like on TV when they show the outside of a house before they show you what's going on inside."

"Yeah, a boring show," Brad said. "We haven't had a decent book since *Treasure Island,* and that was in eighth grade."

Molly's voice popped into Hannah's head, saying Brad wasn't Hannah material. He didn't love to read, that was for sure, but no matter how hard she tried, Hannah couldn't convince herself that made him a loser.

"You're just too impatient," she said. "Let me tell you about this book. It's about shame and guilt and how the world tries to cut you down if you don't follow their rules. Listen to this and you'll see what I mean." Hannah turned the page and read aloud a passage from Chapter 2 where some women were complaining that even wearing the scarlet A wouldn't make Hester Prynne as ashamed as they thought she should be. "They hate her," she said. "They think because she did one stupid thing she should suffer for the rest of her life and it makes them hate her more that she doesn't care what they think." Her throat stung with tears, and she wished almost desperately that she could be half as strong as Hester Prynne.

Brad's eyes darted toward her, then away. "That's a hell of a story," he said. "Maybe I should try it after all."

"Yeah," Hannah said weakly. "It only gets better from there." She played with the edges of the pages. "I wish you'd read it, so I could really talk to you about what it all means. That's the fun part."

"You make it fun," Brad said. "You're a better teacher than Mr. Collins."

"If you say so." Hannah's cheeks got hot, but she was too stuck on the story still to really notice. When she'd read it last summer, she thought that Hester was like Mom because her so-called crime was having a baby with a man other than her husband, and poor little Pearl didn't know who her dad was. Now, she felt like she was Hester because people were spreading rumors about her.

"Where'd you go?" Brad asked, interrupting her thoughts.

"Sorry. I was just thinking about the book. When you read it, you'll see that Hester tries so hard to show them she's a good person but. . . " Hannah looked away. "I can't explain. It's like the scarlet letter is part of her identity, and she's not ashamed, exactly, but she can't escape it either."

"Like me and weed," Brad said thickly. "What I told you before. . . I stopped smoking after, but everyone sees me as a stupid pothead who got arrested once anyway."

Hannah grabbed the bottom of the table as tightly as she could to stop herself from reaching for Brad's hand. "I don't." There was an annoying high-pitched ringing in her ears, and she was glad she was sitting down because she was kind of woozy.

"Even though your friends hate me?" Brad's tone was light. He laughed, but Hannah knew he was upset about that.

"They don't hate you. And anyway, I don't care what anyone thinks. I'm my own person." Hannah's cheeks felt tight and her stomach started doing flip-flops. "I try to be, anyway."

"Me too." The bell rang. Brad grabbed the book. "Thanks for helping me out. Maybe I'll actually read this tonight." As he got up, he added, "I'm doing track clinic after school. If you wanna see me in action, come to the gym."

Hannah bit her lip. "I wish I could. I'm grounded for going to the party." It was as good as an excuse as any, and she wasn't sure it was a lie this time. Her parents had said no hanging out, and didn't watching Brad run on the indoor track count as hanging out?

"Next time, then," Brad said. "I'm there almost every day." He winked at Hannah as he went to the check-out counter. Hannah couldn't help smiling to herself while she waited for him even though her thoughts were going in so many directions they were making her dizzy.

11 – No More Mouse

"I GUESS YOU'RE tutored out after Brad," Molly said when they were at their lockers after school. "Or are you going to surprise me?"

"I told you, I'm grounded. Besides, I'm not in the mood for seeing Mr. Collins again today."

"Why?" Nathan interjected as he walked past. "You failing English too, Slut Hannah?"

Hannah's throat was so tight she could barely speak. "At least I can read Shakespeare properly." Nathan had butchered one of Iago's monologues when he got called on today, reading in a monotone, and Mr. Collins had kept stopping him to say something about it.

That was supposed to piss Nathan off, but he just snickered and said, "News flash: No one with a life cares. That means everyone but you." He purposely bumped her shoulder with his as he pushed past her, making her drop the books she was holding on the floor. "Oops," he said, and walked away, laughing.

Hannah scrambled to pick up the books, her heart pounding.

Molly said, "You were asking for it, Mouse. Why did you pick now of all times to stop ignoring him?"

"Because I'm sick of him," Hannah said, "and of everyone. And it would be nice if you had my back with him."

"I do! You can't let him get to you like this. It's what he wants. Just ignore him."

Hannah rolled her eyes but said nothing. There was no point. She apologized to Molly even though she had nothing to be sorry for and hugged her goodbye before she went out to the bus.

***

When Hannah got home, she went straight to her room to study, but instead, she spent all afternoon re-reading *The Scarlet Letter* in case Brad had any more questions for her. That was the only thing she looked forward to, talking to Brad about a book she loved that he couldn't care less about. What a pathetic loser she was.

She'd felt like that before, she remembered suddenly. It was at the party, right before she'd been drugged. She remembered the crushed look on Jamie's face and how pathetic she'd felt. She'd broken his heart because she was afraid to kiss a boy who wasn't sober, but she'd secretly liked him almost as much as she liked Brad. She hadn't wanted to admit it to herself because she wasn't supposed to like a boy who was old enough to go to college when she was only sixteen, and she definitely wasn't supposed to want to kiss a boy who had beer on his breath.

If her drink hadn't been poisoned, if she hadn't been sedated and out of it, she would have gone after him and maybe she would have had a first kiss she could remember. Except. . .

That nurse or whatever she was thought Jamie had been the boy who raped her. That didn't feel right, but since she couldn't remember, how could she know?

She went out into the kitchen, more because she needed to move than anything else, and grabbed a frozen macaroni and cheese TV dinner out of the freezer. She put it in the microwave for four minutes while she paced back and forth and thought about nothing except how long four minutes was when you were waiting for food. Then, she took it back to her room along with a plastic fork and gobbled it so fast she barely tasted it, ignoring that some parts were still cold as ice because she didn't feel like putting it back in the microwave.

She was almost finished when her phone buzzed. It was probably Molly wanting to know if she was still mad at her, but she picked it up anyway to see.

> **Instagram: sciencewhizkid2004 has**
> **tagged you in a post.**

Sciencewhizkid2004 was Nathan, who Hannah was definitely not following. What the hell?

Her finger hovered over the notification. She wanted to swipe left to delete it, but she was curious enough to open it instead.

It was a stupid selfie of Nathan with his mouth hanging open so wide you could probably see his tonsils if you looked hard enough. The caption read:

> My face at seeing @hannahkollman trying to act like she's not a hypocrite and a liar. Stupid bitch got drunk at a party & slept around but acts like the queen of sobriety. Comment if you hate fake bitches! #whataloser

She threw the phone down onto her desk. *Breathe deep, Hannah. This is bullshit. Besides, Instagram has rules about this stuff, all you have to do is report him.*

The rusty lock on the front door clicked, loud enough for Hannah to hear all the way from her room, and a second later, Mom called Hannah's name.

"I'm in my room," Hannah called back. Her voice sounded halfway normal. Good.

Mom came in. "Did you eat, baby?" Her face fell as Hannah gestured toward what was left of her frozen mac and cheese. "TV dinner again," she said. "What happened to my little food snob who turned her nose up at anything that wasn't fresh and who cooked enough to last us all three days in between homework assignments?"

"I haven't had time. It's almost midterms. I have to spend every minute studying."

"Uh-huh," Mom said. "That explains why you're holed up in this room without even opening a notebook to make it believable." She crossed her arms. "I'm not stupid, Hannah, and I know depression when I see it. What's really going on?"

"Nothing," Hannah protested, but she was weakening. She was tired of lying, so, so tired. Why couldn't everyone just leave her alone?

"There you two are," Eric said, coming up behind Mom. He frowned. "What's wrong?"

"We were just discussing how Hannah's been living on TV dinners all of a sudden," Mom said, her lips thin.

"Oh," Eric said. "I'll make her real food."

"That's not the point," Mom said, but Eric told Hannah to come help him in the kitchen and walked away.

"I have studying to do," Hannah said.

Mom told her, "Go. You need proper nutrition to fuel that big brain of yours."

Hannah shoved herself away from her desk and went into the kitchen.

"Peel some carrots for me," Eric said.

"I'm not your servant, but whatever." Hannah took the peeler out of the drawer and started attacking the carrots.

Eric watched her for a second. "I think you know I didn't just call you in here to help me with dinner. We need to talk."

"There's nothing to say." Hannah's voice was flat. "You already grounded me for going to the party. Why can't that be the end of it?"

"Because Mom and I are even more worried than we were the day after the party." Eric took a pan out and put it on the stove. "We can tell you're not yourself. You're here all the time, Hannah. We know you're not going to after-school tutoring or your other clubs."

"Because I'm grounded!"

"We told you that you could still do those things. And anyway, you're angry and upset a lot of the time. We can see it. So how about you tell me what's really going on with you?"

"NOTHING IS GOING ON!" Hannah slammed the peeler down. "I'm fine!"

"You certainly aren't acting fine," Mom said, coming into the kitchen. "I can hear you all the way down the hall, Hannah, and you're not a yeller. Now stop this nonsense and tell us what's bothering you." Hannah glared at her and Mom said, "Please, baby. I can see you're in pain, and it breaks my heart, and the more you insist you're fine the more worried I get."

Hannah swallowed hard. If Mom knew what had happened, she'd be a billion times more disappointed than she was worried. Besides, if she was going to start telling people, she didn't want to start with her parents. She put the vegetable peeler down, slowly, and said, "Please stop worrying about me. I'll be fine."

"But you're not fine now," Eric said. Hannah shook her head slightly and he said, "Tell us this. Does it have to do with your friends, with school, or something else?"

"All the above, I guess." Hannah bit her lip while she tried to figure out what she could say that would make her parents feel she was confiding in them without telling them the whole truth. "I'm. . . lately, I'm questioning a lot of stuff."

"Like what?"

Hannah shrugged. "Just stuff," she said. "Like, I'm not sure I want to do all this stuff after school anymore. I thought it was me, but maybe it isn't. Besides, people are spreading rumors about how I'm a hypocrite who drinks all the time, and it's not true. But my credibility's kind of shot. Why would Mrs. Marino want me as Vice President of SADD anyway?"

"Has she said something to you?" Mom's face was hard. "Because I swear if they're picking on you because of one mistake . . . "

"Mom. I'm way too old for you to be involved." Hannah turned back toward the carrots. "And no, she hasn't, but I wouldn't be surprised if it's coming." She took out her phone and shoved it at Mom. "This is what I'm dealing with every day," she said, showing her Nathan's Instagram post. "Ever since the party, this is who I am. Hannah the Hypocrite."

Mom's eyes narrowed and she had the same fire in them that Hannah sometimes got in hers. Hannah turned her back on her and went back to peeling carrots so she wouldn't have to see it.

Mom said to Eric, "If she wasn't too old for me to call this boy's parents. . . "

"You'd better not," Hannah said. "It's humiliating enough that everyone knows I went to the stupid party."

"I said 'if', didn't I?" Mom snapped. "And that carrot is peeled enough, don't you think?"

Hannah threw the carrot down and took another one.

Eric said, "Don't do anything rash, Hannah. You can't see past what this idiot has to say tonight, but trust me, if you let people like him dictate what you do, someday you're going to regret it."

"I don't care what he has to say," Hannah said. "That's not the point."

"Okay," Eric said. "Then what is?"

Hannah stared down at the cutting board. "It's that they're not wrong," she said. "I went to a party full of alcohol and drugs. What right do I have to tell anyone else not to?"

"People make mistakes," Mom said. "It's not the end of the world."

"It is when you're supposed to be a role model!" Hannah snapped. "I should never have gone, but I did. Now everything's ruined, especially since. . . "

"Since what?" Mom's voice was soft. Hannah shrugged. "Hannah, SINCE WHAT? What the hell happened at the party?"

"Nothing!" Hannah said, her voice shaking. She grabbed her phone off the counter where Eric had left it. "Your stupid carrots are peeled. Can I go now?"

"Hannah. . . " Mom said, but Hannah pushed past her without waiting for an answer. She ran into her room and slammed her door, then threw herself on her bed and wrapped herself in her blanket, wanting to hide under it like she used to when she was a little girl.

She made herself stop that. She wasn't a little girl. She was a young woman, and she needed to show the world that she could take care of herself no matter what Nathan said on Instagram or what some loser had done to her at a party.

The only question was, how?

She got up and paced back and forth, thinking. Her phone buzzed and she picked it up.

> **Molly:** I just saw Nathan's idiotic post. I reported it & I hope you do too. PS Are you ok?

Really? Molly was telling her what to do? And how many times had she typed and erased "I told you not to stand up to him" before she sent this stupid text?

Hannah threw her phone down on her bed, not wanting to deal with Molly. But that was just more running away, and Hannah was tired of running.

She picked her phone up again, thinking. Pre-party Hannah would have called Molly right away about Nathan bullying her and would have cried on her shoulder if she had a fight with her parents.

The days when she did that seemed like forever ago, like part of another life. Hannah missed Molly so much her chest suddenly ached.

She opened the photo Nathan had tagged her in and scrolled down to see if anyone had defended her.

No one had. All the comments were people laughing at her, people saying horrible things about her, and about how they couldn't stand "bitches like her."

Anger burned in her throat. Molly had seen it and said nothing. She bet Sierra had too. She didn't know if Brad had Instagram, and she hoped he didn't because the idea of him seeing this and not saying a word to defend her hurt even more than the fact that her best friends had already refused to stand up for her.

She stabbed at the three dots on top to report the post. Having to fill out the form to explain what was wrong with the post made her feel tired and like putting her phone down but she told herself NO.

No more Mouse. No more being quiet and just letting people hurt her.

She reported the post, then let her breath out slowly as she opened Molly's text again.

> **I'll be ok. Reported the post.**

She hesitated, her finger over the send button. No.That wasn't what she wanted to say at all.

She deleted that and tapped her phone against the palm of her hand.

It would be so much easier if she'd told Molly she'd been raped in the first place. It was going to be harder now because Molly would be hurt that she didn't trust her and ask her ten million questions she didn't want to answer. But not telling was worse. Not telling was putting a bigger and bigger gap between her and her best friend, and now she couldn't even ask her what to do about her parents because Molly had no clue what was going on with her.

Unless Hannah told her the truth now, there'd be no talking to her about anything important ever again, and she'd lose her best friend.

Hannah started to type something, then stopped. What if Molly didn't want to be friends with her anymore once she knew? What if she didn't believe her? What if she thought she was one of Those Girls and kept her distance? Before the party, Hannah didn't think things like this could happen to girls like her, and she was sure Molly still thought so.

Hannah swallowed hard, feeling the war between Mouse and Hannah start up again in her head. *Look, Mouse,* she told herself. *Maybe you'll lose her if you tell, but if you don't it's a sure thing. So, stop being such a coward.*

Besides, Molly had been the first to welcome her to their fifth-grade class after she'd moved to Cedarwood. She'd felt safe and comfortable for the first time in her life when she met her. So why didn't she trust her now?

Hannah picked up the phone again and texted:

> *I just reported the post. I'm okay, but I'm tired of the way things have been since the party. Can you meet me before school tomorrow so we can talk?*

Thanksgiving

Baskets

T HE NEXT MORNING, Hannah came into the classroom where Molly was folding copies of The Cedarwood Courier and stood in the doorway, crossing her arms against her chest and trying to ignore how hard her heart was beating and how unsteady she felt on her feet.

"I'm really sorry about how I've been acting since the party," she said, making herself come all the way in. "I'm sure you think I'm crazy, but I'm not, I swear. I just. . . " Her eyes flitted to the front page of the paper, then away. "Hey! Henry Ashton writes for this paper. You think he's related to Brad?"

"Who knows and who cares?" Molly tossed another paper into the box. "What'd you want to tell me, besides that you're sorry for acting like an idiot?"

Hannah's mouth felt dry, so dry. There was a water fountain down the hall, but if she went now Molly would think she was crazy and besides, she might never come back. "Um," she said, twisting a lock of hair around her finger. "You know how Hester Prynne had to wear a scarlet A for adultery?"

Molly's eyes widened. "You really had sex that night?"

"No! I mean, yes, but. . . " Hannah pressed her arms tighter against her chest. "I'm not an adulteress. My scarlet letter would be an R."

"R for riddles, which you need to stop talking in. Just say it, Hannah. What - "

"R for rape," Hannah whispered. Her eyes burned like she was going to cry, but she didn't feel sad.

"No way," Molly said. "You were. . . "

Hannah nodded. She watched Molly take a hair tie off her wrist and tie her hair back. Her ponytail was too messy, but Hannah didn't have the energy to say so.

"He drugged me," she said, knowing Molly wanted more details even though she didn't ask. "He put pills in my iced tea and then we had sex. I don't even remember it."

"Wow," Molly said. "Okay. That's why you've been so. . . " She sighed. "Does Sierra know?"

"Yes," Hannah said, an irritated tone creeping into her voice. "I slept over. When Dylan wanted to take me to the hospital, I had to tell her."

"The hospital. Right." Molly crossed her arms. "So, she pressures you to go to some party where you get raped and then gets to play the hero after it happens."

"What?" Hannah said. "That's ridiculous." She picked up a newspaper. "No one forced me to go to that party. I went because I wanted to."

"No, you didn't. You wanted to hang out with Brad, but Sierra wouldn't let you."

Hannah slammed the newspaper down onto the table so she could fold it. "Stop sounding like my mom," she said. "Sierra didn't do this to me."

Molly picked at the corner of a newspaper. "I have to deliver these. Want to come?"

"I'd rather not." Hannah looked away. "I'm not in the mood for dealing with teachers this early."

"Mr. Collins, you mean." Molly threw the last paper into the box. "I hope you know I'm here for you."

Hannah let Molly hug her even though she couldn't wait for her to leave so she could be alone with her thoughts.

***

Hannah sat alone in the classroom until the bell rang, thinking about nothing and everything at the same time and then went to the cafeteria. It was already full, and she had this weird feeling like everyone who looked at her as she walked past could see right through her and know somehow that she'd been raped. Sierra called her but she kept walking, not paying attention to where she was going until she was outside and the wind was hitting her face.

There was a smell like Christmas trees when she stopped by the bleachers to zip her coat. The two long-haired guys who Brad always hung out with were sitting on the bottom bleacher and the one with reddish-blond hair had a cigarette in his hand.

He was smoking weed. Hannah was glad that Brad wasn't with him even though she didn't know why she cared.

The guy asked her if she wanted to join them and laughed. Hannah hurried away from him and onto the track.

Maybe running would do her some good, she thought, pushing herself as fast as her legs could go. Exercise was supposed to be good for your mood, wasn't it?

She only lasted a couple of minutes before her chest felt tight and her ankles throbbed. She slowed down even though she didn't want to, trying to remember what she'd learned in Biology freshman year about why that happened. Something about anaerobic something or other.

Brad's footsteps pounded on the track behind her. Hannah meant to get out of his way, but instead, she stood still, gasping for air.

Brad stopped next to her and said, "You're not having an asthma attack, are you?"

Hannah's face flushed. "No," she said between breaths. "Just. . . out. . . of. . . shape."

Brad jogged in place, watching her. "I wanna make sure you're okay if that's cool. You don't look good."

"Thanks a lot." Hannah wiped her brow with her coat sleeve. She unzipped her coat to try to cool off and made herself breathe through her nose. "Sorry I'm messing up your workout," she said when she could talk properly again. "I'm the least athletic person in the history of the world."

Brad shrugged. "You'd get the gold in the Brain Olympics." Hannah blushed again and he said, "That was super cheesy, but it had to be said."

"It's cool," Hannah said. "I'm just embarrassed that I can't run for more than half a second."

"I can get you trained up if you really want. First things first. What are you doing running with a twenty-ton weight on your back? Get rid of your backpack."

"Oh. Your friends were over there and I didn't think . . . "

"They're cool. They get stoned and act stupid, but they're not thieves." Brad looked Hannah up and down. "But something's up. I can tell. You come out here to tell me you can't tutor me anymore?"

"Of course not. I love tutoring you." The words came out before Hannah could think. "Oh my gosh. I didn't mean it like - "

"It's cool," Brad said. "I mean, a dude could get a swelled head—someone like you actually wanting to spend time with him."

Hannah scuffed her sneakers against the track. "I'm nothing special."

"Yeah, you are." Brad stopped jogging and looked Hannah in the eye. "Seriously, though, if it's not me. . . what's going on?"

Hannah sighed. "You don't want to know. I mean, guys don't. . . "

"This guy does. Look, Hannah, we're friends or whatever so if something's on your mind, I wanna hear it."

"It's too much to tell." Hannah shoved her hands into her pockets to stop herself from grabbing Brad's. "I. . . I told Molly this morning about, you know. . . what happened."

Brad nodded. The expression on his face reminded Hannah of the owl in that stupid glasses place commercial and it almost made her laugh but not quite. He said, "It go bad?"

"Not really." Hannah started walking again. Standing still made her feel too vulnerable. "She meant well but. . . "

"You worried she's gonna tell?"

"Sort of," Hannah said. "I mean, she's my best friend, I should be able to trust her, but I don't think she understands at all. I only told her because I had a big fight with my parents yesterday, and I couldn't talk to her about it without explaining the other thing."

"You fight with yours too?" Brad's tone was too light, and Hannah had a weird feeling that he wasn't really joking. "No way. I thought you were perfect."

"Don't put me on a pedestal. I'm not as great as you think I am."

"I dunno about that," Brad said, "but I think you're pretty freaking awesome." He dug through his pockets. "Here, give me your hand for a sec."

Hannah's heart pounded. "Why?"

"Cause," Brad said, taking a pen out. "I wanna write my digits like I was gonna the day it happened. That way you won't be alone anymore."

Tears welled up in Hannah's eyes, but she was sure it was just from how cold it was out. "I'm wearing gloves," she said, even though she wasn't, and he'd see it as soon as she took her hands out of her pockets. "But I have a phone, you know. You can put your digits in that."

"You making fun of me?"

"Never. I'm 516-555-1712."

Brad pulled his phone out. "Hope I remember that right," he said. "I'd feel bad if a stranger had to deal with my texts."

Hannah smiled despite herself. "How about I give it to you again?"

"You sure?" Brad said. "I might blow up your phone during English or something."

"I'll take the chance," Hannah said. She heard her phone buzz inside her purse and knew Brad had texted her, but she didn't want to look now in case he remembered she'd said she was wearing gloves. Why had she told such a stupid lie?

"That was me," Brad said.

"I know. I. . . I want to read it in private." Hannah looked away. "Come on. Let's see if we can get all the way around the track again before the bell rings."

"K," Brad said. They walked in silence for a few seconds. Hannah could feel Brad's eyes on her, and it made her scrunch over, wishing she could make herself invisible.

Brad said, "I don't want to cross a line or anything, but. . . would it be cool if I held hands with the most beautiful girl in Cedarwood?"

Hannah swallowed hard. "It's not that I don't want to," she said slowly, not looking at him so she wouldn't see the disappointment in his face. "It's just cold."

"And you don't want to cause of what happened. I get it."

"So, you're not going to try to talk me out of it?"

"Nope. That wouldn't be cool, even if you're crushing my dream." Brad played with something in his pocket. "Seriously, we got plenty of time. Maybe someday I'll earn your trust."

"It's not that I don't trust you. It's. . . " Hannah let her breath out slowly, her heart pounding. "I can't explain it, it just feels good to say 'No'."

"So it's not me, then?"

"Not at all."

The bell rang just then, and Brad said, "Wanna race to the bleachers?

"I guess," Hannah said. Brad started running but she stood there, watching him, knowing she'd never catch up. She took her hand out of her pocket and stared at it, thinking, before she walked over to the bleachers so they could walk to homeroom together.

13 – Molly's Huge Mistake

IN HOMEROOM, MOLLY told Hannah she had to tell her something, but they got interrupted by Mrs. Parker, the school secretary, leading everyone in the Pledge of Allegiance over the PA system.

It wasn't until they were done at their lockers and walking to Chemistry that she finally spilled, telling Hannah, "Sierra and I got in a fight this morning. Not a fistfight, obviously, but close enough. I know you didn't want me to, but I confronted her about what happened to you. It was partially her fault, Mouse, she has to understand that."

Hannah looked over her shoulder to make sure no one was close enough to overhear. There were plenty of people in the hall, but they all looked like they were doing their own thing. "I told you, she didn't have anything to do with what happened to me."

"I know, but she put you in a bad situation. You guys didn't stick together, so she couldn't have your back. Anyway, we got pretty loud and Jen had to separate us."

"JEN knows?"

Molly shrugged. "I didn't tell her what we were fighting about. But I might have to. She's my girlfriend. I can't keep secrets from her. Besides, she won't judge you."

"I hope not," Hannah said weakly. They were in front of the Chemistry room. She put her hand on the doorknob, trying to ignore the feeling that something awful was about to happen.

Nathan had his backpack on an empty seat. He took out his notebook as Hannah came slowly into the room, her eyes darting everywhere.

"Well," he said, looking up from what he was doing. "If it isn't the girl who cried rape."

Hannah gasped, but then she made herself raise her head up high and look Nathan in the eye. "Excuse me?"

"You heard me," Nathan said. "Guess I hit a nerve, calling you out for being a fucking hypocrite. So, now to save face you're making yourself look like a victim." He spat on the floor. "It won't work. We all know what you are and pulling the rape card won't change a thing."

Hannah turned her head over her shoulder and looked at Molly, who looked away. She should have known she'd get no help from her. If she was going to stand up to Nathan she'd have to do it herself.

"That's a lie," she said, "and you know it."

Nathan mimicked her and said, "You're going down, slut. Might as well accept it."

Hannah locked eyes with him. She didn't know what to say, but she had to say something. She couldn't let him get away with this.

The bell rang but she couldn't make herself move, not until Mr. Dawson said, "Sit down, Hannah. Don't block the view of the board on the off-chance that someone wants to learn something today."

Hannah threw herself into her seat. She took out her notebook and bent over it, trying to ignore a high-pitched ringing in her ears so that she could hear what Mr. Dawson said if he happened to call on her.

Thankfully, it was a lab day, so she didn't have to put up with him all period long. She sat quietly, thinking about everything and nothing all at once. Mr. Dawson explained the lab and she was listening, but she forgot what he said the next second.

"All right. Get started," Mr. Dawson said, and Hannah got up slowly. Her body felt heavy, and her head ached. She rubbed her temples and shuffled over to the box of safety goggles, suddenly dreading spending time alone with Molly.

They had to weigh a peanut and then weigh the ashes after burning it. Hannah's voice shook for no reason while she told Molly that the peanut weighed two kilograms.

"Don't." Molly put a gloved hand on Hannah's shoulder. "Nathan's an idiot. You can't let him get to you."

Hannah pulled away. "It's not Nathan!" she snapped, grabbing the flint to light the Bunsen burner.

"Then what is it?"

"It's you, okay?" Hannah sniffed. "I told you to keep what happened to me to yourself."

Molly threw ice into a metal can. "I did! I didn't tell anyone, and I definitely didn't share it with Nathan!"

"Yeah, but you yelled at Sierra in front of everyone! What did you think would happen?" Hannah tried to light the Bunsen burner. The flint sparked, but the burner wouldn't catch it.

Molly took the lighter away from her and lit the burner easily. "I didn't mean for anyone to overhear," she said. "I'm really sorry, Hannah."

Hannah stared at the orange flame at the end of the peanut, not feeling like talking. It wasn't like Molly could fix this. What was said couldn't be unsaid. Now the whole school knew Hannah had been raped, even Nathan and all the other assholes who loved any excuse to laugh at her.

"Dish! Quick!" Molly said.

Hannah handed Molly the dish so she could catch the ashes, then Molly gave it back to her to weigh.

"What was the weight of the dish?" Molly asked.

Hannah froze. "Crap. I never weighed it. I'm sorry. I screwed up."

Her voice broke, and suddenly, she was sobbing.

It was a ridiculous thing to cry about, and she told herself to cut it out. Mr. Dawson already thought she was weak and stupid without her crying over a stupid weighing dish that she forgot to weigh.

"Hey, it's okay," Molly said. "Just weigh it after we get rid of this."

"That's not how we're supposed to do it," Hannah sniffed. She turned her head over her shoulder and Mr. Dawson, who had been circulating the room, was standing behind them.

"You okay, Hannah?" Mr. Dawson asked.

Like you care. "Yeah. Fine."

Mr. Dawson looked her up and down, then said, "Hall pass is on my desk. Go wash your face." He walked away.

Hannah bit her lip to make herself stop crying. She held her head up as high as she could as she went to get the hall pass.

BY PRECALC, THE rumors were twice as bad as they'd been in the morning. People in the halls were calling Hannah a slut and yelling things at her like, "You gonna cry? You gonna have another breakdown?" She held her head up high and pretended not to hear, but she didn't know how long she could keep doing that.

She spent Precalc hunched over her notebook, trying to concentrate. It didn't help that Brad defended her against Nathan's latest mean comment when she hadn't asked him to, especially since Mrs. Marino came in and made a big deal out of Brad not being in his seat as if he had started it.

Worse, Jen asked Hannah if she was okay when they were supposed to be working silently and Mrs. Marino caught Hannah whispering back that she was fine and told her to see her after class.

When the classroom emptied out, Hannah was going to go up to Mrs. Marino's desk to apologize, but Mrs. Marino was already settling herself into the seat next to hers.

Mrs. Marino said, "The reason I kept you after class is that I can tell something's wrong. You haven't been yourself in the last few weeks and today you seem especially upset. Would you like to tell me what's bothering you?"

Hannah rubbed her temples, feeling a headache coming on. "Thanks, but I'm fine."

"So fine that you're bursting into tears in Mr. Dawson's class and looking like you're going to do it again right now?" Mrs. Marino's voice was soft. "Teachers hear things too, Hannah."

Hannah stared into space. "Then you've heard all the other stupid rumors about me." She swallowed hard. "I really did go to a party, that much is true. So, if you have to ask for my resignation from the leadership team, it's fine."

Mrs. Marino's eyes widened. "So that's what's going on in that head of yours. No, Hannah, I don't want you to resign. I know you too well to believe rumors that you drink and sleep around on the weekends. Besides, I would never do something like that without even bothering to get your side of the story. That's not how SADD operates, and you know it."

"I guess." Hannah twisted her hoodie string around her finger. "I made a destructive decision, though. I deserve to be punished."

"We all make mistakes, Hannah. Just tell me what happened, and let's see how I can help you."

Hannah bit her lip, not wanting to talk anymore, but too tired to say 'No'. "I. . . I listened to my friend when I shouldn't have and I. . . " Her voice shook.

"Did you break your sobriety pledge?"

"No, but someone broke it for me." Hannah swallowed hard. Then she told Mrs. Marino the whole story, starting with the pills in her iced tea and ending with how Molly had spilled the beans in front of the whole school.

Mrs. Marino handed Hannah a tissue even though Hannah wasn't crying. "I'm honored that you trusted me enough to tell me this."

Like you gave me a choice. "I had to. It affects SADD. People aren't going to listen to us anymore because they think I'm a hypocrite."

"We will find a way to overcome that. This isn't your fault, Hannah, and it would be completely antithetical to everything SADD stands for if I were to accept your resignation over it."

"But no one believes that. Everyone is calling me Hannah the Hypocrite, and as long as SADD is saddled with me, they're going to scoff at the whole idea of sobriety."

"Not necessarily. I believe you, and I'm sure if you told your story, other people would too. Why don't you start with the other SADD officers? I can call an officers' meeting so you can explain. I'm sure everyone would be supportive."

"I-I can't." Molly would be at that meeting since she was the treasurer and telling her once had been bad enough. Besides, Hannah wasn't sure how Katie or the other officers would react.

"Think about it, okay? I won't push you, but if and when you're ready, I will call that meeting for you. I will make it very clear to everyone that I expect them to bring the non-judgmental, supportive attitude toward this that is a cornerstone of the SADD philosophy. In the meantime, don't suffer in silence. I'm here for you any time you need to talk, and I'm sure the school counselor will also make time for you if you want."

Hannah nodded even though she had no intention of talking to the school counselor, now or ever. She took the late pass Mrs. Marino handed her, not bothering to tell her it was her lunch period and mumbled her thanks before she hurried out of the room.

***

When Hannah got to the cafeteria, everyone turned and looked at her and she could see in their eyes they were all thinking that she didn't have any right to be here. *They're wrong*, she thought, trying to walk in like she owned the place the way Sierra had told her. *They're wrong and I'm done caring what they think.* But she couldn't make herself look anyone in the eye.

Molly was sitting at their usual table by herself. She tried again to apologize to Hannah, but Hannah was mad at the whole world and snapped at her. They had the same argument all over again that they had during lab. Then, Molly begged Hannah to sit with her anyway, but Hannah didn't want to.

She walked away without another word, then wished she hadn't because she had no idea where to sit. She'd sat at that same corner table with Molly and Sierra every day since freshman year, and without it, she felt lost in a sea of people, most of whom hated her. There always Katie and the other SADD girls, she guessed, but she didn't feel up to sitting with people she barely knew, especially not after Mrs. Marino had tried to make her tell them what happened to her.

Sierra was sitting at a table by herself, staring into space and twisting her hoodie string. The hoodie was new; Sierra never used to like them, but lately, she was wearing them all the time. She looked up as Hannah threw herself into the seat across from her.

"What are you doing here?" Sierra asked. "I thought for sure you'd be sitting with Molly and Jen at the goody-two-shoes table."

"Nope," Hannah said. "Thanks to Molly and her big mouth, I had to see Mrs. Marino after class. And get this, Mrs. Marino thinks the solution is to tell everyone the truth."

Sierra froze. "You're not going to, are you?"

"No. Telling Molly didn't exactly go well. Why would I humiliate myself any further?"

"Right." Sierra picked at a knot on her hoodie string. "Jake said if it got out, he could get in trouble."

Way to be selfish, Hannah thought, but she didn't want to start a fight with Sierra. "It's already out. People think I'm a slut and a liar. Anyway, what does Jake have to do with anything?"

"Cause." Sierra stared at the table. "It was his house, Hannah, and he let me drink when I'm too young. A-and I love him, and I don't want him to go to jail. So whatever you do, don't tell the cops, and don't let Molly tell them either."

"Who said anything about cops?" Hannah took her sandwich out of her backpack. "I hope Mrs. Marino doesn't call them. I don't want her to."

"Better not," Sierra said. "If I were you, I'd have told her to mind her own business."

Hannah caught Brad out of the corner of her eye, headed for some other table. She called him to come sit with them.

Brad stopped. His mouth opened a little and he looked over his shoulder. "Just checking you weren't talking to some other Brad." He put his tray down and climbed into his seat. "But you sure this one can handle it?" he asked, looking at Sierra.

Sierra ignored him, twisting her hoodie string around and around her finger.

"We're in a fight with Molly," Hannah said, "but I'm sure you don't want to hear about that. Do you have track clinic today?"

"I wish." Brad stabbed at the cafeteria's idea of a meatball with his fork. "Friday's appointment day. Good news is, I get to spend the weekend with my dad once that's over with." Brad opened his milk. "So, what did Mrs. Marino want?"

Hannah shrugged, not wanting to go into it. "SADD stuff, that's all."

"That's sad," Brad joked.

Hannah smiled even though it wasn't funny. "I tried to quit, but she wouldn't let me."

"Why?" Sierra asked. "You didn't get messed up on purpose." She played with the latch under the table, making an annoying clicking sound over and over.

"Bet Mrs. Marino didn't see it that way," Brad said. "Stupid bitch."

Strike two against Brad. He really needed to stop using that word. "Actually, she did. She was really nice and really supportive. She wouldn't let me quit no matter how hard I tried. Though. . . " Hannah stared down at the table, not wanting to look Brad in the eye, and told him about Mrs. Marino's suggestion.

Sierra said again that Hannah shouldn't consider it, but Brad said she should. He said that his dad told him the only way to stop a rumor from spreading like wildfire was by telling the truth over and over until people listened.

"Either way, the next meeting is going to be so awkward," Hannah said. "I'll be worrying about who thinks what the whole time."

"Sucks," Sierra said. Hannah wished she'd offer to come, but Sierra didn't. She just sat there playing with her hoodie string. Hannah bet she had plans with Jake and didn't want to say so.

"I'll come with you," Brad said.

Hannah stared at him. "If you want," she said weakly, trying not to get annoyed at Sierra's half-open mouth. "I wouldn't want you to be bored."

Brad shrugged. "It's cool. I wanna see you in action."

"Mrs. Marino runs it, just so you know," Hannah said, then wished she hadn't. She didn't want Brad to think she didn't want him there.

Brad hesitated. "So, you'll owe me," he said.

"Okay," Jamie said. "But if I win, you have to kiss me."

"Owe you what?" Hannah stammered, sliding her finger under her Friends for Life Bracelet.

"Nothing big," Brad said. His eyes sparkled. "Maybe you could, I dunno. . . come see me jump a few hurdles at track clinic and pretend you're not bored to death?"

"It's a date!" Hannah said and immediately regretted it.

"Awesome! If it's not pushing my luck too much, wanna hang out after school 'til my dad shows up?"

"Sure," Hannah said. Brad fist-bumped her, and she wished he would hug her even though she didn't want him touching her.

15 – Stuck in the Back of the Car

BY THE TIME school ended, Hannah was more than ready to go home. When Brad offered to talk, she told him how tired she was of the dirty looks she got in the halls and how she couldn't tell who believed the rumors about her and who didn't.

"Who cares what they think?" Brad said. "Anyone who matters knows you're not a slut."

"I wish I was that kind of person." Hannah twisted a lock of hair around her finger. "I want to be, but my friends call me Mouse for a reason. I hate being the center of attention, and I hate people thinking stupid things about me even though I don't respect people who let other people's opinions get to them."

"That's cause you have the wrong nickname," Brad said, his eyes sparkling. "You need like, a superhero name."

Hannah thought superheroes were stupid, but she kept that to herself so she wouldn't hurt Brad's feelings. "I'm no superhero."

"Yeah, you are. You stand up for what you believe in no matter who laughs at you. Besides, you're willing to put up with a dude like me." A car honked and Brad said, "That's my dad. Wanna see if we can manipulate him into giving you a ride, so you don't have to deal with the bus?"

"I guess." Hannah got up slowly and followed Brad to the car. It only had two doors and the passenger one was dented. There was also a deep scratch in the hood. Hannah was embarrassed for Brad that his dad's car looked so cheap even though Mom's car didn't look much better.

"Dad!" Brad said as he pulled open the door. "I told Hannah you'd give her a ride. That's cool, right?"

Mr. Ashton's eyes narrowed behind his glasses. His face was a long oval and he had the same brown eyes and chameleon-brown hair as Brad. Hannah couldn't help thinking he looked like the dad in *Dennis the Menace.*

"Of course," Mr. Ashton said. "There's a lever on the side of the seat, Hannah, just pull it up so you have room to get in the back."

"I'll get it," Brad said. Hannah was irritated, but not enough to say she could do it herself. Brad pulled the seat up and said, "Sorry about the antique car."

"It is not an antique," Mr. Ashton said as Hannah climbed into the back seat. "And I told you, Brad, I'm not wasting money on a new car. Slide all the way over, Hannah. Brad can sit in the back with you."

"Oh," Hannah said. "Okay." She bit her lip, hoping that neither Brad nor his dad could tell how freaked out she was by the idea of Brad sitting with her. It wasn't that she didn't want him to, exactly. It was just the lack of doors made her feel trapped, like there was nowhere to escape to if Brad touched her in some way she didn't want, even though she knew he wouldn't.

"So, you're Hannah," Mr. Ashton said as Hannah fumbled with her seatbelt. "Brad's mother says he talks about you all the time."

"I do not!" Brad was turning beet red. "All I said was I made friends with a girl in my math class. Mom exaggerates, Dad. Don't you know that by now?"

"Don't bury your lede," Mr. Ashton said. "Mom told me you said you made friends with a PRETTY girl."

Hannah's stomach felt tight. She turned and stared out the window, making herself breathe in and out and praying she didn't get carsick.

Brad said, "Stop embarrassing her, Dad."

"Sorry," Mr. Ashton said. "You know I have a penchant for embarrassing truths. So where to?"

"Oh," Hannah said. "I live in the Rolling Hills apartment complex on Madison Street. It's right off Main."

Mr. Ashton nodded. "I know where that is."

"Too bad," Brad said. "I was hoping I could make fun of you pulling out a map like this is 1983." He turned toward Hannah. "Dad doesn't believe in GPS."

"I refuse to be dependent on technology," Mr. Ashton said as he pulled away from the curb. "And don't knock the 80s. You don't know what you missed before you were born."

"Yeah, I do, 'cause you're still living there. I'm surprised you got a CD player instead of cassette tapes."

Hannah stared out the window. She could hear Molly saying that Brad was so rude to his father, but she didn't care. She kind of liked it.

Molly. Were they even friends anymore? Hannah hadn't spoken to her since their fight or whatever it was at lunch. Molly hadn't shown up at her locker to try to talk her into doing tutoring today, and she hadn't texted her either.

Could Molly really have given up that easily?

"Guess what Hannah got me to do," Brad said, pulling Hannah out of her thoughts. He grinned. "She's in this anti-drug group, and I'm gonna go with her. When's the meeting again?"

"Thursday," Hannah said, "and it's not just an anti-drug group. It's Students Against Destructive Decisions. We do all sorts of things to help people, encouraging them not to drink or use drugs is only part of it. In fact, we're working right now on putting together Thanksgiving food baskets for people who can't afford a lot."

"It sounds like a positive group to be part of," Mr. Ashton said.

"And Hannah's the Vice President," Brad said proudly as if it had anything to do with him.

Hannah's face flushed. "It's not that big a deal. I . . ." Her phone buzzed, and she glanced at it.

Nathan again. Crap.

"I just organize stuff and make sure everyone knows about the meetings." Hannah kept her voice tightly under control so that Nathan wouldn't get to her.

"What's wrong?" Brad said under his breath.

"I'll tell you when your dad drops me off," Hannah whispered back. "I don't want to involve him." She looked at her phone display again even though she knew she should look away.

Nathan had somehow taken a picture of Hannah leaning on Brad at the flower bed without her knowing. He'd put it on Instagram with the caption:

> Does he know he's dating the school #slut? Oh well, maybe he deserves her. #girlwhocriedrape #stonerboy #biggestlosers

Brad's jaw tightened a few minutes later when Hannah showed him the post. They were standing outside her apartment complex while his dad waited for him to say goodbye to her.

"That fucking asshole!" Brad said. He hit his open palm with his other fist.

Hannah shrugged. "It's just Instagram. Maybe if I keep reporting him, he'll get blocked? Or maybe I should just block him myself so I don't see his crap anymore."

"No," Brad said. "That's not gonna do anything. We gotta fight back somehow."

His dad rolled down the window and said, "I'm sorry, Brad, but we have to go. You can't be late for your appointment."

"Coming!" Brad said. "Guess I know what I'm gonna be talking about in therapy."

Hannah pushed her hair behind her ear. "You won't really waste your therapy session on this, will you?"

"Nah," Brad said. "I'm gonna tell my shrink all about how the most amazing girl in the whole school let me give her a ride home today." Hannah blushed and Brad said, "It won't bother you if I give you a hug, will it?"

"I could use one." Hannah's voice was soft.

Brad held out his arms. Hannah hugged him and he stroked her hair. Her heart pounded and she wondered suddenly whether HE hugged her too while she was out of it. She did her best to push that thought away. She liked the way it felt to be in Brad's arms. She didn't want to let go. That was all that mattered. Wasn't it?

Brad's dad honked. Brad said, "I'd better go before his head explodes." He let Hannah go. "Screenshot that before you report it. You might need evidence."

"Okay," Hannah said weakly. She watched Brad run to the car and jump into the front seat. Mr. Ashton saluted her, and she had no idea why or what that was supposed to mean. Then, he and Brad took off.

Hannah stood watching the spot they'd just been in for a few minutes even though the wind was biting at her cheeks and getting under her coat too. She felt weird, happy and sad at the same time and like she was upset about Nathan but it was an afterthought. She turned and walked slowly away, trying to figure herself out.

16 – The Third Confession

T HE NEXT MORNING, Eric said that if Hannah helped around the house with a cheerful attitude, he and Mom would end her being grounded a day early so she could do something with her friends.

Hannah wanted to go to the mall with Molly. But Molly hadn't called or texted, and Hannah didn't want to be the one to do it first. So that was out.

"I don't know," she said as she put two pieces of raisin bread in the toaster. "It's been so long since I've been allowed out. I don't remember what I used to like to do."

Mom rolled her eyes. "I'd hope being given some freedom back would bring a smile to that beautiful face of yours."

Hannah stiffened. "I'm not beautiful. Not anymore."

Eric turned and stared at her. Mom said, "What do you mean? And don't tell me it's because you went to that party. That's old news by now."

"It's not that, exactly." Hannah picked at a bead on her bracelet. She wanted to be able to tell Mom everything, but she didn't know what would happen then. So, what was she supposed to say instead? "Molly and I had a fight."

"And that makes you ugly?" Eric came over to the table with an omelet for Mom. "Yours is next," he said, "but maybe we should talk first. What was the fight about?"

Hannah bit her lip, wishing she hadn't said anything at all. "You know. Girl drama." But Eric raised his eyebrows at her, so she couldn't get away with that. "It's a long story, but basically I told her something in confidence and she told the whole school."

"That doesn't sound like Molly," Mom said. "More like Sierra. I'm sure she's behind this. And what, pray tell, was this big secret?"

THAT was what Mom had to say? Didn't she have any empathy at all?

"It wouldn't be a secret if I told you," Hannah said coldly. "And for your information, nobody would know about it if Molly didn't yell at Sierra about it in front of everyone."

"So, it did have to do with Sierra, then," Eric said. Hannah shrugged and he said, "We want to help, but we can't if you don't tell us anything. So how about it?"

"Fine," Hannah said, picking at her bracelet. "Molly blamed Sierra for me going to the party. Happy now?"

"Not really," Eric said, "since that doesn't make any sense." He sat down backward on an empty chair. "It's not like people don't know you went to the party, so that wasn't what this is about. So, what's the real story?"

"Never mind. I have studying to do."

Hannah started to get up, but Eric said, "Not never mind. There's obviously something you need to tell us. Besides, you can't study on an empty stomach."

Hannah glared at him, but she sank back into her seat. Arguing was just going to make it obvious something was wrong with her.

Mom said, "What the hell happened at that party? You haven't been yourself ever since, and now you're fighting with Molly and giving us half stories. Nothing we say or do puts a smile back on your face. Please talk to us, sweetheart. Please!"

"I don't know what to say," Hannah said weakly. "I. . . something did happen, but. . . "

"Did you have sex with some boy?" Mom demanded. "Is that what it is? You got three sheets to the wind and jumped into bed with the first boy who gave you attention?"

I'm not you, Mom. I don't think, anyway. "No! I mean, yes, kind of, but not. . . I didn't want to!" Hannah blinked hard.

Mom and Eric looked at each other. "What are you saying?" Mom said. "Eric, what is she saying?"

"I don't know," Eric said, his face grim, "but I think we'd better find out." He turned toward Hannah. "Someone took advantage of you while you were drunk, is that it?"

"Not while I was drunk," Hannah said thickly, "because contrary to popular opinion, I was never drunk." Her heart pounded in her ears and she gulped her orange juice, aware she'd said too much. Too late now, she'd gone past the point of no return like they said in driver's ed when you were in the middle of the intersection and the light turned yellow. "I told you, the only thing I had all night was iced tea."

"Uh-huh," Mom said. "So, you made a stupid decision about some boy sober. Is that what you're telling us?"

Again with the accusations. It was like Mom wanted Hannah to be a screw-up like her. "No!"

Mom said, "This doesn't make sense, Hannah. You're not making any sense. Either you were sober or you weren't. Now, which is it?"

"I was drugged, okay?" The words slipped out of Hannah's mouth before she had a chance to think. She blinked back tears as Mom put her hands to her mouth. "It's my own stupid fault, so you can be mad at me if you want. They told us in school about date rape drugs, but I forgot. I was playing video games with. . . " She hesitated. Mom wouldn't like that she'd been hanging out with a college guy all night and she didn't need her freaking out about that when it was beside the point. ". . . with this guy, and I put my iced tea down. Then when I drank it, I felt weird. I should have been more careful. I shouldn't have let it out of my sight. I should have poured it out just in case, but I didn't. I drank it, and now everything's all messed up."

Hannah put her glass down on the table, harder than she meant to. Good thing it was made of plastic. If it shattered all over the place, Mom would have something else to freak out about. Mom might freak out anyway. She always did, and that's why Hannah didn't tell her things.

It was already starting. Mom had her hands pressed over her mouth. She dropped them and said, "Oh. My. God. So, you. . . some boy was. . . NO! You're not saying what I think you're saying. You can't bc."

Hannah wanted to scream: *Yes, I am! I was raped. That was my big secret. Happy now?* But her mouth was too dry, and her throat was too tight. The best she could manage was a nod. She stared down at the table, tracing the cracks in the wood so she wouldn't have to see the look on Mom's face and know how deeply disappointed she had to be in her. Her eyes filled with tears and no amount of telling herself to cut it out helped. "T-the doctor said I was raped, but I don't remember so maybe. . . "

"Maybe nothing," Mom said. "My poor baby was out of it, and some lowlife took advantage of her." Her face trembled, but then it hardened. "I hope the boy who did this is rotting in a jail cell."

"Yeah," Hannah said. "Me too." There she went lying again. No wonder her parents were disgusted with her. "But that would be a miracle because I told the doctor I didn't want the cops involved."

"Why the hell not? This boy hurt you in the worst possible way."

"I couldn't think! It had just happened and. . . " Hannah bit her lip, not wanting to go into it. "Anyway, what good would it do? I don't have any idea who he is, and I don't remember it happening."

"Someone has to pay for this. That's what! If you'd told me, I would have gone to the police station with you, and I would have come back every day until they got their butts in gear and did something to get justice for my little girl."

I'm not your little girl anymore. "I don't want that. Now can we drop it?"

"No," Mom said. "We can't. This isn't going to just go away. It's always going to be in the back of your mind until you do something about it." She felt in her pocket. "Now what did I do with my phone?" She got up. "Maybe it's in my purse," she said, going up to the ledge and checking. "No. Where the hell is it? Call it, Hannah, see if it's nearby."

"Why? What's the big emergency?"

"I need to call my therapist. That's what," Mom said. "She'll know who to send you to."

"The doctor gave me a list of therapists," Hannah said. She got her purse so she could give it to Mom with the other ER papers. "Not that I want to go."

"You need counseling," Mom said firmly. "You can't get through something like this without it. And then we need to call Dr. Maz and get you in right away for a follow-up."

Hannah shuddered. "Can't I go to a walk-in clinic where no one knows me? Sierra could take me after school."

Mom's face hardened again. "You will not do anything with Sierra," she said. "Not after what she got you into."

"That's what you think!"

Eric held up his hand. "This is not the time to argue," he said, playing peacemaker as usual. "You need us, Hannah, just as much as you need your friends. If you'd rather one of them accompany you to the doctor, fine, but we need to be in the loop. And Mom's right. You need counseling." He turned toward Mom. "We should call her guidance counselor too. He may have some suggestions as to who to send her to."

"No!" Hannah said. "He doesn't . . ."

"Yes," Eric said. "You need support at school and home, and we're going to make sure you get it."

"Whatever." Hannah got up, suddenly restless, and went to the fridge. When she opened it, suddenly she remembered the fridge full of wine coolers at the party and how she was looking for water and couldn't find it when she found the iced tea. She grabbed a yogurt and slammed the door, aware her parents were staring at her. She pulled the silverware drawer out, hard, and took a spoon.

"I'm fine," she said, staring at her reflection in the spoon. "I swear."

"You're not," Mom said, "and you don't have to be, not after this conversation. You can fall apart, baby. It's okay."

"I'm not going to," Hannah said. "Sorry to disappoint you, but I'm not made out of glass." She pushed past Mom. "I'm going to go eat this in my room while I study."

"Hannah . . ."

"Let her go, hon," Eric said. "This was a lot for her. For all of us, really. I'm sure she just needs time to breathe." He brushed Hannah's arm with his fingertips as she walked past. "Hey, if you need us, we're going to be home all day, okay?"

Hannah nodded. She hurried to her room, afraid she was going to cry in front of her parents.

***

Hannah really did try to study, mostly so she wouldn't be a liar. She didn't care about chemical equations or thermal energy or any of it, and she kept getting distracted.

It was hard to stop thinking about the conversation she'd just had. She wondered what Mom and Eric really thought of her, but they were talking so quietly she couldn't hear no matter how much she strained her ears.

She sighed and grabbed her phone. She wanted to text Molly but that would be a weird thing to start off with after a day of silence. Instead, she texted Dylan to ask him to take her to the clinic on Monday after school.

Her phone froze for a sec as she sent the text, then it buzzed as a new text came through. It was Brad checking in to see how she was.

Hannah stared at the phone, wanting to video with him. But she knew she had to look awful. She hadn't showered or even brushed her hair, and he'd be able to tell how close she was to tears.

She called him instead and told him what just happened.

"How'd they take it?" Brad asked.

"I'm not sure. My mom kind of freaked out." Hannah's heart pounded. "I wonder if she found her phone. She was all upset she couldn't. She said she had to call people for me."

"People? What are you, a movie star who's got people on speed dial?"

Hannah giggled despite herself. "No," she said, then sighed deeply. "I can tell you, I guess, since you're seeing one too. They said I have to see a therapist."

"That's cool," Brad said. "How about I come over? You sound like you could use some company."

"I don't know." Hannah wasn't up for explaining to Mom and Eric exactly what Brad meant to her, especially because she wasn't sure. "They didn't exactly say I was done being grounded."

"All the more reason I should show up." Brad's tone was too light. "It'll be too awkward for them to slam the door in my face. Besides, they gotta know they were punishing you for nothing now, right?"

"I still went to the party." But they weren't mad about that anymore, and Hannah knew it. "If you do come over, let's see if we can convince them to let me out. I need to get out of here for a while. But not yet. I still have to shower and make myself presentable."

"I'm sure you're gorgeous even with morning hair, but okay."

Hannah's face got so hot that she thought she might faint. "Maybe someday I'll send you a selfie. But not today. I'll text you when I'm ready."

"You'd better," Brad said. Hannah shuddered even though she knew he was joking.

After they hung up, she picked up her empty yogurt container and hurried to the kitchen to clean it out before she recycled it. She could hear Mom and Eric talking as she went down the hall. Mom sounded like she was crying and said she felt bad that she'd punished Hannah instead of realizing something was wrong.

Eric was holding Mom and stroking her hair when Hannah got to the kitchen. She stood frozen in the doorway, watching, then forced herself over to the sink.

Mom and Eric pulled apart. Mom smiled an obviously fake smile and said, "Toast just popped, baby. I hope it's not too dark for you."

"Oh. Right." Hannah turned off the sink and took the plate Mom handed her. "I completely forgot."

"Well, you've had a lot on your mind." Mom was still talking as if nothing was wrong—as if Hannah hadn't just seen her sobbing in Eric's arms.

"Come sit with us while you eat," Eric added, handing Hannah the butter.

"Whatever." Hannah put way too much butter on her toast. "My friend Brad's coming over. I hope that's okay."

"Friend?" Mom asked. "Or more than a friend?"

Hannah's face got hot. She gulped some water.

Eric said, "Tell us all about this boy, sweetheart. Who is he?"

"He's, you know. . . " Were they really doing this? Were they really pretending she hadn't just dropped a bombshell and that it was a normal

Saturday morning? "He's sweet and funny. And Sierra hates him."

"So, you do like him?" Mom was smiling.

"I need to shower," Hannah said, pushing herself away from the table. Mom didn't argue with her, which was weird and made her feel worse.

HANNAH'S PARENTS HAD moved into the living room by the time Hannah was dressed and ready to go. She'd put on makeup for the first time since the party and the hand-knit silver sweater Grandma had sent her for her birthday, though she'd put on yesterday's jeans again. She didn't have any clean pairs, and she didn't want to wear a skirt. That would make it obvious it was a date, and then Brad might think it was okay to do things with her that she didn't want to do.

Mom smiled. "Finally! It's so good to see you look like yourself, sweetheart. Did you remember to take a picture to send Grandma so she can see how wonderful her gift looks on you?"

"I sent her one to thank her when I got it. And why are you being so weird?"

"I'm not. I'm just admiring how gorgeous my daughter is now that she's willing to wear clothes that show her off instead of ones that make her look like a piece of furniture."

Hannah's heart pounded and it took everything to not run back into her room and change into something that wouldn't give Brad any ideas. "Thanks. I think." She checked her phone. "I think I'll wait for Brad in the lobby."

"Not so fast," Eric said. "Come sit with us for a minute."

Hannah rolled her eyes, but she guessed she should be grateful that her parents were letting her go anywhere at all. She threw herself into the easy chair across from the couch.

Eric said, "We've never met this Brad or even heard of him before. He needs to come say hello before you guys go anywhere."

"He's a good guy!" Hannah protested.

"Nobody's saying he's not," Mom said. "We've always wanted to get to know your friends. You know that."

"And it's doubly important after what happened to you," Eric added. "You're vulnerable right now, Hannah. We don't want you turning to some guy for comfort who might not be good for you."

"I'm not, and anyway he's not like that. He's always so worried that he's going too far. He asks if he can sit with me, and the one time we hugged, he asked if he could first." Hannah's own words echoed in her ears and she wished she could fully believe that. "Now can I go, or do you want to interrogate me some more?"

"Rude!" Mom said. "We can still change our minds about letting you go out, you know."

"We're only asking for your own good, sweetheart," Eric added. "We want to protect you. Is that really so terrible?"

"I don't need protection," Hannah protested.

"You think you don't but look what already happened. Now, where are you and Brad going?"

"The mall. I need new jeans, and he's nice enough to want to go with me even though I'm sure clothing shopping bores him to tears."

Mom reached for her purse as she nodded. She took out her wallet. "I can spare sixty dollars. Will that be enough to cover what you need?"

"I have money," Hannah protested. "You know me. I never spend my allowance, and I still have my birthday money and the money I got babysitting last summer."

"Take it anyway," Mom said. For some reason, she had tears in her eyes as she thrust three bills at Hannah. "Please."

"Fine." Hannah was irritated, but it wasn't worth making a big deal out of. "Thanks." She put the bills away. "Does that mean I can go now?"

"No," Eric said. "We'd rather Brad come to the door so we can at least see what he looks like. Please text him and tell him that."

"Texting and driving is dangerous!"

"If he's the sort of boy who has sense, he won't read it while he's on the road," Mom said. "Text him. Now."

"Yes, Warden," Hannah mumbled under her breath, not daring to say it aloud in case her parents changed their mind and took the whole day with Brad away from her. Eric raised his eyebrows at her, and she looked away as she took out her phone.

> *My parents are being ridiculous and insisting you have to come meet them before they let me go out.*

Her phone buzzed right away.

> **Brad: It's cool. U met my dad,
> didn't u? PS Leaving now.**

"Thank you," Eric said as Hannah put her phone away. "Now, while we're waiting, tell us more about Brad."

"What do you want to know?" Hannah asked cautiously.

"What's he like, for one thing? And why does Sierra hate him?"

Hannah picked at an imaginary dust bunny on her sweater, not sure how to explain. Her parents would freak out if they knew about the rumors about Brad, and they wouldn't want her hanging out with some guy who'd been arrested for drugs. "I can't explain. Sierra just never liked him, and I always did."

"Okay," Eric said. "What do you like about him?"

"He's smart," Hannah said, knowing that was all her parents cared about. "And he's funny, really funny. Sometimes he says something silly in class, and I try really hard not to laugh because the teacher isn't laughing but it makes my day."

"You mean he's the class clown?" Mom asked. "Hannah, really. . . ."

"There's so much more to him than that! Yes, he fools around, but it's just an act. He pretends he's joking, but I can tell he really cares." Hannah looked away as Mom scowled "He makes me feel comfortable. He knows what happened to me, and he's super careful because of it."

"That's good, I suppose," Mom said. "But do yourself a favor and take things slow. Trust me, jumping into something with some other boy to make yourself forget isn't going to end well. It's just going to make things worse."

"Mom!" Hannah's face was hot and her throat felt tight. *I'm not you!* she wanted to scream. *I don't get drunk and jump into bed with guys whose names I don't even know on purpose.* But she didn't dare say that. It would break Mom's heart and besides, Mom wasn't that person anymore and hadn't been in a long time. And anyway, if it wasn't for whatever drunk guy Mom had hooked up with almost seventeen years ago, Hannah wouldn't exist, so how could she be mad at her? "I'm not a slut," she said weakly instead of all the other confusing things she was thinking. "I'm the same person I was before the party."

"I know that. But I don't think you realize how vulnerable you are, sweetheart. Someone took advantage of you less than a month ago! You don't know how easy it is to fall for the first person who makes you feel good after something so earth-shattering, but I do. So please, baby, listen to me. Go slow no matter how you feel about him, all right?"

Hannah wriggled. "Brad should be here any minute," she said, glancing down at her phone. "You can see for yourself he's not evil." She got up and went to the front door, unlocking it and opening it a crack.

"I wish you'd wait 'til he tells you he's here before you do that," Mom said. Hannah ignored her, instead looking out the crack and trying to will Brad to show up.

"And no one said he was evil," Eric added. "There's no need to be overdramatic, Hannah, we're just asking you to keep your eyes open. And if anything makes you uncomfortable, you can always text or call and we'll come get you. So, don't feel you have to stay there with him if you start to feel weird."

"I'll be fine," Hannah said, even though she wasn't sure. The elevator dinged, loud enough to hear it from the apartment. Thank God!

Brad knocked on the half-open door and Hannah opened it the rest of the way. "I wanted to surprise you," he said, "but I guess you beat me to it." His eyes widened as they met Hannah's. "Wow. You look amazing. N-not that you don't usually. "

Hannah looked away, feeling her cheeks get hot. "You'd better come in before my parents yell something totally embarrassing. But thanks."

Brad came all the way in. Hannah held out her arms so they could hug. She held him for a long time, not wanting to let go.

Eric cleared his throat. "Close the door, Hannah, show off your boyfriend just for us and not for the neighbors."

Hannah's face got so hot she felt like turning on the air conditioner even though it was the middle of

November. "I didn't tell them you were. . . you know, that we're more than friends."

"It's cool," Brad said. "I wouldn't mind dating the most amazing girl in school." He rubbed his hands together and turned toward her parents. "I hope you don't mind me saying stuff like that. I, um, I really like your daughter but um, I would never. . . anyway, hi, I'm Brad."

"It's so nice to meet you," Mom said, a wide, phony smile plastered across her face.

Hannah looked at her feet, wishing she had a more normal mom. "And this is my stepdad. He wanted to see what you look like, and now he has. So, we can go."

"Sure he doesn't want to grill me first?" Brad's eyes sparkled and his tone was light.

"I'm sure they both do," Hannah said, "but they'll have to wait 'til we get back." She reached for Brad's hand before she realized what she was doing, then made herself stop. That wasn't something friends did, and she didn't want him to think she wanted more even though she kind of did. "Ready?" she said instead, hoping Brad hadn't noticed.

Eric said, "Wait a second, please. How are you guys getting there?"

"We're taking the bus," Brad said lightly. He grinned as Hannah's face fell. "Just kidding. My dad lent me his car. "

"Brad!" Hannah said and elbowed him lightly. Or at least she hoped she was light. She wouldn't want to hurt him for real.

"You drive, then?" Mom said. The fake smile was back.

"Got my license right here," Brad said. "Believe it or not, they actually gave it to me on the first try." He fished in his pocket. "Here. Feel free to go over it with one of those little flashlights like the cops do."

Hannah did her best to hide the small smile on her lips just like she did when Brad fooled around in Mrs. Marino's class.

Eric said, "You know, we're not being annoying for its own sake. We're protective of Hannah, especially after what happened to her, and I hope you both can understand that."

Hannah crossed her arms, but Brad said, "I get it. Sorry for being rude. Hannah's probably told you I got no filter, and it blows up in my face all the time."

"So I see," Eric said. "Well, there are worse things in the world than that, I guess."

"Let me get a picture of the two of you," Mom said, "and then we can stop embarrassing you and you can get on with your date."

"Mom!" Hannah said as Mom took out her phone. She turned toward Brad, trying to hide how nervous the idea of having her picture taken was making her. "I didn't say it was a date, I swear."

Brad shrugged. "Let's humor them, so they'll get out of our hair," he said. "Okay if I put my arm around you?"

Hannah nodded. She and Brad put their arms around each other, and she did her best to imitate Mom's fake smile even though it made her sick to her stomach.

.

18 – Indian Food and a Fight

THE FOOD COURT at the mall was far more crowded than Hannah expected it to be. Most of the tables were full, and there were so many people waiting for food that they blocked the stands and made it hard to see what was what.

"What are you in the mood for?" Brad asked. "I'm supposed to go heavy on protein and whole grains for track, but pizza's close enough for me."

Hannah suddenly wished Brad would put his arm around her. She bit her lip instead. "Do they still have that Indian food stand?" Sierra had tried to get her and Molly to try some sort of curry last time they were here. Hannah secretly wanted to try it, but she was afraid to say so. She'd promised herself she'd make up for it by buying some of her own next time. That had only been last summer, but it seemed like it was a million years ago.

Brad's eyes sparkled. "Someone else who likes spicy food. Me and my dad love it, but my mom always put her foot down about it. We could never get it before the divorce."

"I've never had it before," Hannah admitted. "But today's a good day for trying new things." Anxiety was creeping up from her stomach and her ears were ringing for no reason. She looked around. "I think we'd better grab a table first—if there's any left to grab."

"I got eyes on the target," Brad said in a ridiculously deep voice that Hannah guessed was supposed to be some guy from an action movie. He gestured toward a table in the middle of the food court where some people were getting up. "Operation grab table will commence in 3. . . 2. . . 1. Go!" He hurried toward the table.

Hannah looked over her shoulder to make sure no security guard was coming this way before she ran after him.

He beat her to the table and was already in his seat when she threw herself into hers. She was hot and sweaty and gross, and she was sure the way she was struggling to catch her breath didn't help. At the same time, she felt good, really good for the first time in forever. "You. . . win."

"I didn't think I was racing YOU," Brad said, grinning. "We both win. We got this table before some vulture swooped down on it."

Hannah put her feet up on an empty chair so she could rub her throbbing ankles. "Sorry to whoever takes this chair next. I need this." She could feel Brad's eyes on her, but he turned his head away from her when she looked up. "You should get food first since you beat me here. I'll hold down the table 'til you get back."

"They got a special at the Indian place, one of those combos where you can get three things and rice for like ten bucks. How about I get that for us to share since you're new to Indian food and all?"

Hannah played with the zipper on her purse, flipping it up and down. There was no reason to get weirded out. Molly had got stuff for her a billion times while she watched the table. So, Brad doing it didn't make it a date. Besides, so what if it did? It wasn't like she didn't like him, and it was obvious he liked her too.

"Sure," she said. "That sounds great."

"Cool," Brad said. "Be right back." He left before Hannah could get her wallet out to give him money for her half of the food.

Her mouth was suddenly dry. She played with the bills she was going to give Brad, wishing she'd thought to bring a water bottle. She'd forgotten to tell him she hated soda, and he was probably going to come back here with a giant one for her because everything he did was big and half of it was to impress her.

One thing was for sure: She could cross him thinking of her as a sister off her list of worries.

You should never have gone to that party, a voice in her head said. *If you hadn't, you could let Brad ask you out and the two of you could live happily ever after.*

Hannah bit her lip to stop the burning sensation in her eyes from turning into tears. That one stupid decision had ruined everything. Molly and her parents were wrong to blame Sierra, but in a way, they weren't. Brad had asked Hannah to come hang out with him that night, and Sierra had said 'No' for her. And she had said nothing. She'd been a quiet little Mouse like her friends expected her to be, letting them call the shots like she always did. And THAT was the fatal mistake she had made. Because if she'd dared to stand up to Sierra and say that she didn't think Brad's party would be so bad and that's where she wanted to go, none of the rest of it would have happened.

"Mouse!" It was Molly's voice interrupting her thoughts. Hannah scowled, not wanting to be called that anymore, but she was glad enough that Molly was talking to her that she didn't feel like saying anything. She turned as Molly came over to her table.

"So, I guess you're not grounded anymore," Molly said. She sat down without being asked. "You here by yourself?"

"Nope," Hannah said. "With Brad."

Molly's eyes widened. "L-like on a date? Are you sure that's a good idea?"

"I'm sure I don't want to talk about it." Hannah's voice had a hard edge to it that she hadn't meant for it to have. "And I'm also sure I want to be alone with him."

"That's fine. I'm here with Jen anyway. I only came over to see if I could smooth things over. But obviously, you don't want that, so whatever. Call me when you decide to come to your senses unless you already deleted my number from your phone."

Molly got up and walked away. Hannah slumped down in her seat, her good mood gone just like that. Why did Molly have to be like that? It wasn't like Hannah didn't want to be friends. She just didn't want Molly inviting herself to whatever it was this was with Brad. Molly was smart; why couldn't she understand that?

Brad came back a second later, holding a tray full of stuff. He had got a combo plate and also a small box of some other food, plus two drinks. "I got us dessert too," he said, grinning. "These are like donut balls soaked in honey. It's the most amazing thing. And they had this hot tea that's made with cinnamon. I figured that was your kind of thing so I got you one."

"Thanks," Hannah said, trying to force herself to smile.

"You don't like tea?" Brad asked. His tone was light but there was concern in his eyes.

"It's not that," Hannah said. "I ran into Molly, or she ran into me, I guess. Nothing's changed between us."

Brad frowned. "What happened between you anyway?" he asked as he opened the to-go box and began dividing it onto the two paper plates he'd got.

"You sure you want to know? It's a lot of stupid drama."

"Course I do. I asked, didn't I?"

"Right." Hannah took a sip of her tea. "The short version is it's her fault the whole school knows about what happened to me."

"The R, you mean?"

"Right. That." Hannah played with the top of the tea container. She told Brad what happened and added, "I'm over it. But every time I see her, we try to make up, and we can't. She didn't understand why I didn't want her to sit with us right now even though she's here with her girlfriend. It's like she thought it meant I don't want to be friends anymore or something."

"That's stupid," Brad said. "Of her, I mean, not you. Here, food'll make you feel better. That's what my mom always says, anyway." Brad handed Hannah her plate. "I got us vegetable samosas 'cause I wasn't sure you eat meat."

Hannah's cheeks got hot again, and she smiled despite herself. "It was nice of you to think of me," she said. "For the record, I do eat meat, but I prefer vegetarian when I can." She reached for her wallet. "How much do I owe you?"

"Nothing. I like the idea of treating you." Brad's eyes were sparkling again. "But if you really feel bad about it you can get mine the next time."

"Thanks," Hannah took another sip of her tea while she put her wallet away. It was taking all her strength not to reach for Brad's hand across the table. "I'm sorry I didn't go to your party instead of Sierra's," she said, her heart pounding so hard suddenly she thought she might die. "If I had, maybe this could be a date after all."

"I don't see why it can't be anyway. Unless you're scared."

Hannah stared down into her plate. Great. Now Brad knew she was a coward. "What's this?" she asked, pointing to something that looked kind of like ranch dressing.

"That's raita. It's got cheese and vegetables in it," Brad said. "You wanna dip bread in it. Don't eat it by itself." He broke off a piece of his bread, which he said was called naan, and showed her.

Hannah nodded. She pulled off a piece of her own bread. For some reason her hands were shaking.

"You ARE scared," Brad said, and this time there wasn't even a hint of a joke in his voice. "Don't worry. I'm lucky to have you as a friend, and I'm never gonna do anything to ruin it."

"I know," Hannah said. She dipped her bread in the sauce—what had Brad said that was called again? "It's not you, you're not doing anything wrong. I just wish I hadn't gone to that party because I. . . I like you, and I wish we could be something." Her voice shook, then it broke. Great. Now she was embarrassing herself in front of all these strangers. "If I hadn't been raped, I would totally want to go out with you," she sniffed.

"That's something, I guess," Brad said. "I just don't get why you think it means we can't."

"We just can't. That's all." Hannah dabbed at her eyes with her napkin. "I keep wanting to hold hands and all that other stuff boyfriends and girlfriends do, but I can't let myself. I don't know how to explain why."

Brad frowned. "You think you're not good enough cause of it, is that it? Cause that's not true, Hannah, you were the most amazing girl ever before and you still are."

"If you say so." Hannah sighed. "I was never really all that special. I just thought I was until this happened to me."

"That's not how I see you, but let me double-check." Brad looked Hannah up and down. "Nope.

Still amazing." Hannah stared down into her food and Brad said, "Tell you what. Let's just pretend this is a date. It isn't, really, but we'll act like it is, so you can get a preview of what you'll miss if you keep being so stubborn."

"Me stubborn?" Hannah couldn't decide if she was irritated or amused. "You're the one who doesn't take 'No' for an answer."

"Yeah, I do," Brad said. "I just don't help my dream girl beat herself up. That's all." He drank some soda. "You don't get carsick, do you?"

"Not in a long time. Why?"

"Cause there's a carousel up on the top floor, and if we were going on a date, I'd totally take you on it, but only if you're not gonna puke on me. Even I've got my limits."

Hannah played with the heat protector on her tea while she thought about it. "Let's go clothing shopping first," she said. "That way my stomach can settle."

"Deal," Brad said. "So, uh, wanna hold hands on this non-date?"

Hannah hesitated, then nodded. She put her hand on the table and let Brad take it while she finished eating.

AFTER LUNCH, HANNAH let Brad put his arm around her while they checked an electronic directory display in the center of the mall. He suggested they checkout Time Warp Clothing, a vintage store he'd always wanted to try. Hannah didn't have a better idea, so she agreed.

Time Warp Clothing turned out to be a small store sandwiched between Bookworm (Hannah's favorite small bookstore) and some store that was playing super loud music. Hannah had passed by a million times before without it bothering her, but today it made her think of the loud music at Jake's party, and she hurried past it as fast as she could.

The music in Time Warp was much more to Hannah's liking. It was classic rock, and right now it was John Lennon's "Watching the Wheels". There were racks of clothing toward the back, and at the front, there were all sorts of accessories, mostly jewelry but also hats, belts, and purses.

"How do you think I'd look with these?" Brad asked, picking up a pair of thick orange suspenders.

"Amazing," Hannah said, smiling slightly. "You play with those. I'm going to go look and see if they have any jeans that don't have holes in weird places."

Brad's jaw tightened. Hannah thought he might argue with her, but he just said, "Cool. I'll be right here when you're done. Unless, you know, you want to show anything off for me before you decide."

"Maybe." Hannah's heart pounded, and she couldn't decide if she wanted that or not. "Be back soon."

Hannah went over to the clothing rack and flipped through pairs of jeans. Most of them didn't look that different from what she had on even though they were supposed to be vintage. Her chest felt heavy. She wanted something completely different from anything she'd ever worn before.

"Can I help you?" a saleswoman said, coming up behind her. Hannah flinched, not liking being surprised like that.

"Oh," she said, pushing her hair behind her ear. "Yeah. I wanted some jeans that aren't as tight as what I've got on." She lowered her voice. "I'm tired of boys staring at my butt all day long."

The saleswoman laughed. "It's going to take more than new clothes to change that. Some guys are pigs. Get used to it." She looked Hannah up and down. "You want to go full vintage? I think you'd rock the flower child look." She explained that girls in the 1960s used to wear flowers in their hair and loose clothing to show how free-spirited they were and showed Hannah a rack full of long-sleeved blouses with puffy sleeves and flowered patterns on them.

"What about jeans?" Hannah asked, irritated that this woman was trying to sell her a whole new wardrobe when that wasn't what she'd come in here for.

"Bell bottoms are on this rack. Though if you ask me, you'd do well with some wraparound skirts too."

Hannah thanked the saleslady, who nodded and walked off. She flipped through clothes. None of this was anything like what she usually wore, but she had to admit she kind of liked it, except that some of the jeans were torn at the bottom on purpose, which she thought was ugly.

Hannah stared at a pair of jeans. It was dark blue, or had been before it had been washed one too many times, and there were peace symbols and flowers sewn around the waist, almost like a belt you couldn't take off. It had big pockets and another flower sewn across the bottom half of the right leg. Hannah giggled to herself. What would Molly say if she came to school on Monday wearing THAT?

No. She couldn't. Nathan and the other bullies would have a field day, and she already was getting too much unwanted attention.

Hannah flipped past the pair of jeans, then back to it. This was exactly what she wanted. She looked over her shoulder to see what Brad was doing, letting her breath out slowly when she saw he hadn't got bored enough to wander off.

She beckoned him over. "Look at these!" she said. "Ridiculous, right?"

Brad shrugged. "One-of-a-kind jeans for my one-of-a-kind girl."

Hannah turned away so he wouldn't see her blush. "I was hoping you'd talk me out of them because I'm this close to trying these on."

"Sorry, but you might as well know now: I'm a bad influence." Brad's eyes sparkled. "I say go for it."

"They're probably going to be the wrong size anyway," Hannah said, but she took the jeans off the rack. "Maybe I'll get a new blouse to go with it." She went over to the rack that the saleslady had called peasant blouses and picked up a white blouse that had black flowers painted on one shoulder. "This one looks okay."

"Don't go crazy now," Brad said, his eyes still sparkling.

"Oh, stop," Hannah said, smiling. She draped the blouse over one arm and went to go find the saleslady. There was a rack of skirts behind her and she stared at it. She wasn't really into skirts, but the brightly colored patterns caught her eye. "The saleslady thought I'd look good in a wrap-around skirt," she said.

"You'd look good in anything," Brad said.

Hannah's cheeks got hot again. She stared down at the clothes she was holding, trying to understand why she suddenly felt like she needed to get the hell out of here before something terrible happened. "I . . . I'll try this one." She grabbed a cream-colored skirt off the rack and hurried to find the saleslady.

The dressing room turned out to be a single-person room that the saleslady had to unlock with a key. Hannah was glad. Back in Florida, Grandma used to take her to this clothing store where the dressing room was like the girls' locker room in gym with nothing in it but a big bench where you sat to get changed and no walls or curtains to hide your body from everyone else. If the dressing room here was like that, she would have decided to forget the whole thing.

The entire dressing room was made of mirrors, or at least it seemed that way as Hannah took off her sweater so she could try on the blouse. She hadn't really looked at her body since that terrible morning when she discovered her breasts were full of bruises and marks she didn't remember getting. But now there was no escaping it because of all the stupid mirrors, and for a blouse that was supposed to be loose and comfortable, there were an awful lot of buttons to open.

She got it open as fast as she could and put the blouse on, then closed all the buttons. As soon as that was done, she let herself look in one of the mirrors, really look.

She. looked. amazing.

The blouse wasn't big at all—in fact, it fit her figure perfectly. The buttons were stylish and went halfway up her torso, and there was a black embroidered flower pattern around the borders of the whole thing, which was white, and which contrasted perfectly with the dark blue jeans she had on.

The only thing she didn't like was that it didn't go up all the way. The buttons stopped halfway up and made sort of a V of open space around her neck, and if she looked closely she could see cleavage even though the blouse itself helped her chest look flat. She wondered if that was allowed in school. The last thing she needed was to get sent home to change when everyone already thought she was a slut.

"I don't care!" she told herself and reached for her new jeans to try them on so that she could laugh at how ridiculous they looked and forget how scared she was to wear the blouse.

But the jeans weren't ridiculous at all. They were comfortable and even though the giant flower across the right leg looked kind of silly she liked it. The black flowers on her blouse popped more because of the pink ones on her jeans and she couldn't stop looking at herself.

It was a perfect outfit. In fact, it was the kind of thing she wanted to wear to school from now on. Yet at the same time, the idea of wearing it anywhere made her nervous and looking at herself in the mirror made her hear in her head how Nathan and some other boys jeered at her in the halls and called her Slut Hannah.

"Stop it!" she told herself. "Stop caring what idiots like Nathan have to say!" She wished she could be a whole new person, one who didn't give a fuck what anyone thought and wore what she wanted and. . . and went out with Brad for real without being afraid when there was nothing to be afraid of.

Why can't I be?

Hannah glared at herself in the mirror. Her heart was pounding, and she felt so lightheaded she had to sit down on the bench where she'd thrown her old clothes so she could try these on. She hugged herself tightly, feeling like a baby on top of feeling like a coward because a little thing like wearing a shirt she looked good in scared her so much.

After a minute she was able to let her breath out slowly and get up. She turned and looked at herself in the mirror, not letting herself look away until she took in everything. She had these big, gray eyes that everyone said were gorgeous, but the rest of her face looked tired and her ponytail was way too tight. Besides, the saleslady said that girls who wore clothes like these wore their hair down.

She yanked her hair tie out and let her hair fall around her shoulders. It hurt a little from how hard she pulled it, but she didn't care. She put the hair tie on her wrist like a bracelet and ran her fingers through her hair to get rid of the shape of the ponytail. Then she looked at herself in the mirror again. She'd stuffed her hands into her jeans pockets like she was hiding them, and she was slouched over a little; the only reason she was holding her head up high was that she couldn't see herself in the mirror if she looked at the floor.

No. That wouldn't do. That was the old Hannah, the girl whose friends called her Mouse and who walked around slumped over like she was trying to make sure nobody could see her. The new girl, the one who wore clothes like this, didn't do that. She stood straight and tall and was not afraid of anyone's eyes on hers. She made herself straighten up and practice walking with her head up instead of down, her body tall instead of half folded over.

The saleslady knocked on the door. "Everything going all right in there, hon?"

Hannah opened it slightly. "Sorry," she said, even though there was nothing to be sorry for. "I got lost looking at myself in the mirror."

"I'm not surprised," the saleslady said. "I knew this look would be perfect for you."

Hannah pressed her arms over her chest, suddenly feeling exposed. "I'm not sure. Maybe it's too much for school." She swallowed hard. "But I want to take these anyway."

"Good choice," the saleslady said. "Would you like me to bring you a few more blouses so you can see what you like best?"

"That would be great. Thanks." Hannah's mouth was too dry to say more, and she hoped she wasn't being rude. "But not too many. I don't want my boy —um—my FRIEND, to get bored waiting for me."

"Oh, he's fine," the saleslady said lightly. "He's having a great time with the accessories. But I'm sure you don't want to be away from him for too long. Be right back."

The saleslady left Hannah to sink back onto the bench in her dressing room and argue with herself about Brad. It felt natural to call him her boyfriend, and New Hannah would talk about him like that because the truth was, that's what she'd wanted since the day he'd transferred into her eighth grade

English class and sat behind her, annoying her by putting his feet on the tray underneath her seat. But Mouse was still in there somewhere, she guessed, because she still wasn't sure about dating him. And anyway, even though it was obvious Brad wanted this to be a date, he'd never said that meant he wanted to be her BOYFRIEND.

"Knock, knock," Brad said, interrupting her thoughts. He was standing at the half-open door. Two more blouses and two more pairs of jeans were draped over his arm as if he didn't know what a hanger was for.

Hannah flinched automatically. "Oh. Hey," she said, hugging herself. "I wasn't expecting . . . not that I don't want you here."

"The saleslady gave me a couple things for you," Brad said, handing her the clothes "But I think she just wanted me to see how amazing you look in what you got on."

Hannah's cheeks got hot. "Thanks," she mumbled, looking away. Then she made herself look him in the eye instead. "I won't be too long, I promise."

"It's cool," Brad said. "Long as you let me take you on the carousel afterward, you can take as long as you want. Besides, I'm amusing myself looking for the perfect necklace to buy you." He looked away from her. "If that's okay, I mean."

"More than okay," Hannah said. Her heart pounded in her ears as she brushed Brad's fingers with her own. "W-we don't have to pretend anymore. I mean, unless you want to, but I . . . it's okay if you want to call it a date."

Brad's eyes widened. "Hell yeah!" he said. He leaned toward her, and Hannah froze, afraid he might try to kiss her and not sure whether she wanted him to or not. Brad backed up. "Sorry," he said. "I should have known you don't wanna put on a show for the security cameras."

"It's okay," Hannah said. She pushed her hair behind her ear. "Um, I'd better try these on before they kick me out of the dressing room."

"Right," Brad said. "And I'd better line up that necklace for you. Don't wanna promise my girl stuff I don't really do." He squeezed Hannah's shoulder. "By the way, love the hair down. It's AWESOME!"

Hannah's heart was going so fast that she didn't think she'd be able to talk, but she heard herself say, "M-maybe next time we hug you can play with it."

"Deal," Brad said. "See ya in a few." He turned and walked away.

Hannah closed the dressing room door, but she didn't get changed right away. Instead, she sat there hugging herself, annoyed that she was so freaked out when there was no reason to be.

"CHECK THESE OUT!" Brad said when Hannah had finally changed back into her regular clothes and come out of the dressing room. He'd put three necklaces on the counter. A silk rope with a silver peace symbol charm. A set of huge blue beads. A chain of white flowers.

"Not the blue beads," Hannah said. "They're too flashy." She stared at the other two for a long time, trying to decide. The flowers were delicate and pretty. She didn't usually like things like that, but for some reason, these were different. But the peace symbol was more like a normal necklace. "The flowers, I guess," she said. "Maybe I can get earrings that look like the other one."

"Cool," Brad said.

Hannah glanced at the handwritten price on the necklace. Fifteen dollars. "Are you sure you want to spend so much on me? These aren't exactly vintage prices even if it is a vintage store, and you already bought me lunch."

"Your smile's worth way more than fifteen bucks. If I can help put it on your face, that's all I want."

Hannah stared down into the pile of clothes, her face getting hot for a change. She checked the price tags. The four pairs of jeans were fifteen each and she didn't see any signs saying there were two-for-one sales like in the department stores, so there went the sixty dollars Mom had given her before she bought the rest of what she'd picked out.

If she got everything, she'd end up spending about two hundred dollars and that was before tax. She had five hundred saved from babysitting last summer and a one-hundred-dollar bill in her wallet that she'd been carrying around since Eric gave it to her for her birthday, but the idea of spending it felt weird.

"Don't think any harder. Your head might explode," Brad said. He frowned as Hannah let her shoulders fall, defeated. "Seriously too expensive?"

"No, I have enough." Hannah played with the buttons on a denim jacket she'd grabbed to go with her new look. "I really don't need this jacket, but if I use my birthday money, it's like a present to myself, right?"

"Totally." Brad's eyes were sparkling. "It looks good on you, so why not?"

"No reason, I guess." Hannah let her breath out slowly. "Come on. Let's do this before I lose my nerve."

It turned out the store gave ten percent off if you spent over a hundred dollars, so Hannah was able to save a little money. It was still the most she'd ever spent on herself in her life. Brad bought her the white flower necklace, and then they left.

The whole way to the elevator, Hannah's mind was on how much she'd spent. Did it make her like Mom used to be, spending money like it was water on sheer impulse? She almost wanted to go return the jacket, but she didn't want Brad to think she was weird. She wasn't up for trying to explain.

Instead, she asked Brad if they could put the clothes in his car before they went to the carousel. She told him it was so she wouldn't leave anything on the carousel by accident, but that was only half true. She wanted to put them away before she chickened out and returned everything.

When they finished putting the bags away and were waiting for an elevator back up, Brad took her necklace out of his pocket. "We forgot to put this on you. Can I?"

Hannah's heart pounded and she felt hot and sweaty. She checked to make sure she was still breathing while telling herself sternly to cut that out, then nodded because she didn't trust her voice to work.

Brad took the necklace out of the packaging. "Turn around, okay?" Hannah did and he said, "I'm gonna have to move your hair out of the way. Unless you'd rather do that yourself."

"It's fine," Hannah said, letting the part of her that wanted Brad to touch her to win for once.

Brad gently pushed her hair out of the way and put the necklace around her neck. It seemed like it was taking forever—was he being slow on purpose so he could keep touching her? She hoped not, but she also wanted him to kiss the back of her neck when he was done with the necklace, except the idea also made the panicky feeling in her chest a billion times worse.

"There," Brad said, letting her hair go. "I'll never understand why they make these clasps so tiny. Don't they want you to be able to actually put the thing on?"

Hannah giggled. "Maybe it's because they want it to be a two-person job," she said, realizing too late she sounded flirty. She stared at her reflection in the elevator doors, pretending to be checking out the necklace but really holding her breath while she waited to see what Brad would do.

"So, what do you think?" Brad asked. "You think it's as beautiful on you as I do?"

"I need to see it in a real mirror," Hannah said, keeping her tone light and trying to hide how warm it made her face feel whenever Brad called her beautiful, "but I definitely like it." She turned toward him. "Thank you."

"No problem," Brad said. "Told you I wanted to buy a minute of that amazing smile."

Hannah could feel how much Brad wanted to kiss her. She played with the back of her earring, suddenly afraid he might even though she wanted him to. God, she was sick of being such a coward.

Maybe she needed to be the one to make the first move. Then she could show herself it was safe.

Hannah took a step toward Brad, but just then the elevator dinged. She let her breath out slowly as she squeezed his hand, pretending that's all she was going to do in the first place.

***

The carousel turned out to be on the opposite end of the third floor from the elevator—across from a kid-sized train ride. Hannah watched the brightly colored trains go around and around, wishing she was still small enough to fit in them.

"Bet you never knew they had this, huh?" Brad grinned.

"Nope." Hannah made herself turn away from the trains. "Are you sure we're not too big for this?" she asked, tilting her head up and watching the brightly colored horses go around and around. Children's music was coming from the center of the ride, and she didn't see any adults on it at all.

"Positive," Brad said. "They make them for all ages. How else are parents gonna get on with their kids? But we don't have to go on if you think it's dumb. We can just watch."

"What would be the point of that?" Hannah asked. She scanned the sign at the front of the carousel with her eyes to find out the price before grabbing a few dollars from her wallet. "I can't believe I never knew this was here."

"That's why I wanted to show you." Brad smiled, but his eyes looked sad like there was no light in them. "It was like, a huge part of my childhood. We'd come to the mall to get clothes and stuff for school every year and go on it after. Dad used to be like a big kid. He'd get this goofy smile on his face when he got on the highest horse they had, and Mom would sit right there watching us and taking pictures. Good times."

Brad's shoulders slumped and he sighed deeply. Hannah put her hand on his shoulder, but he pulled away and said, "Let's get in line."

When they did, Hannah suggested sitting in one of the stationary chariots, so they could talk more easily, but Brad thought that was boring.

"Tell you what," Hannah said. "We can go twice, and the second time I'll get on a horse. How's that?"

Brad smiled slightly. "Cool. But don't think you're getting away with getting on a horse close to the ground. Uh-uh. You have to ride the highest one there is even if I have to help you on it."

Hannah scoffed, ignoring the tight, nervous feeling in her stomach. "Yeah right. I'm pretty tall for a girl. I doubt there's any horse here that can get the better of me."

Brad looked her up and down. "You got the pretty part right, anyway."

Hannah hurried to give her money to the person in the ticket booth, glad that gave her an excuse to look away from Brad.

The chariot was a four-seater car that was fastened to the carousel and didn't move. Hopefully, nobody would want to share it with them. Brad slid in across from Hannah. She wanted to sit next to him, but the ride was already starting.

"I wanted to do this because it's more private," she said, reaching for Brad's hand. "Like the buggy rides in Central Park but better because it doesn't use real horses."

"There goes my idea for our next date." Brad's eyes sparkled. "People on TV are always going on romantic buggy rides in the snow."

"Yeah, well, no one asks the horses how they feel about it. I worry about them. I would love to go to the city sometime, though, if my parents will let you take me. Last year Sierra invited me to see the tree at Rockefeller Center with her, but they said I was too young to navigate the city without them." Hannah rolled her eyes.

"You'll make it there. I just gotta win them over, so they'll trust me with you."

Hannah pushed a lock of hair behind her ear. "It's not you. They don't trust me."

"You? But you've never done anything wrong in your life."

"I went to that party. And when I was in middle school, once I went to CVS with Sierra and bought makeup they thought I was too young for."

"Shocking. And I thought getting arrested was bad." Brad's tone was light, but his voice had a weird note in it. "Seriously," he said as Hannah took his hand again, "why the hell wouldn't they trust you?"

"Because." Hannah twisted her ring, not sure how to explain or if she wanted to. "They think because of what happened that, um . . . that I'm going to jump into bed with the first boy I see." She stared at her feet, not wanting to see the look on Brad's face.

"Cause that's what we're all about, sex and nothing else," Brad said bitterly. He leaned forward. "Hey. You know that's not what I'm trying to do, right?"

"Yeah. Of course." It wasn't entirely a lie. Hannah knew when she was thinking clearly that Brad would never do anything with her that she didn't fully want him to do and that he backed off every time she got scared. The problem was that she got scared too easily. "They said it, not me. They're way overprotective of me. They always have been."

"I bet it's twice as bad now," Brad said. "Mine too. They both watched me like a hawk after I was arrested. You'd think they were still married from the way they came at me." He slumped down in his seat.

Hannah took his hand between hers. "I guess they were scared for you."

"Not like I didn't know how bad it could have been. You think I wanted to go to juvie over a few stupid buds of weed?" Brad blinked hard as Hannah massaged his knuckles. "Sorry for all the drug talk. You probably don't want to hear about crap like that."

"It's okay. It was a mistake, that's all. Like me going to that party."

Brad shook his head. "You didn't do anything wrong. I did."

"But you got a second chance. I'm glad you did." Hannah leaned forward before she realized what she was doing. Her lips were about to brush Brad's when she came to her senses and turned her head, kissing his cheek instead.

She froze, remembering suddenly how angry Jamie had gotten when she'd done that to him at the party. "Sorry. I wasn't trying to . . . "

"It's cool. You being there helps more than you know." Brad smiled, but Hannah could see tears in his eyes. "Just so you know, if you want to kiss, I'm totally open to it."

Hannah swallowed hard, trying to push down her anxiety. "I want to, but. . . " Her eyes darted to Brad's, then away. "I always thought my first kiss would be in the library. Not. . . you know, not while I was passed out."

"That doesn't count. He made you. You didn't want it and you don't even remember it." Brad took Hannah's hand again, running his fingers over the stone on her ring. "I won't ever do that to you. I won't ever do anything you don't one hundred percent want. I promise."

"I know." The carousel was playing an annoying rendition of "Farmer in the Dell" that Hannah was sure was going to be stuck in her head. She twisted a stray lock of hair around her finger. "I wish we were sitting on the same side. I want to cuddle."

"That can be arranged," Brad said, grinning. He got up even though you weren't supposed to stand while the carousel was moving.

"Brad! That's not safe."

"Don't you know by now I never play it safe?" Brad asked, the old sparkle in his eyes back. He crossed quickly to Hannah's side of the chariot and sat down next to her. "There. Now you were saying?"

Hannah giggled despite herself. "I wasn't saying anything." She hugged Brad and put her head on his chest. She could feel his heart beating. It was strong and steady, just what she needed to balance her own. She lay there, letting Brad stroke her hair until the carousel slowed to a stop and they had to get off the ride.

21 – Back to Reality

HANNAH WASN'T READY for the date to end when she and Brad got back to her apartment. Brad offered to help her put her new clothes away and she agreed even though she was sure Mom was going to hover and ask too many questions.

Sure enough, Mom wouldn't let Brad go into Hannah's room to help her. "I'm not ready for you to be alone in your bedroom with a boy," she said. Hannah rolled her eyes even though her stupid anxiety was starting up again. She wasn't exactly ready either, but she didn't appreciate Mom saying so.

"It's cool," Brad said. "Wouldn't want to make you uncomfortable in your own house." But his eyes were narrow, and Hannah could tell he was annoyed too.

"But Mom's going to give you the third degree about our date while you're waiting for me," she said.

"Don't worry, I'll call my lawyer if things get too rough." Brad's eyes sparkled as he gave Hannah her bags. "Hurry back, though. I can't get enough of looking at you."

Hannah's face got hot for a change, and she was sure she was as red as the apple clock in the kitchen.

In her room, she looked around, trying to imagine how Brad would see everything since she wasn't allowed to show it to him. He'd probably think the wall next to her bed was bare and ugly. He'd make a joke about how she didn't have any posters up like a normal girl her age, but he might be impressed with how full the bookshelf next to her desk was.

The desk was too messy. She'd left her Chemistry book open and a pen lying across it, and her highlighters weren't in the drawer where they belonged. She hurried to fix all that, not wanting Brad to think she was a total slob even though he wasn't going to see any of this.

After she was done, she sank down onto her bed, pushing the bags aside. Gosh, she'd bought a lot!

The only person she'd ever known who bought things impulsively was Mom. She loved shopping so much that she used to say that she was glad they lived with Grandma, so they didn't have to worry about whether she spent the rent money at the mall.

Mom hadn't gone on a shopping binge for a long time, and Hannah didn't know how she stopped other than that Mom took medicine every day and saw a therapist once a week. No one really talked about it. It was like the door to the past was closed and locked and Hannah was supposed to forget it ever happened.

But now she needed to know because she'd gone on an impulsive shopping spree too and her moods had been all over the place lately and she wasn't sure if that meant something. What if it meant she was bipolar too? What if it was starting to manifest itself in her now that she was growing up? Was she going to make the lives of everyone who loved her a living hell like Mom had when she was little? What would that do to Brad if she ever got over her anxiety enough to actually be with him, only for him to have to deal with her losing her mind?

She remembered that terrible, awful time when Mom was in the psych ward after her suicide attempt, and Grandma wouldn't tell Hannah anything. Hannah could pick up just enough from eavesdropping to learn that Mom was very sick and might not be coming home ever. It was the scariest, worst thing that had ever happened to Hannah in her life except when she woke up at Sierra's after the rape and didn't know what had happened to her.

And now Hannah was starting to be like Mom.

How could she put Brad through that? And if someday they got married and had kids, how could she . . .

Kids. She hadn't got her period since the rape. What if she was pregnant even though she took that pill?

I can't do this to Brad. I can't.

But the idea of telling him to forget going on a second date made her mad, and another voice in her head said that Brad chose her and that he'd understand.

There only was one thing to do: tell him the truth, all of it, and see if he was up for this.

Hannah ran her fingers through her hair, trying to make herself look decent before she went out into the living room.

"Catholic, I guess," Brad was saying. "I dunno. Dad jokes about his job being his religion. I guess 'cause it's the center of his life. I'm named after some dude that Dad says was a journalistic hero."

"I see," Mom said, while Hannah put her hand over her stomach. If Brad was Catholic, how was he going to react if she was pregnant?

"Um, why are you talking about religion?" she asked. "It's not like we do anything with ours."

Brad squeezed Hannah's hand. "She just wanted to make sure I'm not a serial killer who goes after gorgeous Jewish girls, and I'm not. So, it's all good."

Mom said, "I see where this sarcastic streak Hannah has lately comes from."

"Mom!" Hannah threw her arm around Brad. "When are you ever going to get that I'm my own person? You're always looking for someone to blame for me being myself. God!"

Brad squeezed her shoulder. "And here I thought I was a bad influence." Mom's lips thinned and Brad said, "Just kidding! But seriously, Ms. K, Hannah's way stronger than you think. She doesn't go around doing things just 'cause other people do."

Hannah remembered suddenly Jamie saying the same thing at the party, that he liked that she knew what she wanted and didn't want. She stiffened, wondering again if Jamie had been the guy who raped her.

Mom asked Brad a few more questions, then said she would leave them to say goodbye to each other privately. As soon as she left the room, Brad's dad texted and asked how soon he could expect to be able to use his car.

"I hate to cut this short," Brad said, "but there's always Tuesday, right?" He smiled, but his eyes told another story. "Wanna go out to dinner after track?"

Hannah did. She did so much it hurt. "Only if you let me tell you what you're getting into." She pushed her hair behind her ear. "I. . . . the thing is. . . I want to be your girlfriend but. . . "

Brad took Hannah's hands in his, and she couldn't help noticing that they fit together nicely. Her too-large-for-a-girl hands didn't feel so big in his perfect-size-for-a-guy ones. "Hey," he said. "Don't be so freaked out, okay? I told you, we'll go as slow as you want."

"It's not that. It's just, I have to go to the doctor on Monday after school for a . . . a post-rape checkup, and if I'm pregnant . . . "

"That bastard better not have done that to you!" Brad's nostrils flared as he breathed in and out. "Listen, if you want me to go with you, I'm up for it."

Hannah's mouth dropped open. That was the last thing she'd expected to hear. "Wow. That's sweet of you, but no, I'm okay. Sierra and her brother are taking me."

"You sure? I don't mind. I'll even put up with Sierra if it means being there for you."

"Sierra's not so bad. Not like Molly." Pain shot through Hannah's chest and she looked away.

"What kind of answer's that?" Brad squeezed Hannah's hands, then dropped them. "N-not that I'm pressuring you or anything. I swear."

"No, it's okay. It's just . . . I'd rather we do fun stuff together, not this."

"Me too, but someone else messed that up." Brad's tone was light, but Hannah could tell he knew that wasn't a joke. "All right," he said. "I'll back the fuck off. Just text me soon as you know. And if you change your mind, it's not like I got something so important to do I can't drop it to come hang with you at the clinic."

"Thanks. Really."

There was an awkward pause as if they had both run out of things to say. Then, Brad said he needed to get the car back to his dad and Hannah walked him out. She secretly wished he didn't have to go home.

22 – Weird Conversations

WHEN HANNAH CAME back in, Eric wanted her to help him in the kitchen. He asked her how her date went and admired her necklace, though she could see a frown in his eyes. Then, he told her that Mom had taken Tuesday afternoon off so that she could take Hannah to her first therapy session.

"I can't on Tuesday," Hannah said. "I have plans with Brad."

Eric sighed. "I don't want you spending every waking minute with Brad, and you already had a whole day with him. Besides, your mental health comes first. Any boy who doesn't understand that isn't worth your time."

But she could take care of her mental health a different day. Besides, what if Brad thought she was flaking out like the scared mouse she was trying not to be anymore? "You're not being fair."

"I'm sure you think so. But regardless, it's not going to kill you to spend one afternoon apart from Brad, and that's what you're going to have to do. Now wash the tomatoes for me, and let's get started on this salad."

Hannah's eyes flashed and she wondered what would happen if she went to track clinic with Brad on Tuesday instead of coming straight home like she'd been told, but she knew she'd never have the courage to defy Mom and Eric so openly.

***

After dinner, Hannah went to her room and video-called Sierra.

"Is that necklace new?" Sierra asked as soon as Hannah's video camera came on.

"Yeah." Hannah touched one of the flowers, smiling slightly. "Brad got it for me at the mall today."

"Nice." Sierra picked up a stuffed bear from her bed and hugged it against herself. "What kind of clothes did he pick out for you to go with it?"

"He didn't." Hannah pushed her hair behind her ear, confused. "I got myself a whole new wardrobe, though. Want to see what I'm going to wear Monday?"

"I guess." Sierra ran her fingers through the bear's fur.

Hannah got the blouse and jeans and held them up, not wanting to change in front of Sierra. "What do you think?"

Sierra twisted her hoodie string around her finger. "They're cool, but . . . " She took her glasses off, and Hannah guessed she was wiping them on her shirt since she couldn't see where they disappeared to. "You sure Brad's okay with them?"

"He was right there when I bought them." Hannah's voice had a hard edge to it she didn't like. "Besides, it's not up to him what I wear."

"Maybe not before, but now that he bought you a necklace, things are different. You guys are dating now even if he didn't say so. You need to make him happy."

Hannah touched one of the flowers on her necklace, confused. What Sierra was saying didn't make any sense to her. But Sierra knew more about boys than she did so maybe she was right.

"You don't think he'll be too disappointed I can't make it Tuesday, do you?" Hannah told Sierra how her parents were making her change her plans with Brad so they could drag her to therapy.

Sierra bit her lip. "Tell him to come get you after. If he sees you weren't lying and you really want to spend time with him it'll soften the blow." She fidgeted with one of her braids. "Listen, while I have you on the phone, I. . . I don't think I can go to the doctor with you Monday."

"Why not?" Hannah knew the answer to that. Jake. Sierra always put him first, even after what happened. But she wanted to ask anyway in case Sierra had a real reason for flaking on her.

Sierra's eyes were down like she was staring at something off-camera. Her bedspread, maybe. Or her phone. "You'll be fine without me. Dylan'll be there, and he's better at this sort of stuff. Besides, I bet if Molly makes up with you, you'd way rather have her there than me, right?"

"Sierra!" Hannah was already sick of being in the middle between Sierra and Molly. "First of all, that isn't happening, and second, if it did, I'd want both of you there. And Brad, maybe."

Sierra's eyes widened. "Brad? Are you crazy?"

Hannah stiffened, not appreciating that word. "Maybe," she said lightly, imitating what Brad would do. "He knows everything, Si. He knows I was raped, and I might be pregnant and - "

Sierra's dad came into her room just then. The camera cut off the top of his head so that Hannah could only see the dark skin around his lips, his mouth itself, and part of his gray and white beard.

"Excuse me," Mr. Dunlap's mouth said. "Sierra, I told you before dinner that I expected you to empty the kitchen trash afterward."

"I will!" Sierra said. "As soon as I'm done - "

"NOW!"

Sierra rolled her eyes. "Gotta go," she said and signed off.

***

The next morning, Hannah put on her wraparound skirt. Brad had invited her to study at his dad's, and she wanted to look nice, though she almost changed into jeans because Mom felt a need to tell her that her skirt was too easy to take off. She decided to take the risk anyway, and then Eric teased her about not spending too much time looking into Brad's eyes instead of studying. She hurried downstairs to get away from both of them.

There was a plump, pretty red-haired girl sitting in the lobby when the elevator opened. The girl looked like Molly and Hannah thought that was funny until she got closer and saw it WAS Molly.

"Molly! What. . . what are you doing here?"

"Nice to see you too," Molly said. She crossed her arms. "I had to try one last time. You never text me. You never call me. And you're not happy to see me, so I guess there's no point. But I was kind of hoping we could salvage our friendship."

Hannah played with her bracelet. This wasn't a good time, not when Brad was going to be here any second, and Molly was acting kind of stalkerish. But at the same time, she was tired of the cold silence between them and if there was a way for them to fix this . . .

She threw herself onto the bench next to Molly. "Of course I still want to be friends. It was never about that."

"Really? Then what is it about? Because you don't seem to want anything to do with me, and when I try to talk to you, you get mad."

Hannah played with a button on her jacket, glad Molly couldn't see the new outfit underneath it. "It isn't you. I just feel like the party changed everything. I went and you didn't, and then after what happened to me . . . I don't know, I just felt like everything was different."

"But it's not. I'm still your best friend, or I would be if you'd let me."

But it changed me. Hannah twisted her ring, not sure how to explain. "I know. But I'm different, Molly, and not in good ways. I guess that's why my parents are making me see a therapist."

"They are?" Molly's eyes were wide and bright, the perfect illustration of eyes lighting up. "I'm glad. When?"

"Tuesday."

"Good. Don't bite my head off, but you need help ASAP."

"If you say so. It's not that I'm against it, exactly. I just don't . . . " Hannah's phone buzzed. "Oh. Brad's here."

Molly raised her eyebrows. "You're going out with him again?"

"We're studying at his house."

"Right. So, um, is he your boyfriend now?"

Hannah's face felt hotter than ever. She nodded, making herself smile. "I'll tell you about it later."

"You'd better."

"I'll text you." Hannah double-checked her coat was closed and then walked out. She was sure Molly was watching as she hugged Brad and let him help her into the car. Watching and disapproving. She told herself she didn't care.

23 - Moving Too Fast

LUNCH TURNED OUT to be a sort of buffet. Mr. Ashton had put out every type of bread imaginable: sourdough and wheat and pumpernickel and potato bread, and none of it was the cheap brand that Mom got either. He'd also put out a tray of vegetables and a tray of cheese, and he had got a ton of salads: tuna, chicken, macaroni, and potato.

"I thought Thanksgiving's not for two weeks," Brad said.

"Ha ha," Mr. Ashton said. "I admit I did go a little bit overboard, but I wanted Hannah to feel welcome. Help yourself, Hannah, there are plates on the counter there."

"Thanks." Hannah could feel Mr. Ashton watching as she spooned macaroni salad onto her plate. She was sure he thought she was taking too much.

When they sat down again, Mr. Ashton asked what her plans were for Thanksgiving. Hannah told him that it would probably be just her and her parents. Eric's brother sometimes joined them, but no one had said he was coming. So, she didn't think he was this year.

Mr. Ashton nodded. "I will be joining Brad and his mother at her house this year. I'm sure she won't mind if you join us for dessert."

"I bet she will," Brad said, "but come anyway."

Hannah's ears rang. This was all moving too fast, much too fast. She'd only had one date with Brad. Why was his dad inviting her to Thanksgiving? Her face got super-hot, and she thought maybe she might faint. She drank some more water, trying desperately to cool herself off. "Can I let you know later?"

"Of course," Mr. Ashton said. "I wouldn't want to interfere if your parents have other plans."

The conversation moved on to other things. Hannah said she liked that they were having an indoor picnic today, and Mr. Ashton said he wished he'd had time to cook instead, but Brad said that he always said that and never did it.

"Speaking of, burgers okay on Tuesday?" Brad asked Hannah. "I got a place I want to take you to."

Hannah's heart pounded. She wanted to go with Brad to have burgers instead of to the stupid therapy appointment. She wanted that so bad her chest hurt. "Um. . . " she said. "About that. . . I kind of need to put it off."

Brad's face fell. Hannah looked away. "I'm not flaking on you, I swear. My parents made an appointment for me without bothering to ask when I was free, and they won't change it."

"Course they did. Parents, right? No offense, Dad."

"None taken," Mr. Ashton said. He took another bite of his sandwich. "I'll be out of your way as soon as I finish this. You two can complain about how we parents go out of our way to make your lives miserable all you'd like."

"You don't have to rush." Hannah felt terrible about making Mr. Ashton feel unwelcome at his own table. "It was so nice of you to put this together for us. You should enjoy it too."

"It's all right. I'm used to eating at my desk." Mr. Ashton stood. "You two needed brain fuel for the studying you're doing, I didn't mind providing that. I'll be in my study if you need me, Brad." He walked away.

"Wow," Hannah said. "My parents would be all over us."

"Yeah. Dad's pretty hands-off. Probably why he and Mom couldn't stay married. Anyway, so what's this big important appointment your parents won't let you get out of?"

"Oh. It's. You know. . . " Hannah didn't know why she couldn't get the words out of her mouth. It wasn't like Brad wasn't seeing a therapist too. "What I told you before about how they want me to see someone about dealing with the thing that happened to me."

"You know what's cool about that? It only lasts an hour, so even if you hate it, it'll be over pretty fast."

Hannah put her hand over her stomach, feeling anxiety bubble up again. "Want to come get me after, so you can see I'm not blowing you off?"

"Nope. I want to come get you so we can make up for lost time." Brad reached for Hannah's hand. "I'm gonna be at my mom's, which means it's fifty-fifty whether I can pull it off, but if I can, I wanna treat you to a burger with whatever you want on it."

A voice in the back of Hannah's head said she'd better stay home and do her homework. "Mine might not let me go either. They think I'm putting you too close to the top of my list anyway." Ugh. Why did she have to make herself sound like such a baby? "Actually, never mind. I don't care what they say. I want to have dinner with you and I'm going to."

"Knew I'd corrupt you!" Brad's eyes sparkled for real as he dumped ranch dressing on his plate to dip his vegetables in. "Come on. Let's finish eating, so I can show you how much I've read of *The Scarlet Letter*."

***

After lunch, Hannah and Brad moved into the living room to study.

"Let's do this!" Brad said, tossing *The Scarlet Letter* on the table. "You were right. This book isn't so bad if you look past the stupid way he writes to the actual story."

Hannah giggled. "That was just the style back then. You should read Dickens when you get finished with this. My favorite is *Great Expectations*." Her tongue suddenly felt dryer than sandpaper. "It's about this romance that should have happened but doesn't because this woman's been raised to be cold and cruel, and that's not who she really is."

"You really should be a teacher. You make thick books sound worth reading." Brad's smile faded. "What's wrong?"

Hannah stared at the ground, hoping Brad didn't think she was too high maintenance. "I was supposed to be her that night. Estella from *Great Expectations*. Sierra lent me a dress even though she thought it was a ridiculous idea and he tore it when he . . . " She bit her lip. "But it's okay. Dylan said it just needed a few stitches and it would be as good as new." She blinked hard. "Anyway, let's study. How far did you get?"

"I finished." Brad's eyes sparkled. "Wanna quiz me?"

"I trust you. Besides, Mr. Collins doesn't just want us to memorize the story. He wants us to be changed by it. He likes to ask things like which character you identified with most and why."

"Dimmesdale," Brad said. "Definitely him. He couldn't get rid of how bad he felt about what he did and it killed him." He looked away from Hannah. "I kind of liked Pearl too. She was all messed up 'cause her parents weren't together."

Hannah wasn't sure that was why Pearl acted out, but something told her not to argue. "How long have your parents been divorced?" she asked. Brad's head jerked up and she said, "S-sorry. It's not my business."

"No, it's cool. And since last fall. My sister went to college, and a couple weeks later, it was over." Brad swallowed hard. "It wasn't my fault."

"Of course not." Hannah put her hand on Brad's shoulder. "Did they fight a lot before?"

Brad pressed his hands together. "I get enough of this at my shrink's. Can we not?"

"Right. Of course. Sorry for prying." Hannah stared into space, wanting to say something but not wanting to say it. "I'm glad at least you know who your dad is. I don't, and I probably never will." Her heart pounded harder. "There's something I have to tell you, and if you can handle it, maybe I can get over being afraid to kiss you."

Brad's eyes widened. "Go for it," he said.

Hannah nodded. Her mouth was dryer than ever, and she didn't think she could get the words out. She squeezed his hand and said, "My mom is bipolar. The only reason I'm here is because one time when she was manic, she jumped into bed with some guy whose name she didn't even know. He left right after and a few weeks later she found out she was pregnant."

"Wow," Brad said. "Okay. But that's her. It has nothing to do with you and me. Besides, that dude did the world a favor, making you."

Hannah's face got even hotter. "That's sweet, but . . . " She fidgeted, interlocking her fingers and twisting her hands back and forth. "I could be bipolar too. I'm moody and impulsive lately, and I don't know if it's because of, you know, the R, or because that's who I really am. I just can't hide it anymore after what happened to me. And if I am, you need to run away from me, far far away, because until it's under control, I could really hurt you in ways I don't want to talk about."

"Uh-uh," Brad said. "If you are, we just gotta face it together." He put his hand on Hannah's shoulder. "Your mom seemed okay to me. You telling me she still does that stuff?"

"No, not anymore. She hasn't in a long time. She's on medicine now that controls it. But sometimes her medicine needs to be changed, and she starts to be a little bit more unpredictable 'til they fix it."

"I'm cool with unpredictable. If that's what you are, I mean."

"Yeah, but you don't know the whole story. It's not just being unpredictable. It's way more. When I was six, she got it in her head I needed to see Santa at the mall so I wouldn't feel left out at Christmas, and she drove like a maniac. Then, when we got there, she started fighting with the crowds and we almost got kicked out. And then a few months later, she got in one of her down moods and she took a whole bottle of pills. If my grandma hadn't been home, she'd be long gone."

"Holy shit," Brad said. "Thank God she's okay."

"Yeah." Hannah stared at the coffee table, tracing the grains in the wood with her eyes. "Anyway, if I'm bipolar too, I could put you through that, and I can't ask you to risk it."

"Your mom and stepdad make it work," Brad said. "Besides, I'm not like my dad, I don't walk out on the woman I love."

He loves me! Hannah didn't know whether to be thrilled or scared. "Your dad's the one who filed for divorce?"

"I guess. They had a big fight, and he left for a couple weeks. When he came back, they told me together he was moving out permanently." Brad thumbed through the pages of the book. "You never told me which character you identify with. No fair if I do and you don't."

"Oh. Right. I used to think I was Pearl because I didn't have a dad and sometimes people looked down on my mom because of it. But now, I don't know . . . maybe I'm Hester?"

"Definitely." The sparkle in Brad's eyes was back. "It says right here she held her head up high and walked with a quiet dignity even when they were trying to shame her, and that's totally you."

"I don't know about that. I haven't exactly held my head up high in a long time. I'm not quiet because I'm dignified. I'm quiet because I'm scared not to be."

"You, scared? What have you got to be scared of?"

"Everything." Hannah reached for Brad's hand. "You're the first person I ever told about my mom, so please don't spread it around."

"I won't. I told you, you can trust me." Brad played with Hannah's knuckles. "I'll tell you something about me, that way if I ever betray you, you can get me back."

"You don't have to do that. I know you won't tell."

"Maybe not, but I want to." Brad swallowed hard. "Some assholes call me gay as like, an insult or whatever—like I'd be any less of a dude if I was. But, um, they're only half wrong. I'm not into dudes but sometimes. . . " He looked away from her. "I'm not a hundred percent straight either."

Hannah nodded, not sure what to say. "So, you're bi?"

"I guess. But I'm totally into you, I swear."

"I believe you." Hannah squeezed Brad's hand. "I'm sorry I haven't been ready to kiss you. It wasn't because I didn't think you were really interested. I just can't stop being afraid no matter how hard I try. In the mall, I thought maybe if I made the first move, I could do it. But then the elevator came and I lost my nerve."

"How about a do-over, then?" Brad leaned forward.

"I-if you're sure you want someone with as many problems as me."

"Hey. That's my line." Brad smiled that heart-melting smile again. "If you'll have me, I'll have you. How's that?"

"Perfect." The scared part of Hannah's brain screamed at her not to give in, but she couldn't fight it any longer. She leaned forward and let Brad put his lips on hers. His were soft, and it scared her a little when he pressed his mouth against hers so they could kiss. At the same time, it felt right, so right. She closed her eyes, concentrating on the feeling of his lips on hers as she breathed in and out. She could feel how much he loved her, and it made her want more. She reached up and ran her hand through his hair, and he did the same, stroking hers as they kept kissing.

Afterward, he stroked her cheek and asked if she was okay, and she nodded and said, "Better than okay." Then she hugged him, ignoring both the voice in her head that wanted him to peel her skirt off her and the one that was terrified that she'd already gone too far.

24 – The Rift Grows

THE NEXT MORNING, people were laughing and whispering as Hannah walked through the cafeteria, looking for somewhere to sit. Hannah wasn't sure if they were laughing at her clothes or calling her a slut, but she made herself hold her head high and tell herself over and over she didn't care.

But then, she passed by Molly and Jen's table. Jen had her hand half over her mouth and was snickering at something and Hannah didn't want to be paranoid, but she was sure it was about her.

"What's so funny?" Hannah demanded, crossing her arms against her chest.

"Nothing," Jen said. "But that's an interesting outfit Brad talked you into." She giggled.

Hannah locked eyes with Molly, wanting her to say something.

Molly looked away. "Your clothes, your business," she said. "Though you have to admit, it's very different."

"So?" Hannah snapped.

"So, no need to bite our heads off," Jen said. "We're just pointing out the obvious, geez."

Hannah had had enough. "For your information," she said, hating herself because her voice shook when she wanted it to be loud and firm, "Brad didn't talk me into anything. I picked this out myself, and I'm wearing it because I happen to like it. And anyway, you guys are supposed to be my friends, so why the hell are you laughing at me?"

"Relax, will you?" Jen said. "It's just some good-natured teasing, though you haven't been acting like much of a friend recently."

"Jen," Molly said quietly. "Don't. Hannah and I made up yesterday, you're going to . . . "

"Sorry, hon," Jen said, raising her voice so she drowned out Molly's. "Someone has to stand up for you. I don't know what the hell stick got up your ass, Hannah, but you've been a first-class bitch ever since that stupid party. Molly keeps trying because she remembers how you used to be, but I'm done. You've changed and not for the better. So when you're ready to be sweet, quiet Hannah that we all loved again, let us know. Until then, stay the hell away from us."

Hannah was so mad her throat hurt. She forced it down and said to Molly, "I thought you wanted to make up."

"I do." Molly played with her ponytail, tightening it when it was already tight. "I swear I do. But like I said yesterday, we always end up fighting s-so maybe I should give you space. I don't know."

"Yeah," Jen said. "You're angry all the time and you don't seem to know who your real friends are." She reached for Molly's hand. "Don't let her suck you into her drama, babe. Come on."

Molly stared at Hannah for a second. Then she took Jen's hand and they walked away together.

The rest of the morning was super awkward. Hannah had to sit next to Molly in homeroom and again in Chemistry, and she didn't know what to say to her. She was glad at least it wasn't a lab day, so they didn't have to interact at all. After that, Hannah went out to the track to run with Brad and try to get her mind off things, but it was too cold out for her. She couldn't last, so she ended up going back to the cafeteria and watching him run through the window while she drank a hot chocolate that she bought from the machine.

Worst of all, Mr. Nesbitt, her guidance counselor, called her to the office and told her Mom called him. Hannah told him she was fine even though she wasn't. He didn't argue with her, which made her think he was a sucky counselor because he should have seen right through that and realized she was the opposite of fine.

The longer the day dragged on, the more aware she was that soon she was going to the doctor to find out if she was pregnant. During PreCalc, she wondered if this was how people on Death Row felt on the day they were supposed to be executed, then felt bad for thinking that. If she was pregnant, a life was growing in her. It was the opposite of being put to death. And Mom said that getting pregnant with Hannah was the best thing that had come out of a bad situation. Could it be the same for her?

She put her hand over her stomach and did her best to pay attention so that Mrs. Marino wouldn't have a reason to keep her after class again.

After school, Hannah met Sierra at her locker.

"Well, this is it," she said, trying to make herself smile. "As soon as Dylan gets here, we're going to find out if my life has changed forever. You sure you can't come with me?"

"I wish I could." Sierra played with her phone. "I feel shitty about leaving you hanging, but Jake thinks it's better I don't get all stressed out. He's right, I guess. I'll feel horrible if it turns out that you're pregnant, and I just can't deal with sitting in the clinic with you waiting to find out."

"It must be nice to have a choice." But that wasn't fair, and Hannah knew it. Sierra had been there for her all this time, and it wasn't her fault Hannah might be pregnant.

"Come on, Mouse. Don't be like that." Sierra looked away. "I know I'm being an awful friend. But I really can't take it. I'll just sit there the whole time wishing I hadn't ruined your life."

Hannah had a sudden urge to kick Sierra's locker as hard as she could. She held her breath until it passed. "I ruined my own life, okay? Not you. I went to that party. I drank that drugged iced tea. Now I have to deal with it. And I'd rather you be there, but since you obviously don't want to . . . "

"It's not that I don't want to. It's that I can't." Sierra twisted her hands together. They went back and forth, back and forth, while Hannah glared at her, trying and failing to talk herself out of being mad. "I'll be there for you afterward, but I can't do this. Please don't be mad."

"I'm not," Hannah lied. She felt more than ever like kicking the locker or maybe kicking herself. There she went being a stupid little mouse again. "But I better go. I don't want to miss my ride." She turned and walked away as fast as she could.

It was still freezing cold out, but now she had to deal with it. It wasn't like she could wait inside for Dylan to come get her. She sat down on the raised flowerbed and pulled out her phone to text Brad, but it was hard to type with gloves on, and her autocorrect kept changing her mistakes to words that had nothing to do with what she wanted to say.

"Where's your boyfriend?" Nathan jeered as he walked by. "Did he finally figure out you're a slut and dump you?"

It took all her energy not to jump up and deck him.

She wished Dylan would hurry up and get here. Maybe he was going to forget? Maybe she was going to get left here by herself and need to call a taxi? She hugged herself tightly, feeling a lump in her throat and praying her tears didn't freeze to her face.

"There you are," Brad said, throwing himself down next to her. "Been looking everywhere for you."

"Why?" Hannah's voice held a bitter note. "Don't you have better things to do?"

"Nothing better than supporting you." Brad put his hand on Hannah's shoulder. "Hey. It's gonna be okay."

"I doubt that." Hannah hated herself for being so weak and whiny in front of Brad, but she was tired of pretending to be fine when she wasn't. "Sierra stood me up, and I wouldn't be surprised if her stupid brother did too."

"If he does, I'll call my dad. He won't like being bothered when he's trying to work, but if it's for you, he'll chill out about it."

"No! Your dad likes me. I don't want him to know I'm a slut who might be pregnant."

"He won't know that 'cause it's not true."

"You're the only one who thinks so." Hannah kicked at the bottom of the ledge. Brad's forehead creased with worry, and she said, "Sorry I'm being such a bitch. I just don't appreciate Sierra flaking out when I need her most."

Brad put his arm around Hannah. She leaned on him, wanting comfort even though she was afraid Mr. Collins would bother them again if she stayed in his arms too long.

Brad stroked her hair. "I know it's not the same as having another girl by your side, but if you want, I'll come with you."

The idea of Brad sitting in a clinic with her waiting to hear whether she was pregnant was weird even though she'd been planning to ask him. Then again, the whole thing was weird and even now, after all this time, she couldn't quite believe it was happening to her, that she'd been raped and might be having a baby. "If I'm pregnant, everyone's going to think you're the daddy."

"Let them." Brad squeezed Hannah's hand. "You're way more important than what some losers think."

Hannah's face got so hot that she almost took her hat off.

A car honked and she said, "There's Dylan. Thank God."

"That a 'Yes'?"

"You're relentless," Hannah said, a note of admiration creeping into her voice. "But I'll be fine now that my ride's actually here."

Brad's whole body deflated, and Hannah could tell he was crushed. "Whatever you say. If you change your mind, call me. I'll hop on my bike and pedal over as fast as I can."

Hannah couldn't help smiling at that. She let Brad kiss her before she went to meet Dylan.

THE WAITING ROOM at the walk-in clinic was even more crowded than the one at the ER had been. There were pamphlets in a rack on the wall. One of them said: I'M PREGNANT—NOW WHAT? Hannah stared at it, unable to make herself take it.

If Molly was here, she'd say that if Hannah was pregnant, she'd have to get rid of it.

But it's not that easy, Molly, she answered her in her head. *I know being pregnant when I'm still in high school would ruin everything, but if my mom had done that I wouldn't be here. And what if there are protesters? What if I decide to have an abortion and people spit in my face and call me a slut like Nathan does all the time? I couldn't deal with that on top of having to wonder the rest of my life what my baby might have been like.*

The door to the exam rooms creaked open and a nurse called, "Hannah K?"

Hannah got up. Dylan wished her luck and held his arms out to hug her. Hannah wasn't in the mood to be touched, but she let him.

In the exam room, the nurse asked Hannah all the same questions she'd been asked in the ER, which made her so sick she thought she might throw up. She hadn't expected to have to do this all over again—couldn't they look up her medical record on the computer or something?

The nurse asked her if she'd been given anything to prevent HIV and she couldn't remember. The nurse wrote that down and left her to freak out while she waited for the doctor.

The doctor turned out to be an older woman, gray-haired and wearing thick glasses. There were wrinkles in the peach skin around her eyes.

"Hannah, right?" she said when she came in. "Can you verify your last name and date of birth for me?"

Hannah did even though it was ridiculous. The nurse had already asked her. It wasn't like there was someone else hiding under the exam table that she could switch places with.

They got started after that. The doctor was even worse than the nurse, asking a ton of questions in an all-business tone that made Hannah feel like she didn't really care about the answers. They went through how regular Hannah's period was (super regular except for it being three days late now) and whether she had any symptoms of sexually transmitted diseases (she didn't.) Then, she ordered blood work. She said it would take two or three days to come back, but she could get Hannah an answer today about pregnancy if she did a urine test and a pelvic exam.

"I'd insert a speculum into your vagina and take a look at your cervix," she explained when Hannah asked what a pelvic exam was. "If you're pregnant, even at three or four weeks it'll be softer and have changed color."

"I'll skip that, thanks." Hannah hugged herself, suddenly cold. She couldn't deal with the idea of someone putting something inside her right now. But was that being irresponsible? She didn't know.

The doctor didn't argue. She just nodded and told Hannah she'd send the nurse in to do the urine and blood tests. Then she and her business-like attitude left the room until after Hannah was finished peeing into a cup and getting blood drawn.

When she came back, she closed the door and sat down across from Hannah. "You had trace amounts of HgC, the pregnancy hormone, in your urine. Given those extremely low levels, I think it's likely that you were pregnant, but you aren't anymore."

"I don't understand." Hannah's voice shook for no reason.

"This happens sometimes early in pregnancy. It's called a chemical pregnancy because your body gave off the chemical signs of pregnancy, but then you miscarried so early on that it was like you were never pregnant."

"M-miscarried?" Hannah's throat stung when she swallowed. "So, it's like I had a baby growing inside me, and it died?"

"This early, it was more like a clump of cells than a baby." The doctor was still talking in that same detached tone. "It may have happened today or yesterday, which would explain why you still have a little bit of HgC in your urine."

"So why don't I have my period then?"

"The chemical pregnancy could have delayed it, and so could the morning after pill or the stress from having been sexually assaulted. You'll probably get it in a few days. You should know that it may be heavier than usual." The doctor smiled slightly for the first time. "I know it doesn't seem like it, but this is good news. You're sixteen. You didn't need to be saddled with a baby on top of everything else."

"Right." Hannah's voice was flat, but her mind was racing. The doctor was right and she knew it. If she'd been pregnant, she probably would have ended up terminating it anyway. So why was she so heartbroken that she felt like she didn't even have the energy to get off the exam table so she could go home?

The doctor patted her shoulder before giving her some paperwork. "Bring this to the front desk. And if you need anything at all, feel free to call."

Hannah took the doctor's business card even though she was sure she'd never use it. The doctor left the room to give her a chance to get her things together before she left. She stared at her phone, wondering what the hell to tell Brad, or anyone else, about her pregnancy that wasn't.

WHEN DYLAN DROPPED Hannah off, she went around the back of her apartment to the playground instead of going inside.

It was too cold and too dark for anyone to play there now. Hannah threw her backpack down on the ground and got on an adult-sized swing. It creaked as she scraped her feet against the dirt. She swung slowly back and forth, trying to figure things out and trying not to think at the same time. She wanted Brad to come over but she didn't want him to think she was as pathetic as she felt right now, so she didn't text him.

A car pulled into the lot behind the building, blaring music so loud that Hannah couldn't think. She slid off the swing, annoyed, and headed for the lobby.

"Hannah!" Sierra called, getting out of the loud car. "Wait up."

Hannah crossed her arms as she turned. "What are you doing here?"

Sierra's face crumpled. "I SAID I'd be there for you after, didn't I? Dylan got on my ass too about being a shitty friend so I came over to make things right. But if you don't want me here . . . "

"I didn't say that!" Hannah needed Sierra more than she needed to be mad at her. "Come on. Let's talk in my room."

"So . . . " Sierra said when they were sitting cross-legged on Hannah's bed.

"So." Hannah swallowed hard. "You'll be glad to know I'm not pregnant."

"Thank God!" Sierra said. "Wait . . . you look heartbroken. Brad said something, didn't he?"

"No!" Hannah made herself breathe, trying to get rid of the hard edge in her voice. "I'm not pregnant—anymore. The doctor said I had a miscarriage before the baby was big enough to be anything." A tear rolled down her face. "No reason to be sad, right? I mean, a baby would have ruined my life, and this wasn't even . . . it was nothing."

"I wish I knew what to say." Sierra twisted her hoodie string around her fingers. "Please tell me you're okay."

"I will be. I guess." Hannah picked up her pillow and hugged it the way she wished she was hugging Brad right now. "I never thought anything like this would ever happen to me."

"Yeah." Sierra played with the edge of Hannah's comforter. "Should have been me, right?"

Hannah's insides burned with anger. There was no reason for Sierra to be saying stuff like that.

The front door creaked open and Mom called, "Hannah? Are you home yet?"

"I-In here!" Hannah called. She kicked the bottom of the bed, mad at herself for her shaky voice.

Mom came down the hall and came in without knocking. "Oh, sweetheart . . . " Her face hardened when she saw Sierra, then she put on a super-wide smile. "Sierra. How nice to see you again."

"I was just leaving," Sierra said. "Hannah didn't need to be alone right now." She got up. "Cheer up, all right? I don't want to see you moping around school tomorrow for Nathan to mess with."

"I'll try," Hannah promised. She let Sierra hug her. Then, Sierra left.

"Sorry, Mom. I know you don't like her, but she's my best friend and she showed up to check on me and I needed her."

"The news must have been terrible." Mom sat down next to Hannah. "Tell me all about it."

Hannah shrank back. "I'm tired of talking."

Mom put her arm around her. "I'll just hold you then like I did when you were little. I used to sing to you, remember?" She sang a few bars of some song Hannah had no memory of, something about God granting them peace.

"Since when do you believe in God?" Hannah sniffed.

"Ssh . . . I love you. I love you so much." Mom stroked Hannah's hair. "Tell me the truth, sweetheart. Are those tears in your eyes because you're pregnant or because you're not?"

Hannah raised her eyebrows so high her face hurt. How the hell did Mom know? "Neither," she said and told her what the doctor had said. Halfway through she couldn't hold the tears back. She clung to her, wishing she was little enough to climb into Mom's lap.

Mom rubbed her back. "I am so sorry, baby. You are too damn young to know this kind of pain." She kissed the top of Hannah's head. "But it's going to be all right. It really is. I won't say it's for the best, but at least now you won't have to deal with the consequences of what some man did to you for the next nine months."

"I don't understand any of this. The rape, the pregnancy, the miscarriage. What did I do to deserve it?"

"Nothing." Mom's voice was firm, and her lips were pencil-thin. "None of this is your fault. None of it! Do you understand me?"

"If you say so."

Mom rocked Hannah back and forth as if she were still a baby. "How could my sweet Hannah be to blame for any of this, hmm? I've never met a person with a bigger heart. You see the good in everyone, and you've never said a mean thing to anyone in your life. There's no way a girl as beautiful as you deserves anything but the greatest happiness this life has to offer."

"That seems far away." Hannah wanted to add that she doubted she'd ever be happy again, but she didn't want to scare Mom. She wasn't suicidal like Mom used to be, but it might sound that way to her and then she'd freak out.

"I know. I know." Mom stroked Hannah's hair. "Tell you what. Take it easy the rest of the day, and then tomorrow if you want to play hooky from school, you and I can have a mom-daughter day to try to take your mind off all of this. How's that sound?"

Hannah bit her lip. "I'll be so behind if I do that. Besides, it's not like I'm sick."

"Your mental health comes first. I learned that the hard way." Mom kissed the top of Hannah's head again. "You just let me know, okay? I may not always be the greatest mother in the world, but I'm here for you as best as I can be."

"Don't put yourself down. I wouldn't want any other mom than you."

Mom had tears in her eyes. "You don't know how much that means to me to hear you say that, baby." She stood. "I'll be in the kitchen making dinner if you want to join me."

"I need to be alone for a little bit, but I'll be out soon."

"All right. But no hiding in here." Mom ruffled Hannah's hair like she used to when she was a little girl. Then she left.

Hannah let her breath out slowly. She went into the bathroom to wash her face so she could give Brad the news over video without embarrassing herself.

27 – Out of Balance

THE NEXT MORNING, Hannah let Mom give her a ride to school to make up for not listening to her about staying home. When they got there, she promised about a million times she'd call if she needed her and hurried to the bleachers behind the school building to hang out with Brad. She didn't feel up to running, but she let him sit with her and hold her while she cried some more. It was weird, almost like they were grieving for a baby they'd lost together even though Brad had nothing to do with it.

After a while, Hannah felt better enough to go to the cafeteria. Molly was sitting with Jen. Her eyes met Hannah's as Hannah and Brad walked past.

Molly said something to Jen, then jogged up to Hannah. "Um, Mouse, listen . . . "

"Don't call me that!" Hannah snapped. "It's not Mouse. Not anymore."

Molly's eyes widened and Hannah could see tears in them. "Wow. Okay. So, I really can't say anything right, can I? You know what? Never mind. I'm done being used as a punching bag. I should have listened to Jen and steered clear of you."

"I'm not! If you would listen to me for two seconds you'd understand!"

"Goodbye, Hannah." Molly turned and hurried away.

Hannah's shoulders shook. That was it, she guessed. It was over, six years of friendship down the drain just like that. And on top of that, people were staring. People had seen the whole thing. Katie and the other SADD girls were at a table behind her, and only God knew what they thought. And if this fight made its way back to Nathan . . .

"What a freaking bitch," Brad said.

"She's not." Hannah's voice shook.

Brad put his arm around her. Hannah leaned on him, telling herself to stop crying. Molly wasn't worth it. Brad led her to the table, and she sat down with him even though she really wanted to be alone.

***

When the bell rang for Chemistry, Mr. Dawson told everyone to take out a piece of paper for a pop quiz.

It was hard to concentrate on the quiz questions. Hannah kept forgetting what she was writing halfway through, and no matter how much she told herself to stop thinking about other things, she couldn't get focused.

She was only halfway through the last question when Mr. Dawson called time. She kept writing anyway.

"That means you, Hannah," Mr. Dawson said. "Your fate is sealed. Put your pen down."

Hannah threw her pen down onto her desk. She was sure she'd failed for the first time in her life, and worse, she didn't have Molly to talk her down from it like she usually did after a disastrous quiz.

Mr. Dawson walked down the aisles, taking everyone's paper and giving them a lab sheet instead. "Don't worry," he said quietly as he took Hannah's paper. "None of your fellow students knows anything either."

Hannah's throat felt tight, but Mr. Dawson was gone before she could think of anything to say. She hunched over her lab sheet, not wanting to be Mouse anymore but not sure that talking back to him would accomplish anything anyway.

Lab was even worse than the quiz because Hannah had to work with Molly.

She watched Molly put a couple of graduated cylinders on the lab table. "That quiz was hard, huh?"

"Let's divide up the work," Molly said, ignoring that. "How about you do the HH calculation for the first part?"

Hannah crossed her arms, pressing them hard against her chest. "I'll get my calculator." She shuffled to the front of the room and took as much time as she dared, looking through her backpack even though she knew her calculator was in her pocket.

Molly looked up from what she was doing, then back down at the lab sheet when Hannah finally got back to the lab. The old Molly would have teased Hannah about taking so long. Then again, the old Hannah wouldn't have had to waste time hiding in the front of the room because Molly wouldn't be mad at her.

"We're looking for a pH of 6.9," Molly said.

Hannah nodded. The calculator was all blurry because of the tears she was struggling not to let fall. She bit her lip hard. She didn't need Mr. Dawson catching her crying in lab for a second time. She followed the formula on her lab sheet and pressed all the right buttons, or hoped she did, to tell Molly how much acid to use.

Mr. Dawson stopped behind them as Molly titrated the base into the acid. "This is supposed to be a group effort, not one of you working hard while the other is hardly working. Switch places, ladies. The idea is for both of you to have a chance to risk this concoction blowing up in your faces." He watched as Molly dipped the pH probe into the buffer. "That means you risk touching the probe too, Hannah."

Hannah felt something snap inside. She bit her lip again to stop herself from knocking over the flask and hurting someone.

Molly said nothing as she handed Hannah the probe. Hannah could feel Mr. Dawson's eyes on her as she put the probe into distilled water to clean it. She wiped it off and put it into the buffer. "6.8," she said as Mr. Dawson walked away. "We're a little off."

"Add sodium hydroxide," Molly told her.

Hannah added the salt and stirred. "This is like us. Not the right balance."

Molly wrote something on the lab paper. "You measure first this time."

Hannah swallowed hard as it sank in that Molly really meant it about not being friends anymore. She reported that their buffer was now at 7.0 like it was supposed to be and stepped back so Molly could measure it too, determined not to say another word that didn't have to do with the lab.

28 – The First Therapy Session

O LIVIA, THE THERAPIST Hannah met with after school, turned out to be a woman who was Mom's age or a little older. She looked like a teacher with long, dark hair tied back into a half-ponytail, an ocean-blue blouse that was not too fancy and which made her brown eyes pop, and a white pearl necklace around her neck that stood out against her tan skin. She came out into the waiting room and introduced herself almost as soon as Mom told the receptionist they were here.

Hannah shook hands with her and thought maybe she wouldn't be so bad, but then Olivia said, "I'd like your mom to join us just for a minute."

"Why?" Hannah asked. "I thought I was the one who needed to talk to you."

"I always like to get the parent's perspective," Olivia said. "After that, I'm all yours. I promise."

Hannah didn't like that at all, but what could she do? She was too old to throw a tantrum in the waiting room and anyway, she didn't want Olivia to think she was completely crazy.

Olivia led her and Mom to her office, which wasn't anything exciting. There was a leather couch against the wall and a couple of easy chairs catty-corner to it. Olivia's desk was in a far corner, and there was a bookshelf against the wall. The office had a big window overlooking the parking lot, but since it was already starting to get dark outside, there was nothing to see out of it.

Hannah threw herself on the couch as far away from Mom as she could get away with, while Olivia took an easy chair facing both of them. She explained again that Mom would only be sitting in this one time and only for a few minutes, then went over the confidentiality rules. Mom wouldn't be allowed to know anything about what went on in Hannah's sessions unless Olivia thought Hannah was in danger of hurting herself or someone else or Hannah gave her permission. That made Hannah feel better, though she was still mad at Olivia for inviting Mom in the first place.

"So, Debra," Olivia said when she'd finished going over everything, "what made you decide to make an appointment for Hannah?"

Hannah's throat felt tight as Mom began, "The last month or so she's seemed very depressed and withdrawn. At first, she told us it was because she felt guilty about sneaking out to a party with her so-called best friend, but t-then she worked up the courage to tell us that . . . "

"It's my story to tell!" Hannah snapped, unable to take it anymore. "I was raped, okay? I didn't tell my mom for a long time and when I did, she said I had to have therapy."

Olivia said, "I hear how furious you are that your mom started to tell me something so personal and painful about you, Hannah. Hold on for just a minute, okay? I just need to finish getting your mom's perspective."

Hannah traced the pattern in the floor tiles with her eyes while Mom told Olivia how worried she was that Hannah spent so much time in her room and that Hannah insisted on being friends with Sierra and spending all her free time with Brad. Mom was especially unhappy that Hannah wanted to spend time with Brad on Thanksgiving when they'd just started dating.

Olivia explained that it was normal for a girl Hannah's age to refuse to accept her parents' opinions about her social life, but before she sent Mom out of the room, she promised she would work with Hannah on coping better with the rape.

Score one for Mom, Hannah thought bitterly.

When Mom was gone, Olivia said, "I heard a lot about what your mom thinks, but our time together is really for you. What are you unhappy about in your life that you would like to change?"

Hannah played with her ring, twisting it back and forth. "I, um. . . I guess I want to get past some things."

"Like what?" Olivia balanced a yellow pad of paper on her knees. Hannah wondered what she was writing about her—if she thought she was bipolar like Mom or what.

Hannah wiggled. "Like the way it changed me."

"It? You mean the sexual assault?"

Hannah nodded. "Everything's different since then. I'm different, I guess. I used to feel close to my best friend, but now it's like we're strangers. And a lot of the things that used to be important to me just aren't. Like, I don't care about the stuff I used to study for hours because really, what difference does it make?" Hannah's voice shook but she managed not to cry in front of Olivia.

Olivia handed Hannah a tissue. "It sounds like you feel kind of lost since the rape."

"I guess." Hannah bit her lip. She'd already said more than she planned to and now she wished she was still a little girl so she could crawl under the couch. "I don't want to be Mouse anymore," she blurted out without meaning to. "That's what my friends call me because I'm so quiet nobody even knows I'm there. Sometimes I think that's why it happened."

Olivia raised her eyebrows. "You blame yourself for the rape because you were so quiet you were almost invisible. I want you to know that even if you were the world's quietest person, that doesn't make what happened to you your fault."

Hannah rubbed the back of her neck, feeling a headache coming on. "I wish Molly could get that I don't want to be Mouse anymore."

"We can talk about that. But I meant what I said before. Mouse or no Mouse, this wasn't your fault." Olivia leaned forward. "I want you to tell me that so you can start to get it in your head. Say, 'No matter how quiet I was, it wasn't my fault someone raped me.'"

This was silly and pointless, but Hannah repeated the words anyway. Tears welled up in her eyes as she did.

"That's right," Olivia said. "I want you to tell yourself that in the mirror every morning until it sinks in."

Hannah rolled her eyes, but she promised she would anyway.

The rest of the hour passed quickly. Olivia explained that everyone had deep-seated beliefs about themselves and the world and that these beliefs helped drive their behavior. She said that by uncovering Hannah's, they could learn what made her be so quiet and mouse-like and find ways to help her be comfortable with speaking up more.

Then, she asked Hannah a ton of questions, starting with where she'd grown up and what it had been like to live with Grandma and Mom when she was a little girl and how it felt then to not know who her dad was. Hannah was careful to dance around the edges of the truth, afraid that Olivia might ask her too much about her own symptoms if she knew Mom was bipolar even though she was beginning to trust her with her secret. She was glad when Olivia moved on to how things were with Mom and Eric now and what was going on with her friends. It was a lot easier to talk about that than how she felt when she was little.

When time was almost up, Olivia gave Hannah a notebook small enough to put in her purse. "This is a journal I give all my clients after our first time together," she said. "I want you to write in it at least once a day."

"About what?" Hannah thought of the journal entries Mr. Collins made them write. He always put a question on the board for them.

"About anything that's on your mind. It can be helpful to get all those thoughts and feelings that you tend to keep inside out on paper."

Hannah bit her lip. "Are you going to read it?"

"Not unless you want me to. But if there's ever something you want me to see, I'll be happy to take a look."

Olivia told Hannah she was glad she'd got to meet her and asked her whether Tuesdays were good. Hannah's heart pounded, but she ignored that, explaining that she wanted to hang out with Brad at track clinic from now on. Olivia said since it was Hannah's therapy, it should be at a time that was convenient for Hannah and made a new appointment for the next Monday.

In the waiting room while Hannah was putting her coat on, Mom told her to invite Brad over for dinner instead of asking him to pick her up. Hannah didn't want to, but she didn't want to fight with Mom. Anyway, she'd gone over to his dad's for lunch so it wasn't THAT unreasonable. But when she called Brad he was in a bad mood because his mom wouldn't let him borrow her car, which meant he had to cancel their date.

Mom put her hand on Hannah's shoulder. "Disappointed?"

"I guess." Hannah didn't want to talk about it, not with Mom. She missed Molly so much her stomach hurt because that's who she wanted to call and couldn't.

Mom squeezed her shoulder. Hannah said, "I'm FINE, Mom. Can we just get out of here?" She pulled away and walked out without waiting for an answer, not sure who she was madder at: Brad's mom or her own.

MOLLY KEPT UP the silent treatment for the next couple of days, even when they got their quizzes back and Hannah got the first C she'd ever got in her life. Then one day, she came up to Hannah at lunch and asked if Hannah still wanted SADD to co-sponsor the All-Nighter since that would mean working together.

"No, it's okay." Hannah felt pathetic about how quickly she answered. It probably looked to Molly like she was trying to spend time with her when clearly their friendship was over. "Keeping people safe on Prom Night comes first, right?"

Molly nodded slightly. "Thanks. See you at SADD then." She stood there for just long enough that hope shot through Hannah that she'd say something else, then she turned and walked away.

"What did you let her off the hook so easy for?" Sierra asked. "After everything she did, you should tell her to go to hell."

Hannah twisted a lock of hair around her finger. "I didn't want to be petty, not when it comes to SADD projects."

Sierra shrugged. "She's still a backstabbing bitch, and only weak people let people walk all over them."

Hannah stared at her. That didn't sound like Sierra at all. It was . . . mean. "I'm not! I'm just putting the project first."

Brad interrupted, "What's the All Nighter? A bunch of kids sitting around studying all night?"

"No, silly," Hannah said. "It's like Prom but without alcohol or drugs." She looked down at the table, sure Brad thought it was boring. "We dance and play games and stay at school pretty much all night."

"Awesome!" Brad said. "I'm in. If you wanna go with me, that is."

"I'd like that. Except . . . I wasn't sure I was going to go. The last party I went to didn't exactly work out. Anyway, you guys still coming to the SADD meeting with me today? You can learn all about it."

"Wouldn't miss it for anything," Brad said, "especially after my mom made me flake on you."

"Sierra?"

Sierra played with the zipper on her purse, flipping it up and down. "I wish. Jake called earlier and reminded me we had a date."

"Hold up a sec," Brad said. "You're blowing Hannah off for the dude who had the party where she got messed with? Seriously?"

"Brad," Hannah said quietly, not wanting her friends to fight. "It's okay, really."

"It's not," Brad said. "She's supposed to be your best friend. It's bad enough she didn't have your back the night of without putting the dude who made it happen over you!"

Sierra slammed her milk container down. "Jake didn't rape her! Stop trying to put wedges between him and me. How would you like it if I did that to you and Hannah?"

"He's not!" Hannah said. "And just so you know, Jake made me feel weird even before the pills in my tea."

Sierra's eyes narrowed. "Jake said you'd try to blame him for what happened to you, but I didn't believe it 'til now."

"I'm not!" Hannah's voice rose. "I'm just . . . "

"Whatever. I need dessert." Sierra pushed herself away from the table so hard it moved before she stomped off.

Hannah groaned. "Great. Now I have no friends left."

"Nah," Brad said. "You got me." He brushed Hannah's fingertips. "Besides, she just left to cool off, she'll be back."

"I hope so."

"Forget her," Brad's eyes sparkled. "Let's talk about what's really important. You going to this dance with me or not?"

"If I go, it'll be with you."

"Cool. Now, let's see how to get you out of this mood. We could go out to the track. Or, I know . . . " Brad picked up his spoon. "We could have a food fight!" He flicked a little bit of mashed potato at Hannah. It didn't come close to her and she was sure he'd done that on purpose.

Hannah giggled even though she was scared a teacher would come over and give them both detention, or worse, send them to Mrs. Garcia's office if she let Brad get her into a food fight. She couldn't risk that, not with the meeting this afternoon.

"Track sounds good," she said, "even if it is freezing cold out."

"'K." Brad jumped up. "Race you to the trash first. Winner gets a head start once we get out."

"That'll be you, but okay." Hannah grabbed her tray and Brad grabbed his, and they hurried to the trash. Hannah could feel the lunch monitor's eyes on her, but she didn't care. She ran all the way to the trash and threw her things away, shocked that no one had stopped her from going too fast.

30 – Only One Thing to Do

SIERRA WAS ALREADY in her seat when Hannah got to Mr. Collins' room half an hour later. She sighed to herself and shook her head at something on her phone.

"What's wrong?" Hannah asked, even though she was afraid Sierra would tell her to mind her own business.

"Nothing." Sierra looked at Hannah, then away. "I want us to be cool again. So, um, you think you can stop saying stuff about Jake?"

Hannah wanted to shake her, but she didn't have the stomach for another fight. So, she went into Mouse mode and said, "Yeah, of course." She turned toward the board and looked at the journal question, so she wouldn't have to think about what a coward she was.

The question was:

Why do you think Othello didn't realize Iago was sabotaging him?

In the play, Iago was supposed to be Othello's best friend, but he told him a lot of lies that ruined everything. Reading the question made Hannah think of how Molly listened to Jen about dumping Hannah as a friend.

Before Hannah knew it, she'd written all about her Molly drama and how much she missed Molly and how she wished she was still the kind of person she could tell things to. She'd written about how scared she was she might be bipolar because of her mood swings and impulsive behaviors since the rape and how Molly could never understand that. Then she started to write about everything else that she couldn't tell Molly.

How she was feeling good right now, but she had been super sad about the miscarriage even though she didn't want a baby.

How relieved she was not to be pregnant.

How she hadn't wanted Molly to know about the rape because Hannah used to think this couldn't happen to girls like her and was sure Molly still thought that way.

Mr. Collins called her name and Hannah heard people whispering and giggling. She wondered how many times he'd called her before she came out of her thoughts. She ignored Nathan staring at her as she folded the page over and turned toward the front of the room, trying to pretend everything was normal.

***

After school, Hannah went to the cafeteria to wait for Brad. After she texted him where she was, she took out her journal and re-read what she'd written. She wanted to show it to Olivia next week. When she got home, she'd have to copy it over into the little journal she was supposed to use for therapy.

Suddenly, Nathan grabbed her journal out of her hand. "Judgment day, Slut Hannah!" he grinned. "Let's see what you wrote here."

"Give that back!" Hannah demanded, jumping up, but Nathan held it out of her reach, laughing. He opened it and began to read aloud, "It's hard to tell the moment when your best friend stops being your best friend and turns into your enemy. Just look at me and Molly."

"STOP!" Hannah shrieked, then hated herself for sounding so shrill instead of strong and decisive. She jumped to try to grab the journal back from Nathan, but he jumped back, laughing.

A whole crowd of people gathered around as Nathan went on reading Hannah's journal out loud. Some of them were frowning, but nobody told Nathan to cut it out or to give her back her journal when they could all see he was embarrassing her. And worst of all, Hannah could see Molly right outside the crowd as Nathan told the whole world all about how Hannah didn't think Molly could understand that she missed the baby that she had miscarried or that she was afraid she was bipolar like her mom.

"I SAID STOP!" Hannah shouted, desperate to drown out Nathan's voice before Molly could hear. "Give that back. It's mine!" She jumped again and this time managed to knock the journal out of Nathan's hand. She scooped it up and threw it in her backpack, barely able to control her tears.

"Score one for the slut," Nathan said, "though I read all the good parts. So, you're a psycho as well as a bitch, huh?"

Hannah pushed past him, trying to get to Molly so she could explain, but Molly was gone. She kept running, not knowing where she was going, and smashed right into Brad.

"Whoa," Brad said. "What do you think this is, the track?"

"Sorry," Hannah said, pushing down her annoyance. How could Brad make jokes at a time like this? "I need to get to the meeting."

"Wait." Brad touched Hannah's cheek. "You're like, way upset. Talk to me before you do something crazy."

"I'm not crazy!" Hannah snapped.

Brad held up his hands. "I know that. Believe me, I know crazy. I live with myself."

Hannah made herself take a deep breath. It was bad enough things were ruined with Molly. She didn't need to ruin them with Brad too. "Nathan knows about the bipolar," she said, her voice cracking. "How Mom is and how I might be. Everyone does. He read my journal out loud in front of a million people and I think Molly heard."

"Fuck!" Brad said. "That asshole!"

"Don't. I don't need your anger." Hannah bit her lip. "D-do you think I am? Bipolar, I mean."

Brad shrugged. "I don't know anything about it. I mean, you seem stable to me, but I'm the dude who couldn't deal with anything after his parents split up. So . . . anyway, what I'm trying to say is, it doesn't matter if you are or not. You're still the same awesome, beautiful chick you were before I ever heard the word." He put his arm around Hannah. "Try to forget him, okay? We got way more important things to do than worry about his bullshit."

Hannah put her hand over her stomach. "He knows about the miscarriage too." Brad scowled and she said, "Maybe there's only one thing to do since everyone knows anyway. When we get to the meeting . . . " She let her breath out slowly. "They might as well hear it from me if they haven't heard it from someone else."

Her heart pounded and she felt shaky, but she told herself she had no choice. She grabbed Brad's hand for courage and let him walk her to the meeting room.

There were a ton of people already there when Hannah and Brad arrived. Molly was sitting with Jen and a bunch of other girls, talking. She stopped when Hannah came into the room with Brad. Her eyes flitted to them, then away.

Hannah crossed her arms, not sure whether she was angry or upset. "Um, Molly, listen," she stammered. "I don't know how much you heard, but . . ."

"It doesn't matter." Molly's voice had no emotion in it whatsoever, but she wouldn't look at Hannah. "At least now I finally know how little you think of me." She glanced at Jen who gave her an encouraging nod. "It would have been nice if you said it to my face, but at least it's out in the open now."

"I didn't say it to anyone but myself," Hannah said, "and you could have told Nathan to cut it out instead of standing there listening."

Molly's face softened but Jen interjected, "Now you want her to fight your battles for you? She was willing to before, but you didn't want anything to do with her."

"Maybe she didn't know how to talk to you guys. You ever think of that?" Brad said. "It's not like she just stubbed her toe. What happened to her was a big fucking deal, and you guys keep making it all about you and how your freaking feelings are hurt that she's not how she used to be."

"Shut up, stoner," Jen said. "We all know you're only at this meeting to try to get into Hannah's pants."

Hannah's eye pulsed. "That's not true, and it's also not the way we're supposed to talk to prospective members." Her heart pounded as she turned toward Molly. "Get your girlfriend in line or ask her to leave."

Molly pushed her hair behind her ear. "Hannah's right. We have to tolerate him," she said to Jen. She turned back toward Hannah. "But don't you dare think this means I'm taking your side. This is SADD business. No more, no less."

"Whatever," Hannah said. "Brad needs some new member info." No one moved. "So, I guess I'll get him some." She took Brad's hand, feeling like she was giving up as they walked away.

Mrs. Marino was sitting by a little table where they had some brochures and flyers about what SADD was. Hannah's eyes flitted toward her, then away, sure Mrs. Marino wouldn't be happy that Brad was here. But Mrs. Marino treated him like any other new member, smiling widely and giving him a button along with a welcome packet.

"That's a lapel button," Hannah explained after they'd thanked Mrs. Marino and walked away. "I-if you want to wear it."

"No way, I get to be one of the cool kids right away?" Brad smiled. "Put it on me?"

"Gladly." Hannah pinned the button on Brad's shirt. She kissed him lightly.

The Sergeant-at-Arms, Elizabeth, was calling the meeting to order so they had to scramble to find seats. Hannah took Brad's hand as they sat down, secretly hoping Molly was watching. There were already agendas on their desks. Hannah knew what was on the agenda—she'd written it and handed it in a few days ago—but she read it again anyway, trying to calm her nerves.

Katie came up to the front of the room to open the meeting. Hannah's ears buzzed with anxiety as she led them through the opening and an icebreaker game so that all the new people could get to know everyone.

Katie said, "Next we're going to hear from our Vice President, Hannah Kollman, who is going to update us on our current projects."

Everyone stared at Hannah as she made her way to the front of the room. It was only about ten feet, but it felt like she was walking ten miles. She always got nervous standing up in front of the entire meeting and today it was twice as bad because she didn't know who thought what about her.

"Thanks, Katie," Hannah said, surprised her voice sounded halfway normal. "We're doing our annual Thanksgiving baskets for the needy next week. We'll be meeting on Monday during fourth, fifth, and sixth periods to put them together and we need volunteers to sign up to deliver them. We also are going to be working with Molly Layton, our Treasurer, on the All Nighter." Hannah's heart pounded as Molly started to get up. "You know what?" she said. "Before I call Molly up here, I want to say something about something else."

Molly looked at Jen, who shrugged, and some of the other people were whispering to each other.

Hannah grabbed onto the edge of the desk at the front of the room, sure she was going to faint. She made herself breathe deeply and find Brad who was leaning forward to listen to her. "If you were in the cafeteria right now, you heard a lot of stuff that was supposed to be private, but since someone read my diary out loud, I might as well set the record straight. I didn't drink at that party. I was drugged. And then. . . well, if you paid attention to our campaign about date rape you know what happened to me." Hannah's eyes burned, but she didn't let herself cry. "I-I don't know what else to say, b-but I wanted you all to hear the truth i-in case you didn't respect me anymore." Her cheeks felt hotter and hotter. She was just embarrassing herself more. "Anyway, back to business. Here's Molly."

Brad stood up and started chanting, "Hannah! Hannah!" like she was a celebrity or something, and other people started joining in. Hannah came slowly back to her seat, not sure what to make of that.

AFTER THE MEETING, Katie came up to Hannah to thank her for what she said. "You did what I've been scared to do for about two years."

Hannah watched Katie shift her super-heavy backpack on her shoulders. It was sagging and she was afraid it might rip. "What do you mean?"

"You know how I lug this thing around?" Katie stared at the ground. "It's not because I'm a weirdo who doesn't believe in using my locker. It's because a couple years ago, I was putting my books away and this boy came up behind me and. . . and he touched my breasts. No, not touched. He. . . he rubbed them like. . . " Katie swallowed hard. "Anyway, that's why I don't go to my locker."

"Oh, Katie." Hannah had no idea what to say. "I'm sorry."

"No, don't be. I just wanted to say, I'm sorry for what happened to you, but it felt good not to be alone." Katie patted Hannah's hand. "Girls like us should stick together. Don't let anyone get you down." She shifted her backpack again.

"That looks awfully heavy," Hannah said. "How about we go to your locker together, and I'll keep an eye out?"

Hannah saw the same fear she'd been carrying around for a month in Katie's eyes. Katie pushed her hair behind her ear and said, "I'll miss the late bus if I go now, but thanks."

Hannah watched her hurry away, a small smile on her lips even though she felt bad for Katie that she wasn't ready to face her fear. A few minutes later, Mrs. Marino told Hannah she was proud of her and Hannah knew she deserved it even though she felt this weird emptiness because Molly wasn't there to be proud of her too.

***

The next morning, school started two hours late because it had snowed overnight. Hannah had to take the bus since there was no one to drive her, which meant she had to put up with people whispering about her and the bus driver had to tell some girl to take her bag off the seat next to her so Hannah could sit down. The girl rolled her eyes and said she didn't want to sit next to a psycho slut and didn't move her bag until the driver threatened to kick her off the bus.

And if that wasn't bad enough, Hannah had to deal with Molly and Jen standing at their lockers together, whispering and staring at her while she went to hers.

Katie came up to Hannah while she was fumbling with her lock and trying to pretend she didn't give a fuck about Molly and her stupid girlfriend. "I thought I'd . . . " she said, then cut herself off. "What's wrong?"

"Nothing." It was only the second time Hannah had ever talked to Katie except for when they worked on SADD projects together, and she didn't want her to think she was a drama queen. "Just an ex-friend staring at me. I don't like it."

"Come with me, then," Katie said. "I want to go to my locker after all."

Hannah hurried to switch out her books so she could. She could feel Molly's eyes on her as she and Katie walked off.

***

Nothing happened at Katie's locker except Katie felt embarrassed about being afraid for so long, but Hannah told her how hard it had been for her to start dating Brad and how sometimes she still freaked out when he touched her. That seemed to make Katie feel better. Afterward, Katie gave Hannah a pep talk about Mr. Dawson while they walked to their science classes together. She said that he was all bark and no bite, and if Hannah ignored that he was an asshole and did her best work, he'd have nothing to say.

Molly's eyes flitted to Hannah, then away, when Hannah slipped into her seat.

"How long is this going to last?" Hannah demanded. She knew she shouldn't say anything, but she'd had enough. "You giving me the silent treatment except for lab, I mean."

Molly shrugged. "I feel awful about what happened to you," she said, staring down at her notes. "I really do. But you let it ruin our friendship, and you can't just throw me away and then expect me to act like nothing happened when you're ready to pick up where we left off."

"I didn't throw you away!" Hannah's voice rose without permission, and she struggled to hold onto what was left of her good mood.

"You did! You think I'm Iago, and now you're busy replacing me with people who you think are better than me." Molly still wouldn't look at Hannah. "I know you can't help it. It's part of being bipolar or whatever, but I can't deal with it. So, as I said, business only."

The bell rang. Hannah turned toward the front of the room, trying to get herself together before Mr. Dawson had something to say. But she couldn't stop thinking about all those recesses in fifth grade when Molly would tell her to close her book and come play with her. Molly always pushed Hannah to do things Hannah was scared to do. Even yesterday, half the reason she said what she did was that Molly was there. How could their friendship be so fragile that a misunderstanding between them could grow and grow until it broke them?

"All right, everybody," Mr. Dawson said. "We're continuing the lab from last time. Hopefully, you've managed to keep track of your lab sheets." As Hannah took hers out of her notebook, he said, "Everybody means everyone except you, Hannah. Leave Molly to her own devices for a minute and come up here."

Hannah's heart pounded. Now what?

Nathan shouted, "Watch out, Mr. D. She might go psycho on you!" Hannah gritted her teeth but otherwise ignored him.

Mr. Dawson said, "Lab's that way, Nathan."

Hannah raised her eyebrows. Mr. Dawson standing up for her, even in a small way, didn't make any sense. He always played favorites when it came to Nathan. Of course, he hadn't actually punished him or done anything meaningful about him bullying Hannah, but still.

Mr. Dawson crossed his arms. "It's like this, Hannah," he said quietly. "Classes like this only look good on your college applications if you do well in them, and lately, you've been slipping. Last couple of labs, you've been scattered, and this last quiz wasn't your best work, to say the least. Now your guidance counselor says I have to be sensitive because you've been through a lot, but facts are facts. This is an advanced science class, and if you're too emotional to keep up, then it's not the right class for you right now."

And there it was. Mr. Dawson thought Hannah was too stupid and emotional to be a scientist. And how dare her guidance counselor, who knew nothing about her except what classes she wanted to take, say anything! Hannah wished Mom hadn't called him when she was trying to find the right therapist for Hannah. Now he was just one more person putting his nose in Hannah's business.

Mr. Dawson said that if Hannah dropped this class, she could try it again next year, and that made Hannah angrier. She said she was going to pull up her grades, and he said he hoped so because he could only give her a B for lab and that was being generous. If she dropped any lower, she'd be kicked out of the AP science program altogether.

Hannah made herself hold her head up high and lock eyes with Mr. Dawson even though she was secretly shaking with fear. If she flunked out of AP science, she'd never live it down.

"I'll get an A next quarter," she said. "You'll see." She turned and walked away, determined to prove Mr. Dawson wrong.

***

"It's not like you need that class for anything except to show off," Sierra said at lunch. "It's not worth the stress. Besides, if you get rid of it, you won't have to deal with Molly anymore."

"Still not the point." Hannah played with her milk carton, opening and closing it over and over. "Mr. Dawson resents that he has any girls in his class at all. If I quit now, it'll prove him right. Don't you see that?"

"Yeah, but . . . "

Katie came up to the table. "Sorry to interrupt, but I was wondering if I could talk to you a sec at my table."

Hannah bit her lip to push down the anxiety bubbling up in her chest. Katie wouldn't call her over so her friends could make fun of her, would she? She was in SADD, but still. It had happened before.

"Um, sure," she said, starting to stand up. "Oh, this is my friend Sierra, by the way."

"Hi," Katie said and held out her hand. "I'm Katie. I work with Hannah in SADD."

As Sierra shook hands with Katie, her sleeve bobbed up and down and Hannah saw or thought she saw a bruise on Sierra's wrist. It was small, and it went by so fast that Hannah couldn't be sure.

"What happened to your wrist?" she asked Sierra under her breath.

Sierra looked away, but not before Hannah saw her eyes widen. "Walked into my car door. Stupid me, right?"

Hannah had this weird feeling like Sierra wasn't telling her the whole truth, but she didn't want to make a big deal out of nothing, especially not in front of Katie, so she just told Sierra she'd be right back.

"You don't have to come back to the outcast table if you don't want to," Sierra said as Hannah started to follow Katie.

Hannah swallowed hard. She didn't want Katie to think she was an outcast. But maybe she hadn't heard.

On the way to the table, Katie asked about it, and Hannah explained about one of their friends blaming Sierra for the rape. Katie said she would sit with Hannah and Sierra another time. Then, she took Hannah over to the table and introduced her to Elizabeth and the rest of the SADD members that she sat with every day.

Elizabeth reminded Hannah of Molly because she had the same round face and long hair tied back into a ponytail, only her hair was brown instead of red, and Joy had darker skin than Sierra did and wore her hair piled up on top of her head. The other two girls, Amanda and Lucy, didn't look like Hannah's friends at all. Amanda, who was more peach than white, had pink and purple streaks in her hair and a nose ring. She didn't look like the kind of person who would be involved with SADD at all, but Hannah had seen her at almost every meeting. And Lucy, who told Hannah her name was short for Lucinda, had jet black hair that fell straight down and the most gorgeous eyes that Hannah had ever seen.

"Hi," Hannah said and shook all their hands, hoping she didn't forget anyone's name. She sat down next to Katie. "What's up?"

Elizabeth put her soda can down. "We wanted to talk to you about what you said at the meeting," she said, and fear shot through Hannah again that this was a trap, that they were going to laugh at her or call her a slut.

"Yeah," Joy said. "We all wish we could have. . . " She fidgeted. "The thing is, all of us, um. . . we've had weird experiences with guys. Not. . . not like what happened to you, but we've all had guys rub against us 'by accident' or say or do other stuff that made us uncomfortable."

"Yeah," Elizabeth said, "and none of us ever told anyone until after the meeting. We were talking about what you said, and all of us had these stories. So, we thought there might be more girls like us. We kind of were wondering: We want to make like, an assembly to talk to the whole school about the stuff that happens, and Katie thought you could help us."

"Wow," Hannah said. "Um, what did you have in mind?"

Lucy explained that they wanted to teach the whole school what happened to girls when someone touched them sexually in a way they didn't want and how to stand up for each other. Katie added that since Hannah had done such a great job telling her story at SADD, they had hoped she'd be the main speaker.

Hannah's heart pounded. She wished she had brought her milk over with her, so she could buy herself some time by drinking it.

"S-speak in front of the whole school?" she stammered, then looked away. These girls thought she was brave, and she didn't want them to know that they'd made a mistake.

Elizabeth reached across the table and patted her hand. "I'm shy too. I get it. But you made such a big impact at SADD and it, like, rippled outward already. We thought if we could somehow do it on a bigger scale, it would impact even more people."

"Yeah," Katie said, "and your story is more powerful than ours. I even feel bad putting ours in the same conversation. I mean, you were drugged and everything. All that happened to me was an asshole touching me."

"No, that's bad too," Hannah said. "Guys stare at my butt when I go up to the board and I hate it. It makes me feel like that's all I am to them just like that's all I was to HIM, whoever he was."

Katie nodded. Elizabeth said, "Not to push or anything, but that's why we need you. You can help people see that this is a big deal in a way we can't."

Hannah bit her lip, thinking. Mrs. Marino had said she demonstrated real leadership and almost everyone cheered her on after she made her speech. That was because Brad had started it, but no one would have repeated it if they didn't mean it too. But still, she'd practically fainted while she was talking to twenty-five people. So, how could she possibly get up in front of the entire school and tell them she had been raped, especially when there were people like Nathan in the audience who would probably try to drown out her voice by screaming SLUT at her?

Who cares what he thinks?

It wasn't like keeping her mouth shut was going to make Nathan think any more highly of her. He thought she was a slut either way, and he was always tearing her down. And hadn't she just told Sierra that dropping Chemistry would be like giving in and that she didn't want people like Nathan to win?

But still. Talk in front of the whole school? Her, the girl Sierra had nicknamed Mouse freshman year? The girl who was so quiet that no one but Molly had ever noticed she was even there, reading her book instead of playing games with the other kids? The girl who longed to be bold but didn't think that could ever be her even though holding herself back hurt like hell?

No more Mouse, Hannah told herself. *That was who Molly thought you were. You're not, not anymore.*

Her voice shook, but she said, "Okay. I'll do it."

"**Y**OU'RE REALLY GOING to do this?" Sierra asked on the way to English. "Look what happened when you told Molly."

Hannah bit her lip. "I'm tired of letting assholes like Nathan win." But a voice in the back of her head said she was going to back out before the assembly. She was a scared little mouse and she knew it.

"Assholes always win, no matter what. Trust me." Sierra rubbed her temples.

Way to be supportive, Hannah thought, but she didn't feel like saying so. "Maybe, maybe not. Look what happened when I spoke at SADD."

"Yeah, but that was a ready-made audience. Losers stay out." Sierra played with her backpack strap. "Look, if I can't talk you out of doing this, you gotta promise me you'll keep my name out of it. Please? Molly already hates me. I don't need the whole school agreeing with her."

Hannah squeezed her backpack buckle. She wanted to tell her story, her whole story, but didn't she owe it to Sierra not to embarrass her? "I guess," she said uncertainly as they rounded the corner toward Mr. Collins' classroom.

"Is it pushing it to leave Jake's name out too? He didn't do anything and anyway, people are gonna think something about me they shouldn't if they know I have a boyfriend like him."

Hannah stared at her. Shouldn't Sierra be proud of who her boyfriend was, no matter what anyone thought? Hannah didn't try to keep it secret she was dating Brad, even if she did wish certain people would give him more of a chance.

"Nobody's going to think . . . " she began as they came into Mr. Collins' room.

Nathan was standing in the doorway. Hannah tried to push past him, but he slid to the right so she couldn't and back to the left when she tried to get around that way. "Pay the toll, psycho," he said. "Admit you're batshit crazy."

"Takes one to know one," Sierra said. "Now let us through or my hard head's gonna crush your nose."

Nathan scowled. Mr. Collins' footsteps echoed down the hall and Nathan finally got out of the way.

"Thanks for standing up for me," Hannah said to Sierra as they came in, even though she was mad. She didn't want Sierra talking for her. She wanted to solve her own problems.

Sierra shrugged. "Least I could do. From now on I got your back." She bit her lip. "Even if I end up at St. Anthony's, I'll find a way."

Hannah frowned. "St. Anthony's? What?" St. Anthony's was a Catholic school on the other side of town. Hannah was sure Sierra's parents wouldn't want to pay for it, and anyway, Sierra was the last person who would fit in at Catholic school.

Sierra picked at her bracelet. "I'm not happy," she said flatly. "Maybe a different school will help."

Hannah didn't know what she was talking about, but the bell rang before she could ask.

***

Sierra left after class while Hannah was still putting her books away. By the time Hannah got into the hall, it was so crowded she couldn't have pushed through to catch up with Sierra even if she could find her, which she couldn't. So, she had to wait until after school. But when she approached Sierra's locker, Sierra was on the phone, telling someone in an annoyed voice that she wasn't arguing and that she knew they only wanted what was best for her. Hannah assumed Sierra was fighting with her parents and left her alone when Katie called 'Hi' to her.

Katie told her she was going to Elizabeth's. Hannah wasn't sure if she was invited or if it was a point of information, but in any case, she wanted to hang out with Brad. So, she only walked as far as the pick-up circle with them. They left and she cuddled with Brad, but he could tell something was wrong and asked her what was up.

Hannah sighed. "Nothing really. Sierra said something weird. That's all."

"Sierra weird? No way."

"Ha ha." Hannah put her head in her hands. She totally trusted Brad to keep secrets, but she wasn't sure how much she could tell him before she'd cross the line into betraying her best friend. She told him what happened in English anyway and added, "I hope me doing this assembly won't make her even more unhappy. She asked me to leave her and Jake out of it."

Brad said, "Fuck that. Why the hell should you be worried about protecting Jake's ass when he sure as hell didn't protect yours?"

"True, I guess. But what about Sierra? She's my best friend, and she wants me to keep it to myself that she went to the party too."

Brad shrugged. "Sierra's way cooler than I used to think, but if you ask me you gotta start putting as much effort toward watching your own back as you do toward watching hers."

Hannah wasn't sure whether she was glad Brad actually liked Sierra or annoyed by the other half of what he said. She kicked at the ledge she was sitting on. "For the last time, it's not her fault I was raped!"

"I get that. I'm just saying, you put her first all the time, and it's totally not fair to you."

"Right." Hannah stared out at the pickup circle, willing Brad's dad to come so they could get out of this conversation, but it was still empty. "Um, you want to help put together baskets during lunch on Monday? There's going to be pizza."

"No way. PIZZA?" Brad's eyes sparkled.

"Yep. The real stuff, not the kind they have in the cafeteria."

"I was gonna come anyway, but now that sealed the deal." Brad grinned. "Look at you, turning me into the kind of dude my parents always wanted me to be."

Brad's grin melted what was left of Hannah's bad mood. Just like that, she was feeling good enough to giggle. "You more than make up for it. I'm starting to be bold because of you. I might even stand on top of this flowerbed someday."

"Do it!" Brad said. "I'll spot you."

Hannah put her backpack and her purse down and let Brad help her onto the flowerbed. He took her hand and said, "How's the view from up there?"

"Exhilarating!" Hannah tilted her head back. She was so close to the sky that she felt like she used to when she was a little girl on the swings. "I can touch the clouds!"

Brad's dad honked.

Brad helped Hannah came carefully down off the flowerbed. She was feeling dizzy, but in a good, excited way, and she thought next time she might jump down instead.

Was she manic like Mom used to get?

"Race you to the car!" she called to Brad, pushing that thought down, and took off before he could answer.

33 – The Basket Making Party

B Y THE TIME lunch rolled around on Monday morning, Hannah felt so down in the dumps it was hard to move, and even holding hands with Brad on the way to the basket making party didn't help. She'd had a fight with her parents on Sunday because they didn't want her to risk getting hurt by telling her story at the assembly, and her mood had got worse from there. Plus, Sierra was out sick, and Molly was still not talking to her, just staring at her like she was from outer space whenever she was with any of her new friends.

There was mushroom pizza at the basket making party. That was Hannah's favorite, and she knew that SADD had got it just for her. But she couldn't seem to make herself feel grateful for it. She took two pieces anyway and poured herself a cup of cream soda even though she usually hated soda, just to try something different.

"Hannah!" Katie called and waved her and Brad over to a round table where she was sitting with Elizabeth.

Hannah came over to them. "You remember Brad, of course," she said. "My boyfriend."

"Of course. The new guy." Elizabeth smiled. "I'm so glad you came back."

"No place I'd rather be than with Hannah," Brad said. "So, what are we doing to save the world today?"

"Putting together baskets for people in hospitals and homeless shelters," Katie explained. "We got lots of donations. They're over there." Katie gestured toward the other side of the room. "Someone even donated a bunch of chocolate turkeys to brighten up people's holiday."

"Aww," Hannah said, suddenly feeling better. She guessed the pizza in her stomach was helping. "Come on. Let's get started."

"While we're doing this, I thought we could talk about the assembly," Elizabeth said, and Hannah explained to Brad what they were planning.

"Awesome!" Brad kissed the top of Hannah's head. "I knew I was dating the world's bravest woman."

"I'm not sure about that, but okay," Hannah said. She could feel a pair of eyes on her. Molly was looking at her. Again. Throwing the card she was about to write down, she said, "That's it. If Molly's going to stare at me, she can spit out whatever it is she wants to say."

Brad put his hand on her wrist. "You sure you wanna do that?"

"Yeah," Katie said. "Let her see you having a better time without her."

"I guess," Hannah said, and picked up her pen again. But then she put it down. "Still, though, if I'm going to talk in front of the whole school, I have to have the courage to speak up to one person who's being. . . "

"A bitch?" Elizabeth asked. "You can say it, Hannah. It's okay."

"It isn't really. I don't like that word. And she used to be my friend, anyway." Hannah pushed the card away. "Be right back."

Molly looked up as Hannah came up to her. "I hope you're here to talk about the All Nighter," she said. "I told you, Hannah. Business only."

Hannah crossed her arms. "I wouldn't be over here at all if you weren't staring at me."

Jen said, "She wasn't. You're really not that important, Hannah."

"She was," Hannah said, "and it wasn't the first time. And don't you think she can speak for herself?"

Jen's eyes narrowed and Hannah knew she'd got her.

Molly said, "Of course I can. And you're right. I was staring. I guess I still can't get over the fact that I don't know you anymore. I mean, look at how you're dressed and who you hang out with."

"What's wrong with any of that?" Hannah pressed her arms against her chest. "It's bad enough that I have to explain myself to my mom. I don't need my friends doing it too."

"Good thing we're not friends anymore, then," Molly said. "Go back over there with your cooler-than-me new friends since you think they're so great."

"You don't have to be jealous. You could come join us."

Molly hesitated, but then she said, coolly, "No thank you."

"Yeah," Jen said. "Your new friends aren't our kind of people."

Hannah didn't know what that meant, and she didn't want to know. *That's your loss*, she thought, but she didn't have the energy to say so.

When she got back to her seat, she threw herself into it and picked up her pen. "You were right. I should just ignore her."

"Here," Katie took one of the chocolate turkeys out of the bag of donations they were working with. "These are supposed to be for people in need, but no one needs chocolate more than you right now."

"Thanks." Hannah opened the chocolate turkey even though she felt a little bad about taking something away from someone who had a lot less than she did. She bit into it, trying her best to be grateful for her new friends.

***

Hannah meant to ask Olivia about the bipolar thing that afternoon, but instead, she ended up talking about everything that was going on with Molly. Olivia said it was brave for Hannah to be herself even though Molly didn't like it and might never make up with her.

"I don't feel brave. I just feel sad." Hannah fidgeted. "You really think I should just forget about her?"

Olivia shook her head slightly. "Only you can decide that. But you need to ask yourself if this relationship is worth it, and if it is, what makes you want to continue to be friends with her? What is it you like about her?"

Hannah bit her lip. "She used to be the one to get me out of my shell. She never let me hide in my books or run away from opportunities. I wouldn't be Vice President of SADD if it weren't for her. I wouldn't even have run."

"She was supportive and encouraged you not to hide from the world in the past. What about now?"

"She doesn't understand anymore." Hannah's voice was thick with pain. "We were best friends for six years, and now she hates me." She blinked back tears.

Olivia handed Hannah a tissue. "I know that hurts. But sometimes relationships change, Hannah. Sometimes as you change, someone who you once loved very much just can't follow you down your new path. When that happens, often the best thing to do is to let yourself mourn the loss and then move on."

"I don't want to," Hannah sniffed. "I want Molly." She looked away, sure that Olivia thought she was acting like a baby.

"I know you do." Olivia stood. "I'm going to make a copy of your journal pages that you wanted me to read if that's all right, and then next week we'll talk about them. In the meantime, this week your assignment is to keep writing about Molly. Write about everything you loved about your friendship and how heartbroken you are that it seems to be ending."

Hannah nodded slightly, but when Olivia got up to make the copies she slumped down in her seat. She wanted to think Olivia was wrong, but she knew she wasn't. Her friendship with Molly was over. Period. She had to accept that.

Now she just had to decide what to do about seeing her in school all the time.

THE NEXT MORNING, Katie and her friends called Hannah over as soon as she came into the cafeteria. Joy and Lucy had made a flyer announcing the assembly, and they wanted Hannah's input on it and then they wanted to go to the principal's office to get Mrs. Garcia's approval. Hannah didn't see what the big rush was. But Katie and Elizabeth insisted that they had to do it before they all left for Thanksgiving break, so she went with them.

Mrs. Parker said that Mrs. Garcia was too busy to see the girls right now. Katie gave her the flyer anyway, and she said she'd pass it on. She wasn't sure Mrs. Garcia would allow them to have an assembly about such a heavy topic.

"T-that's why we need to talk to her," Hannah stammered, surprising herself. She hadn't been planning to speak at all. "This is really important, Mrs. Parker. I was raped and being silent about it made things a hundred times worse. We have to do this, and not just for the people who haven't been raped. For the ones who have, so they know they're not alone."

Mrs. Parker sighed. "I'll see if she's available, but she's probably going to tell me to make an appointment for all of you after break. Go ahead and have a seat."

"Good job!" Elizabeth said to Hannah.

"Yeah," Katie said. "You convinced her it's important."

Hannah shrugged. "The proof'll be if we get our meeting."

Mrs. Parker came back. "Mrs. Garcia doesn't have time to see you this morning," she said. "But she WILL see you first thing Monday morning. She wants to see an agenda for this proposed program, so make sure you write something up over Thanksgiving."

"Seriously?" Katie said. "She can't give us two minutes now?"

"It's fine," Hannah said. "We'll just have to get together over break. I'll be around over the weekend maybe."

"I'll be out of town," Katie said. She opened her phone. "But I can set up a document for all of us to work on. Add ideas when you get a chance, and then when I get back Sunday night, we can go over them." She smiled at Hannah as the girls got up and turned to go. "Nobody get discouraged. Hannah helped us get a meeting. This is huge."

Hannah felt so good about Katie praising her that it didn't even bother her that Molly was in the office delivering newspapers to teachers' mailboxes when the girls all left.

***

Hannah was supposed to help Brad review for his English test when they met in the library second period, but he was too nervous to concentrate. They ended up spending half the period talking about the assembly. Brad said that he'd heard rumors that a teacher at the middle school had been fired for touching boys inappropriately and convinced Hannah that they needed to have boys talking about sexual assault too at the assembly, just in case. After Hannah made a note to herself to ask Katie about that, Brad changed the subject to Molly, but Hannah thought they'd better study. She suggested they go out to the track and play a game where Brad had to answer questions while running.

While they jogged in place, Hannah said, "Okay, so who's the main character, and what's her problem?"

"Hester Prynne," Brad said, his feet hitting the ground in time with each syllable. "Everyone looks down on her cause she slept with another dude while her husband was away at sea."

"Two points," Hannah said. They started running for real. Hannah was getting stronger, and she could last longer without losing her breath or having to stop. She kept shooting questions at Brad, and he kept answering without even stopping to think.

Hannah's shoelace came untied. She slowed to a walk and turned her head over her shoulder. "You're doing great. I'm just gonna - "

Oof! She stepped on her untied shoelace and went flying.

"Shit!" Brad said as Hannah threw her hands out so she wouldn't fall on her face. He tried to grab her, but it was too late. He ended up falling on top of her.

Hannah froze, her heart pounding so hard she could barely breathe. Brad's weight was pinning her down, and he could do whatever he wanted to her. She was so scared that she couldn't even form the words to tell him to get off her, much less scream.

She squeezed her eyes shut, her body stiffening to try to protect itself from Brad.

Brad rolled off her. She felt like she could breathe again but she lay still anyway.

"You okay? You didn't break anything, did you?" Brad knelt beside her. "I'm so sorry. I was trying to stop you from falling, and I think I knocked you down."

Hannah looked away. Of course Brad hadn't been trying to rape her. How could she have thought he was? "No," she said, sitting up and hugging her knees to her chest. "It was my own stupid fault. I stepped on my shoelace before I could get it tied. Sit with me a sec?"

"Course." Brad sat down next to her. Hannah took his hand, squeezing it to try to calm herself down. "It wasn't just my shoelace. I. . . when we fell I kind of had a panic attack."

Brad put her hand between both of his. "My stupid ass on top of you probably made it hard to breathe."

"Yeah." Hannah stared out at nothing. "It wasn't just that," she said. "I. . . I thought. . . " She bit her lip. "I don't want to hurt your feelings, but it made me think of HIM." She played with Brad's knuckles. "I know you would never hurt me, but you had me pinned down and. . . "

Brad scowled. "I wouldn't do that to you, Hannah! Ever!"

"I know." Hannah looked away. "Nathan's not wrong when he calls me a psycho. I mean, I'm not in touch with reality. You fall on me and I think it's HIM. . . "

Brad's breath was making little clouds of frost as his nostrils went in and out, and Hannah knew he was trying to calm himself down.

"You're not a psycho," he said. "You told me from the beginning you freak out 'cause of him, so what the hell did I expect?" He scratched at the ground with a twig. "I was only trying to break your fall, I swear. But I should have known me grabbing you from behind was gonna freak you out. I suck."

"No," Hannah said. "I suck because I can't tell the difference between you and the asshole who raped me."

"Whatever." Brad kept scratching at the ground and Hannah knew he was hurt.

"We're not fighting, are we?" Hannah said, tears in her voice. "I took you out here to help you with your test. Please don't hate me."

"I don't." Brad laughed a short, bitter laugh. "One good thing, now that I fell on you and didn't do anything, maybe you can get over it."

"Maybe." Hannah didn't like the way Brad was talking, but she didn't want to fight with him either. "Can we just forget this whole stupid thing and go back to run-studying? I don't want you to mess up your test because of me."

Brad pulled at a tuft of dead grass and threw it onto the track. Hannah looked away, wishing he wouldn't do that. "How about we just sit? You should take it easy after a fall anyway."

"I guess." Hannah stared at her sneakers. Her knees were beginning to throb, but she didn't want to roll up her jeans to see what was wrong with them.

"Want a hug?" Brad asked.

Hannah nodded. Brad put his arms around her and kissed the top of her head while she wondered how long it would take before he got sick of her freaking out and gave up on her.

35 – A Thanksgiving Surprise

AFTER SCHOOL, HANNAH told Brad that she hadn't been able to shake the feeling all day that she was too much work for him. "Come here," Brad said. "Put your head on my chest while I say the world's corniest thing." Hannah was sure he was gonna make a big joke out of how afraid she was, but she leaned on him anyway. Brad kissed the top of her head. Then he stroked her hair and said, "Ready?" His voice vibrated in Hannah's ear, and she almost laughed even though she felt like crap. She nodded and Brad stroked her hair and said, "Here goes. I wanted you to hear my heart beating 'cause it wants you and only you. Pretty cheesy, right? But it's true."

Tears sprung to Hannah's eyes. "I just hate that I freeze up and stuff. I feel like I'm always holding myself back because of HIM. I hate that you have to get around this stupid ghost of some asshole I don't even remember." Her shoulders shook and the only reason she didn't cry was because Nathan could be watching.

Brad held her. "It's cool. It really is. Look, I couldn't deal with anything after my parents split, all right? More than once, I sat out here smoking weed and staring into space when I should have been in class, and even when I didn't skip, I was checked out mentally. I was so screwed up I flunked out of AP English, and if you'd told me a girl like you was ever gonna give me a second look, I'd have thought you were messing with me. So, if the price for being able to call you my girlfriend is backing off when you get freaked out, it's more than worth it. Okay?"

"Okay." Hannah hugged him. "Someday I won't be freaked out so much. I promise."

Brad kissed the top of her head and rubbed her back. Hannah was sure he was feeling her bra clasp through her blouse, but she didn't care.

Someone honked loud.

"Shit!" Brad said, and Hannah jerked up, sure whoever was making all that noise was about to get into a major accident.

"What the hell?" she said when she saw it was just Mom. Her body felt heavy as she came over to the car. "Did you forget to take your meds?" she snapped. "There's no reason to be so obnoxious."

Mom's eyes narrowed. "Get in the car," she said, "unless you want me to embarrass you in front of your boyfriend."

You already embarrassed me. Hannah threw her backpack on the floor and herself into the car.

"You will not use my illness against me," Mom said. "EVER. You can be as angry as you want. You can do the whole surly teenage thing because you don't want your friends to think you have a decent relationship with your mother, but you will NOT make nasty comments about me needing to be on medication, not after how hard I fought to get better enough to take care of you. Do you understand me?"

Hannah stared at her scuffed-up jeans. "Yes, Mom. Sorry."

"I hope you are." Mom let her breath out slowly. "Now, the reason we're in such a hurry is we have to get to the airport."

"The airport?" Hannah frowned. "I hope you didn't buy us tickets somewhere on the spur of the moment. I can't leave town, Mom. I have plans with Brad and on Sunday I'm supposed to . . . "

"Relax. Even I'm not that impulsive. No, I bit the bullet and told my mother what's been going on with you. Unlike us, she has money to burn, and I couldn't talk her out of flying up to spend Thanksgiving with us."

Hannah wasn't sure how she felt about that. She'd wished a million times Grandma was here to talk to, but she was so different now than she'd been last Passover. If Grandma didn't like the new her, it would break her heart. "I thought New York is too cold for her."

"It is. She's willing to make the sacrifice for you." Mom's voice was soft. "And so am I. A whole week of her is almost more than I can bear, but if it helps you . . . Anyway, I don't want to be late. You know how she is. That's why I was in such a rush to get you."

Traffic was terrible and Mom irritated Hannah by asking a billion times for the name of the terminal and the airline. When they finally got to the airport, Mom refused to park in the underground lot even though there were spaces and insisted on going all the way up to the top floor, which was above ground. Then they had to get an elevator all the way back to street level and follow the signs for arrivals.

A digital sign in the arrivals area said that Grandma's plane wasn't going to get in for another half an hour.

"Why did we have to be here so early?" Hannah complained, throwing herself into an empty seat.

"I didn't know there would be so little traffic," Mom said as if the traffic jam they'd sat in the whole way here hadn't existed. "Stop being such a grumpy pants." While Hannah was rolling her eyes at Mom's attempt to sound like she was still a teenager, Mom pulled some bills out of her wallet. "Here. Go get yourself a snack. Maybe that'll put you in a better mood."

Hannah didn't want Mom spending money on her, but she didn't feel like arguing. So, she took it and went to check out the concourse. She wished Brad was here. They'd had so much fun at the mall that day, and he would make her laugh so she would stop freaking out.

She stopped at a smoothie place and tried to figure out why she was in such a bad mood while she read the menu. Grandma coming should have been the best news she had in a long time. But what if she was disappointed in her? Grandma had high standards and Hannah tried so hard to live up to them even after she and Mom moved. What would Grandma think if she knew Hannah was a miscarriage away from repeating history by getting pregnant way too young? Or if she knew Hannah had wanted to go to the party and refused to give up her friendship with Sierra after? Or, worst of all, if she knew Hannah might be bipolar like Mom?

"What can I get you?" the person behind the counter asked, pulling Hannah out of her thoughts.

"Oh." Hannah had no idea what she wanted. She scanned the list as quickly as she could so she wouldn't hold the line up. "Um, a small banana and oat shake with peanut butter, please." She couldn't remember if she'd had a banana at breakfast this morning, but it was too late. She'd already ordered.

The smoothie cost ten dollars and Hannah couldn't shake the feeling that she was wasting money after she handed over the bills Mom had given her. She stepped back to wait, staring at a display of protein bars and wishing she'd bought one of those instead. They were a lot cheaper. Her eyes landed on the peanut butter and chocolate ones, but that made her think of how Molly used to share those with her, and she had to look away.

"There you are," Mom said when Hannah finally got back with her smoothie. "I was about to text you if not send out a search party."

Hannah's smoothie was way too cold. She rubbed the back of her neck, trying to get rid of the brain freeze. "They took a while making it. That's all. It was super expensive. I spent all the money you gave me."

"That's what I gave it to you for. Anyway, Grandma's plane landed. She's on her way to meet us right now."

"Great." Hannah managed a smile. She took another sip of her smoothie to calm her nerves as Grandma came toward them.

Grandma looked the same as she always did. She was maybe an inch taller than Hannah with the same gray eyes and oval face with a pointed chin. Her hair was short and gray, but Hannah could still see curls in the back that were almost like hers. Her peach-almost-tan hands were wrinkled a little more than Hannah remembered but were the only real sign that she was old.

Grandma pushed Hannah's hair away from her face as she hugged her hello. "My beautiful Channa," she said, using the Hebrew pronunciation for Hannah's name. "I'm so sorry, sweetheart. I wish I'd been here to pick up the pieces after it happened."

"Do you have luggage to pick up?" Mom asked. "They're announcing Carousel C."

Grandma locked eyes with her. "It'll still be there in five minutes. My granddaughter is more important. Don't you think?" She turned back to Hannah without waiting for an answer. "I'm here now and I'm a good listener. So, if you want to go for a walk - "

"It's twenty degrees out," Mom interjected.

"Or go out somewhere, just you and me," Grandma went on, ignoring Mom, "I'd be delighted to take the time." She slipped her arm under

Hannah's. "Come, my dear. Walk me to the carousel, so we can get my bags and get on our way home."

Hannah could feel Mom's eyes on her back as she let Grandma walk her toward the baggage claim. It reminded her of Molly, and she didn't like it. She bit her lip so she wouldn't say so and made herself hold her head up high so Grandma wouldn't worry about her.

36 – A Drama-Filled Day Out

THE NEXT MORNING, Grandma wantcd to take Hannah out for coffee. Hannah wasn't sure she wanted to, but when Grandma said she could invite Brad she agreed to go.

The closest coffee shop was the one in the strip mall across the street from school where a lot of kids hung out during their free period. There was no school today, of course, but that didn't mean she'd be the only high schooler in here, and she really didn't feel like running into anyone. But Grandma thought it sounded like a good idea, and it felt easier to go along with it than try to explain that Hannah wasn't in the mood for being anywhere near school. Besides, Brad knew where it was, so it made meeting him there easy.

Waiting for him felt awkward anyway. Hannah had wanted hot chocolate, but Grandma said, "Live a little, darling!" and ordered two caramel lattes for them. Now Hannah was drinking a too-cold drink for the second time in as many days while the wind blew against the building and made a lot of noise.

"I can't believe you wanted a cold drink in this weather," Hannah said.

Grandma shrugged. "I've never been one for hot drinks. Of course, Florida doesn't get this cold." She reached across and patted Hannah's hand. "You know, if everything's too much for you after the rape, you could always transfer to Miami for your senior year. I'd be happy to let you stay with me."

Hannah chewed on her straw. "Thanks, but I wouldn't want to leave Brad. Besides, I'm working on not running away anymore."

Grandma raised an eyebrow. "When did you ever run away from anything?" She smiled slightly. "I remember a little fireball who absolutely would not accept my attempts to protect her from the truth about her mother's illness. You put your little foot down and made it clear the only way I was ever going to get any peace was if I took you to see your mother so you could understand for yourself how bad off she was."

Hannah stirred her too-sweet latte with her straw. "I felt like such a spoiled brat."

"You weren't. You were just determined, that's all, and you were right. I shouldn't have tried to protect you from the truth. But that's enough about the past. My point is, you still have that determination, and I hope you won't let what happened to you dampen it one bit."

Did Grandma know the whole story? Hannah doubted it. If she did, she had to be disappointed that Hannah had gone to the party. "I'm trying. I'm even working with some of my friends on putting together a program at school about sexual assault."

"That's wonderful!" Grandma said. "Tell me all about it."

Hannah's heart pounded. "W-we don't have a complete plan yet. On Sunday, we're going to start putting together a rough draft of our idea. B-but I'm going to speak and . . . " She trailed off, sure she sounded stupid and ridiculous.

The bells on the door chimed as someone came in. Brad! Thank God. Hannah stood and called, "Over here!"

Brad came over. Hannah hugged him tightly, showing off for Grandma how much she loved him. Grandma asked him about the charity thing he and Hannah were doing. After he explained, he asked Hannah again if she was coming to his house for dessert, and she said she would. Grandma said Hannah needed to bring something and offered to help her bake.

"Never go to a party empty-handed, *sheifale*," she said, and Hannah's face got hot. *Sheifale* was a Yiddish word that meant "lamb". It was a better nickname than Mouse but still. What would Brad think about Grandma suddenly speaking in a foreign language?

The door chimed again. "Crap," Hannah said under her breath as Molly and Jen came in, holding hands.

Brad squeezed her hand. "They're not gonna start anything. Not with your grandma here."

"What are you two whispering about?" Grandma interrupted.

"Nothing," Hannah said. "Just some people I'd rather not see just came in. That's all." She pulled her cup closer to her, reminding herself that Grandma expected her not to be Mouse. "But don't worry. I'm ignoring them."

Grandma frowned. "I'm guessing you mean Molly," she said, and Hannah remembered that Molly had come to Passover a couple of times. "Your mother said you had a falling out."

Hannah groaned. "Is there any part of my business Mom didn't tell you?"

Grandma chuckled. "You sound just like her at your age. Anyway, I wasn't entirely surprised. There was always something about that girl I didn't like. She seemed phony, too good to be true."

"She is not." Hannah secretly thought Grandma might be right, but she still felt too loyal to Molly to say so. "She just doesn't understand. That's all."

"What she is, is coming this way. She's going to put on a show for my benefit. You just watch."

Hannah took Brad's hand, so Molly would see she wasn't the only one on a date. Molly's eyes flitted to it, then away.

"Hi, Mrs. Kollman," Molly said, ignoring Hannah and Brad altogether. "Are you in town for the holiday?"

"I wouldn't miss it for the world." Grandma's lips were thin and her voice hard.

"I'm glad. Hannah needs all the help she can get right now." Molly lowered her voice and said, "Did she tell you - "

"Molly!" Hannah said. "Telling the whole school isn't enough?"

"I wasn't going to ask about you-know-what!" Molly's voice rose.

"Maybe not," Grandma said, "but you're clearly upsetting my granddaughter, and I'm sure you're doing it on purpose."

"She isn't," Hannah said, not wanting Molly to think she needed Grandma to fight her battles for her. "I don't know what she's doing, but it isn't that."

"Thanks for believing in me that much," Molly said. "That's something." She crossed her arms. "I came over here because even though Hannah's written me off, I haven't written her off. Despite everything, I do still care about her." She twisted her necklace. "And I'm worried about her."

"Seriously?" Brad said.

"Hannah," Molly said, ignoring Brad, "hasn't been acting like herself since Halloween. I guess maybe she can't help it." She lowered her voice again. "Hannah thinks she's bipolar, and I think maybe she's right."

Hannah stared at Grandma while she tried to catch her breath, but she couldn't tell from the look on her face whether Grandma thought it was true. She would know, too. She'd raised Mom, bipolar and all.

"I was going to talk to my therapist about it," Hannah whispered.

Grandma patted Hannah's wrist while putting her finger to her lips. "Is that what you came over here for? To embarrass Hannah in front of me as if she wasn't humiliated enough by what some boy did to her?"

"No!" Molly sounded genuinely upset. "I told you, I'm worried about her. She isn't acting normal, and I thought since you're here you should know so you can intervene."

"Uh huh," Grandma said. "Well, you told me. So, how about you go back to your own table, and we will deal with this without you."

Molly's eyes narrowed.

"Yeah," Hannah said. "And just so you know, now that you did this . . . we're done."

"Hannah!" Molly's voice shook. "Don't . . . please don't. I swear I'm only trying to help."

"You wanna help so bad, learn to keep your mouth shut!" Brad said. "Hannah didn't need you telling the whole world her other secret, and she didn't need you telling her grandma this one." He squeezed Hannah's shoulder. "You have any idea how broken up she is over you giving her the silent treatment? And then on top of that, you go blabbing shit that's not your business to tell? What the hell is wrong with you?"

Hannah slumped down in her seat. "Everyone stop. I don't want a scene."

"No scene," Molly said. "I'm going. But just so you know, I've never tried to be anything but a good friend to you. When you come to your senses, I hope you'll finally see that." She turned and hurried away, and Hannah knew her well enough to know she was holding back tears.

Hannah groaned. "God! You'd think I was her girlfriend instead of Jen, the way she talks. What does she have to be like that for?"

"Let's not waste energy on her. We have more important things to discuss." Grandma leaned forward. Lowering her voice, she asked, "Did you really say you were afraid you were bipolar?"

Hannah nodded. "I'm going to ask my therapist, I swear."

"I see." Grandma had no expression on her face. Not being able to tell what she thought scared Hannah worse.

"D-do you think I am?" Hannah stammered.

Grandma shook her head slightly. "I'm no psychiatrist, *sheifale*. But I always knew something was off about your mother, that there was something in her that I couldn't ever reach. I just didn't know what it was or what to do until it was almost too late. And I don't get that same feeling from you. But I'm glad you're getting help before you do something you can't take back." Grandma took Hannah's hand. "And I want you to know that no matter what this psychiatrist says the problem is, you are still my Channa that I love almost more than life itself."

"I know," Hannah said, even though she hadn't been sure until just then. "Um . . . Mom doesn't know. I didn't want her to worry."

"I assumed that." Grandma played with Hannah's ring. "I certainly understand not wanting to deal with how she might react. But your mother is not the enemy either, darling. She loves you so much that she was willing to give you to me to raise even though she hated having to, just because it was what was best for you. And if it turns out you are bipolar or anything else, she will love you through that too. Now, I won't say anything because unlike some people, I understand that certain things are not my business to tell. But if you want me there when you tell her, I'm happy to be by your side."

Hannah squeezed Brad's hand. "I'm not ready yet. I want to see what Olivia says first."

Grandma nodded. "I'll be back in Florida by then. But you can always call me after." She patted Hannah's hand. "Now, what do you say we forget all this and the three of us do something fun? I'll treat you two to an afternoon at the bowling lanes if you won't be too embarrassed getting your pants beat off by an old lady."

Brad grinned. "I knew I'd like your grandma!" He reached for Hannah's hand. "C'mon, let's get out of here."

***

Hannah texted Sierra on the way to the bowling alley to ask her if she was feeling up to meeting them, but she didn't answer. When they got there, the attendant had to search forever for shoes Hannah's size, which put her in a terrible mood, and then Grandma wouldn't let her get away with asking for bumpers like they put up for little kids or picking up the lightest ball the alley had.

"You need some confidence," Grandma said, "and you don't get that by playing the easy way." She handed Hannah a green ball. The holes were big enough for Hannah's fingers, but she was sure it was too heavy.

She was wrong. The ball was heavy enough that carrying it wasn't easy, but she could do it.

"Told you that you are stronger than you think." Grandma smiled. "Now, which lane are we?"

"Seven." Somehow Hannah didn't mind Grandma asking twice like she did when Mom did it.

Lane seven was between a lane that some family full of kids had and a girl Hannah's age. The girl was light-skinned black and was wearing a hoodie with the hood part down over her back, and had a ponytail made out of a bunch of small braids.

It was Sierra. And she was with Jake.

Hannah said to Brad, "Nice of Sierra to text me back."

Brad shrugged. "She probably figured you didn't wanna hear about her going anywhere with that freaking loser." He hit his palm with his fist. "You know what? Let's pretend they aren't there. It's way better I take it out on the bowling pins than on his face." He turned toward Grandma. "You wanna go first, Mrs. K?"

"Oh, call me Julia," Grandma said. "And I think I'll go last. No use making the two of you feel hopeless before you begin."

"We'll see who makes who feel hopeless," Brad said. "Watch me, Hannah. See if you can pick up how it's done."

"I won't, but okay." Hannah could watch Brad all day. Besides, staring at him meant not acknowledging that Sierra and Jake were there.

Except that was impossible because Jake was loud, and he wasn't very nice. "Another gutter ball for you," he said to Sierra. "You're really crappy at this."

"Jake!" Sierra said.

"Don't get an attitude. Sucking at bowling's not a crime. You're still the prettiest girl I've ever met. That's what counts."

Jake leaned in for a kiss. Sierra had the same disgusted look on her face that she had at the party, but she kissed him just like she did then.

Hannah was about to go over there. She had no idea what she was going to do but she had to do something.

"Earth to Hannah," Grandma called. "Come in for a landing, it's your turn."

"Oh." Hannah went to get her ball. She threw it as hard as she could, thinking about Jake and the asshole who raped her and how Nathan had treated her ever since all at once. At first, it looked like she was actually going to get a strike, but at the last second, the ball veered to the right. She ended up hitting just one pin.

"Told you I suck," Hannah said.

"You'll get it," Grandma said. "Take your second turn, *sheifale.*"

Again with the Yiddish nickname. And where Sierra could hear, too. Hannah grabbed the ball and tried again. This time it went to the left, and she got three pins.

"Four is more than zero," Grandma said, "which is what some Negative Nelly predicted. Now, watch me." She took her ball and went up to the foul line. Hannah watched as Grandma lined it up with one of the arrows on the floor. She threw the ball perfectly, going down on one knee as she let it go, and it hit the center, knocking all the pins down at once.

"Not bad for an old lady, huh?" Grandma said, smiling slightly as the display on their scoreboard showed STRIKE!!! "Now next time it's your turn, let me help you, and we'll see if we can get more than a few pins knocked down."

The game went on like that. Hannah kept one eye on Jake and Sierra. She could feel something was wrong there, but they weren't fighting anymore, at least not loudly enough for her to hear, though Jake wouldn't stop gloating about how much better he was doing than Sierra. Meanwhile, Hannah managed to get a couple of pins every round, which was nothing compared to Brad, who hit seven or eight, or Grandma, who played a near-perfect game.

By the time the game was finally over, Hannah was starving. Grandma said she wasn't hungry, but Hannah knew she was giving her and Brad time alone. She promised to hurry back even though she knew Grandma would tell her to take her time.

In the food court, Brad got them both a couple of hot dogs and gushed about how awesome Grandma was. "The way she handled Molly was badass, and she bowls like she's half her age." He reached for Hannah's hand. "You having a good time?"

"Trying to. It would be better if. . . you know." Hannah gestured toward Jake and Sierra, who were sitting a few tables away. Jake had broken a piece of square pizza in two and was giving Sierra the smaller half. "Can you watch this while I go say 'Hi'?"

"I'll watch it go into my mouth," Brad joked. He kissed Hanna and then she headed to Sierra's table.

"Smile," Jake was saying. "You'd think you're at a funeral. God."

"I don't feel like smiling." Sierra sighed. "I'm pretty miserable actually."

"Just because I teased you a little? Learn to take a joke, Sierra. This is supposed to be fun, remember?"

Hannah wanted to scream at Jake to leave Sierra alone. Instead, she said, "Sierra! I thought that was you."

Sierra turned her head. "Oh. Hannah. Hi. Jake, you remember . . . "

"Course I do. She's even hotter sober." Jake looked Hannah up and down, staring way too long at her breasts. She crossed her arms over her chest, protecting herself.

Jake's smile faded. "How you doing after . . . you know."

"After I was raped?" Hannah snapped. "I'd be better if you stopped staring at my chest. Thanks."

"Sorry. I can't help that you have such amazing tits."

"Jake," Sierra said. Jake glared at her, and Sierra stared down at the table. "I'm not telling you what to do, I swear. B-but Hannah doesn't get your humor. She's uncomfortable."

"Don't be," Jake said to Hannah. "It's a compliment. Don't you get that?"

Hannah bit her lip to stop herself from asking Sierra what the hell she was doing with this asshole. "There are better compliments," she said. "By the way, do you know the asshole who did it to me?"

Jake's grin faded. "I told Sierra to make it clear to you I had nothing to do with it. The guy was a loser who had no business being there, all right? I didn't even know him."

"Yeah," Sierra said, "so leave him alone."

"Relax, baby," Jake said, putting his hand on Sierra's arm, tight enough that Hannah could see tears in Sierra's eyes. Sierra didn't object, though. She just bit her lip like she was trying not to cry. Jake kept squeezing her arm while he went on, "It's not like she's gonna turn us into the cops. Right, Hannah?"

Hannah stared at Jake's hand on Sierra's arm, remembering the bruise she'd thought she'd seen the other day. Jake had put it there. She was sure of it.

"I don't have anything to tell them," she said coldly. She tried to look Sierra in the eye to silently tell her it was going to be okay, but Sierra wouldn't look at her. "Unless you know something."

"Can't help you, sorry." Jake took a French fry. "Lighten up about it. It was no big deal."

"N-no big deal?" Sierra asked. "She was a virgin, Jake. Your friend - OUCH."

Jake was squeezing Sierra's arm even tighter. "SHUT UP!" He dropped his arm suddenly. "I'm sorry, baby. I didn't mean to hurt you. But I have to protect you. You know his name. That makes you an accessory. So, if she goes to the cops, you're going to go to jail. Is that what you want?"

Sierra's eyes widened with fear.

Hannah said, "D-don't listen to him."

"He's right, though," Sierra whispered. She took her glasses off and rubbed her temples, then put them back on. "I'm such a shitty friend. I'm half to blame." She turned toward Jake. "I have to talk to Hannah alone. I have to make her understand . . . "

"Like hell you do!" Jake said. "She's gonna try to convince you it's my fault, and I can't trust you not to turn on me. So, no. It's her or me, baby. If you choose her, it's over."

Sierra froze.

Hannah said, "Let him go, then. Doesn't he always come crawling back anyway?"

Jake's eyes flashed. "Fuck you both. You're too immature for me anyway." He stormed off.

Sierra put her head in her hands. Hannah sat down next to her and put her arm around her. "Forget him," she said. "Look at how he treats you, Sierra. You don't need . . . "

"YES, I DO!" Sierra snapped. "He's the only one who'll ever have me. Don't you understand that?"

"That's not true! You could do so much better than him. Look what he did to you just now!"

Sierra stared at her. "So, it's true. You do hate him so much that you want to break us up." She blinked back tears. "How could you do this to me? He was the only good thing in my life, and you ruined it!" She jumped up.

A voice in Hannah's head was screaming *Don't make a scene, don't make a scene, don't make a scene* but her body didn't listen. She blocked Sierra's path. "Don't go after him."

"I'm not," Sierra said. "Like you said, he always comes crawling back." She grabbed her phone. "I'm calling Dylan to come get me. In the meantime, leave me the hell alone!" She pushed past Hannah, bumping her shoulder hard.

Hannah stood frozen, not sure if she should go after Sierra or not. She didn't want to piss her off more, but what if Sierra chased after Jake?

By the time she decided she had to go after her, Sierra was long gone.

HANNAH WAS TOO upset to tell Brad what had just happened, but he asked.

"I might have lost Sierra for good. That's what." Hannah gulped her root beer, wincing as the bubbles burned her throat.

"Nah." Brad took her hands in his. "You stood by her when everyone wanted to blame her for what happened to you. She's gotta remember that."

Hannah shook her head slightly. "Not the way she's being about Jake. It was like she was on drugs or something. She was saying things that don't make any sense, and she got mad at me when she should have been mad at him."

"It would help if I knew what happened," Brad said. "Tell me? Please?"

Hannah chewed on her straw, thinking. She didn't want to embarrass Sierra. But then she thought about Jake's hand on Sierra's arm. She had been sure he was hurting her on purpose, and a good friend wouldn't let that go. What was that they said in health class freshman year about keeping secrets?

Better an angry friend than a dead friend. That's what.

Jake wouldn't literally kill Sierra but still. He was dangerous and for all Hannah knew he'd been the one who raped her.

Nope. She had to tell, even if it meant Sierra never talked to her again.

She told Brad the whole story. By the time she finished, his eyes were on fire, and he was holding onto the edge of the table with all his might. Hannah was afraid he was going to do something crazy, or even worse, go smoke weed to chill out. But he didn't. He just said Jake was more of an asshole than he thought.

Brad thought they needed to tell Dylan what Jake was doing to Sierra. But Hannah didn't want to be a snitch, and she definitely didn't want Sierra to be any madder at her than she already was.

"Fuck how she feels about it," Brad said. "This dude sounds dangerous. Who the hell knows what he's gonna try to do next?"

Hannah bit her lip. Didn't they say that once someone started getting violent, it would only get worse?

"Okay, I'll text Dylan," she said. She stared at her phone for a long time, trying to think of what to say. There was too much to tell, but if she called him, Sierra might hear, and she wanted to get her help without making her mad. Finally, she texted:

> If you haven't already, I think you need to check on Sierra. She & Jake had a big fight and she's super upset.

That was the coward's way out, and she knew it. But she didn't want to totally betray Sierra even though she'd promised herself she'd tell everything. So, she hit send anyway.

Brad told her he was proud of her and kissed her and she let him even though she knew it was a big lie.

***

Hannah was quiet the whole way home. There was something else she could do about the Sierra situation, something that she wasn't sure she had the guts to do.

She could tell the cops that she'd been raped and that Sierra's boyfriend knew the rapist. That would get her justice and get Jake away from Sierra.

But it would also make her a snitch, and anyway, Sierra would probably never talk to her again if she did that.

When she came into the apartment, Mom was in the living room watching something or other on TV. She turned it off and asked how Hannah's day was, but when she found out that Hannah wanted to bake with Grandma, she wouldn't let her.

Just like that, Mom and Grandma were fighting. Grandma thought Mom was being selfish when Hannah needed to talk to her, and Mom was convinced that Grandma wanted to manipulate Hannah into moving back to Florida. Eric came out of the kitchen and got in the middle of it, but that just made Grandma and Mom start fighting about whether Mom moving to New York to be with Eric had been a good idea.

"STOP!" Hannah shouted. "I'm not moving back to Florida, and Brad'll live if I don't bring apple fritters tomorrow. I don't need to do that. All I need is for you guys to take me to the police station."

Everyone froze. "The police station?" Mom asked.

Hannah nodded. "I've been thinking about this the whole way home. I want to tell the cops I was raped."

"Why, sweetheart?" Mom asked. "You told me you didn't want to. What changed your mind?"

Hannah fidgeted. If she told Mom the whole truth, she'd freak out about Sierra being a bad influence. "You don't want me to, do you?"

"I didn't say that," Mom played with her necklace, twisting the charm around and around. "All I want is for you to be whole and happy and like you were before, and I just don't know what's going to get that for you."

Eric brushed Mom's fingertips with his. "What Mom's trying to say is that she's afraid of what it could do to you. We want justice for you. We want to see this asshole rot in a jail cell. But we also want to protect you."

"Protect me from what?" Hannah pressed her arms so tight against her chest that it hurt. "I already lost my best friend and had my diary read in front of the whole school. What could be worse than that?"

"You don't even know." Mom's voice was soft. "Going to the cops won't be easy, and it also won't be the end of this nightmare. It'll just be the

beginning because if they even make an arrest—
which I doubt they will, given the circumstances—
there's still a trial to get through, still my baby on
the witness stand getting torn apart by some
defense attorney who wants to win by tearing her to
pieces. And even if he's found guilty, what if the
judge doesn't care enough to do more than give him
a slap on the wrist for ruining your life?"

Hannah stared at the ground. She hadn't
thought about what would happen if Jake and his
friend were arrested, just that she wanted them to
be punished.

But could she do this if it meant getting up in
court and getting attacked by some defense
attorney? She wanted to be the kind of person who
had no fear, who could just get up on the witness
stand like it was no big deal, but she wasn't. She
was still Mouse no matter how much she wished
she wasn't.

"You really think there's going to be a trial?" she
asked.

"We don't know," Eric said. "First there has to
be an arrest, and we don't know for sure the cops
will even do that much. That's why we're not a
hundred percent behind this, Hannah. If you go to
the police it's going to be very painful for you, and it
could be for nothing."

"Someone has to take a stand," Grandma
interjected, "and if not Hannah, then who? Don't
forget where we came from, Debra. Six million of
our people died in the *Shoah*, six million
exterminated and you know what allowed that to

happen? Millions more who refused to stand up for what they knew was right before it was too late."

"That has nothing to do with this!" Mom snapped. "Why do you always have to turn everything into something bigger than it is?"

Look who's talking, Hannah thought, but she didn't have the energy to say so.

Eric said, "Let's not get sidetracked. This is about Hannah, not about either of you, and definitely not about what happened in Nazi Germany." He turned toward Hannah. "This is really your decision to make, and Mom and I will stand by you no matter what you decide. But I really think you should wait until after your next therapy session so you can talk to Olivia about it and get an objective perspective."

Hannah twisted a lock of hair around her finger, thinking. Eric sounded reasonable, and it would be a relief to put this off. The part of her that was still Mouse thought so, anyway. But apparently, Mouse was outvoted because she couldn't let herself wait another minute. "I don't need Olivia's opinion. That'll just waste time."

"You've already waited a month to consider reporting this. What's another few days?" Mom asked.

"I'll lose my nerve. That's what." Hannah grabbed her purse. "Who's taking me to the police station?"

SIERRA TEXTED HANNAH while she was waiting on a hardbacked chair in the lobby of the police station, sandwiched between Mom and Grandma:

> It's bad enough you told Dylan I broke up with Jake. Leave my name out of this or I WILL NEVER FORGIVE YOU.

Hannah slumped down in her seat. She was going to lose another friend. She was sure of it.

A cop came up to her just then. Hannah's eyes slid over his uniform, trying to take in the fact that this was really happening, that she was really talking to the cops about what someone had done to her. His badge had the name "J. Prescott" on it and Hannah distracted herself wondering what the J stood for while she got up and shook his hand.

"Do you want us to come with you, sweetheart?" Mom asked.

Hannah hesitated. She didn't really want Mom there but she didn't want to hurt her feelings. "I'll be okay," she said. "I hope."

She turned and followed the officer, staring at the back of his head. He had sandy hair that wasn't quite blonde, and it looked like he had a small tattoo on the back of his neck in green ink that

312 | REINVENTING HANNAH

stood out against his white skin. Hannah watched it bob up and down, but she couldn't quite make out what it was because it was half-hidden under his uniform. Since when were cops allowed to have tattoos? she wondered.

Officer Prescott took her to a small room. "We're gonna meet in here for privacy," he said, closing the door behind him. The room had a table in it like on TV when they interrogated suspects.

Officer Prescott opened a laptop that was on the table and asked Hannah for her ID and her full name and address. She felt so dizzy as she took out her learner's permit she could barely see. She wished Officer Prescott would open the door and let her get some air but she didn't dare ask.

Officer Prescott handed her back her ID. "So, you're reporting a sexual assault?"

Hannah nodded. Officer Prescott told her he needed to get some details, starting with when, where, and what happened. His voice was soft, but she wasn't convinced he cared at all, and she definitely didn't think he was going to believe her.

She launched into her story anyway.

Officer Prescott made her describe Jamie and the other guys she'd been playing video games with. She barely remembered the other guys, though Jamie was imprinted on her mind forever because she'd almost kissed him. She hoped she described them right.

When she told him that Jake gave her the iced tea, Prescott asked her what Jake's last name was.

Hannah scrunched up her forehead, trying so hard to remember her brain hurt, but she was pretty sure Sierra had never told her.

"I don't know," she admitted, picking at a loose thread on her sleeve. "He goes to Cedarwood Community. I think. Anyway, his house was on Roosevelt Avenue in Eastwood. It was the last one on the block." She bit her lip, trying to remember the exact address.

Officer Prescott made Hannah describe Jake. "And you never met him before?" he asked when she had.

She told him she hadn't.

"What's the name of this friend that invited you?"

Hannah stared down at the table. "She was drinking. I don't want her to get in trouble."

"She was drinking, and you weren't? So, you were what, the designated driver with a learner's permit?"

"I was going to call a Lyft." Hannah shifted in her seat, feeling like she was the one in trouble.

Officer Prescott locked eyes with Hannah. She held her breath, but she refused to look away. After a minute, he said, "Moving on. You said after you drank the iced tea you felt weird. Weird how?"

Hannah told him the little she remembered: how she couldn't walk or talk properly and how she woke up at Sierra's (she almost said her name but caught herself just in time) and how Dylan made her go to the hospital. Her voice shook and she couldn't understand why she was so close to tears when she hadn't cried when it happened.

Prescott asked Hannah what Dylan's name was and she knew that if she told, it would lead the cops straight to Sierra and that would be that. But Dylan had seen exactly what Hannah was like after the rape, so he might be able to fill in some blanks the cops needed to arrest the asshole who did it.

"Dylan Dunlap," she said, staring down at her hands and trying to convince herself she hadn't just betrayed Sierra.

"Was he at the party?"

"No. I guess Sierra called him to come get us."

"Sierra. That's your friend?"

Crap. Hannah had been so flustered she'd forgotten to keep Sierra's name out of this. She nodded, blinking back tears.

Prescott made her tell him Sierra's last name and she did. She'd already screwed up, might as well go all the way. Then he asked her a bunch more questions. Who poured the tea? Where did she put it? Who was around when she was playing with Jamie? Hannah wasn't sure of any of it, and she was only half paying attention because she was too freaked out about how mad Sierra was going to be.

Prescott asked her the same questions over and over, or at least, that's what it felt like. Then, he told her the detectives would be in touch when they had reviewed the case.

"How long?" Hannah didn't want to spend all day at the police station, so she hoped it would be quick.

"Depends how long they take reviewing your case. Usually, they make contact within a day or two."

"A day or two." Hannah's voice was flat. "So, they won't do anything today?"

"Probably not. They gotta review everything first on top of the cases they're already working." Prescott left to go make copies of Hannah's ER paperwork and her ID.

Pain radiated from the back of Hannah's neck, making her head hurt. She rubbed it, wincing.

She'd gone through all this for nothing. The detectives probably weren't even going to call, and on top of that, this stupid patrol officer had treated her like she was the suspect. And she'd given them Sierra's name too. It was an accident but still. It had been an accident when Molly had told the world that Hannah had been raped, and that hadn't made it hurt any less or made it any easier to forgive.

Molly. Had Hannah been too hard on her? Hannah bit her lip, not knowing what to do. She'd told her two hours ago they were done forever and meant it but now she wanted to talk to her.

She took a deep breath and called her.

The voicemail came on after one ring, which meant that either Molly's phone was off, or she declined the call. Hannah thought it was best to just hang up without saying anything but she didn't want to be a coward, so she overrode Mouse again and said into the phone, "Um, Molly, it's me, Hannah. I . . . I wanted to say I'm sorry. I didn't mean it when I said we were done. I was just mad.

And, um, even though I still think you were wrong to yell at Sierra in front of everyone, I was wrong to not let it go after you apologized. It was an accident. So, I forgive you, and I hope you forgive me."

She hung up. A second later, her phone buzzed.

```
I don't want to be friends anymore.
    Please don't call me again.
```

Hannah's eyes filled with tears. She swallowed them and sat up straight as Prescott came back with her medical papers.

39 – A New Threat

WHEN SHE GOT home, Hannah flopped back on the couch and stared at her phone, scrolling through posts on Instagram and trying to be grateful that Nathan hadn't posted anything obnoxious about her today. Molly had forgotten to block her on social media, she guessed, since she was able to see twenty billion photos of her and Jen. Maybe she'd left Hannah unblocked on purpose just to rub it in her face that she was way happier without her. Hannah didn't know.

Grandma clapped her hands. "Funk time's over. Come with me, *sheifale*. Let's get those fritters made."

Hannah didn't feel like it, but she knew Grandma wouldn't leave her alone until she came into the kitchen, so she gave in. Grandma told her to get a bunch of apples out to core and slice into rounds.

When Hannah picked up a knife, Grandma said, "You need a corer like I have at home. You just put the apple on a skewer and turn the crank and presto! Cored, peeled, and sliced." She smiled slightly. "I guess I know what to get you for Chanukah."

"Great." Hannah tried to force a smile, but she could tell from the way Grandma's eyes clouded over that she wasn't fooling her. She cored and sliced the apples the old-fashioned way, aware of her grandmother's eyes on her back.

"Do you remember watching me do this when you were little?" Grandma asked. "You used to beg me to let you help. When you were big enough, I let you mix the batter, and you were so proud of yourself." She sighed. "Times have changed. Now it's me who's begging you to let me help you, the same way I used to beg your mother when she was in one of her dark moods. What happened at the police station, darling? You've been down ever since. It must have gone badly."

Hannah bit her lip, ashamed of the tears in her eyes. "I just don't think they're going to do anything to help. That's all. I wish I hadn't gone."

"Never, ever regret taking a stand," Grandma said. "It takes strength and courage and it can be lonely, but at least you fought for a better world. That's more than you can say if you keep quiet."

"My friends want me to be quiet. I think." Hannah threw the apple slices into a bowl. "That's why Molly hates me now, and I think Sierra does too." Hannah's voice broke and a tear rolled down her face. She told Grandma everything: how she'd screwed up, how Molly had rejected her attempt to apologize, how Sierra hadn't answered her phone when she tried to call her on the way home.

"And it's all for nothing," Hannah sobbed, "because the cop said the detectives will take days to get back to me, and I doubt they're going to do anything at all."

"Well, don't let them get away with that," Grandma said. "Standing up for yourself is not something you do once and never again. Sometimes you have to fight the same fight over and over until something gives. So, if the police won't take you seriously enough to investigate this case the first time, keep bothering them until they get moving. And if you really want to be friends with these girls, fight for that too."

"How?" Hannah asked. "Molly told me not to contact her, and Sierra isn't calling me back. I can't force them to spend time with me."

"No, you can't do that. But a girl as smart as you can find a creative way to get her message across to them. Now come over here and fold the eggs into the flour. These fritters won't bake themselves." Grandma squeezed Hannah's shoulder. Hannah went over to the sink and washed her hands again even though she'd washed them before they started so she could try to start over.

***

The next morning, the SADD group met at Panera Bread to get their baskets and their route assignments. Hannah had planned on going just with Brad, but Elizabeth texted and invited them both to go with her and Joy, and she figured it was better not to alienate what friends she had while she had them, so she gave in.

"I got great news for us," Brad said when they picked him up.

"For 'us' us or for the group?" Hannah asked.

"Both, I guess." Brad grinned. "Dad's gonna cover what we're doing for his paper. He's got a photographer lined up and everything. I told him Panera Bread. Is that the best place?"

"Yep," Elizabeth said. "That's going to be our central meeting point, so everyone'll be there. You should talk to him, Hannah, since you're VP and Katie isn't here."

"Right." Hannah made herself smile. There was no reason to be nervous. It was just Brad's dad, not a reporter she'd never met before.

"What smells like apples?" Joy asked, interrupting Hannah's thoughts.

"Oh. My Grandma and I baked apple fritters last night. She gave us some to share." Hannah took a small bag off her lap. "They're like donuts but with fresh apples."

"Nice," Elizabeth said as Joy took one. "Let's eat them in the car before we go in."

Hannah stared out the window as another car pulled up. It was a small red car, so small it didn't have any backseat at all with a tiny trunk and a spoiler on the back. The passenger door opened, and Molly got out.

Hannah quickly looked the other way, hoping Molly hadn't seen her. "This is going to be awkward," she said under her breath to Brad.

"What is?" Joy butted in.

"Molly just got out of the car next to us." Hannah bit into her fritter, but even the sweet taste didn't cheer her up.

"Don't worry," Elizabeth said as Brad took Hannah's hand. "Katie told me that putting you two in the same group would be a bad idea. I made sure it didn't happen."

"Thanks." Hannah stared at her too-beat-up sneakers, wondering what her friends really thought. She let Brad put his arm around her.

When they were done eating, Elizabeth opened her trunk, and they all grabbed boxes of baskets to bring into the Community Room at Panera Bread and divide among the volunteers. Hannah and her friends put the boxes on a long table against the wall and then sat down at a smaller table in the center of the room.

Hannah couldn't help looking around to see where Molly was. She and Jen were at another table, holding hands. Molly looked away as soon as Hannah's eyes met hers. Jen put her arm around Molly and kissed her ear as if Hannah was the one who had hurt Molly instead of the other way around.

Elizabeth started the meeting and called Hannah up to the front of the room, and her nerves started going, worse than they had when she told everyone she'd been raped. She managed somehow to get through telling everyone about signing in for their community service hours and encouraging them to eat the snacks Panera had donated for them, but she couldn't wait to sit back down.

"And my dad's coming!" Brad said as Hannah started to walk away.

"Oh. Right," Hannah said. "Brad lined up some interviews with the *Cedarwood Courier*. Everyone sit tight and wait for him, and in the meantime, we'll give you your assignments." She hurried back to her seat.

Hannah's phone buzzed as Elizabeth came back up and started calling people's names. She had a new voicemail from an unknown number. She checked her visual voicemail, so she wouldn't have to listen to it.

> **Hey slut girl, you know you wanted it. Stop crying rape, you stupid bitch.**

Someone poked her. Hannah jerked her head up, startled.

"Sorry," Brad whispered. "My dad's here so you probably don't want the photographer catching you on the phone."

"Right." Hannah ran her fingers through her hair as she let her breath out, hoping she could keep herself together until after the interview.

HANNAH ANSWERED MR. Ashton's questions while the rest of her brain tried to work out what to do about the voicemail. She wondered if it was Jake or Nathan. It sounded like the kind of thing Nathan had been saying but at the same time it didn't, and Jake gave her just as bad a feeling. She guessed she'd have to listen to the message to see, but she wasn't sure she could stomach hearing it.

Toward the end of the interview, Mr. Ashton asked Hannah what motivated her to do things like this. Hannah meant to tell him that it was important to her to help other people, no more, no less. But somehow, she ended up telling him how hard it was for her when Mom was in the hospital and how she wanted to make things easier for other kids who weren't having a good Thanksgiving because of someone being sick. She was afraid Mr. Ashton would ask why Mom was in the hospital, but he just said what she was doing was noble and asked her about what the next activity after this was. Hannah told him about the Tree of Life they were having in December to encourage people not to drink and drive over the holidays, and then Mr. Ashton finally thanked her and went away to talk to the photographer.

"You were awesome!" Brad said, putting his arm around her. "That was so freaking brave, talking about your mom like that."

"If you say so." Hannah sighed.

Brad kissed her ear. "What's wrong? This should be, like, one of the happiest days of your life. I got you a ton of publicity, and we're doing something awesome for kids who don't have anything."

"This, that's what." Hannah thrust her phone at him. "I should be used to it by now but as usual I can't make myself not care."

Brad glanced at the message, his face darkening. "These fucking assholes ever gonna leave you alone?"

Hannah shrugged. "Like I said, I should be used to it." She bit her lip. "Want to listen to it for me and tell me if it's Nathan? I can't bring myself to do it."

"Whoever it is better have been smart enough to disguise their voice, or they're gonna answer to me."

"Don't! I told you, I hate that macho crap."

"Just saying how I feel. I wouldn't really do anything. Don't worry. Think I wanna take another ride in the back of a cop car?"

"I hope you're joking," Mr. Ashton interrupted, coming back just then. "Though what happened last summer is not something to joke about."

Brad's eyes flashed. "You know me, Dad. I can't help making everything a joke." Mr. Ashton raised his eyebrows and Brad said, "Someone's messing with Hannah. I was just saying I don't like it."

"Messing with her how?" Mr. Ashton asked.

Hannah had the same sinking feeling she had in the police station like she was being interrogated and forced to say things she wanted to keep to herself. "It's not a big deal," she said. "Someone left me a nasty voicemail. That's all. I'll just delete it."

"Wait," Mr. Ashton said. "I don't want to get into your business, but if someone's harassing you, that's serious. I don't want to see it escalate. Don't delete the voicemail. Let me hear it."

Hannah wanted to tell Mr. Ashton, "Thanks, but no thanks," but the words wouldn't come out. She felt like she was paralyzed even though she knew she wasn't.

Brad said, "We got it under control, Dad."

"No. You don't. Hannah is clearly scared to death. This is serious business, Brad. It's not the kind of thing two kids should be dealing with on their own." Mr. Ashton put his hand on Hannah's shoulder. "We have a few minutes before you have to leave. Come sit with me and tell me what's going on. Off the record. I promise."

"It's too much to go into," Hannah said, finding her voice at last. "S-something happened to me on Halloween, and ever since certain people have been bullying me." She could feel Molly staring at her from across the room. Great. She forced herself to hold her head up high. "This isn't the time to talk about it. Today is supposed to be about other people, not me. B-but I've been telling the world, and I even told the cops yesterday, so I guess I can tell you. A month ago, I was raped." She told him the rest of it, emphasizing how much Brad's support meant to her.

Mr. Ashton's eyes softened but his face hardened. "Oh, Hannah," he said. "I'm so sorry. Let me see the message you got. Please."

Hannah handed her phone over.

Mr. Ashton scowled when he read the message. "Looking at this with a reporter's eye, it occurs to me that this and your reporting the rape to the police yesterday may be connected. Someone may be trying to intimidate you out of pursuing this matter." He patted Hannah's shoulder. "Try to put it out of your mind until after this event is over. But if you need me to, I will go to the police station with you to report this latest incident and make sure they take it seriously."

Elizabeth came up to them ready to go before Hannah could answer, but Hannah was pretty sure her answer was No.

***

At the hospital, Hannah's group gave Thanksgiving baskets to families who had a kid in the hospital. They had a list of room numbers, and they came into each room and said 'Happy Thanksgiving' and handed the basket to whatever adult was in the room with the child. Most of the parents looked sad, but they managed watery smiles and thanked Hannah and her friends, and if their kids were able to, they made them say thank you too. One little boy hugged Hannah and wouldn't let go until his mom made him.

It was lunchtime by the time they got all the baskets delivered.

"That was awesome!" Brad said, jumping from the second to last step instead of going downstairs properly. "You see the smiles on some of those kids' faces?"

Elizabeth laughed. "You got bit by the community service bug, huh?"

"He sure did," Joy said.

"Wait 'til you see what we're doing next month," Hannah told him. "The Tree of Life is part of our holiday celebration. You'll definitely want to be there for that." She was feeling good, really good. This was more like the way things used to be: hanging out with a whole group of friends who were into the same kinds of things she was. No stupid drama like with Molly and Jen.

Joy wanted to go out to lunch to celebrate and everyone agreed, but then she asked, "What's Sierra up to? If she doesn't have plans, maybe she'll want to hang with us."

Hannah's stomach sank. "I'll ask her," she said, pushing her hair behind her ear, "but I don't know."

Joy frowned. "Don't tell me you had a fight with her too."

"Kind of," Hannah said, looking away. Her new friends probably thought she was a drama queen. Great. "I made a mistake that could backfire on her, and now she's not exactly talking to me." Joy and Elizabeth turned toward her. Hannah was stuck now. She couldn't get out of explaining this. She told them how Sierra didn't want to be involved with the cops and how she'd screwed up and told them her name by accident.

"She said she'd never forgive me if I did, and she hasn't called or texted since," Hannah said.

"She's not mad. Trust me," Joy said. "She's scared. Black people have a different experience with cops than white people do. We're guilty 'til proven innocent. For her, being a witness is a big risk because they'll find a way to make her the bad guy and if not her, her brother."

"But Dylan wasn't even there. He picked us up. I told them that."

"Doesn't matter. Black guys being accused of raping white women's a big part of our history."

Hannah bit her lip. This didn't feel right. She'd known Sierra a long time, and she'd never talked about people being prejudiced, ever. Besides, her fear was because of what Jake said. Wasn't it? But still, that cop had asked her about Dylan a million times. What if Joy was right, and Hannah had got him in trouble when he'd done nothing but try to help? She should have kept her big mouth shut.

She stared at her feet. She needed to talk to Sierra. If Sierra would even talk to her.

Elizabeth jingled her keys. "So. Lunch?"

"Sounds good," Joy said. "You guys in?"

"Two huge meals in one day!" Brad said. "Hell, yeah."

"Me too," Hannah said. "I'll text Sierra on the way."

Sierra answered her text as she slid into the car next to Brad. Hannah stared at her phone, her eyes widening.

> This is Sierra's mom. I am sorry but she is grounded until further notice. And I am calling your parents too. How DARE you cover for her with Jake and with this party, especially after what happened to you?

41 - A Line in the Sand

ANNAH'S PARENTS WERE sitting in the living room, their jaws set and stern looks on their faces, when she came home.

"Grandma wants you to help her in the kitchen," Eric said, "but she's going to have to wait a few minutes. Sit down, please."

Hannah sank into the easy chair across from the couch. "Sierra's mom called, didn't she?"

Mom nodded. "I only wish she'd come in person so I could have had the pleasure of throwing her out of my house. Be that as it may, she said some things that Eric feels - "

"Both of us really." Eric squeezed Mom's hand. "Sierra's mom had a lot to say about this boyfriend of Sierra's, and we hope you have the sense to stay away from him even if Sierra doesn't. But that's not our main concern. As you know, we've been worried all along that you're moving too fast with Brad, especially after what happened to you, and before we let you go to his house for dessert tonight we need to clear some things up."

"Like what?" Hannah's jaw was so tight that speaking hurt.

"Like," Mom said, "is it true he does drugs?"

"What? No!" A pulse started up behind Hannah's right eye. "Come on, Mom! You met him. You saw he was sober!"

"I think you're protesting a little too much," Eric said. "Now as much as we don't like Sierra, we seriously doubt she'd make up a story about Brad being a stoner out of whole cloth. So, let's try this again. What's the truth?"

Hannah's throat felt tight with anger. How DARE Sierra betray her like this, especially after she'd kept her mouth shut about Sierra dating Jake this whole time? She guessed it was revenge for her giving Sierra's name to the cops, but still.

"He used to smoke weed," she said weakly.

"Used to?" Mom crossed her arms. "How do you know he doesn't anymore?"

"Because I actually spend time with him instead of listening to rumors. Come on, Mom, you know he's good for me. And you should know more than anyone that people can change."

"I also know that people don't change unless something terrible happens. For me, it was swallowing a whole bottle of pills. What was it for Brad?"

Hannah stared at the ground, not wanting to betray Brad, but Eric said, "Mom asked you a question, and I would appreciate it if you answered it."

She wasn't five years old anymore, but whatever. They weren't going to leave her alone. She had to tell them the truth.

"He was arrested," she mumbled.

"Arrested," Mom said. "And this is the boy you love?"

Hannah's head jerked up. "Yes," she said, staring Mom in the eye. "It is."

Eric held up his hand. Again. "Whether you love Brad or not is not what worries us. It's that you seem to surround yourself with people who use poor judgment, and you've already been badly hurt once by going along with something you knew was a bad idea. Tell us this, Hannah. What would you do if Brad ever offered you weed?"

"He doesn't smoke anymore, so this is stupid. Besides, I don't do drugs! I'm Vice President of SADD, remember? And Brad joined because of me. He was super excited today after we delivered the baskets, and he's looking forward to working on the Tree of Life next month."

Eric and Mom looked at each other. Eric said, "Well, that's certainly encouraging. But it isn't enough, Hannah. You've made a series of poor decisions lately, and we need to know that we can trust you. And on top of that, you're spending too much time with Brad. Some ex-stoner that you think you're going to save isn't the answer to your depression. So, you're not going over there for dessert and from now on, you'll only spend limited time with him, and only when his parents can supervise you."

Hannah jumped up. Stupid Sierra, making all this trouble. "That's what you think. I'm not eight anymore, and you aren't going to control what I do. Keep it up, and I'll take Grandma up on her offer to move to Florida. Is that what you want?"

Mom's face crumpled. "You don't mean that," she said.

"Just try me." Hannah's head was buzzing, and a little tiny part of her brain was screaming at her that she was going way too far, and she'd better stop. But she couldn't make herself listen. The best she could do was say, "I'm getting changed and then I'm going down to the lobby to meet Brad. Thanks to you, I'm not spending Thanksgiving here at all." She turned and ran to her room, slamming the door as hard as she could.

She could hear her parents talking to Grandma, but she couldn't hear what they were saying. *Hannah's worse than we thought,* maybe. *This is how it started with you, Debra. You'd better cancel Thanksgiving and get her to the hospital right away.*

She sank down onto her bed, covering her eyes with her hands and trying desperately to push the tears back. "I'm not crazy," she said to herself. "I'm not!" She wanted to call Brad and tell him to come get her, but she couldn't because she couldn't let him see her like this, couldn't let him see that she was totally broken down because then he might leave her and she'd really have nothing.

She took out her phone anyway, sniffing hard to try to get herself back under control, and stared at it. She dabbed her eyes, telling herself to stop crying and stop acting weak. And no matter what, do NOT miss Molly because Molly was not her friend anymore, and she was just going to have to figure things out without her.

She could start by putting on the clothes she'd planned to wear to Brad's in the first place, she decided. And she did, making sure to put the t-shirt and jeans she'd been wearing in her laundry basket instead of leaving them on the floor. Then she went into the bathroom and washed her face before coming back to do her makeup.

She nodded at herself in the mirror. Mouse was gone, and a beautiful girl with striking gray eyes and dark hair that fell in soft waves onto her shoulders had taken her place. She stared at herself a while longer, smiling slightly, and then texted Brad before she went to face her family.

***

Grandma insisted on taking Hannah into the kitchen to help her cook while she was waiting for Brad. She had a ton of ingredients laid out on the kitchen table: cottage cheese, eggs, raisins, and apples. "I'm already boiling the water for the noodles," she said. "I need you to put everything else together."

Hannah shuffled her feet over to the drawer where Mom kept all her measuring cups.

"No, no measuring cups," Grandma said. "Just eyeball it. If you ask my opinion, a real cook doesn't get too caught up in following the recipe exactly."

No one asked your opinion, Hannah thought, but she didn't want to be rude, so she didn't say so. She dumped half a canister of cottage cheese into a bowl and hoped it wasn't too much.

Grandma nodded approvingly as Hannah broke a few eggs into the cottage cheese and whisked it together. "You know," she said, "when your mother first met your stepfather and decided to take you to New York to be closer to him, I fought it with everything I had. I thought she was running away like she'd done so many times before, only this time her choices could land you in a bad situation. I pulled out all the stops. I even threatened to sue her for full custody."

"You did?" Hannah opened a can of mixed fruit and went to the sink to drain it.

"I did, and it only made her more determined to leave." Grandma sighed. "One could hardly blame me, I suppose. It was all too easy to love you, my darling, and I didn't want to ever see you hurt, even if it meant severing the very fragile ties between me and your mother forever." She dumped a box of noodles into the pot of boiling water. "There is a kind of delicious irony in you threatening to run away to live with me because she doesn't approve of your choice of boyfriend, but I cannot in good conscience encourage it."

"I know." Hannah stared down into the concoction she was creating. "I said that to hurt her."

"Oh, I know you did. I told her history is repeating itself in front of her eyes. Stick to your guns about Brad, *sheifale*. Your parents will see that they're wrong about him eventually. I did about Eric."

Hannah thought she heard a soft knock on the front door. She dropped her whisk and hurried to the front room.

In the hall, Brad's dad had his hand on Brad's shoulder. "Brad told me you had some concerns about his past," he told Mom, "and I thought perhaps it would help you to hear direct from the horse's mouth what we've been doing to make sure he stays on the right path."

"Dad!" Brad said. He looked over Mom's shoulder at Hannah. "I told him this was totally unnecessary, but do parents ever listen?"

"Not helping your case," his dad said. "May we come in?"

"Yes, of course." Mom turned to Hannah. "Are you and Grandma done in the kitchen?"

"No," Hannah said, "but I want to make sure you don't twist what Brad's dad says all out of shape."

"Here we go with the exaggeration again," Eric said. "Hannah seems to enjoy casting us as villains who live to make her miserable."

"She's sixteen," Mr. Ashton said. "That's her job." He patted Brad's shoulder. "Go to the kitchen. I'll do my best not to say anything too embarrassing."

Hannah took Brad's hand to show him that she was on his side and they went to the kitchen. She strained her ears to try to hear what Brad's dad was saying to Mom and Eric, but they were keeping their voices low. She could only hear bits and pieces. Mr. Ashton said something about Brad's mom being on the same page even though they were divorced and that they made Brad go to therapy after he was arrested. Mom said something

Hannah couldn't hear at all, though she was sure she was saying that she and Eric made Hannah go to therapy too. Later, Mr. Ashton said he thought Hannah and Brad were good for each other, and he hoped Mom and Eric would give Brad a chance. Grandma opened the oven just then and told Hannah to put the kugel in, so she couldn't hear Mom's answer.

When the kugel was done and cooling on the counter, Mr. Ashton stuck his head in and said that Mom had invited him and Brad to dinner. He was going home so that Brad's mom wouldn't be offended, but Brad could stay.

"Does that mean Hannah's parents get I'm not a monster?" Brad asked.

"No one thought you were a monster," Mr. Ashton said, "but yes, I think I smoothed things over." He said goodbye to Brad and Hannah and left.

Brad picked at the top of the kugel. Hannah watched him, wondering what Mr. Ashton had said to Mom and Eric and whether they really were going to leave her and Brad alone.

THERE WAS SO much food on the table that Hannah could skip the turkey without anyone noticing. Grandma had made all sorts of side dishes on top of the stuffing and mashed potatoes that Mom and Eric had made: potato latkes, which were pancakes made out of potato that Jewish people usually only ate at Chanukah; a spinach quiche; and of course the noodle kugel, which she made Mom put all the way on the other side of the table so that it wouldn't be anywhere near the turkey.

"I forgot how much you used to cook for us," Hannah told Grandma after she'd had her third piece of noodle kugel. "Oh my gosh, I've missed it. Not that you're not a good cook too, Mom. Grandma's food is just different."

"Oh, stop," Mom said. "We both know you're the one who inherited her cooking ability. I can follow a recipe but that's about it."

"Hannah used to do all the cooking," Eric added, patting his mouth with his napkin. "Before . . . you know."

Couldn't they have one night off from talking about that? "Maybe I'll have time to cook again soon," Hannah said weakly.

"You finished?" Brad asked, patting her hand. "Mom'll freak out if we show up too late."

Hannah had been picking at the edges of the kugel pan. She dropped her fork, guiltily. "Oh. Yeah."

Brad took her plate and his. "Anyone else want me to take their plate into the kitchen?"

"Don't be silly," Mom said. "You're our guest. Let us do that."

"Nah," Brad said. "What kind of guest leaves the house worse than it was when he walked in? Be right back." He kissed the top of Hannah's head and took her plate and his into the kitchen.

"He really is a nice boy," Mom said in a low voice. "It's a shame he got caught up with drugs last year."

"Just weed, Mom." Hannah also kept her voice low even though she was sure Brad knew they were talking about him.

"Even so, he could have had real problems. It's only by the grace of God he didn't end up in juvenile hall."

Hannah glared at her so hard her eyes hurt. "What did his dad say?"

"Nothing earth-shattering," Eric said. "But I'm glad he came over. It makes us feel a lot better to know Brad's parents are involved in his life." He took a sip of his wine. "They're just as concerned about his choices as we are about yours. Nobody wants to see either of you ruin your lives. So, we'll leave you guys alone about dating. But please don't let Brad's opinions replace the voice in your head. If he tries to talk you into doing something you know you shouldn't, you need to stand up to him."

I'm not Mouse. I'm not as weak as you think I am. "He's not going to, but whatever."

"I hope not," Eric said, "but I want you to be prepared just in case."

Brad came back just then, so Hannah had to settle for rolling her eyes.

"I don't wanna rush you," Brad said to Grandma, "but the longer I'm over here, the more freaked out my mom's gonna be so. . . "

"Of course." Grandma put down her wine glass.

Hannah frowned. "Are you sure you can drive?"

"She's only had half a glass," Mom said.

"No, Hannah's right," Grandma said. "I should set a good example. Debra, do you mind if we let Brad borrow - "

"Absolutely not!" Mom said. "He's not covered by our insurance and anyway, a teenager out on Thanksgiving with all those drunk drivers . . . no."

Hannah's phone rang. Thank God! That would get her out of this stupid conversation. Better yet, it was Dylan, so that solved two problems at once.

"Hey," she said, answering it. "You have good timing. Brad and I need a ride."

"That's good," Dylan said, "'cause I got my mom to relent and let Sierra out for half an hour, so you and her can straighten some things out."

***

Sierra was sitting on the bench in the lobby when Brad and Hannah got downstairs. She looked weirdly small to Hannah like she was trying to shrink into herself. Her eyes flitted to Hannah, then away. "Gonna give me hell for badmouthing your boyfriend?"

"Uh-uh." Hannah couldn't be mad at Sierra, not when she seemed so fragile. "We have a lot to talk about, but I'm not throwing you away. Don't worry." She sat down next to Sierra and turned her head over her shoulder. "Is it okay if I talk to Sierra alone for a minute?"

Brad nodded. "Just so you know, she's way more forgiving than I am," he told Sierra. "You better treat her right." He squeezed Hannah's shoulder. "Text me when you're ready."

Sierra stared at the ground as Brad walked away. "I deserved that," she said. "I tried to ruin you guys on purpose."

Hannah shrugged. *It's okay,* she wanted to say, but that was Mouse's idea and not really how she felt. "You were getting back at me, I guess." She patted Sierra's hand. "I'm sorry I told the cops on you. I didn't mean to. It just happened. Like what Molly did, I guess."

Sierra stiffened. "Do me a favor and keep Molly's name out of your mouth. Fucking phony do-gooder."

"Wow. Okay." Hannah didn't know what to say. "I figured you were madder at me than her, but I guess not."

"Nope." Sierra hugged herself. "I was pissed at you, but I was a shitty friend to you. So, I kind of deserved what I got. I-it was so weird, Hannah. It was like I was drunk even when I was sober because I thought so much off-the-wall crap about you. I thought you drove Jake away on purpose because you were jealous or something and when you told Dylan on me, I figured you were twisting the knife in more. B-but now you're willing to sit with me when I totally tried to screw you over and I . . . I don't know what was wrong with me."

"I do." Hannah bit her lip, not wanting Sierra to get defensive. "Jake happened. That's what. Remember in that stupid play we just had to read how Iago acted like he was Othello's best friend, but he was telling him a bunch of lies? That's what Jake did to you."

"Jake's no Iago," Sierra said. "I mean, yeah, he can be an asshole, but he can also be so sweet."

Hannah twisted her ring some more, not wanting to say the thing that had just popped into her head. Finally, she decided to go for it anyway. "Did Dylan tell you about the message Jake sent me?"

"Yeah. Sorry. Like I said, sometimes he's an asshole." Sierra stared down at the ground. "Anyway, Dylan made me tell our parents about the party. He said it was better they hear it from me than find out when the cops show up. They were livid. My dad got me and Dylan a lawyer in case they question us, but he's determined to make my life a living hell. As far as he's concerned, Dad Jail should be worse than if I actually went to jail. I'm only out 'cause my mom gave me a reprieve while he wasn't home."

"I'm sorry."

"Don't be. I'm the one who's an idiot." Sierra sighed. "My mom has my phone, so I don't know if Jake's been calling me or not."

"You still want to be with him after everything that happened?"

Sierra rubbed the spot on her arm where Jake had grabbed her. "He left a bruise. I keep pressing on it to remind myself I'm better off without him, but it doesn't work. I still miss him anyway. I'm sorry I'm so fucked up, Hannah. I mean to be a good friend, I swear, but something's wrong with me."

"Nothing's wrong with you." Hannah put her arm around Sierra. "Maybe you're just used to Jake being there."

"I guess. Dylan said you need him to take you and Brad somewhere?"

Hannah nodded. "Brad's dad invited me for dessert."

"That's cool." Sierra smiled even though there were tears in her eyes. "At least one of us has a date for Thanksgiving, right?" She got up, ignoring Hannah's outstretched arms. "Come on. Let's get you there before Dylan's gotta run me back."

***

Brad's mom had a real house, not just an apartment, and Hannah couldn't help thinking about the walk down the block to Jake's the night of the Halloween party as she and Brad got out of Dylan's car. Everyone's shades had been drawn, and it had made her feel so isolated and alone even before anything happened.

"You're awful quiet," Brad said, taking Hannah's hand. "Nervous about meeting my mom?"

"Kind of," Hannah said. She didn't feel right letting Brad think that was the only thing bothering her and added, "I have a lot on my mind."

"I bet." Brad squeezed her hand. "You don't have to stay long if you don't want. Just say hey to my mom and sister, and then I'll see what I can do about begging my dad for his car to take you home."

"No," Hannah said. "That's what Mouse would do, but I'm not her anymore." Brad's eyes clouded over. Hannah said, "That's what Molly used to call me."

"Yeah, I know. I never liked that freaking nickname. It wasn't you."

"It used to be, I guess. Mouse is—was—super scared of the world. She always ran away and hid in her room instead of doing anything she wanted to do."

Brad squeezed Hannah's hand. "I think I ran across her a couple times. She freaked out about us dating, and I had to keep promising her I was cool with taking it slow."

Hannah's face flushed. "Yeah. Sorry about that."

"It's cool." Brad stroked Hannah's hair. "You being shy didn't turn me off one bit. I just had to learn to be patient for once in my life. That's all." He kissed her ear. "Come on. Let's go meet my family and get it over with."

Hannah took his hand, feeling more and more like a little girl as they came into the house. She couldn't stop thinking about Jake's party, how the music was too loud and how everyone was milling around looking like they were half out of it. *This isn't that*, she thought, following Brad into the living room. *This isn't that!*

Brad introduced Hannah as his "amazing girlfriend" to his sister, Emily, who was a few inches shorter than him and who had blond hair with cranberry streaks in it and a suntan Hannah was jealous of.

Emily was watching a football game on TV with Brad's dad who was drinking a beer. His mom came into the room and turned the TV off, then asked Hannah to come in the kitchen with her to help her with dessert.

When she gave Brad's mom a container of apple fritters, his mom said she was sad that it was the only homemade dessert on the table. Nobody really came to eat dessert anyway. They all filled their plates and went back to the TV room, and Brad's mom complained to Hannah about his dad drinking a beer and Emily watching TV when there was company. So, Hannah didn't feel like staying and was relieved when Brad asked his dad for the car keys so that he could take her home.

"Dessert sure was a bust, huh?" Brad said when he dropped her off. "Sorry my family's not cool like yours."

"It's fine," Hannah said. She reached for Brad's hand, wanting to give him something because he seemed so upset. "Come on. I want to show you something."

Hannah took Brad to the playground. "I like to sit on the swings when no one's around. It helps me feel better when I'm upset."

"Wanna see who can swing higher?" Brad grinned.

Hannah pushed her hair behind her ear. "I don't know. I don't want to fall."

"You won't," Brad promised. "I won't let you." He reached for her hand. "Come on. Let's swing together."

Hannah clung so hard to the metal chain with her free hand that it hurt, but she pumped her legs in time with Brad's anyway. They swung higher and higher, and Hannah was sure they were going to fall or else knock over the entire swing set, but nothing horrible happened. She actually felt sad when she and Brad came back down to Earth so he could go home.

THE WEEKEND PASSED quickly and before she knew it, Hannah was in the car with Mom, taking Grandma back to the airport. Before she left, Grandma told Hannah that if she felt scared or overwhelmed, she wanted her to remember that Grandma believed in her and try to feel it all the way on the other end of the East Coast.

Hannah reminded herself of that when she woke up on Monday, missing her and not feeling like going back to school at all.

When she got there, Hannah went to the office with her friends first thing to talk to Mrs. Garcia about the assembly. Mrs. Parker was talking to a woman Hannah had never seen before when the girls came in. The woman was tall, with blonde hair cut at an angle so that it framed her oval face. She had pale white skin and deep-set blue eyes. She reminded Hannah of the way Mom had looked when Hannah was a little girl.

"Hannah!" Mrs. Parker smiled as she turned around. "I'm glad you're here. I was about to text Mrs. Wolfe to send you down when you get to homeroom." She lowered her voice. "This is Detective Lindstrom from the Special Victims Division. Go with her into Mrs. Jefferson's office, and I'll make sure you have privacy." Mrs. Jefferson was the assistant principal, who Hannah guessed wasn't here yet.

"Oh." Hannah pushed her hair behind her ear. "Okay. But what about our meeting with Mrs. Garcia? You know, about the assembly."

"We can handle it," Elizabeth said. "We have copies of the agenda."

"Yeah," Katie said. "You do this. We'll do that."

Hannah's stomach sank with disappointment. She'd worked so hard on the agenda, and she wanted to be the one to explain it to Mrs. Garcia. But she was outnumbered, she guessed. And anyway, this detective had gone out of her way to meet her at school, so it would be rude to make her wait. "Okay."

"Hey," Katie said. "Good luck."

Hannah made herself smile. "You too." She watched as her friends went into Mrs. Garcia's office, missing Molly more than ever. But those days were gone, and Hannah had an interview with the cops to get through. She made herself stop thinking about Molly and follow Detective Lindstrom into Mrs. Jefferson's office.

While Detective Lindstrom opened her file, Hannah twisted her hair around and around her finger, trying not to think about the message Jake had sent her. Sierra would be furious if she told the detective about it, but maybe it was the right thing to do.

Detective Lindstorm made her tell her all over again what happened. The only question that was different this time was that she wanted to know if there were any other boys Hannah's age at the party or if they were all Jake's age or older.

Hannah crossed her arms across her chest. "I don't know. I mean, I only met a few, and they were all too old for me. But someone from school must have been there because people were spreading rumors about me getting drunk and having sex when I came back to school on Monday." She blinked back tears, sick of having to tell this story over and over and sicker of feeling bad about it. "I'm sorry I went, okay? I know I didn't have any business at a party like that. I should never have agreed to go."

Detective Lindstrom handed her a tissue even though she wasn't crying. "I don't care that you went to this party. I care about what happened there. It sounds like there were a lot of older boys and a lot of alcohol and drugs flowing freely. That was a bad situation waiting to happen, and I have a feeling you might not be the only girl who was victimized that night."

Hannah bit her lip, thinking of Sierra. "It was fun at first," she said weakly. "I played video games with this guy, and he didn't care that I wasn't drinking."

"Jamie?" Detective Lindstrom asked, checking her notes. "Did he tell you anything we might be able to use to identify him, like where he went to school or where he worked?"

Hannah told her that Jamie went to Cedarwood Community. Detective Lindstrom wrote that down and moved on to Jake. She asked if Hannah had ever found out his last name and when she hadn't, she said she'd have to find out from Sierra. "I'll let Mrs. Parker know we're looking for her. In the meantime, describe Jake for me."

"Gross." The word slipped out of Hannah's mouth before she knew she'd even thought it. She shuddered. "I didn't like him from the second we walked in. He smelled like beer, and he was flirting with me when he was supposed to be with Sierra. He kept calling me Hot Hannah, and it made me feel weird. And then in the bowling alley . . . " Hannah hesitated, still not wanting to betray Sierra, but she couldn't let Mouse win that one. Jake had hurt Sierra enough, and Hannah too.

She told Detective Lindstrom everything: how uncomfortable Jake had made her feel, how sure she was that he was hurting Sierra, and how he said they were both immature because nobody agreed with him that Hannah's rape was no big deal.

Detective Lindstrom wrote it all down. "Well, he's wrong about that," she said. "Your rape is a big deal, and if he had anything to do with it, he is going to face some consequences." She leaned forward. "Hannah, you said Jake was hurting Sierra. Do you think he ever did to her what someone did to you?"

Hannah gasped. "That's one thing he didn't do to her. I don't think, anyway." She played with her phone, thinking, then nodded to herself. If Jake was sending her nasty voicemails, who knew what else he might do? "He sent me this," she said, showing the visual voicemail to the detective. "My boyfriend's dad said I should report it."

Detective Lindstrom's jaw got tighter and tighter as she read it. "I'm going to forward this to my phone, okay?"

"I guess." Hannah watched while Detective Lindstrom did. "Do you have any more questions for me?"

"I do actually. I want to go through what happened the next morning again."

Hannah sank back into her seat, her heart pounding. "'K."

Detective Lindstrom made her tell the story again of how she learned she'd been raped, interrupting every now and then to ask a question. She asked a lot of questions about Dylan: how long Hannah had known him, whether it made sense to her that he hadn't taken her to the hospital right away, why she believed him when he said he thought she'd been raped.

"Dylan had nothing to do with this," Hannah said. "He wasn't at the party, and he felt bad that he thought I was drunk when he picked us up."

"Just covering all the bases," Detective Lindstrom said, but Hannah didn't believe her.

Detective Lindstrom asked her some more questions about the hospital and what they did for her there and made her sign a form giving the hospital permission to give the evidence they'd saved to the police department. Then she asked her about the bullying. Hannah didn't know what that had to do with anything, but she told her about the things Nathan said and did anyway.

By the end of it, Hannah wanted to go back home and go back to bed. Her body felt so heavy that she didn't see how she was going to go down the hall to her locker, never mind get through a whole day of school.

"Do you think you'll be able to do anything?" she asked.

"Well, this won't be an easy case. The good news is you went to the hospital as soon as possible after the incident, so they were able to collect a lot of physical evidence. Hopefully, we get a DNA match once we get ahold of a suspect. But in a situation like this where there were a lot of people going in and out and you don't remember enough for us to go on . . . it could take a while. Now we're going to talk to Sierra and her brother and see what light they can shed on this, but I'm not hopeful, especially if Sierra doesn't cooperate. If I were you I'd try to get her to see that this isn't the time to be loyal to her boyfriend, 'cause chances are he committed a serious crime against you, and you're not gonna get justice unless she helps us track Jake down."

**

Hannah's friends met her in the cafeteria at lunchtime. They insisted on taking her to the McDonalds across the street to celebrate her talking to the cops. It annoyed Hannah that they thought that was anything to celebrate, but she agreed anyway.

As they were walking through the cafeteria, Nathan blocked her path. "What the hell, slut?" he snapped. "Why'd you tell the cops maybe I raped you? Like I'd even want to touch your dirty ass."

"I didn't, first of all," Hannah said, "but maybe if you didn't keep messing with me - "

"I'm not a fucking rapist!" Nathan shouted, so loud that people sitting at nearby tables turned their heads. "Just cause you can't take a joke - "

"A joke?" Hannah's voice rose despite her best efforts. "A joke? That's what you call reading my diary aloud in front of the whole school and posting photos of me and Brad on Instagram without our permission? That's what I told the cops because it's true. If they thought anything else, you did it to yourself by being an asshole."

"You shouldn't have told them anything, you stupid bitch. You're gonna be sorry you were ever born!" Nathan stormed away.

"Wow," Katie said. She put her arm around Hannah who was shaking even though she kept telling herself not to let Nathan get to her like that. "Here, come sit down a second and try to forget him."

Hannah let her lead her to a table. She didn't understand why she wasn't mad that Katie didn't stand up for her while Nathan was screaming at her. She would have been livid if Molly had been there and not said a word to defend her.

"I can't believe that asshole," Hannah said, too upset to care whether her friends approved of her language or not. "Who the hell does he think he is?"

"Forget him," Sierra said. She pushed her glasses further up on her face. "Come on, let me buy you a strawberry milkshake."

"I guess." Hannah didn't see how a milkshake would help anything, but she was too tired to argue.

As the girls got up, Mrs. Parker came up to them. "Oh good. I caught you before you went out."

"It's our lunch period," Hannah said, "we're allowed."

"No one said you aren't." Mrs. Parker lowered her voice. "You're needed in the office, Sierra. A police detective wants to talk to you."

Sierra's eyes were wide with fear. "My dad said not to talk to cops without a lawyer."

"You can tell the detective that when you get there. Mrs. Garcia said to come get you."

Sierra turned her head over her shoulder. "Meet me at McDonald's. This won't take very long cause I have nothing to say."

Hannah hoped she was right.

44 – Trying to Start Over

HANNAH TRIED TO have a good time at lunch with her friends, but it was impossible. She kept turning her head over her shoulder to see if Sierra was coming, and she had no idea what her hamburger tasted like after she ate it because she wasn't paying attention. The longer it went on, the more scared she was that Sierra was in trouble, and it was her fault. She should have listened to her and kept her name out of it, or better yet, not told the cops at all.

But then she walked into English and Sierra was already in her seat. Thank God!

"Did they just let you go?" she whispered.

Sierra nodded without turning to look at Hannah. Her hands were shaking as she took her glasses off and wiped them on her shirt.

"What happened?" Hannah put her hand on Sierra's shoulder.

Sierra pulled away. "Nothing. I'm being a big baby. No wonder Jake thinks I'm immature." She laughed bitterly. "He should be glad how I tried to stand up for him though. That detective didn't like me. I could tell, and when I didn't want to help her pin what happened to you on him, she about lost it." Her eyes flashed. "I TOLD her I wasn't talking to her, but she had to make me feel like crap, telling me if I didn't, the guy who raped you would get off scot-free, and it'd all be my fault."

Hannah picked at her bracelet, not knowing what to say. "I'm sorry. I wanted someone to do something about what happened to me, I didn't mean for you to get interrogated."

"Yeah, I know. Too bad I don't have my phone to call my dad with. Not that he'd help." Sierra sighed. "I wish Jake was here."

Hannah bit her lip to stop herself from blurting out that Sierra had said the other day that Jake was bad for her. "They tried to ask me if he'd done anything to you like what happened to me."

Sierra stiffened. "You'd better have told them 'No', cause he didn't." She stared straight ahead. "Anything we did, I wanted. I swear I did. And we didn't go that far anyway, he said he couldn't even though I was jailbait."

What an asshole! "Not even the night of the party?"

"No! I didn't want to, so we didn't. All right?" Sierra tapped her pen against her desk. "I'm not a slut! Don't you dare say that I am."

"Of course not." Hannah patted Sierra's hand.

Mr. Collins came in then and put a journal question on the board, but Hannah didn't bother to see what it was before she took out her journal. She had way too much on her mind to care.

***

By the time school ended for the day, a million new rumors were floating around about Hannah, probably thanks to Nathan. People shouted stuff in her face about being a snitch and some people screamed, "MAKING FALSE POLICE REPORTS IS

A CRIME!" when they passed her in the halls. A few people even bumped her hard enough with their shoulders or elbows to hurt, but there was no way she could prove it wasn't an accident, so she said nothing.

She understood how Katie used to feel about going to her locker, she thought as she opened hers, looking over her shoulder to make sure no one was planning on shoving her into it. She got her books as quickly as she could and slammed her locker shut, then double-checked the lock.

When she turned around, Molly was standing behind her. Hannah gasped so hard that it felt like a hiccup got stuck in her throat. "Oh my God. I didn't see you come up."

"Clearly." Molly twisted her ring. "Um, are you okay?"

"I will be as soon as I catch my breath." Hannah swung her backpack over her shoulder.

"I mean in general." Molly hurried to catch up with Hannah. "I. . . I heard what Nathan said to you and how some people have been treating you, and, um, I was worried."

Hannah froze. "I thought you don't want to be friends anymore."

"So, I can't worry?" Molly's voice rose. "Look. Obviously, we grew apart, but we were friends a long time, and I still care about you."

"When Jen's not around, you mean." Hannah grabbed tight to the banister as she went down the steps. "Whenever she is, you don't care about anything but what you can get out of me."

"THAT IS NOT TRUE!" Molly ran after Hannah. "Hannah, please . . . "

"Please what?" Hannah crossed her arms. "Please act like you're my best friend when you haven't acted like it for a long time? Telling Sierra was an accident. I get that. But telling my grandma you thought I was bipolar wasn't and . . . "

"I told you. I was trying to help."

"And telling me you were done when I tried to apologize to you wasn't either." Hannah bit her lip. "And on top of all that, you never stood up for me, Molly. Not once since this started. You didn't even tell Nathan off on Instagram, never mind when you saw him bullying me in person."

"What good would that have done? He wasn't going to listen."

"That's not the point! Even if it wasn't really going to help at least you would have been on my side!"

"I was on your side! I just didn't want to give him the satisfaction of seeing he got to us. That's what he feeds off of, don't you get that?" Molly crossed her arms. "Look, that's all in the past. There's no point in arguing about it now. Can't we let bygones be bygones and just, I don't know, start again?"

Hannah hesitated. She'd waited forever for Molly to come around, but something in her didn't want to let her off the hook so soon. "Maybe," she said coldly. She turned away, ignoring the voice in her head telling her that she was being mean for no reason. "I have to go. I have therapy." She hurried across the campus to the pick-up circle.

***

Therapy didn't make Hannah feel any better. Olivia said she read the journal pages and asked her what she wanted to discuss about them, but Hannah was too chicken to ask whether Olivia thought she was bipolar. So, Mouse won but not really because Olivia brought it up.

She said she didn't think Hannah was, which Hannah guessed was good news, but then she read this checklist aloud and made Hannah say 'Yes' or 'No' to each one. Hannah had none of the manic symptoms except racing thoughts and restlessness, but she had almost all the depressed ones. Olivia said that wasn't surprising and explained that Hannah's moods might be all over the place because of what happened to her.

All of that took up almost the whole session, so Hannah didn't have time to talk about the latest Molly drama. She left feeling more annoyed at the world than ever. It was a waste of a perfectly good hour she could have spent with Brad.

The next few days were more of the same. Sierra told her that Dylan had gone with a lawyer to answer the police's questions. Other than that, she heard nothing about her case. She and Molly settled into a cold truce, working silently together in lab but otherwise not talking, and Molly stopped staring at her all the time. Hannah missed it but didn't tell her friends that when they said they were glad Molly wasn't bothering them anymore.

On Friday, Mrs. Garcia finally gave the girls their go-ahead for the assembly. Hannah and her friends went out to lunch at the pizza place to celebrate, but Hannah wished that Molly was there even though it was her own fault that she wasn't.

Joy kicked her under the table. "Hey! This is supposed to be a celebration."

"Yeah," Katie said. "You have a lot to be happy about, especially today. This assembly is going to change the world, and you're a big part of that."

"I know, but . . . " Hannah sipped her soda to buy herself time. "I can't explain," she said weakly. "I guess I shouldn't care, but so many people being assholes is really getting to me and God knows what Nathan's going to do."

"Fuck him," Brad said. "He can't do anything to you, Hannah. Okay?"

"Nobody's stopped him from everything else he's done to me." Hannah bit her straw. "I wish I didn't care what he does, but I do. And if I can't deal now, how am I ever gonna be able to speak in front of the whole school? Someone's going to shout something, and I'm going to melt into a puddle." God, she was such a coward. She'd never hated anyone as much as she hated the girl who lived in her head.

"You can do it," Katie said. "You did that day in SADD, remember?"

"Yeah," Elizabeth added. "And you'll have all of us supporting you."

"Thanks." Hannah pushed her hair behind her ear. "I miss Molly. I should have forgiven her when I had a chance."

Elizabeth said, "She's the one who decided to be a bitch."

"Yeah," Katie said. "She could have been friends with all of us instead of shutting you out except when she needed something."

"I guess," Hannah said.

Joy picked up her glass. "Toast, everyone. Out with the old, in with the new."

Hannah raised her soda cup and clinked with the others even though she didn't feel like it.

***

There was a big crowd of people in the hall, standing around and blocking the path to Hannah's locker when she tried to go after lunch.

"Something must have happened," Brad said.

"Nothing to do but push through anyway, I guess." Hannah grabbed Brad's hand and started to do just that.

Molly broke away from the crowd and came up to them. "Um, Hannah," she said, and Hannah knew her well enough to know she was struggling to keep her voice from shaking, "you don't want to go to your locker right now."

"Why?" Brad demanded. "What the hell did you do?"

"Not me," Molly said. "Nathan, I think." She bit her lip. "He graffitied it, and it's really ugly and mean. You don't want to see it. Trust me."

"Yeah, I do," Hannah said, even though she thought Molly might be right. "I might need to take pictures of it."

"What for?"

"'Cause this stops here," Brad said, "that's what. This asshole's gotten away with too much as it is. Now, get the hell out of our way."

Hannah bit her lip, not liking the way Brad was talking to Molly even though she wasn't sure why she cared. "Can you not?" she said to Brad. "Or you either," she added, turning toward Molly. "Look, friends or not friends, you were nice enough to tell me Nathan did something, and I get that you're trying to help. And the last thing I need is you and Brad at each other's throats. So can the two of you declare a truce 'til this is settled?"

"No problem," Molly said. "As long as you declare one with Jen."

"Jen and I aren't fighting, but whatever." Hannah turned toward Brad. "You see Sierra anywhere? I want her."

Molly scowled. Brad said "Over there, trying to get through. I'll go help her, okay?" He kissed the top of Hannah's head. Hannah kind of wanted him here, but she wanted Sierra too. So, she let him go.

Molly said, "So. . . "

Hannah looked away. "I need to deal with my locker before we talk."

"Right." Molly pushed her hair behind her ear. "I really am sorry about everything. I guess we'll never be best friends again, but if you still want to be friends at all. . . "

Hannah did. More than anything. "Maybe," she said.

Brad came back with Sierra.

"You wouldn't believe . . . " Sierra began. Her eyes widened. "What is SHE doing here?"

"Helping with the Nathan situation," Hannah said. "We declared a truce. Now help me get through this crowd, so we can see what the hell he did."

"Right. Okay."

Brad took Hannah's hand and they started pushing through the crowd, Molly and Sierra following behind them. Someone said, "Here comes the slut now!" and a few people laughed. If anyone stood up for Hannah, she couldn't hear them over everyone else whispering and laughing.

When they got to Hannah's locker, it took her a few seconds to take in what she was looking at. At first, all she saw was spray paint all over her locker. Then she saw that someone had sprayed: *LYING SLUT!!!* in big letters going diagonally across the door. The vandal, whoever he was, had taped a photo to her locker, too, underneath the message, a horrible photo that might have been photoshopped but might have been from when she was out of it. The photo showed her lying on a couch. A guy who she couldn't make out was lying on top of her, kissing her neck. The guy was naked. On the bottom of the photo, someone had written in marker:

YOU WANTED THIS.

H ANNAH BACKED AWAY, feeling like she'd been punched in the stomach. "That's not me," she managed to say. "Is it?"

She reached for the photo to take it off her locker, but Brad said, "Don't, okay?"

"People are staring at it," Hannah said, her voice breaking. "I want it gone."

Brad put his arm around her. "I know. But . . ."

"Brad's right," Molly said. "It's evidence, Hannah, let the cops take care of taking it down."

"T-the cops?" Hannah felt like her brain was wrapped in gauze. It was impossible to think. "D-do we need. . . "

"Of course we do," Molly said. "If that isn't photoshopped, they can use it to find the person who raped you. And anyway, vandalizing your locker like that is against the law."

Hannah nodded, but she was looking at Sierra, who looked away as she wiped her glasses on her shirt.

A pair of heels echoed on the floor. "All right, people," Mrs. Garcia said. "Why are we all standing around when the bell's about to ring?"

"C-cause," Hannah said. "L-look what someone did . . . " She stared down at her sneakers. She didn't want Mrs. Garcia to see that terrible photo. No, that wasn't true. She didn't want to CARE that Mrs. Garcia saw it.

"My God," Mrs. Garcia said. She patted Hannah's shoulder, then wheeled around, suddenly fierce. "Who in this big crowd of people saw the person responsible for this? Nobody? Move along then, or I'll assume the guilty party is among you and take you all to my office for questioning."

People grumbled, but they moved. Mrs. Garcia turned toward Hannah and her friends. "I'm so sorry this happened, Hannah. Let's go to my office, okay?"

Hannah's heart pounded. She looked from Molly to Sierra.

Sierra's eyes were wide, and her lips were partially open. Hannah was sure she was thinking about Jake and how that photo could get him in trouble.

That pissed her off more than anything. Jake had hurt Sierra so badly, and he had made her keep it to herself that Jake knew who had raped Hannah. And for all she knew, Jake had taken that awful picture. Except he didn't go to school here, and Nathan had threatened Hannah too, so that part didn't add up. But still. Hannah had more than enough of Jake and of Sierra refusing to let go of him after everything he'd done to both of them.

"I want Officer Dalton," Hannah sniffed. Officer Dalton was the school resource officer. He was a cop, but supposedly, he was also there to help kids make good choices. Everyone pretty much avoided him, and Hannah felt like a snitch for asking. But at the same time, she was too mad to care.

"Are you sure?" Mrs. Garcia asked. "He may want to arrest someone."

Hannah hesitated. She'd been terrified for Sierra that day that Sierra had been taken to the office to talk to the cops, and she knew from Sierra's crossed arms and half-open mouth that Sierra might never forgive her if the cops arrested Jake over this. But enough was enough. Jake had hurt and scared Sierra on purpose on top of pretending he didn't know who had raped Hannah and making her feel uncomfortable whenever she got around him. If Sierra wanted to cling to him despite all the crap he'd done, that was her problem. Hannah was done getting dragged down with her, and if Sierra didn't like it, she'd survive just like she'd survived a whole month of Molly giving her the silent treatment.

"Yes," she said, turning her back on Sierra so she wouldn't lose her nerve. "I want to press charges."

"All right, then," Mrs. Garcia said. "Let's go."

"I'm coming too," Brad said. Mrs. Garcia raised her eyebrows, but he said, "Hannah needs me. No way I'm leaving her side."

"Me too," Molly said, and Sierra agreed too.

As Sierra turned to follow Hannah, something rattled in her backpack.

"Hold on a minute," Mrs. Garcia said. "What do you have in there?"

Sierra shrugged. "I guess I got an old Snapple bottle in there I forgot to throw out or something. I suck at cleaning out my backpack."

"Then you won't mind opening it for me so I can see."

Sierra's eyes flashed.

Hannah said, "Why are you bothering her? It's not like she had anything to do with this."

"Something in her backpack sounds like it could be a bottle of spray paint. Open the bag, Sierra. Now."

Sierra slammed her backpack down onto the ground. It was half-open. "What the hell?" she said and opened it the rest of the way.

There was a can of spray paint sitting on top of her books.

Her eyes widened and she gasped. "I never saw this . . . someone had to . . . I didn't do this to you, Hannah. I swear I didn't."

Before Hannah could say she believed her, Mrs. Garcia said, "Come with me, Sierra. You're going to have to wait in my office for your parents." She picked up Sierra's backpack and gestured with her head for Hannah to follow her too.

***

The chairs in the main office were hard and uncomfortable. The ones at the police station had been too, and Hannah vaguely remembered the ones in the ER where her mom was in Florida were just as bad—or was she thinking of the ones in the ER here?

"You okay?" Molly asked, interrupting her thoughts. Hannah glared at her and Molly said, "Stupid question. I know. I just don't know what else to say."

Hannah shrugged. "I don't either," she said, "and no, I'm not okay." She looked at Molly, then back at nothing. "You know Sierra wasn't involved, right?"

"You said she's not, and you seem sure." Molly crossed her arms. "The only thing is, where'd the paint come from?"

"Her bag was half-open when she put it down, so obviously Nathan put that can in when she wasn't looking."

"I guess." Molly fiddled with her earring. "As mad as I was at Sierra, I never thought she was capable of anything like this. Besides, why would she?"

Sierra's parents came in, interrupting the girls' conversation.

Her dad's eyes flitted toward Hannah, then away. "My daughter's in there?" he asked, gesturing toward Mrs. Garcia's door. Hannah nodded, too freaked out by how he was being to speak.

"That was weird," she said under her breath as the Dunlaps went into Mrs. Garcia's office.

"Getting a call your kid's in trouble with the cops does that," Brad said. "Trust me."

Hannah squeezed his hand but said nothing. Molly looked at them like she wanted to say something, but she didn't speak either. Hannah looked away from her, tired of Molly staring at her but not wanting to fight with her right now.

Officer Dalton came in. "Be with you in a sec," he told Hannah and went into Mrs. Garcia's office. He was in there for a long time. Hannah strained her ears, but she couldn't hear a single word of what was going on.

When he came back out, he made Hannah come with him to the conference room. He told her that he'd looked at the security tapes and seen a person wearing a hoodie vandalize her locker. He'd only seen them from the back and hadn't seen their hands, so he didn't know for sure if the culprit was black or white. But Sierra was wearing a hoodie and she had the can of paint, so as far as he was concerned, he had proof she did it.

"It wasn't her," Hannah said, fidgeting. "It was Nathan Walsh. I'm sure of it."

"What makes you think that?"

Hannah bit her lip. There was no explaining unless she told Officer Dalton the whole story, and she was tired of telling that story. But if she didn't, Sierra would probably be arrested. She couldn't let that happen.

She let her breath out slowly and said, "It's a long story but here goes." She told Officer Dalton that she'd been raped a month ago and that Nathan had threatened her after she reported it and explained about the crowd and Sierra's backpack being open before Mrs. Garcia searched it. "He put that can of paint in her bag. I'm sure of it," she said. "Sierra didn't have anything to do with it."

Officer Dalton nodded. Hannah wasn't sure if he believed her or not. "There's more," she said. "Um, Sierra's boyfriend, the one who had the party. He's really bad news. I don't know if you can do anything about him, but I was kind of hoping you could." She told him about Jake hurting Sierra and how Sierra said she missed him even though sometimes she also said she knew he was bad for her.

Officer Dalton's face was grim when she finished. "All right," he said. "Here's what we're gonna do. Number one, I'm gonna pass on everything you told me to the detective working your case and make sure she gets that lewd photo Nathan or whoever put on your locker. Number two, I'm gonna suggest Mrs. Garcia call Nathan in for a chat while I look into if there were any prints or anything left behind when your locker got hit. But before I do that, I wanna take another pass at Sierra and see if I can get her to turn on this Jake for her own good."

***

"I dunno what's gonna happen now, but Sierra's dad is pissed," Brad said when Hannah came back out to the lobby area. "He was yelling pretty loud. Molly and me heard everything."

Hannah sank into her seat. "I wish I hadn't told Mrs. Garcia to call Officer Dalton. I didn't know Nathan framed Sierra, or I wouldn't have."

"But you had to," Molly said. "Sierra or no Sierra, you couldn't let Nathan get away with this."

"I know that!" Hannah snapped.

Molly slammed her purse onto an empty seat. "Here we go again. Even now I can't say anything right, can I?"

"That's not true!" Hannah's voice rose but she made herself take a deep breath while she reminded herself that she and Molly were supposed to be in a truce. "Look, ever since I was raped, I get mad super easy, okay? I'm trying to control it, but it just comes out." She stared at the ground. "That's part of why I thought I was, you know, like my mom. My therapist said I'm not. She said I'm all over the place because of what happened to me. But I don't know how long it'll be before I'm anything like myself again."

Molly's eyes widened. "Is that you saying you're sorry?"

"I guess." Hannah was still staring at the floor. "I'm tired of fighting with you. Can we not? Please?"

Molly nodded. "For what it's worth, I'm glad you're not bipolar. And that you actually told me what was going on with you. My mom said it was something like that, but I figured she didn't know. It's not like she's at school with us. Anyway, I guess I can try not to take it personally when you lash out."

"Thanks. I'll try not to be so mean too. You're not who I'm mad at." Hannah bit her lip. "Friends again?"

For one awful second, she thought Molly would say 'No', but then Molly said, "God, you don't know how long I've waited to hear you say that. Can I . . ." She held her arms out.

Hannah nodded. Molly hugged her.

Mrs. Garcia's door opened as they pulled apart. Sierra came out, slowly, followed by her parents and Officer Dalton. Hannah was glad Sierra wasn't in handcuffs, though when Sierra raised her head it was obvious she'd been crying.

"Sierra!" Hannah ran up to hug her. "Thank God you're not in trouble."

"Don't!" Sierra snapped, pushing Hannah away. "Jake's going to jail thanks to you being a snitch. Now he'll never forgive me, no matter what."

"Better him than you," Mrs. Dunlap said. "As it is, you're going to have a lot to live down."

Sierra rolled her eyes.

Mr. Dunlap said, "None of those faces, young lady. You'd better be grateful you have parents who will fight to protect you, because God knows no one else will do it." He locked eyes with Hannah. "Especially not your so-called friends."

Hannah took a step back. "What? I went to that party to watch Sierra's back!"

"You should have come to us! It was our job to protect her, not yours, and anyway, you helped Jake keep hurting her."

Hannah's mouth dropped open. She wanted to scream at Mr. Dunlap that he was being unfair, but she couldn't find the words.

"Hold on, Mr. Dunlap," Molly said. "I don't think any of us know what you're talking about. How could Hannah tell you anything if she didn't know anything?"

"She knew Sierra was hooking up with some college boy," Mr. Dunlap said, "and that he got both of them to go to the kind of party where people get hurt. She was assaulted herself, for God's sake! And yet she said nothing."

"Because Sierra told me not to!" Hannah said. "I was trying to be a good friend."

"Yeah, well, you failed. There are some secrets you don't keep, Hannah, and I guess you girls had to learn that the hard way." Mr. Dunlap shook his head. "It doesn't matter now. What's done is done, and now I'm going to enroll her at St. Anthony's like she's been begging me to do and see if I can undo the damage you helped Jake do to her."

Hannah's eyes burned with tears she refused to let fall, not while Mr. Dunlap was being so mean to her. "Y-you're going to Catholic school?" she asked Sierra.

Sierra nodded. "It was Jake's idea. He thought I'd look super-hot in a Catholic school uniform. Guess he'll never get to see it now."

"Stop it, Sierra," Mrs. Dunlap said. "I don't want to hear that boy's name come out of your mouth another time. And you're going to St. Anthony's to learn, not to model clothing for some boy who isn't worth it. Now let's go."

Sierra stared at the floor as she shuffled away.

Hannah stared at the door to the main office as it swung closed. So that was that. No more Sierra. Her chest hurt worse than it did when Molly wasn't talking to her, and she wasn't sure she could hold back the tears. But Mrs. Parker said they all needed to go to class now so she bit her lip and let her friends walk her out.

The Tree of Life

FTER SCHOOL, MOLLY wanted to take Hannah out for coffee so they could catch up, but Hannah had to turn her down because she had plans with Elizabeth to go to Brad's track clinic. She invited Molly to come too, but she said she might as well tutor if Hannah was busy. Hannah promised to text her later and gave her a hug. Then she headed down the steps, thinking about how weird it was that a week ago, Molly wanted nothing to do with her, and today, they were hugging like there'd never been any rift between them at all.

"What was that all about?" Elizabeth asked her, joining her on the steps.

Hannah shrugged. "We made up. Maybe one day, she'll come sit with us for real instead of staring at us."

Elizabeth said nothing. The silence was uncomfortable. It made Hannah feel like Elizabeth was trying not to say she hated Molly. "You heard about Sierra?"

"Yeah. Sucks." Elizabeth put her hand on Hannah's shoulder. "I heard about your locker too. You okay?"

"I guess." Hannah's whole body ached with exhaustion and she wanted to go home and go to bed, but she wasn't feeling that heavy depressed feeling in her chest that she'd been carrying around for weeks. She didn't know why. She was too tired to be depressed, she guessed.

Elizabeth noticed and asked if Hannah wanted to skip track clinic and go home, but Hannah didn't want to flake on Brad again, so she promised she'd tell Elizabeth if she needed to leave early and then they headed to the gym.

The gym was set up like a track except it was split into sections. There was a relay race section where boys ran for a little bit, then passed a baton to another boy; a section full of hurdles to jump over; and a section where a few boys were racing down an imaginary track marked with blue duct tape. In the other half of the gym, there were the same sections, only girls were competing instead of boys, and in each section, there was an older student who was helping coach everyone.

Brad jogged up to Hannah and Elizabeth. He was wearing a black tank top and blue gym shorts and sweat made his hair stick to his forehead even though it was twenty degrees outside. "You guys made it!" he said, while Hannah traced his muscles with her eyes. They looked even bigger and more attractive up close with no shirt sleeve to hide them. He hugged Hannah and called, "Coach! This is my girlfriend, Hannah. She's been running with me every morning."

Brad's coach jogged up. His head, which was bald, was shiny with sweat, and his skin was a shade darker than Sierra's. He reminded Hannah of Dylan, only he was closer to her parents' age than her age. He introduced himself as Coach Anderson and asked Hannah if she was going to try out for the girls' track team in the spring.

"No," Hannah said, making herself laugh. "I'm not nearly athletic enough to be on a team. Ask Brad, I tripped over my shoelace last week."

"So, wear Velcro to your tryout," Mr. Anderson said, grinning. He blew his whistle and called for an assistant coach who worked with the girls and told her to take Hannah over to the girls' side and try her out on the hundred-meter dash to see how she did.

Hannah went with the assistant coach and did what she asked her to even though this was ridiculous. She didn't need to do track just because Brad did. But running did help her mood, so who knew? Maybe she'd join the track team and maybe she wouldn't, but she couldn't rule anything out, not when she'd changed so much already.

When track ended, she crashed back down to Earth, remembering suddenly that Sierra was gone. Brad wanted to go out to dinner, but Hannah felt too sweaty and gross. He insisted on getting her a milkshake from Potbellies, and Elizabeth said she didn't mind stopping to get it. So, they did.

No one was home yet when Hannah got back. She put her milkshake in the refrigerator and went to take a shower. When the hot water hit her body, tears sprung to her eyes. The more she washed, the more she needed to cry even though everything that happened at school was a long time ago already. She sank to her knees and sobbed while the water massaged her back. She felt bad about using so much water, but she didn't want to get out. She stayed in until the water got cold.

Mom was in the kitchen when Hannah went to get her milkshake. She handed Hannah a peanut butter and jelly sandwich as she sat down. "I made this for you while you were in the shower. I heard you crying, sweetheart. What's wrong?"

"I was just getting some things out of my system." Hannah took a bite out of her sandwich. "You'll be thrilled to know that Sierra's parents decided she doesn't need me in her life. They're putting her in Catholic school just to keep her away from me."

"Of all the nerve," Mom said. "What the hell bug got up their asses? You're the one who's a better friend than their daughter deserves."

"Not helping," Hannah said, even though part of her liked the way Mom was standing up for her. "Anyway, what got into them is that they decided the stuff Jake did to her was my fault because I didn't tell them she wanted to go to his party before it happened. Anyway, that was the least bad thing that happened today." She told Mom about the graffiti, doing her best to make the photo sound less bad than it was so Mom wouldn't freak out, and how she'd reported it to Officer Dalton. She finished by explaining how all she'd accomplished was making Sierra mad at her because now the cops were after Jake. "On the positive side," she said, trying to soften the blow, "Molly and I are friends again."

"That's something," Mom said. "Let's turn on News 12 and see if they're reporting anything about anyone being arrested in connection with your case."

Hannah stiffened. "You really think my story will be on the news?"

"Only local," Mom said. "If even that. But that could be a good thing. It could get the cops' butts in gear if they know all of Long Island is waiting for them to arrest someone. You can take your sandwich into the living room if you want to watch with me."

"Okay," Hannah said even though she'd lost what little appetite she had.

The news wasn't reporting anything about Jake getting arrested or even that the cops were looking for him. Hannah sat through an hour's worth and then checked News 12's website on her phone for breaking news too, but there was nothing. Eric came home and Mom went into the kitchen to help him with the groceries. They spoke in low voices the whole time and Hannah knew Mom was filling him in. She hoped she got all the details right.

Eric called Hannah to come help him with the groceries. She brought her empty plate into the kitchen with her and busied herself washing it while she waited for his lecture.

Eric handed her some TV dinners to put in the freezer. "Mom tells me you went through an ordeal today."

"Yeah," Hannah said. "Sierra's dad said I helped Jake hurt her. He thinks I'm the worst friend in the world."

Eric sighed. "Parents say things they don't mean when their kids scare the hell out of them. Mom and I said a lot of things about Sierra that probably weren't fair either. Hang in there. Maybe he'll see things differently once Jake is behind bars."

"I doubt it. He's putting her in a whole other school."

"Still, though," Eric said. "Things can always change, Hannah. You can't let the way they are right now get you down."

Hannah thought about that while she put away some frozen vegetables. "That's true, I guess. I mean, I changed, and it took Molly a long time to catch up. But by the end of the day today, it was like we hadn't fought at all."

"See?" Eric said. "And you were so convinced you'd lost a friend." He squeezed Hannah's shoulder. "Chin up, Hannah. No more thinking whatever's wrong today will be wrong forever."

"I'll try," Hannah promised, mostly because she wanted Eric to stop going on about it. She wasn't in the mood for a pep talk.

"That's all we ask, sweetheart," Eric said. "And Hannah, thank you for telling us what happened today. We're on your side always, but we can't help you if you don't talk to us."

"I know. I didn't want to hide anymore."

"I'm glad. Now, Mom says all you had for dinner was a peanut butter and jelly sandwich. So, how about you go rest while I make us some real food?"

"I don't need . . . "

"Maybe not but I want to give it to you anyway," Eric said. "Please let me."

Hannah's eyes widened and she thought of all the times Mom had given her money that she didn't need either. Suddenly it hit her: Her parents gave her stuff because they didn't know what else to do for her.

"Okay," she said, determined to be more grateful from now on. "Thanks."

***

Hannah dreaded Chemistry the next morning more than usual because she was sure Nathan was going to be worse than ever after getting away with graffiting her locker and framing Sierra. He looked smug too, sitting straight up in his seat and smirking. Hannah was sure he was planning the next obnoxious thing he was going to do to her.

He has no power over me, she told herself while Mr. Dawson went over the lab instructions. *None.* But she couldn't stop freaking out about him anyway.

There was a knock on the door. Mr. Dawson pulled it open and Mrs. Garcia and Officer Dalton came in. They went right to Nathan's desk.

Don't stare. You didn't like it when people did it to you. Hannah turned her head anyway, along with the rest of the class.

"Stand up," Officer Dalton told Nathan. "Mrs. Garcia's here to witness me taking you into custody."

"For what?" Nathan demanded.

"We know you vandalized Hannah Kollman's locker," Officer Dalton said, "and you disposed of the can in an innocent person's backpack. Now get on your feet."

Nathan's eyes snapped as he stood. "This is bullshit! Whatever that bitch told you, she's lying!"

Officer Dalton ignored him, instead handcuffing him and patting him down. "Come on, Hannah!" Nathan said. "I was just having a little fun with you, and you know it." Officer Dalton told him to be quiet and then he and Mrs. Garcia took him away.

BY LUNCHTIME, A ton of rumors were going around about Nathan getting arrested. Hannah did her best not to listen to them, but she couldn't help thinking it was what Mr. Collins would call poetic justice. Besides, it almost made up for the people who still bumped her in the halls and called her a lying slut or a snitch.

Katie told Hannah she heard that Nathan was going to be charged with sharing porn because he put that photo up. It annoyed Hannah, but before she could figure out how to explain why, some freshman girl came up to the table and told Hannah that she felt like she could stand up to bullies too because of what Hannah had done. The girl hugged her, then ran away to sit with her friends.

"Look at that," Brad said. "You're some freshman's hero now."

"There's no reason for me to be," Hannah said, "but whatever."

"Oh, stop," Katie said. "This isn't a reason to be depressed. Besides, if you're already making a difference now, just wait 'til our assembly!"

"I don't mean to be Debbie Downer," Hannah said as Brad's phone rang and Brad walked off to answer it. "I just don't think Nathan getting arrested made that much of a difference. Maybe I'll feel better once Jake is arrested too. I don't know.

As long as the people who actually raped me are at large, it doesn't feel like I won."

"Have you heard from Sierra since yesterday?" Elizabeth asked.

Hannah shook her head. "My parents think once hers cool down, they'll let her be friends with me again, but I don't know."

Brad came back to the table, his face grim. "That's gonna be a while," he said.

"Why?" Hannah asked. "What was that phone call?"

Brad reached for her hand. "That was my dad. He's not on the crime beat, but he hears stuff cause of working at the newsroom."

"And?" Hannah's nerves were too jangled to put up with the long-winded way Brad told stories.

"And," Brad said, "he heard that Jake ran away. Cops went to his house, and there was no sign of him or his car. They're looking for him, but his family's got money. He had a head start. Dad doubts they're ever gonna catch up with him. He said for all they know, he made it up to Canada."

Hannah's eyes widened. "So, I'm never going to get justice. And we lost Sierra for nothing." She bit her lip. Sierra. "Oh my God. You don't think Sierra would run away with him, do you?"

"Her parents are watching her like a hawk," Brad said. "Trust me, she's done with him."

Hannah nodded, but under the table, she texted Dylan and hoped his parents wouldn't take it out on Sierra if they found out about it.

Some number Hannah didn't recognize tried to call while Molly was walking her to the bus after school. Hannah didn't answer in case it was Jake or some other asshole. Five minutes later, her phone rang again. This time it was Mom. She said a district attorney had called about Nathan and wanted to see Hannah right away, so she was coming to get her.

"I hope my mom doesn't have to keep taking time off from work because of this crap," Hannah told Molly, who was waiting with her and Brad at the pick-up circle.

"You're more important than work," Molly said. "You just don't see it."

Hannah bit her lip. Molly had this way of saying things that made her sound super bossy, but she didn't know how to tell her to cut it out without getting into a fight all over again.

"I hope the DA's gonna tell you she's sending Nathan to real jail," Brad said. "Not juvie. Rikers or some shit like that where he'll get beat up all the time."

"Brad!" Molly said. "That's not exactly nice."

"So?" Brad shot back. "Look what he did to Hannah!"

"How about you two don't fight?" Hannah snapped. "I'm stressed out enough."

"No one's fighting." Brad squeezed Hannah's hand. "You got any idea what the DA wants?"

"Nope," Hannah said. "All my mom said was she's coming to get me so we can go." She leaned forward, staring out at the pick-up circle. "What the hell is taking her so long? It would have been faster to take the bus!"

"She'll be here," Molly said. "Time slows down when you're nervous." She patted Hannah's hand.

Hannah felt another pair of eyes on her. She turned as Molly dropped her hand. Jen was standing there.

"I knew it!" Jen said. "You're more into Hannah than me. That's why you wouldn't give up on her when she was being a total bitch to you."

Hannah said, "In case you haven't noticed, I have a boyfriend. And I'd never . . . "

"That doesn't mean anything," Jen said. She turned toward Molly. "I tried so hard to get you to see she wasn't worth it, and you wouldn't listen. Now I know why." She turned and hurried away.

"Oh God," Hannah said, rolling her eyes. She made herself stop when she saw how hard Molly was struggling not to cry. "You wanna go after her?"

"I would never cheat on her, and even if I liked you that way, you're not attracted to girls, so it wouldn't matter." Molly sniffed. "Are you going to be okay if I go?"

Hannah nodded and Molly hurried away.

Hannah said, "I hope I didn't break them up."

"Nah," Brad said. "They did it to themselves if it goes that way." He stroked Hannah's hair. "Nathan's the one who's gotta freak out about the DA, not you. Jump through whatever hoops you gotta to get him behind bars forever."

"I'll try."

Brad stroked her back. "There's your mom," he said. "Sit up before she has a fit."

"Like I care what she thinks. Kiss me for good luck before I go."

Brad did. Hannah held him for as long as she dared before she went over to Mom.

***

ADA Golden turned out to be a woman whose age was in between Hannah's and Mom's. She was white with a big forehead and high cheekbones, and she wore her long brown hair tied up in a bun.

"I wanted to talk to you about how this case is going to proceed," she said. "But first, I want you to know that I'm personally disgusted by this whole thing. I am going to fight as hard as I can to get you justice." She explained that there was a ton of evidence against Nathan and that she was charging him as an accessory to Hannah's rape on top of everything else because that photo was evidence he'd watched it happen. She also said she was going to try to convince a judge to keep Nathan in jail until his trial, but if the judge didn't listen, she would get a restraining order so he couldn't keep harassing Hannah. "But that's just the first step," she said. "Mr. Walsh is likely going to plead not guilty, and if he sticks to that there will be a trial."

"Right." Hannah made herself keep breathing while in her head she told Mouse to shut up about being scared.

"Will she have to testify?" Mom asked.

"Let's not get ahead of ourselves. It'll be about a year before we get that far, and I'm hoping I can get him to take a plea before then. That would be the best-case scenario because if he does, he'll have to confess in court to harassing your daughter and branding her as a liar when he knew damn well she had been raped, and we won't have to worry about tracking down any of her friends who have graduated to testify against him in court."

"What kind of plea are we talking? He's not going to get away with a slap on the wrist for his part in what he did to my little girl, is he?"

"Mom!" Hannah's cheeks were so hot she was afraid she was about to faint.

"Your mom's just looking out for you," ADA Golden said. Hannah breathed in sharply to stop herself from telling the woman to mind her own business. "And no, I do not intend to allow Mr. Walsh to get away with a slap on the wrist. I want him to face reasonable consequences for his part in this without having to put your daughter through the ordeal of a trial. So, my hope is that he has information about who actually raped her that he'd be willing to trade in exchange for a lesser sentence."

"I'd be happy if he helps you catch Jake." The words came out of Hannah's mouth before she knew she was thinking them.

"Hannah," Mom said.

"I would, Mom! Brad's dad said that Jake could be in Canada and that the cops might never find him. And what if Sierra runs away to be with him?"

"Jake?" the ADA interrupted. She glanced through her notes. "Oh. Jacob Parsons, the young man who hosted the house party. He certainly would be a big fish that our office would love to use Nathan Walsh to catch, but we'll see."

"Are we done here?" Mom snapped. Hannah looked at the floor, wishing her mother would do a better job of hiding her irritation.

"Almost," ADA Golden said. "I need to go over the statement your daughter gave to the police to make sure I have everything I need. Would you mind if I spoke to her alone? Sometimes it's easier if no one else is in the room."

Mom's lips were thin, but she said, "I understand." She kissed the top of Hannah's head and said, "I'm not going far, baby."

Hannah patted Mom's hand to show her she still loved her even though she secretly wanted her to hurry up and go.

After Mom left, ADA Golden said she needed Hannah to tell her everything she could remember about what Nathan had done to her after the rape. Hannah told her about the rumors and the mean things Nathan said and did, sometimes backtracking and going all out of order. ADA Golden asked her for the screenshots of his Instagram posts and downloaded them onto her computer. She wanted to copy the journal pages Nathan had read aloud too. Hannah didn't want to let her, but ADA Golden said it would help show how badly Nathan tormented her, so she gave in.

At the end of the interview, ADA Golden asked Hannah for a list of people who she thought might have heard or seen Nathan bothering her. "Tell your friends I'm going to be calling them, so they don't get blindsided. I need to have all my ducks in a row before the pre-trial hearing."

Hannah kept it to herself that Sierra probably wouldn't be allowed to testify, much less talk to the ADA, as she nodded.

***

Nothing much happened with Hannah's case over the next couple of weeks. Brad's dad talked to a reporter that covered court cases and found out that ADA Golden had stopped the judge from transferring Nathan's case to juvenile court, and the ADA called Hannah herself and told her that Nathan had been released on bail. However, the judge had issued the restraining order they'd talked about in her office. Other than that, there was no real movement forward other than Molly telling her that ADA Golden had called her, and she was going to testify against Nathan if the case went to trial.

Jake had not been caught, either. Hannah texted Dylan every few days to check in and make sure Sierra was still where she was supposed to be, but she tried not to do it too much because she didn't want to make things any worse with Sierra's parents.

In the meantime, she had plenty to do to keep her mind off things. She was working on the Tree of Life holiday event with SADD, which was going to be the Friday before Christmas break, and she asked Mrs. Marino for permission to add something new. Traditionally, at the Tree of Life ceremony, people lit candles for everyone who had been killed by drunk drivers and made pledges to stay sober over Christmas break. Hannah wanted to also light candles for people who had been sexually assaulted by someone who was drunk or high.

"I don't want to dilute the power of our message," Mrs. Marino said.

"Oh," Hannah said, then decided not to leave it there the way Mouse wanted her to. "But it won't, Mrs. Marino. It'll add to it. I mean, dying is the worst thing that can happen, but it's not the only thing. If people get drunk over the holidays, something like what happened to me could happen to them. So, it's another important reason to stay sober."

Mrs. Marino hesitated, then said, "If you want to invite people to join you in lighting candles for sexual assault victims, I guess you can."

Hannah wished Mrs. Marino would be more enthusiastic about it, but she guessed this was the best she could do. She had another plan for the Tree of Life too, but this one was a surprise for Brad. So, she couldn't say anything in front of him and had to wait until she was alone with Molly to take care of it.

Besides the Tree of Life, which was a huge event that took up a lot of her time, there were her morning runs with Brad and track clinic once or twice a week; meetings at lunch or after school with Katie and Elizabeth to plan the assembly for April; letting Molly tutor her in Chemistry so she could get her grades back up before it was too late; and Sunday morning breakfasts at the diner with her parents, who had decided to make it a weekly thing so that they could get closer as a family.

Two days before Christmas break, Molly met her at her locker after school. "Your pin came," she whispered. "Are you sure Brad's ready for this?"

"He's been sober six months," Hannah said. "I think. Anyway, however long it is, he's not going back to weed. So, I'm sure he won't be offended." She took the pin and card from Molly and put them in her backpack. "I'm sorry you don't have anyone to give one to anymore."

Molly shrugged. "Not your fault. I shouldn't have listened to Jen in the first place. Maybe then I would have been a less crappy friend this whole time." She bit her lip. "Here comes Katie. You want me to . . . "

"No. This is silly. I'm friends with both of you." Hannah slammed her locker shut as Katie came up to her. "Ready to discuss last-minute stuff for the Tree of Life?"

"Sure," Katie said, "though I'm sure you got it under control." She glanced at Molly. "Is she coming to the meeting too?"

"Thanks, but I'm not on the committee," Molly said. "I don't want to butt in."

"You wouldn't be," Hannah said. "Besides, I want your input." She glanced at Katie. "I hope that's okay with you because I already went through one ridiculous tug-of-war between Molly and Sierra, and I don't want to go through another one."

"It's fine," Katie said, but her crossed arms and narrow eyes told another story. Hannah didn't want to push it, so she ignored that as the girls went out of the school building.

***

In the coffee shop, Hannah filled everyone in on her conversation with Mrs. Marino. Katie and Elizabeth were excited, but Molly was worried that people might not want to admit in front of the whole school that they'd been sexually assaulted.

"Right." Hannah couldn't believe she'd forgotten already what it took to tell even one person she'd been raped. "This was a stupid idea, I guess."

"Don't give up so easily," Elizabeth interrupted. "We'll figure this out. Any ideas, Molly, since you brought it up?"

"I do, actually." Molly tightened her ponytail.

"Of course you do," Katie said. She sighed. "Let's have it."

"Well," Molly said as if Katie didn't have an attitude, "what if we did this? Ask everyone to close their eyes and then ask anyone who has ever been sexually assaulted while they or their partner was drunk to raise their hands. Then you just count them, so you know how many candles to light. That way nobody knows who else raised their hands."

The door chimed, and Dylan came in with Sierra. He had his arm around her, and she looked like she was unsteady on her feet.

"Hannah?" Katie said. "You still with us?"

"Sorry," Hannah said. She gestured toward Sierra's table. "You guys keep talking. I'll be right back."

Dylan turned as Hannah came up to the table. "Hannah, hi!" he said, smiling a sad sort of smile. "I'm glad you're here. Can you do me a favor and sit with Sierra a minute?"

Hannah's stomach sank. "Sierra's in trouble, isn't she?" she said under her breath.

"Better with me than with our parents," Dylan said. "She hasn't been doing so well, I guess. Came a few minutes early to get her from school. She had a bottle of wine in her hand she was passing around with three other girls. I got her out of there before she drank too much, but I can't trust her not to run off so if you can. . ."

"I will." Hannah sighed. "I guess you have to tell your parents this time."

"Dunno what I'm gonna do yet. After how hard my dad was on her after the paint thing happened, I'm afraid he's gonna make things ten times as bad. But I told her after the party I wasn't covering for her a second time. Anyway, be right back."

Hannah pulled out the chair across from Sierra and sat down. "It's good to see you," she said awkwardly.

"Is it?" Sierra stared down at the table. "Your life is probably way better now that I'm gone. You have a lot of awesome friends. What do you need me for?"

"Sierra, stop. I've missed you like crazy." Hannah patted Sierra's hand. "Were you drinking because you thought I didn't?"

Sierra stiffened. "So, Dylan told you. Asshole."

"He's worried about you! Sierra, he loves you. Don't you know that?" Sierra shrugged. Hannah said, "Talk to me. Tell me about your new school or about your new friends or whatever."

Sierra blinked hard. "Whatever, Dr. Mouse." She took off her glasses and rubbed her temples while Hannah pushed her anger down so she could help. "I don't want to talk about school. It sucks except for all the bad kids. Leave it to me to find the other losers, right?"

"Stop that. You're not a loser, Sierra. You're not." Hannah's ears were buzzing and she couldn't think. She had to make Sierra feel better somehow but she didn't know how.

Sierra shrugged. "I wish I'd run away with Jake. It would have served my stupid parents right to never see me again, and I'd be down in South Carolina where it's nice and warm. None of this cold winter crap."

Hannah's body jerked up without permission when she heard Jake's name. "Jake's in South Carolina?"

"Oh, yeah. His family has a summer home there." Sierra laughed to herself. "The stupid cops think he went to Canada. They'll never find him." She sighed again. "I should have gone with him. He said it was my last chance or else I'd never see him again. He even grabbed my arm, see?" Sierra rolled up her sleeve. She had five little bruises on her arm. "He tried to put me in his car, but I got away. Why didn't I let him? Being with him would have been so much better than this shit."

Fear shot through Hannah, making her sit straight up. She had to have misunderstood, or else Sierra didn't know what she was saying because she was drunk. As bad as Jake was, he wouldn't really try to kidnap Sierra, would he?

"You don't really want to be with Jake after everything he did, do you?" Hannah did her best to keep her voice neutral.

Sierra shrugged. "At least he's sweet sometimes." She leaned forward. "I'm glad I can trust you not to tell anyone. Not like Dylan. I can't trust him anymore."

"Trust me with what?" Dylan asked, coming back with a bottle of water for Sierra.

"She's mad because you told me about the wine," Hannah said, her heart pounding. This was no time to give in to Mouse, but she didn't know what else to do. "Um, I need to get back to my other friends now, but you know where I live. You come over any time you need, okay?"

"If I can," Sierra said, "I will. You're the only true friend I ever had."

Hannah gave her a quick hug before hurrying back to her table. She hoped nobody noticed how freaked out she was.

48 – Trying to be a Good Friend

WHEN ELIZABETH DROPPED Hannah off after the meeting, Molly insisted on getting out too, and after Elizabeth pulled away, she asked to come up so they could talk.

In Hannah's room, Molly said, "Look, Hannah, this is probably none of my business, but I can tell something upset you when you went to say 'Hi' to Sierra. Will you tell me? Please? I won't tell anyone this time, I swear."

Hannah hesitated. Sierra would never forgive her if Molly told the world that Dylan caught her drinking, never mind the rest of it. But at the same time, Hannah needed to tell someone. Lying about this was wrong, all wrong. Sierra was in trouble. She was drinking and insisting Jake was a good guy and if she ran away with him and got hurt worse . . .

Well, then Sierra's dad would be right about Hannah being the world's worst friend because she knew and kept her mouth shut.

"She really is miserable," she told Molly, cautiously. "So miserable that Dylan caught her drinking with her new friends."

"Oh, God." Molly rolled her eyes.

"Don't, okay?" Hannah crossed her arms. "Yeah, she's being stupid, but judging her won't help."

"I wasn't," Molly said. "I swear."

She was, but Hannah decided to let it go. She had more important things to worry about. "The thing is," she said, hugging her knees to her chest, "Sierra knows where Jake is, and I'm afraid she's going to run away to be with him."

"Jake? As in her loser boyfriend the cops are looking for?"

Hannah nodded. "There's more. I think Jake . . . " She swallowed hard. "He tried to do something even worse to her." She told Molly about the bruises on Sierra's arm and what Sierra said. "I could be wrong, but it sounded like he tried to take her with him when she didn't want to go. I keep thinking he could try it again."

"Even he can't be that stupid." Molly crossed her arms. "The cops know Sierra's into him. They have to be watching her to see if he contacts her. Anyway, you have to do something. It's not fair to you for Jake to be wherever he is instead of in jail for what he helped do to you. And if she runs away with him . . . "

"He could do something really awful to her. I know." Hannah fidgeted. She needed to be alone to think things over, but did Sierra have time for that? For all she knew, she was planning to sneak out tonight. "How is she going to get to South Carolina without anyone knowing anyway?" she asked. "It's not like she has money for a plane ticket."

"South Carolina? So that's where Jake is?"

Crap. Hannah had been thinking aloud and forgot Molly was there. Too late now. "Maybe. Sierra said his family has a summer home there."

"Which he's probably totally trashing," Molly said. "We can't let Sierra go down there, Hannah. He'd have her exactly where he wants her, alone with him a million miles away while her family has no clue where she is. He could do whatever he wanted to her, and there'd be no one to help her. No Dylan, no you. Nobody."

Hannah's eyes widened, thinking about that.

Jake had already hurt Sierra over and over, and he'd tried to kidnap her. Hannah didn't know what else he was capable of.

What if he'd made up the friend who raped Hannah? What if he'd done it himself?

And what if Sierra went to South Carolina, and he did it to her too?

Hannah couldn't let Sierra risk it.

"Better an angry friend than a dead one, right?" Hannah's voice shook even though the saying didn't really fit. Jake wouldn't kill Sierra. Would he?

She opened her purse and got the card out that the detective had given her in case she remembered anything else that would be helpful for her case.

Twenty minutes later, Detective Lindstrom sat with Hannah in the kitchen while Molly waited in the living room so she could keep Mom company if Mom came home before the detective was gone. She made Hannah tell her the whole story all over again. Hannah left out that Sierra had been drinking. Sierra was going to be mad enough at her for telling on Jake. She didn't need to get her arrested for underage drinking too.

"I'm glad you called me," Detective Lindstrom said. "There are two things I need to do now. One is to make sure that Jake is found and arrested. We have a better idea of where he went now, and we can work with law enforcement down in South Carolina to catch him and return him to New York. But I also need to make sure your friend stays safe. I'll reach out to some patrol officers and see who's in the area to do a welfare check on her. If God forbid she's disappeared, we'll put out an Amber Alert on top of working with Missing Persons to find her and bring her home."

***

Molly had to go soon after Detective Lindstrom did. She offered to stay anyway, but that would have meant explaining to her parents why she couldn't come help with dinner. Hannah didn't want to risk it. So, she told Molly she'd be fine even though she was secretly freaking out about Sierra. Molly was so grateful that Hannah let her help at all that she didn't seem to notice. She hugged Hannah goodbye and left.

Mom came in a minute later, holding a box of donuts. She'd bought them for Hannah because she'd been through so much lately.

Hannah felt too sick with worry to even think about eating donuts. She was tempted to try to force herself so that Mom wouldn't know anything was wrong, but she knew better than to listen to Mouse about that. As Eric said, her parents couldn't help her if she kept her problems to herself. So, she told Mom the cops found out about Jake's summer house, leaving out Sierra's involvement with that discovery, and that she was too anxious about whether they'd catch him to eat. Mom said it might take a few days since they'd have to search the whole state for him and that she wasn't allowing Hannah to go on a hunger strike until he was found. Hannah felt better enough to eat even though she didn't like the way Mom was bossing her around.

By bedtime, she still had heard nothing from the cops, and there was nothing on any of the news sites either about Jake or Sierra. Sierra hadn't called to curse her out either, so she guessed that no news was good news.

She had trouble sleeping anyway. When she finally did drift off, she dreamed that Jake was holding a gun to Sierra's head. He said he would kill her if Hannah didn't do what he said and made Hannah handcuff her. Sierra screamed at her that she was the worst friend in the world, then turned into a fox and tried to bite her.

She jerked awake, glad that was just a nightmare. She was afraid to close her eyes again when she saw the clock said it was 3:38 AM.

The next day was Saturday, and Hannah planned to sleep in. However, her phone rang around ten in the morning, waking her. She jerked up and answered it, hoping and fearing that that was the cops.

It wasn't. It was Elizabeth. She wanted to go candle shopping and asked if Hannah could call Molly. Hannah said she would and asked if she could invite Brad too, which was fine with

Elizabeth. They hung up and then Hannah texted Brad and Molly. She didn't think this was such a big emergency that she had to wake them up if they were still asleep. Then she checked the news. Nothing. How long was it going to take to catch Jake?

Hannah made herself get into the shower, hoping it would wake her up. By the time she was done, she had texts back from Brad and Molly telling her to let them know when she was ready for them to head over. She hurried to get ready, ate breakfast, and told her parents she was going out.

"Oh, good," Eric said. "We finally get to meet the mysterious Elizabeth."

Hannah rolled her eyes as she opened her yogurt. "Sorry, but no. Brad's picking me and Molly up and we're meeting Elizabeth at the mall." Her phone buzzed and she glanced at it.

> Dylan: I need to talk to you. Can you come downstairs for a couple minutes?

HANNAH COULD TELL Dylan was stressed out when she got downstairs. He hadn't shaved and he was standing against the wall, his arms crossed.

"What the hell, Hannah?" he snapped before Hannah could ask if Sierra was okay. "Why'd you call the cops on my sister?"

Hannah took a step back. "What was I supposed to do? Jake tried to force her into his car, and she still wanted to run away to be with him."

"You could have come to me instead of getting the cops involved!" Dylan's nostrils flared, and Hannah knew he was taking deep breaths to try to control himself.

"What happened?" she made herself ask even though she was afraid of the answer.

"She's not in jail. Don't worry. No thanks to you." Dylan turned his back on Hannah. "They said they got a tip she was gonna run off with Jake, and they wanted to search her room to see if she had a bag packed or whatever. I'm telling you, if Dad let them, they probably would have found some BS excuse to arrest her. And that's 'cause you had to go calling them instead of keeping it in the family."

Hannah stared at the ground. "I didn't mean for that to happen. I just wanted Jake caught before he could hurt her."

"I know you meant well. It's just my family handles stuff itself. We'd way rather deal with Sierra our way." Dylan took a few more deep breaths. "After Dad threw the cops out, he said he didn't need a warrant to search his own damn self, and he found a knapsack in the back of her closet. She had clothes and a wad of money. Who knows how soon she was gonna take off? Dad took it away and locked her in her room, but that's no solution, not unless the cops put as much effort into catching Jake as they did into finding out what she was up to." Dylan rubbed his temples. "This isn't like her. Going to that party was normal teen stupidity, but this is a whole other ballgame. What the hell's going on with my sister?"

Hannah swallowed hard, trying to shake the feeling that this was all her fault. "I guess it's been hard for her. People blamed her for what happened to me, and Jake was terrifying her."

"And she never came to me." Dylan crossed his arms. "Do me a favor and talk to me next time even if she won't."

"I will." Hannah pushed her hair behind her ear. "Can I ask you something? How mad at me is she?"

"Right now, she's not talking to anyone. But that'll pass." Dylan patted Hannah's shoulder. "I know you were trying to be a good friend to her even if you screwed up. She'll see it too one of these days."

Hannah doubted it, but she nodded anyway.

An hour later, Elizabeth waved as Hannah came into Yankee Candle with Molly and Brad. She was trying to decide between tea lights and jar candles and wanted to talk to Molly about how much SADD could spend and which candles were better.

Hannah knew she should participate in that discussion, but she was too restless to put up with it and wandered off to check out some other candles.

She found a section in the back that had snow globes. She picked one up and shook it, thinking about how Sierra's mom had a shelf full of them that she showed Hannah one Christmas when she came over to see Sierra's tree.

"There you are," Brad said. "Whatcha doing?"

"Thinking about Sierra. Her mom has a lot of these."

Brad put his hand on Hannah's arm. "Want to get one for Sierra? We could go over after this to give it to her and see how she is."

Hannah shrugged. "It's going to take a lot more than a snow globe to fix this. Besides, her parents probably won't let us see her." She smiled slightly. "She'd probably like this one with the teddy bears, though. She still has stuffed animals on her bed."

"Get it, then," Brad said. "If anyone could use some Christmas cheer, it's her, right?"

Hannah picked up the snow globe. "I guess."

Molly called her just then to tell her they were ready to buy candles. Hannah started to put the snow globe down, then changed her mind.

After the girls bought the candles and Hannah bought the snow globe, Detective Lindstrom called, interrupting Elizabeth's suggestion that they play Secret Santa for each other. The detective wanted to tell Hannah that Jake had finally been arrested. Elizabeth insisted on buying Hannah a slice of pizza and a soda at the food court to celebrate the good news.

"So, what happens next?" she asked as they sat down. "They're going to get out of him and Nathan what they know about your rape, right? And then you can finally get justice?"

"I guess." Hannah took a sip of her Mountain Dew. "I mean, so far nothing happened since Nathan was arrested except Sierra going nuts." Her eyes widened. "Sierra. I'd better go try to see her and make sure she's okay now that Jake's been arrested."

"Waste of time," Molly said. "Her parents won't let you. Besides, she's already so mad at you she's not talking, so what's the point?"

"I have to try. That's what. I can't just sit here doing nothing while Sierra's having a nervous breakdown."

"That's the Mountain Dew talking," Elizabeth said. "Come on. Let's put that energy to good use and do our Secret Santa drawing."

Going Christmas shopping was the last thing Hannah wanted to do. It didn't feel right, not when Sierra was in trouble. But when Elizabeth gave her a piece of paper to put her name on, she did it. *You win, Mouse*, she thought as she put her paper in the pile.

They all picked one, and Hannah got Elizabeth's name.

She wandered around the mall aimlessly, thinking about Sierra and Jake and Nathan and the rape and wondering whether her life would ever be normal again. Telling the cops that she'd been raped was supposed to make things better, but it had done the opposite. Now her life was a whirlwind of calls from the police and trips to the DA's office, and every time they made progress at all on her case, it reminded her that this whole thing was far from over and might never be.

She ended up buying Elizabeth a gift card at the Cheesecake Factory on the top floor of the mall. Elizabeth seemed to like going out to eat, so hopefully, she'd like that and not think it was a stupid gift that Hannah hadn't put any energy into getting.

Afterward, she went into a sports store and got Brad a combination watch/stopwatch he could use while he was at track clinic. The salesperson showed her a smartwatch that tracked his steps electronically, but that was way too expensive. So, a regular watch had to do. She was two for two on crappy gifts, she guessed.

That left Molly and Katie, and of course, Mom and Eric and Grandma. But not now. It was almost time to meet her friends at the food court and she didn't want to be late.

Molly was the only one there when Hannah made it back. She was sitting at a table by herself eating a huge chocolate chip cookie. She offered

Hannah half and told her that she'd tried to make up with Jen while she was waiting, but Jen was rude to her. Hannah felt bad that she'd been so worried about Sierra that she'd forgotten that Molly was heartbroken about Jen. She hugged her and told her that she hoped she found someone else soon. Then she asked her how she made out with her Secret Santa.

"You'll find out when we have our Christmas party," Molly said, and Hannah knew that meant Molly had got her name. "You?"

"We'll see," Hannah said.

Brad came up to the table just then. "Ooh, cookies," he said. "Mind if I. . . "

"Go for it," Molly said. Elizabeth came back too, and they all shared the cookie before they put their gifts in Elizabeth's trunk one at a time so that nobody would see them.

***

On Tuesday, ADA Golden asked Hannah to come in after school. She told her and Mom that Nathan had made a deal for a lighter sentence in exchange for telling them everything he knew about Hannah's rape. He'd pleaded guilty to criminal mischief and to harassing Hannah, and he'd been given a year of probation, a fine, and community service. He'd also waived his right to a hearing before Mrs. Garcia expelled him from school.

Mom said, "No jail time? You promised us he wouldn't get a slap on the wrist!"

"We had to make a trade-off," ADA Golden said. "We needed his information to help us make sure the person who actually raped your daughter is caught. Besides, he'll have an expulsion and two misdemeanors on his record. That's not inconsequential."

"What did Nathan tell you?" Hannah asked.

ADA Golden sighed. "Mr. Walsh knew full well that you had been raped when he began bullying you and claiming you made the rape up. For what it's worth, he was adamant that I tell you that he's sorry."

"Well, that's worth about as much as the breath he wasted saying it," Mom said.

"I agree," ADA Golden said, "especially given the other half of the story. Hannah, Jake took pictures of his friend raping you. Lots of them."

"So that's where Nathan got the photo." Hannah's voice was flat. "Did Jake rape me too?"

"No. He watched and took photos. Then he gave some to Nathan and told him to threaten to show them to the whole school unless you kept your mouth shut about what happened to you. Nathan came up with the plan himself to vandalize your locker instead, but Jake told him to put the paint can in Sierra's bag as a warning about what would happen to her if she turned against him."

Hannah nodded while ADA Golden explained all the charges she'd filed against Jake. She should be angry at him and Nathan and at Sierra too for dating that asshole, but she felt nothing at all.

"What about the boy who raped me?" she asked. "Did you arrest him?"

"Yes. We did. His name is Tyler Washington, and he is being processed as we speak. Does that name mean anything to you?"

Hannah shook her head.

ADA Golden leaned forward. "It's going to be a long hard road before you get justice for any of this. Mr. Parsons and Mr. Washington most likely are going to fight the charges and may try to drag your name through the mud before they even get to trial. But we have a strong case against them. We have Nathan's testimony and a lot of physical evidence, plus the threatening message Jake sent you. All that will help fill in the gaps in your memory, and I promise I will fight hard for you to get the justice you deserve."

"Fight hard?" Mom snapped. "Like the way you let Nathan get off with nothing worse than a fine?"

"We got your daughter's rapist thanks to that deal, didn't we?" ADA Golden's voice was quiet. "That's a big win."

"For the moment," Mom said. "Let's go, Hannah."

Hannah's head was buzzing, and she had this weird feeling like none of this was real as she followed Mom out of the room.

***

Mom had to go back to work after the meeting, but she promised Hannah she'd be home as soon as possible to talk to her about what had happened. Hannah was just as glad to be home alone. She didn't need Mom hovering and worrying about her.

She wanted to text Grandma, but Grandma would know right away she was upset even if she didn't say so. She decided to wait. Instead, she practiced what she would be doing for the Tree of Life ceremony on Friday to try to keep her mind off everything else.

There was a loud knock on the door. Hannah froze.

Jake was in jail and she had a restraining order against Nathan. There was nothing to be scared of.

She looked out the peephole and saw Sierra standing there. Sierra didn't appear to be wearing a coat even though it was twenty degrees outside. She was hugging herself.

Hannah opened the door. "I guess you heard the news about what Jake did to me," she said. "Are you okay?"

Sierra laughed. "Am I okay? No, I'm not okay. Does it look like I am?" She pushed past Hannah and threw herself onto the couch. "Jake's gone forever," she said, "and I want to be mad at you, but I can't because I don't want you to remember me that way."

"Remember you? What are you talking about?"

"I came to say goodbye. That's what." Sierra fidgeted. "I'm sorry I was such a crappy friend. I tried, but . . . anyway, you'll forget me soon enough."

Hannah froze for the second time in as many minutes. "Please tell me you're not going to try to kill yourself."

Sierra's eyes widened. "I knew you were smart," she said flatly, "but I didn't think you'd catch on that quick."

Hannah sat down next to her on the couch. "Please don't do that," she said, her voice shaking. "Please. I love you, Sierra. I've been heartbroken since your parents interfered with our friendship. I even got you a Christmas present. I was going to give it to you the other day but Dylan said it wasn't a good time to come over."

"Course he did." Sierra bit her lip. "Keep your present, whatever it is. I didn't have anything to give you to remember me by, so I guess you can use it for that."

Hannah's heart pounded. She had to stop Sierra somehow, but how? "I don't want something to remember you by. I want you here, alive. We're having a Christmas party on Friday and I want you to be part of it. I want to graduate with you next year."

Sierra's face trembled. "I don't know why you'd want me."

Hannah put her arm around her. "I don't know why you think I'd be happy if you died. Let me call Dylan, okay? He can get you the help you need."

"No. Dylan's disappointed enough in me. I don't want him to see me like this."

You'd rather he see you next at your funeral? Hannah couldn't believe this was happening. "Then let me call Brad. You know he won't judge you. Please, Sierra. You sat with me in the hospital when I didn't want to go. Now let me do it for you."

Sierra stared down at the ground. "You're too good a person. You should hate me. Everyone else does."

"Sierra! Why are you being like this? What's wrong?"

"Everything, but the last straw is Jake going to jail. Things are going to come out now that I just can't . . . " Sierra bit her lip. "I'm not strong like you. I'm sorry."

"You're plenty strong. I couldn't have got through what happened to me without you."

"Wouldn't have happened if it weren't for me dragging you to that party." Sierra swallowed hard. "I didn't know Jake took pictures. I swear."

"I believe you. Want to tell me what you're afraid is going to come out?"

Sierra stiffened. "I don't want to talk about it. As it is my parents won't let me forget it. My dad thinks so little of me now, and my mom thinks I betrayed the entire black community by acting like . . . " She sighed. "Once I'm gone, they'll forget their shame, I guess."

"My mom tried to kill herself too, and it just broke my heart." Hannah took Sierra's hand. "Don't do this, Sierra. Let me help you."

Sierra pulled away. "This is better for everyone. Trust me." She got up. "Just know you were a good friend, Hannah—better than I deserved." She started toward the door.

Hannah blocked her path. "I am not letting you do this to yourself. If you do, Jake wins. Don't you see that? He wanted to break you down, and he did."

"Too late for that," Sierra said. "He already broke me." Hannah didn't move. She just raised her eyebrows at Sierra. Sierra said, "I have it all planned out. I'll break into my dad's liquor cabinet and get a bottle of wine. After I drink some for courage, I'll break the glass and slit my wrist with the broken part. When they find me, they won't be surprised because all I am to them is a bad kid who makes them more and more ashamed every day."

"That's so not true," Hannah said. "My parents punished me too after the party and Brad's punished him after he was arrested last summer, but it wasn't because they were ashamed. It's because they care. They don't want things to get any worse. Don't you see that?"

"Maybe." Sierra's voice wavered. "But maybe not." She rubbed her wrist. "Do you think it'll hurt?"

"It sounds painful," Hannah said. "And it'll hurt me to lose you."

Sierra hesitated. "I don't want to, but I think I have to anyway."

"You don't," Hannah said. "I swear you don't. Whatever Jake did to you, it's okay. I won't think any less of you, I promise. And I'll stand up for you. But you have to stay alive, Sierra. I can't do anything for you if you're gone."

Sierra sank into the couch. She sighed deeply and put her head in her hands. "I don't want to die, but I can't. . . "

Hannah put her arm around her. "You don't have to. Let me call Dylan. Let him help you, so you make it through today."

"I guess." Sierra leaned her head on Hannah's shoulder.

Hannah stroked Sierra's hair while she called Dylan. Then she held Sierra while they waited for him, trying not to think about what would happen when he got there.

MOM CAME HOME at the same time as Dylan showed up. Hannah tried to ask to go to the hospital without cluing Mom into what was going on, but Mom said she had to stay here. Dylan said he could take care of Sierra by himself, so she had to let her go without her. She hoped he was really taking her to the hospital and not just taking her home.

Mom said, "Okay. Want to tell me what was really going on?"

Hannah did, she did so much her chest ached. But Sierra hadn't said she could tell Mom and she wanted her to trust her, even if Mom was the one adult who could understand because she'd been through the same thing. "She's depressed about what her boyfriend did to me. She feels horrible about it."

"As she should." Mom said. "What about you, sweetheart? How are you doing with everything?"

Hannah shrugged. "Okay, I guess. I mean, it doesn't change anything, really. I thought having the name of the boy who did it would make me feel better, but I don't feel anything at all."

Mom sighed. "I don't know that you'll ever get closure, sweetheart. That boy is just a name to you, a name of someone who did something terrible to you that you can't remember and never will."

"He made a baby that died," Hannah said, her voice flat. She hadn't even thought about her miscarriage in a long time. Now she remembered Sierra coming over and comforting her after her appointment. She should be with her, dammit, not here talking to Mom. "He turned my life upside down. And I don't really know who he is or why he did it."

"He did it because he thought he could get away with taking what he wanted from you. Nothing more, nothing less." Mom's voice was hard. "That ADA had better do right by you this time."

"Does it really matter?" Hannah crossed her arms, irritated. "Even if he goes to jail for a million years it won't change what he did to me. Honestly, I don't care if they all make deals if it means I don't have to deal with the cops or the DA anymore."

"You were the one who wanted justice. I tried to tell you it wouldn't do you nearly as much good as you thought it would. But now that you started, you might as well finish." Mom lowered her voice as Hannah glared at her. "Why so angry, sweetheart? Is learning the truth about what happened to you hitting you hard?"

"I don't know." But Hannah did know, kind of. She was angry because calling the cops hadn't done anything good. Yeah, Jake was in jail and so was the other boy, but was it worth it? Sierra hadn't been suicidal before the cops got involved, and Hannah was no closer to feeling like anything was resolved than she'd been months ago. So, what the hell was the point? "I'm sick of all this, I guess. I want to put the rape behind me and live a normal life, but how can I when it might be years before these assholes go to trial?"

Mom put her hands on her shoulders. "You just do. You move on and you hold your head up as high as you can, and you forget about the things you can't control."

Hannah's face trembled. Mom hugged her tightly while she felt awful about not telling her that part of why she was crying was that she wasn't sure Sierra was out of danger yet.

The next couple of days leading up to the Tree of Life ceremony were a blur. Dylan texted Hannah that Sierra had been admitted to the mental hospital across town. Sierra had tried to downplay how bad it was when she was in the ER because she didn't want to be hospitalized, and Dylan and his parents had to fight with the ER staff to get them to believe that Sierra would hurt herself if she was allowed to go home. And once she'd finally been admitted, they had to wait a million years for an ambulance to take her to the mental hospital.

She was safe now. That was the important thing, but Hannah didn't want to think about it or about anything. She spent most of her spare time studying and wishing she could still get lost in a book and forget the world like she did when she was a little girl and Mom was the one hospitalized for being a danger to herself. She did her best to stay upbeat in front of her friends so they wouldn't worry that she might be suicidal too, which she wasn't.

Then it was Friday, the last day before Christmas break. The Tree of Life ceremony took place at lunchtime in the school auditorium, and parents were invited. Mom had used up her personal days going to the DA's office with Hannah a billion times so she couldn't come, but Eric was coming and so was Brad's dad, who was covering it for his paper.

Hannah, Katie, Molly, and Brad sat on chairs on one side of the stage. The podium was on the other side and there was a curtain behind it so that nobody saw the Tree of Life until they were ready to dedicate it.

Mrs. Garcia came up to the podium and said she was grateful for the entire school community and wanted them to stay safe, then turned the assembly over to Katie.

Hannah's leg bounced up and down while she checked her note cards. She wished that speaking in front of people didn't make her so nervous.

Katie took forever explaining that the Tree of Life was an annual SADD tradition and why they did it. Finally, she said, "And now, let's open the curtain so you can see this year's Tree of Life."

The curtain opened. There was a large tree behind it that Molly and Hannah had helped put white lights on earlier in the day. Katie said softly, "Look how brightly these lights are shining." She pressed a button and the lights went out. "It would be a shame if any of our lives were snuffed out by alcohol, but sadly, every thirty-three minutes, someone dies in an alcohol-related car accident.

Don't let it be you. Don't drink and drive this holiday season." She paused while Hannah scanned the faces of the audience to make sure nobody was laughing at how corny that sounded. Katie turned the lights back on and invited Hannah up to start the candlelight vigil.

Hannah's heart pounded as she came to the podium. "As Katie said, every thirty-three minutes, someone dies in an alcohol-related car crash. We talk a lot about drunk driving, but that's not the only way alcohol can ruin people's lives. A-as many of you know, last Halloween I was raped. There was a lot of alcohol and drugs at the party I was at and . . . "

Just then, the door to the auditorium swung open. Hannah breathed in sharply while she waited to see who had come in late.

It was Sierra's dad.

Eric slid over to make room for him. Hannah waited until he was settled while her mind raced, trying to figure out what he was doing here. "As I was saying, the boy who raped me was probably drunk. I know the boy who took pictures of it was." She looked Mr. Dunlap in the eye, then looked away. "That's why this year, in addition to lighting candles in memory of all those who have died in car accidents, we're going to light candles for all those who have been sexually assaulted while either they or their attacker was under the influence. Molly, could you come up to help me with the candles?"

Molly did and Hannah said, "We're going to start by lighting candles for those killed in drunk driving accidents during the past year. Here are some of their names." As she read each name out, Molly handed her a candle in a holder. She lit it and handed it back to Molly, who put it near the base of the tree, just far enough away to not risk a fire. Molly put a space between each candle big enough for another candle.

When they were done, Hannah asked everyone to close their eyes and then asked for people to raise their hands if they or someone they loved had been involved in an alcohol-related sexual assault.

At first nobody raised their hand. Hannah's stomach sank. She wasn't sure if this was a terrible idea or if she was the only one in the whole school who had been raped by someone who had been drinking. She raised her own hand to encourage everyone. Then a girl raised her hand, slowly, and another girl who was peeking through her fingers raised hers.

Ten girls raised their hands, not counting Hannah. Hannah was about to tell everyone to open their eyes when suddenly Mr. Dunlap raised his hand too.

Was he raising it for Sierra? What the hell had Jake done to her?

Hannah bit her lip while she breathed in and out. She couldn't lose it when she was supposed to be leading the ceremony. She thanked everyone for their bravery and told them to put their hands down so everyone could open their eyes. Then she and Molly lit twelve candles for sexual assault survivors.

"The reason we're doing this is because in a way, you die when you're sexually assaulted. The person you once were is gone, and you have to rebuild a whole new you." Hannah's face started to get hot and her ears started buzzing. She grabbed onto the podium to steady herself and said, "Please don't drink and do something that changes people's lives forever."

There was dead silence in the auditorium for a second and then suddenly everyone was standing and clapping. Hannah saw spots in front of her eyes. It was the flash from the photographer taking photos of her and the tree.

She drank some water to calm her nerves. "One more thing. We'd like to invite you all to give your loved ones the Gift of a Lifetime. This is a small pin you can give to someone to show them that you love them and want them to stay sober, healthy, and alive this holiday season. It comes with a pledge you can both sign. If you don't have a pin and would like to purchase one for someone, please go to the table at the front of the room. All proceeds benefit SADD."

Hannah's heart pounded as she turned the podium over to Molly, so she could explain what the money SADD would get from the pins went toward. Then Mrs. Garcia came up again to close the ceremony.

Afterward, Hannah wanted to give Brad the pin she had in her pocket for him, but Mr. Ashton wanted to get more photographs with her for his story.

"Off the record, I am incredibly proud of you," he said after he'd had his photographer take some more pictures. "It was a brave thing you did, telling people your story."

"Just wait until April," Hannah said nervously. "We're doing another assembly for Sexual Assault Awareness Week." She took the pin out of her pocket. "You might want to see this too. I'm about to give Brad the Gift of a Lifetime."

Mr. Ashton's Adam's Apple bobbed up and down. "Do you think it would embarrass him too much if you called him onto the stage and let his old man take some pictures?"

Hannah smiled slightly. "You know Brad. He loves being the center of attention."

Mr. Ashton went to get Brad. Brad came onto the stage with Hannah and hugged and kissed her. "You were awesome," he said.

"You're awesome every day," Hannah told him. "I have something for you." She took the pin out. "This is the pin I was talking about. I love you, Brad, and I know you're committed to your sobriety. But I wanted to ask you if you would wear this pin and sign the pledge promising to stay sober, healthy, and alive this holiday season."

Brad took Hannah's hands in his. "I love you too. I'm not gonna drink or get high this Christmas. I promise. Pin me." He let his dad take a picture while Hannah took out the pin and put it on his shirt, over his heart. "You putting this in your paper?" he asked his dad. "Cause I wanna do this, and I'm not sure Hannah wants the whole world to see." He leaned forward and kissed her.

"That one will be for our private album," Mr. Ashton said. Hannah thought suddenly of Jake taking pictures of her rape. She bit her tongue to make herself stop that and then hugged Brad tight and kissed him again.

***

A little while later, Hannah came over to Eric. "Brad and I are going to catch a ride with Elizabeth. We're having a little holiday party, but I won't be home late, I promise."

"Fine with me," Eric said, "as long as you let me embarrass you by falling all over myself telling you how much I love you and how proud I am of you."

Hannah shrugged. "If you have to, but it really wasn't that big a deal."

Eric put his hands on her shoulders. "Don't put yourself down, sweetheart. You used the worst thing that ever happened to you to create something positive that would help other people. I'm sure there are far more people affected by sexual assault than the few who raised their hands, and I have no doubt that you helped some of them take the first step toward getting the help they need to deal with what someone did to them. I'm sorry that Mom couldn't be here to see it too, but I took a video on my phone to show her later. I know she will be as proud of you as I am."

Hannah had tears in her eyes. She'd been so, so afraid of disappointing her parents after the party. She'd never have guessed then that Eric would ever be proud of her again or want to share what she was doing with Mom. "Can you send it to Grandma too?"

"I will." Eric hugged Hannah. "Have a good time, sweetheart."

Mr. Dunlap was coming back from the merchandise table as Hannah turned to go. "Hannah," he said, shifting his weight uncomfortably. "Do you have a second?"

"I guess." Hannah crossed her arms, not sure what Mr. Dunlap wanted. "Um, how's Sierra?"

"She's getting there. She's gonna come home next week, but the doctors say she's still got a long road ahead of her once she does." Mr. Dunlap turned the pin over and over in his hands. "I got this for her. She can't have sharp objects up there in the hospital, but when she comes home, I want her to have it." He stared down at the pin. "What I wanted to say was that I was harsh toward you that day in the principal's office. You girls were both Jake's victims, but I treated you like the enemy."

Now it was Hannah's turn to wriggle uncomfortably. "My parents explained it to me. They said that adults say terrible things when they're scared for their kids."

"That's for sure. You don't know how it was for me to hear that story come out of Sierra's mouth. I'm afraid people aren't going to be as fair with her as they were with you when it all comes out. They're going to say she asked for it, sneaking out to see a much older boy, and some are going to say hateful things about girls like her all being promiscuous. Hell, if Jake hadn't messed you up too, I don't know the cops would even take it seriously. But none of that was on you, and I know you're not the bad influence tempting her to do things that reflect badly on her. I owe you an apology, Hannah, and my thanks. If it weren't for you, I wouldn't have a daughter anymore to worry about."

Hannah's eyes widened. "I'm glad I got through to her. I wasn't sure she'd listen. She was so convinced everyone was better off without her."

There was pain in Mr. Dunlap's brown eyes, just for a second. He said, "Thank the Lord above you did. Listen, the doctors say she's gonna need a lot of support once she gets home. You think you might be willing to come over one night for dinner after she gets back?"

"I'd be happy to."

"Thank you. For everything." Mr. Dunlap patted Hannah's shoulder and walked off. Hannah watched him go, trying to get her bearings before she went to meet Elizabeth.

51 - No More Fear

ELIZABETH HUGGED HANNAH and Brad when they came to the door. "I'm so glad you guys could make it! Come on in and see my tree."

Brad squeezed Hannah's hand as they followed Elizabeth into the living room. It was bigger than Hannah's, with beige carpeting covering the floor and a flat-screen TV against one wall. A coffee table in the center had a pile of wrapped gifts on it, and there was a Christmas tree in one corner, which hadn't been decorated yet.

"Katie and Joy wrapped our Secret Santa gifts for us since they weren't there when we did it," Elizabeth said, "and then the three of us did some more Christmas shopping."

"We got something for Sierra too," Joy said. "When she comes home maybe you can bring it to her for us?"

"I will," Hannah promised.

"We'll exchange ours in a bit," Elizabeth added. "First, I thought we could decorate the Christmas tree together." She picked up her iPod from the table. "I put together a holiday music playlist, but let's pass it around and everyone add their favorite holiday song."

Hannah wondered whether it would be weird to add a Chanukah song since they were decorating a Christmas tree, but when it was her turn, she saw that Elizabeth had already put a couple on the list. She added "Light One Candle", a folk song from the 1960s she loved about honoring the sacrifice and strength it took to fight for justice. Then she passed the iPod to Brad.

Elizabeth's mom came in while everyone was taking turns decorating the tree. She looked like an older version of Elizabeth except her face was rounder and she wore her hair in short layers.

"It looks like your party's in full gear," she said. "I just want to say hello to everyone, and then I'll leave you to it." Elizabeth introduced Hannah, Brad, and Molly, who were the only ones who had never been to Elizabeth's house before. Her mom hugged Hannah and said, "I heard your presentation this afternoon. I'm so honored to know you."

Hannah didn't know what to say to that, so she just thanked her.

After the tree was decorated, Elizabeth plugged in the lights and turned them on. "Our very own Tree of Life," she said. "Who's ready to exchange presents?"

There were a ton of gifts on the table. Molly gave Hannah a necklace with her name on it, and Brad gave her the peace symbol earrings she'd been eyeing in Time Warp on their first date. Hannah put them on. Then she gave Brad his watch and gave Molly a scrapbook that said Best Friends on the cover. Inside, she'd put a lot of pictures and notes that she'd kept since they met. Molly had tears in her eyes as she thanked Hannah.

Elizabeth gave Hannah a water bottle that said "I'm a survivor!" on it and had a teal ribbon for sexual assault awareness next to the words. Hannah felt bad about giving Elizabeth such a stupid gift when Elizabeth had given her such a nice one, but when Elizabeth opened hers, she said, "Awesome! I'll save this for when Sierra is better and then we can all go out to dinner together to celebrate her coming home."

That was the start of an awesome holiday break. Hannah let her family take her out to dinner as their gift to her one night and gave them the presents she'd picked out for them when they came home.

A few days later, Hannah's present came in the mail from Grandma. It was a picture frame that had a quote from Proverbs on it:

She is clothed in strength and dignity and she laughs without fear of the future.

Grandma had put a photo of Hannah in the frame that she'd taken when she visited on Thanksgiving. Hannah was shocked at how wide her smile was and how high she'd held her head because she thought she'd been depressed that whole holiday.

My dearest Hannah, (Grandma wrote on the inside of her Chanukah card)

When I saw this photo frame, I knew it was exactly what you needed. Put this on your desk and look at it any time you feel discouraged. Never ever forget how much strength and courage G-d has blessed you with, my darling, and may you always hold your head up high no matter what obstacles this world of ours throws in your path.

Hannah read it aloud to Mom and Eric. Mom kissed the top of her head and said, "I think we found something your grandmother and I can agree on." Hannah blushed and hurried to put the card and photo away in her room.

The best present of all was that Sierra graduated from inpatient care to a partial hospitalization program, which meant she still had to spend most of the day in the hospital, but she was allowed to come home at night. Hannah came over and gave her her snow globe and her gifts from the rest of the group. Katie and Molly had both bought her friendship necklaces, and she also got a coffee mug from Elizabeth with a saying about becoming a butterfly and a small stuffed bear from Brad that said FRIENDS FOREVER on its shirt. And Joy had given her a print of a painting from Ghana of two friends standing in front of a hut.

"Wow," Sierra said. "All this stuff for me?"

Dylan, who was sitting in the living room with them, frowned. "You getting overwhelmed, Si?"

"No," Sierra said. "I'm okay, I promise. I'm just. . . " She twisted a stray lock of hair. "I can't believe everyone cares so much," she said, her voice breaking. "When I went in, I thought no one was going to miss me."

"Well, you were wrong," Hannah said. "We all love you and Elizabeth's saving the gift card I gave her for when you're completely better, so we can all go out to dinner."

"That might be a while," Sierra said. "But it's something to work toward, right?" She gave Hannah a watery smile.

***

All too soon, Christmas break was over. It was a new year now, and in a few months, Hannah, Molly, and Brad would be seniors and Elizabeth, Katie, and Joy would be graduating. But first there was the Sexual Assault Awareness assembly to worry about on top of keeping up with school and hanging out with friends.

Hannah had a new routine now. Lunch with her friends, therapy on Mondays, track clinic on Tuesdays and Thursdays (except when there was a SADD meeting), and hanging out at Elizabeth's house on Wednesdays and Fridays. On the weekends, Brad took her ice skating and to the movies and wherever else they felt like going, and she and all her friends took turns spending time with Sierra so that Sierra would see how many people loved her.

One day, Mrs. Marino asked Hannah to come to see her at lunchtime. She told her that she wanted her to apply for SADD National Student Leadership Council.

"I think this would be a wonderful opportunity for you," she said. "You'd get to work closely with the national leadership team to create new SADD initiatives and help make our organization even stronger, and you'd also have the opportunity to attend conferences and speak to national media about important issues."

Hannah gulped. "S-speak to national media?"

Mrs. Marino nodded. "Don't get intimidated," she said. "There will be a lot of media coming to your assembly in April, and I'm sure you will handle it just fine." She patted Hannah's shoulder. "You're a real leader, Hannah. The way you've been advocating for sexual assault survivors since your rape just solidifies what I already knew. All you need to do is believe in yourself the way I believe in you."

"That's what my grandma says too," Hannah said, thinking of the quote on the photo frame. "Okay, I'll do it."

***

That afternoon, Olivia said, "It sounds like you're starting to put the pieces of your life back together in positive ways. How does the part of you that you like to call Mouse feel about the changes you're making?"

Hannah bit her lip. "Are you sure it's okay to talk about Mouse like she's really a separate person who lives inside my head?"

"Everyone has lots of different versions of themselves," Olivia explained. "We all have parts of ourselves we don't like or want to change. I think that the way you differentiate between Mouse and Hannah is a creative way of expressing the tension you sometimes feel between the woman you want to be and the girl you've been in the past."

Hannah thought about that. She guessed Olivia was right that growing up meant not letting Mouse's fears stop her from doing what she needed to do for herself. But something about it made her feel bad.

Olivia said, "You look upset. Did something I said bother you?"

"Not exactly." Hannah picked at a bead on her bracelet. "It's just . . . getting raped was awful, but if it hadn't happened, I might never have given up being Mouse. But that makes it feel like it's a good thing that happened to me and it wasn't."

"I see." Olivia wrote something in her notes and Hannah was sure she was buying herself time. "I agree that your rape was a terrible experience and that there is nothing to celebrate about it. But you know, that's not the only way to look at what's been happening for you. I think that your tendency to make yourself invisible was never really who you were, and it was making you unhappy to be that way. So, maybe instead of the rape being a 'good thing', it was the catalyst that caused your unhappiness to reach a boiling point so that you felt you HAD to change."

"Like a critical mass in chemistry?" Hannah asked. "That's what you need to sustain a nuclear reaction. If you don't have enough fissile material, the reaction can't keep going." She couldn't help feeling proud of herself for being able to explain that so well. Now that Nathan wasn't in her way and Molly was her friend again, Hannah was back to getting A's in Mr. Dawson's class.

"Exactly," Olivia said. "I won't pretend to know how it works in nuclear reactions, but with people, I know that most of the time when they have a crisis that makes them want to change, it's because frustration has been building for a long time. And then something happens that makes them not able to deal with the way things are anymore."

"The way I was before I was raped feels like it was so long ago even though it was only three months ago."

"You've changed a lot. Some of the ways you changed had to do with feeling out of control after your rape, but some of it had to do with feeling like your Mouse persona just wasn't working for you anymore." Olivia leaned forward. "I want to push back on one thing you said earlier. Mouse isn't really another girl who lives inside your head. She's just the name you've given to the shy, quiet part of Hannah. So, it's not that you chose to give up Mouse after the rape. It's that you chose to no longer give in to the urge to be quiet at times that it didn't feel good to you to stay silent. How do you feel about that?"

Hannah thought suddenly of how mad she'd got that time that Molly had called her Mouse and how Molly had backed off and refused to talk anymore. "That's why Molly and I almost stopped being friends. She was quiet too. I felt like I had to throw her away because I wanted to throw Mouse away."

"You felt pressured to be the way you used to be, and you didn't like it. But what about now? Do you still want to throw Mouse away?"

"Not exactly." Hannah bit her lip. "I mean, I don't want to be her anymore but sometimes when

I'm quiet I kind of laugh to myself and think, score one for Mouse."

"You know, there are times when it's good to be quiet. Maybe it would be helpful to learn when to listen to that voice in your head that says let's be quiet and when to ignore it. That's something you and I could work on in the coming months, learning how to work with Mouse instead of being all one way or the other. What do you think?"

"I'd like that," Hannah told Olivia about the National Student Council Leadership application and added, "I don't want Mouse to hold me back anymore. I'll miss too many opportunities if I do."

"Well, then, let's make it our new goal to learn how to balance your new desire to make the most out of opportunities to be a leader with your natural inclination to be quiet and not draw attention to yourself," Olivia said.

Hannah nodded, barely able to contain her excitement.

***

Over the next two months, Hannah felt better and stronger than ever. She made Honor Roll, finished her application for National Student Council Leadership, and worked with Molly and Elizabeth on planning the All Nighter on top of finalizing her plans for the assembly.

Plus, the assistant coach at track clinic convinced her that the girls' team needed her to win relay races and Brad laughed when she asked if he minded her trying out for the same sport he did and said, "Don't you get that was my plan all along?" So, she did even though she wasn't sure she'd have time for practicing with a team on top of everything else.

About the only thing Hannah wasn't happy about was that nothing major had happened with her case. Jake and Tyler had both pled not guilty. Jake was denied bail because he had run away before, and Tyler's lawyer had tried to say that he deserved to be released on his own recognizance, but the judge hadn't listened and set bail at $25,000. As far as she knew, he hadn't been able to pay it, but the ADA had told her that even if he did, she had nothing to worry about because a condition of his bail would be that he had to stay away from her. Hannah was glad she was too busy to think about it because after the way Jake had tried to intimidate her, she was scared his friend might come after her or Sierra anyway.

She heard from Dylan a few days before the assembly that Sierra was coming home full-time soon. Dylan said that Sierra had missed so much school she was going to have to repeat her junior year but that the more important thing was making sure she felt strong enough to deal with that. Hannah didn't have time to tutor her to try to help her catch up, but Molly said she would do that on Tuesdays and Fridays instead of the general tutoring she was doing, and Hannah was glad to hear that Sierra accepted her offer.

The assembly took place on a Thursday afternoon in early April. Mrs. Marino had helped her write press releases for it, and Brad's dad was far from the only reporter there.

Hannah's heart pounded worse than ever as she looked out at all the faces in the audience. The whole school was there. Every teacher had taken the class they were supposed to be teaching to the assembly and sat with them, and the assistant principal, dean of students, and all the secretaries were in the front row. Mrs. Parker caught Hannah's eye and gave her a wink and a thumbs up while Hannah made herself breathe in and out and told Mouse in her head that it was going to be okay and that Mouse could trust her not to let her get hurt. That was something new that Olivia had suggested she try next time she felt freaked out about standing up for herself, and she thought now was as good a time as any to try it out.

Hannah's eyes slid over all the people in the audience while Mrs. Garcia opened the assembly. Mrs. Garcia made everyone say the Pledge of Allegiance, then had them all sit down so she could make her opening remarks, which Hannah didn't listen to. Instead, she looked at Brad and thought about how scared she'd been to let him be her boyfriend and how glad she was that she'd taken the risk.

Her ears perked up when she heard her name and then the entire school was applauding for her. Hannah swallowed hard as she came up to the microphone.

"For those of you who don't know me," she said, playing with the edges of her note cards to try to calm her nerves, "my name is Hannah Kollman and last October . . . "

"SLUT!" some boy shouted, and a teacher said, "HEY!"

Hannah froze while the teacher told the boy to get up. Suddenly, strength surged through her and she said, "No, he can stay. He needs to hear this." She put her note cards down and leaned out into the audience, making eye contact with the boy. "I knew when I decided to do this that some people might call me names. Words like 'slut' hurt people like me. They make it so we're scared to tell our stories and so we blame ourselves for what happened to us. And the worst part of it is, silence literally kills us. Somebody I know almost ended her life because she was afraid of what people might say about her.

"I'm not a slut and I'm not a whore, and neither is anyone else who has been sexually assaulted. I wasted a lot of time being ashamed but now I know that the only people who deserve to be ashamed are the boys who raped me." Hannah paced back and forth on the stage, trying to calm herself. "I went to a party my parents wouldn't approve of. That's it. And two boys who were old enough to know better did something to me that turned my life upside down. One of them put pills in my iced tea while I was playing video games. Those pills messed me up so bad that everyone around me thought I was drunk and nobody did anything to stop it while the boy who raped me took me over to a couch and took my clothes off and his friend took pictures of us having sex.

"I don't remember any of that. It's what the cops told me happened when they arrested the boys responsible. What I do remember is waking up the next morning sore and bruised and having no idea what happened the night before. What I do remember is being afraid to tell anyone what happened to me. And what I do remember is going to the doctor for a follow-up appointment and finding out that my rapist got me pregnant, but the baby died before it was big enough to be anything."

Hannah's voice shook. She made herself take another deep breath. "Now, I'm sure we've all had health classes where we talk about how we need to watch our drinks at parties. I used to think it was my fault I was raped because I didn't do that.

"But here's the thing: All of those warnings are about what we should do to protect ourselves from getting raped, and that's wrong. Not that being careful isn't good, but . . . has anyone ever talked in health class about what to do if you're a guy at a party who wants to have sex with a girl?" She looked out at the audience. No one raised their hand. "Ever heard a teacher talk about why words like slut are so hurtful? No? Well, today we're going to go over all of that. But most important of all, I want you to know that if you're someone who has never told anybody that you were raped or sexually assaulted, you're not as alone as you think you are. I thought I was alone too until the first time I told my story, and then I discovered that there were a lot less people who screamed SLUT at me than there were people who understood and cared. The mean ones were just louder."

Hannah let her breath out slowly as Mrs. Garcia came back to the podium to say that Hannah and the other people involved in this program were devoting a lot of time and energy to sharing a painful part of their lives and that she expected the audience to treat them with respect. Then Hannah started the program for real. They had a skit where the stage was darkened while she, Katie, Elizabeth, and a few other volunteers each stepped into a spotlight and said one sentence about what someone had done to them. Then they showed a video about consent and Hannah led the audience in a Q & A about it. After that, Brad came up to the podium to talk about how guys didn't have to be disrespectful to girls to be manly and introduced two male volunteers who told their stories and talked about how hard it was to come forward because they were afraid of what their friends would think of a boy who had been raped.

Hannah took the podium one last time. "I want to thank everyone who came forward today. This isn't easy to talk about at all. I've told my story a million times, and it's still not easy. But hopefully hearing all of our stories and all of our thoughts about how to change things helped someone today."

Mrs. Garcia told everyone to show her their gratitude. The audience clapped and clapped, and a lot of people gave standing ovations. Afterward, reporters wanted to talk to everyone who had spoken.

A reporter asked Hannah, "Do you plan to create community events related to sexual assault awareness over the summer?"

Hannah hadn't thought about that. She paused for a second to focus on her breathing because the idea of exposing herself to the ridicule of the entire community scared her. "Maybe," she said. "I want to make sure that other people that went through what I went through know they're not alone."

Another reporter asked her about Jake and Tyler and whether she was afraid they wouldn't be punished. She was, a little, but she decided the world didn't need to know that. "I try not to think about what's going to happen to them. That's not up to me. I just hope I can help the next person not go through what I did because of them."

The interviews felt like they went on forever. Brad's dad was the last to interview her, and then he invited her to dinner with him and Brad. Hannah accepted eagerly, smiling to herself as she thought about how scared she would have been to spend time alone with them six months ago.

She thought about what she'd said to the reporters as Mr. Ashton unlocked the car. She really didn't know what was going to happen with Jake and Tyler or even what was going to happen this summer. But it didn't scare her anymore either.

"Brad tells me you have your learner's permit," Mr. Ashton said. "Would you like to try driving? I'll be right next to you in case you have a problem."

Hannah nodded. "I want to get my license this summer," she said, "so I might as well start now."

Mr. Ashton switched places with her.

It felt good to be doing something so normal, she thought as she adjusted the seat and put on her seatbelt. She hadn't thought she'd ever be normal again after her rape.

She started the car and drove out of the parking lot behind school, headed toward whatever was going to happen next.

THE END

If You Are a Real Life Survivor...

THANK YOU FOR reading. I know that it if you've experienced something like what Hannah experienced, this book may not have been easy for you to read.

While I certainly hope people found this story entertaining (nobody wants to hear their work is boring!), I wrote it partially to help survivors know that **they are not alone.**

Statistics show that rape and sexual assault are far too common. Approximately 1 out of 6 women and 1 out of 33 men have reported an attempted or completed sexual assault, and the numbers are even higher for transgender people and for Native Americans.

Yet, like Hannah, survivors often feel alone, ashamed, and anxious. Sexual assault survivors are at greater risk for depression, substance abuse, anxiety, eating disorders, and PTSD.

Survivors are also 4 times more likely to contemplate suicide. If you are feeling suicidal, please reach out to your doctor, therapist, or one of the resources below.

Whatever the circumstances of your sexual assault were, they were not your fault and you deserve compassion, support, and to be able to continue to move forward in your life.

Hotlines
NATIONAL SEXUAL ASSAULT HOTLINE
1-800-656-4673
NATIONAL TEEN DATING ABUSE HOTLINE
1-866-331-9474
1-866-331-8453 (TTY)
NATIONAL SUICIDE PREVENTION HOTLINE
1-800-273-8255
TREVOR PROJECT CRISIS LINE (LGBT/YOUTH)
1-866-488-7386
***

Websites
RAINN (Rape, Abuse & Incest National Network) www.rainn.org
NSVRC (National Sexual Violence Resource Center) www.nsvrc.org
***

A Special Note for Domestic Violence Survivors

Some sexual assaults occur within relationships.

Your significant other does not have the right to demand sex of you. If you were afraid to say 'No' or were forced by an abusive partner, that is sexual assault.

I implied that this happened to Sierra because I wanted you to know that you aren't alone either. Dating abuse and violence is, unfortunately, fairly common among teenagers. Girls between the ages of 16 and 24 are among the most likely people to be abused by their partners.

Here are some signs to watch out for that might indicate an unhealthy and abusive relationship:

1. Your partner is extremely insecure or jealous and/or gets angry when you spend time with other people. They might even stop you from spending time with your friends or family.

2. Your partner has a bad temper and you find it hard to predict what will set them off.

3. Your partner invades your privacy and/or monitors your whereabouts (e.g. constantly calling to check in or tracking you on their phone.)

4. Your partner blames you for all the problems in the relationship and/or falsely accuses you of bad behavior.

5. Your partner breaks your things, hits you, or threatens to do it.

6. Your partner pressures you to have sex or forces you to have sex you don't want to have.

It can be confusing to figure out whether or not your relationship is healthy, because most abusive relationships aren't like this ALL the time. There are times where your relationship seems good and your partner makes you feel very special, and you might love them, feel they love you, or doubt your own feelings about the bad times.

You never deserve to be mistreated.

If you are involved in an abusive relationship, some of the resources above may be able to help you. You can also get help from the following websites:

Break The Cycle breakthecycle.org

Love Is Respect loveisrespect.org

(Safety note: if your partner is monitoring your Internet use, it may not be safe to access these resources from your phone or computer.)

If You Know A Survivor...

I
T CAN BE hard to know how to be a good friend to someone who confides in you about sexual assault or who you think may be in an abusive relationship.

That's why Molly and Hannah had such a big falling out. Molly meant well, but her reaction to Hannah's confiding in her made everything worse.

If you find yourself in this situation, these tips can help you support your friend.

***

1. Believe what your friend tells you. You might have seen the hashtag #BelieveSurvivors on Twitter or other social media. That hashtag exists partially to tell survivors that there are people who WILL believe them, because sometimes people think they're making it up, and survivors sometimes have a hard time telling anyone what happened because they are afraid they won't be believed. You can help your friend just by believing what they tell you happened to them, even if they're accusing someone you're friends with.

2. Tell the survivor it is not their fault. Many survivors feel ashamed and guilty. It can be helpful to tell them that the attack is not their fault and that you don't blame them for what happened to them.

3. Accept where they are at. Some survivors may have a hard time trusting people or may be depressed, anxious, or want to be alone a lot. Don't push them to do things they don't want to do, but do let them know you're there for them. Use supportive statements like, "It must have been scary." to let them know you understand and accept their feelings.

4. Don't push for details. Many survivors feel a loss of control, and it helps them to be able to tell their story on their own terms. Plus, something like sexual assault is hard enough to talk about without someone wanting to know details that the survivor isn't ready to disclose.

5. Don't give advice. Many people automatically jump into fix-it mode when their friend tells them something scary and painful that they are going through. But survivors often don't want or need to be fixed -- in fact it can make them feel uncomfortable or overwhelmed if you throw a lot of advice at them. It's better just to listen and express support and empathy unless your friend specifically asks for advice.

6. Ask if the survivor needs medical attention. Survivors may need help going to the doctor or hospital after a sexual assault. Let the survivor decide whether or not they want to go, but don't be afraid to bring it up. (Note: in some states, hospitals may have to call the police if a sexual assault survivor is under age.)

7. Don't push your friend to report the crime. Many survivors decide not to report their sexual assaults to police for a variety of reasons. This is their choice to make, and it's helpful to support their decision rather than push them to report.

8. Respect their privacy. Don't make the mistake Molly made. It can take a lot for a survivor to confide in anyone about their sexual assault, and it's important that you keep what they told you to yourself unless they give you permission to share it.

9. Know the signs of suicide. In most cases, it's best to give survivors space to make their own decisions. But if your friend is displaying signs that they are considering suicide, you may need to get emergency help for them.

Signs of suicide include:

Withdrawing from friends, family, and activities they used to enjoy

Giving away prized possessions

Expressions of guilt, shame, and self-hatred

Statements like people would be better off without them or they wish they were dead.

Obsession with death

Taking risks that could lead to death

If you suspect a friend is suicidal, it's okay to ask! You cannot make someone suicidal by asking if they are considering suicide. You may need to tell an adult such as your friend's parents or a teacher if you have reason to believe your friend is considering suicide. You can also call the suicide hotlines above and/or offer to take your friend to the hospital. As a last resort, you can call 911, but don't do that unless you have no other options and you think your friend is in immediate danger.

Make sure to take care of yourself. It's stressful to deal with a friend's serious problems. You may feel like you're being selfish if you can't talk right now or need a break from your friend's emotions, but you're not! You can't be helpful to your friend if you are exhausted, overwhelmed, or depressed yourself because of focusing too much on them and not enough on yourself.

Acknowledgements

I T'S TAKEN ME about two years to turn *Reinventing Hannah* from an abstract idea about a girl who has to overcome being sexually assaulted to a finished novel. There are so many people whose help was invaluable.

There would be no book without my friend, accountability partner, and fellow artist **kat pérez**; my friend, critique partner and fellow author **Michelle Burden**; or my friend, editor, and fellow author **J.M. Brister**.

I'd also like to thank everyone on the Facebook groups **Trauma Fiction**, **Legal Fiction**, and **Cops and Writers** for their help getting the medical and legal details right.

And of course, thank you, my readers, for reading!

I hope you've enjoyed reading *Reinventing Hannah* as much as I've enjoyed writing it. If you have, please consider leaving a review on the site you purchased this book from.

If you'd like to help me be able to write more books like this, please join my Patreon (http://www.patreon.com/jackaori). Your monthly contribution helps me be able to devote time and energy to further books as well as helps me pay for everything that goes into turning a story into a finished book.

Thanks again for reading. I'd love to hear your thoughts about *Reinventing Hannah*. Feel free to hit me up on Twitter (@heroicmuse2016), Instagram (@heroicmuse) or Facebook (@heroicmusebooks). You can also email me at jack@jackaori.com with your feedback!

About the Author

JACK A. ORI writes about young people dealing with tough issues such as mental illness, violence, and prejudice. In addition to *Reinventing Hannah,* he is the author of *Mama's Illness,* a short story about a six-year-old girl dealing with her mother's hospitalization for suicidal ideation. Jack is also a staff writer for the online TV magazine TV Fanatic, a full-time freelancer, and a life coach who helps empower young adults to overcome real life challenges and live life on their own terms. He currently lives on Long Island, New York, where he plays violin with a local orchestra in between writing sessions.

Printed in Great Britain
by Amazon